A WAY WITH ALL MAIDENS

·······································

A SATYR'S ROMANCE

·······································

by Barry N. Malzberg

STARK HOUSE

Stark House Press • Eureka California

A WAY WITH ALL MAIDENS / A SATYR'S ROMANCE

Published by Stark House Press
1315 H Street
Eureka, CA 95501, USA
griffinskye3@sbcglobal.net
www.starkhousepress.com

ISBN-13: 978-1-951473-52-5

Book design by Mark Shepard, shepgraphics.com
Cover art by Titian
Proofreading by Bill Kelly

First Stark House Press Edition: January 2022

A WAY WITH ALL MAIDENS

David Perkins didn't intend to join S—'s acting troupe. He started out as a thief. But circumstances being what they are, he is forced to lay low for a while. And what better place to lay low than as an extra in the back of a theater production. Which is how Perkins finds himself a member of the cast of S—'s new play, The Tempest. All is well and good until S— decides that, against the better judgement of the director, he wants Perkins to be his Prospero. Now Perkins has all these nonsensical lines to learn for a part he doesn't really understand, rehearsed by a director who has absolutely no faith in him. Thank goodness he has Jane, who provides a most delightful distraction to all this theater business. Otherwise, he'd surely go mad.

A SATYR'S ROMANCE

It all begins in Times Square on New Year's Eve. Harry Wheeler is ushering in 1970 with the crowds when someone lights a firecracker behind him. A young lady falls into his arms in a dead faint. What is he to do? Seizing the moment, he carries her off to his basement apartment. And there Harry's seeks to explain himself to this young actress, Rona Smith, whom he has so conveniently abducted. Sex is part of it, but Harry believes there is so much more here that needs to be said. He tells Rona the story of Idiom, his alter ego—his sexual history, his search for connection. But after the sex is over, Rona finds she has no patience for this man who barricades himself behind his words. Because Harry, she decides, is very likely crazy.

A WAY WITH ALL MAIDENS

by Barry N. Malzberg

Writing as Mel Johnson

"You gave me speech and all the good I got on't is I learned to curse."

—Caliban, in *The Tempest*

"This smooth stone supports Emily's pelvis. We have not kept up with his later work."
—"Stone and Cutting Were All Our Thought"
Trim Bissell, *Yale Review 1967*

PROLOGUE

My cock zoomed into her then with enormous skill, already distended toward that distant source of its energy, and I felt myself moving into her with an almost illustrious speed, all gasps and moans to the contrary, fixated on the target. Her breast was enormous in my mouth, the nipple huge and pointed, my teeth chewed down on it, and it was as if, from this angle, I am totally surrounded by her flesh. Her aspect under clothing, indeed, gave no clue as to the enormity of this thick flesh. "I'm always ashamed of my breasts," she had said when she disrobed. I think they're too large. I'm embarrassed for them." And when she had emerged from the tight straps of her garment, the film of her chemise, it had indeed been an astounding sight, beyond the borders of all reasonable expectation. I had had to assure her with my mouth, my hands, my bursting cock that there was indeed nothing whatsoever to be ashamed of in her breasts; anything that can so well suit form to function, suit need to consequence, must be very well made indeed.

But that was before we had sucked, we had gone the round of the positions, we had explored like honest laborers all of the byways and implications of the placement of the bodies. And then we did the fucking itself. I was deep in the timeless saddle, poised over her, rising to enormous heights, and then falling through valleys of sensation atop her, up and down, the click of some joint in the area of my thighs adding a note of contrapuntal enthusiasm to the endeavor. Underneath me she was screaming and wailing like the tormented Caliban himself; her mouth grunted in a full range of words and notes; her hips thrashed. I restored the rhythm which had broken down to unevenness from the franticity of her response, placed my calming belly atop hers, and they rubbed together until she settled into a more monolithic pace. And then, once again, I fucked her, rose ceilingward in splendid pursuit of the posture, and she was spreading, spreading before me, the limp channel of her being, all open, all discovered.

"Fuck!" she screamed at length, and I did what I could to oblige her, momentarily forestalling my load by remembering other times, other fucks, other circumstances. Her breasts reminded me vaguely of those on a barmaid in Milan whom I went to bed with a long time ago under entirely different circumstances; it was in the reflection of those breasts, that fuck, that I found the trigger of the present situation held up. But her mood was insistent, her body demanded, and her mouth opened to scream for my climax. So all attentive to my work I bowed my head and worked into her with something approaching real energy, real enthusiasm ... and I poured all the way into her.

I poured all the way in, from every gutter of being, realizing that, at the moment I come, I have no real idea of who the girl is, her name, even the circumstances underlying our joining. She could just as well have been the Queen of England as some trollop from the brothel down the street; the anonymity is the same, the indirection, the confusion ... but there was no time to think of that, damned little time to think of anything as her thighs bucked and surged against me and I spilled, spilled, spilled the vanished seed, my teeth sinking into the huge softness of her left breast, raising marks upon it. For a long time I remained quiescent on top of her, listening to the even sound of her breathing and the sound of carriages in the street below....

"Oh," she said, "that was good; that was very good. But where were you? Toward the end you seemed to drift away from me."

"Oh," I said, shifting my weight off her; revolving to lie beside her, I placed a hand on her pendant breast, "it happens now and then. It's an old problem and has nothing to do with you. It's just that other things come to mind."

"Actors," she said. "Yes, actors. I know what you must go through."

"It has nothing to do with being an actor either. It's just the way that things get sometimes."

"Oh yes it does," she said, a hand reaching down to rub gently along my inner thigh, drawing it up to my balls, making them arch. "Don't be offended. I consider it an honor."

And then it all came back to me. Strange how the energy of fucking cancels thought—to say nothing of reason. Then it all slid into place. She was one of the actresses in the company, of course, the little company we have, and, because I am the lead actor not to say the founder, there was no problem in getting her to bed and no reason why she should not fuck me, and that explained all the circumstances. She was very good too. More and more often, however, I have been subject to these strange twitches of amnesia, strange submersions of memory at the time of vigorous acts, leading to a kind of disconnection—to say nothing of dread and intimidation. This could have been a sign of some nervous disorder, although I put it down to the strains and stresses of organizing and managing an ambitious but essentially untalented flock of actors as they scurry through the provinces. At any rate, everything was all right; balance, perspective, and a sense of history have been restored; all that is missing is a sense of destination.

"Do it again, David," she said snuggling against me, the warm surfaces of her body felt like heated cake against my palms, all of it open and attending to me. With a kind of distant energy I began to stroke her shoulders, rub my mouth against her breasts, partake of the nipples, and I felt the wetness of her cunt, still dripping my recent come as she wiggled against me. I slid into what could only be called a purity of accommodation, a sweet negation of thought, a sanctity of connection, and I could have rested beside her and stroked her body for a very long time, but at some crucial instant she pulled away from me, rolling over to her side of the bed and then, pulling her legs up, sat cross-legged and regarded me with a bemused kind of attention that was not without humor.

"You're not even present." She pouted. "It's as if you're not even here; you're some place far away. It doesn't matter to me, but I am concerned for your sake. Why don't you tell me what's wrong?"

"Nothing's wrong," I said to her and reached to touch her, but she is deft, she is cunning, and she rolled away from me and knelt in a protective posture, her forearms huddled against her breasts, her eyes mischievous, her face curled, her box shrouded by the curve of her thighs. "No," she said, "not now. Why don't you talk to me? I thought when I joined this company I'd get an education. That's what you said, that I'd have an opportunity to learn all about the stage. So educate me and we can fuck later."

"I have nothing to say. Come here."

"I'm taking risks, you know. You told me the penalties and problems we might get into having female actresses playing the female roles. But I took the chance anyway. I admired you. And I came right up here with you after rehearsal. Don't you think I deserve to be talked to?"

"It isn't that," I said. "It's just that I don't feel very much like talking. I find it very difficult to talk."

"Better now than later," she said and put a cool hand on my knee. It became apparent to me then, not for the first time either, that I was losing control of a situation. Perhaps this has something to do with age, although if pressed I would have another explanation. "I want to have a chance to know you. What excited me about you is that you were acting with S— during the last plays, but you never talk about him."

"Not all the last plays," I said, "just the very last one, and it wasn't much of an experience. I was too young then to understand what was happening, and besides I barely knew him until the very end."

"But he must have been fascinating!"

"No he wasn't." I was somewhat appalled at the retrospective turn the conversation had taken. "He really wasn't; he was just an ordinary man in many ways. None of us liked his play very much, and he was impossible at rehearsals. Anyway, it all happened a long time ago."

"You mean he wasn't what everybody says he is?"

"What does everybody say he is?"

"Oh, for heaven's sake." She gestures irritably. "He was a genius. He was the greatest genius of his time. Everybody knows that—everybody who wants to get into the theater."

"Well ..." I paused somewhat annoyed, the returning rush of perspective had led to the strange feeling that I should not, after all, have been in that bed with that girl at that particular time. I am old, old, beyond my time, and in the bargain my association with S— had none of the effects which she seemed to have attached to it. "None of us really thought so; he was just a difficult cranky old man and almost impossible to work for. I was in the last play, and we went into Stratford, and we did it, and it was a mess, and then all that business happened, and the company fell apart—and that's the end of it. That was a long time ago. That was in 1612. It really doesn't affect me anymore."

"Now you're talking. Tell me more. Tell me what it was like then, what the play was like, what it was like to act for him. Don't you understand how valuable this can be?"

"I don't care about value," I said. "I don't care about most things these days, I fear." And I reached for her then with real determination, damned not to be denied and got my arms on her, clutched her flesh, put myself against her. In a half-penitential posture I dragged her down to the sheets impressing the slight arch of her back against them. Seeing the rising of her breasts, I returned all energy to her nipples, grappling with them, my excitement now restored. I should have been grateful; after all it was a coup not only to take the chance on female actors for the crucial parts—but to find a blessing such as that to join the company was justification and more.

Yet, even as I sucked on her nipples, she would not stop talking. Everything was fine; everything could have moved along until the burst of creation, that is the end of the act, but she would not stop talking: "You have to tell me," she said. "You must tell me what it's like. I've got to know. It's important to me!" I pressed my belly down on hers, flatness to flatness, my curved dong seeking her opening and still: "It's too valuable, too important! You must tell me about this," she protested, wrenching away slightly; her very nipples were curled in petulance.

So I say, finally, only to quiet her, "All right, hush! I can't and won't talk about it now, but I'll write it all down. I'll put down everything just the way it happened to me. I have some notes somewhere, and I'll get them in order." I was reaching, reaching and trying to make that first fragile connection.

"Will you, then? Will you write it all down so that I and the others can read it?"

Not even wondering about the question of *others*, I say, "Yes, yes, of course. Now just be quiet! Be quiet and let me make love." My prick winged its way in like mercury, way into her core. As I began to work toward the climax again, beating on her flesh like a wingless butterfly, trapped in some shell of abstraction I found myself saying, "Yes, yes, I'll get it all down. I'll take it out of the trunk and put it in order and give it to you, yes, yes." Anything to quiet her ... and then the swell of my coming and true fucking begins, and I am incapable of speech, feeling the hard knots of her nipples bounce and jounce off my face as I emerge into a long, swooning corridor of generation....

But of course it would all end, and my promise would hold because she was right. That is the point, the precise point: she was absolutely right. Part of the current problem is that I have wrongfully relegated all of this to a history it cannot be buried in. In the time of reckoning I knew I would have to produce my notes, and I knew then that when all of that was over, when the girl had gone, when other days had come upon me, it would be necessary to go into all of it again: the madness of Milan, the agony of Stratford, the music of Sorrento, and the sounds of that tortured summer when all of us, all uncaring, sent S— on his final journey while we tried to uncover our own destiny. There is little good to be achieved at it but yes, it is clear that I now want to unearth it because at some time it might have scholarly value. Then too, the amnesia is a seizing disease, and at any moment I might lose all of it ... all except the pain and the mystery.

Padua? Sorrento? Milan? Rome—I think it was Rome. Of course I am not sure of any of these; they may all be mental rather than physical places. The horrid sameness of all of this! The horrid blandness! How coldly it focuses on a frieze of the soul!

Enough rhetoric. One must start somewhere. One evening the detestable S— himself, a short, fat man wearing false garments and what I take to be a kind of plaster on his nose gathered the entire cast around him after a rehearsal and, gesticulating violently while Thorpe stood numbly behind him, spoke to us as follows:

"Now listen, gentlemen, you realize that you are doing this entirely wrong. You have no conception of my play. Time and again I have lectured Thorpe, told him what to do, what interpretation must be made, but he insists upon misapprehensions and communicating his banalities to the players. Still, he is the director, so I have stood aside respectfully and watched him work this out. But no longer, no longer! We go to Stratford in four days for the premiere, and the play persists in its wretched performance. I cannot possibly be disgraced before my own audiences.

"You do not understand any of this. The play is not an actual happening, it is like a dream. The island is merely a state of mind, and Prospero is a creature of the imagination. I have gotten into some very deep theological material here. And you don't understand any of it.

"The demeaning literalness of all of this! You there, the chap playing Caliban, I can't stand it anymore, for weeks I have stood aside respectfully while you play this dwarf as if he were a dog. He is not a dog but a spirit of earth and water! He is the key to the play.

"Gentlemen. I have written many plays, and more than thirty of them have been produced, but I have never seen any of my work disgraced. You have distorted *The Tempest* during these weeks. I warn you now that from here on in I will be more than keeping an eye on you. I shall be actively taking part in the rehearsals; I shall be discussing matters with the director. We cannot allow this travesty to continue, or it will be the ruination of us all. You have your reputations to consider as well. Don't you have any pride in yourself as a company?"

And so on. After this was over Thorpe himself stood forward to stand next to S— and, taking off his hat to knead it uncomfortably, said that he extended apologies on his own behalf and on that of the company for what had been a "fundamental misapprehension," in the working out of the text. Thorpe promised that there would be no repetitions of this in the future, and there would instead be a general coming to terms with the body of the drama. He told Caliban and Prospero that he wished to see them for special exercises at the conclusion of this rehearsal, and then he dismissed all of us, warning us to stay out of the town and to avoid drunkenness. He cautioned that the other principals would be similarly tested.

Fortunately, since I was merely playing one of the sailors I was able to make a rapid exit and found myself soon enough with a small uncomfortably chattering group of supernumeraries in the nearest local pub. Usually as a matter of procedure I avoided those foul relationships which existed as the undercurrent of the traveling company, but I was too tired that evening, too shamed, and too dispirited to engage in the effort of isolation. At least half of them, as is to be expected, were faggarts, so they spent the remainder of the evening excitedly discussing Thorpe's humiliation, S—'s arrogance, and the general implications of recent events upon the future of the company. Unwillingly I found myself being drawn into the discussion, and a small, graceful fellow who said his name was George began to regard me with unusual intentness as the evening and the ale progressed.

"You," he said at one point, "we haven't seen much of you around here. You *are* in the company, of course, but where have you been?"

"Oh, mostly I keep to myself," I replied. "I haven't been part of the group for long. I just joined in London."

"Oh yes, of course, I remember now. Well, what do you think of our little organization? What do you think of S—? What plans do you hold for the future?"

"I just joined the company to get some training," I said, detecting an ominous glint in his eye which spoke volumes, to say nothing of attendant, corollary difficulties. "I've always wanted to be an actor, and I was fortunate enough to find a vacancy when the troupe was in. Actually, I don't know if I'll want to go beyond finishing out this tour. It's been disappointing."

"Oh, I'm terribly sorry. What's your name by the way?"

"David Perkins," I told him, and then perceiving his features had set into an even more determined cast—apparently the possession of my name seemed in his mind to place him in a more than casual relationship to me. I hastily made what excuses had to be made—what I did was to claim cramps and incipient vomiting—and pushing my way rapidly through the growing crowd at the pub I made my escape into the open air. I paused at the river to wash my face briefly and then proceeded in the general direction of that dismal inn where the company was being quartered during their engagement.

It occurred to me then to wonder, for the first time, exactly what in hell I was doing there and precisely what I intended to gain by the entrapment, but I didn't want to think about that too much. I didn't want to think about anything actually, so I distracted myself by humming several cheerful tunes in a quavering tenor. The almost oiled ease of drunkenness lent speed to my limbs, not to say grace of passage to my voice, as I lumbered back to my room. For the first time that day, feeling the release of isolation from the tension of the rehearsal and the inn, I began to feel well, well with a distinct fullness of spirit which indicated that a decision was upon me. By the time the inn had forced its way into my gentle gaze the decision itself had been made: I realized that I was going to quit the company when the performances ended in Stratford and would then make my way back to London. I suddenly understood, and understood with an almost farcical completeness, that I had never cared for acting that much anyway—and if S— was any representation of a playwright, Thorpe any representation of a director, and that tortured imp, Garrick, any indication of a principal actor, then I was certainly making a proper decision in getting out of the craft early rather than late. I have a certain small gift in my hands: I can cobble, work in wood and leather, and otherwise engross myself in small mechanical tasks, and my father's moderate means would certainly enable me to begin some kind of trade in London.

So simply did the gnawing of a lifetime's rage settle down within me, then. It is a sad thing, however, to be twenty-three and to realize that you could have saved yourself all of the trouble. It was a shrugging epiphany, though, aided by the slickness and ease of liquor, and when I came into the almost empty pub I was in high spirits indeed, so high that for the first time I glanced at the barmaid with something approaching meaningful appraisal, wondering if, after it was all over, the wench would really be worth the trouble. In the act of pouring a disreputable-looking pair of travelers some beer from a pitcher she caught my gaze and returned it with an appraisal of her own, rendered nonetheless interesting by the high angle of her breasts against the thin garments she wore. What seemed to be a rosy wink descended upon her features, and I made plans to go to my room, change into something slightly more appropriate—I was wearing my costume, still unchanged from the final scene—and go down to examine this terrain with circumspection.

But bounding into my room with a leap already in search of fresh clothing, I found all this easy speculation and lighthearted energy was reduced to the level of fool's tokens because there, sitting on my bed itself, was S— himself, his head sunk in his hands, his hands led down to elbows which rested on his knees, and those knees were so solidly enjambed into the bedspread that he looked ensconced for eternity.

He looked up at me with alertness in his features. "Well, there you are," he said. "Come back after hours of carousing, no doubt. I must say that this is unconscionable behavior for a young actor. You will dissipate your talents. I could tell you stories by the score of actors more gifted than you who have done that."

My original state of shock persisted long enough to leave me absolutely numb; I was only able to take a seat beside him through the careful ritualization of my acts and by suppressing all the wild conjecture which skirted through and around my mind. As little as I liked S— and as disturbing as I have found contact with him from the first, there was no question but that there was something impressive about this man; he was, after all, the head of an important troupe of actors, was once a notable actor himself, and his plays do show a certain facility.

"You wonder why I am here, Perkins," he spoke up after a moment. "I came up some time ago and wished to speak with you. I have now been sitting uncomfortably in this clammy room for some time awaiting your return, wondering if my initial impulse was not, perhaps, the wrong one.

At any rate, I will be frank now. I will be to the point, for it is very late. I have decided to give you a major role in this production immediately."

"You are?" I was amazed. "But I only joined up in London!"

"Yes, I know that perfectly well. I know your birthplace and parents' names and probable motivations for joining our company as well. I have made it my business to learn almost everything about my actors' backgrounds and lives, Perkins, and, therefore, I have no need of your biography. On the other hand, a discussion portends. What do you think of *Tempest?*"

"I don't quite know what to say," I said and hated the way the word "sir" then fell into the end of that sentence as if it had been some kind of mote caught irritatingly in its eye. "I don't think I understand it. It's fantastic but it's too fantastic. And all that unhappiness—"

"Precisely!" S— bellowed. "That is precisely the point!" He gave me a clout on the back which set my insides to shaking. "You have arrived at the basic paradox of the play! It involves misery, true, but the misery is disguised in fantasy. But that lout who is playing Prospero insists upon stressing the dreamlike elements in his performance to such a point that he carries on like a faggart, and the play loses all masculinity, all drive. This company is full of faggarts," he added irrelevantly and leaned back against the wall to produce a particularly foul cigar from his waistcoat which he lit with enjoyment. "At any rate, Perkins," he said, "I have firmly made a decision. You are youthful, and you have a certain intelligence. Also you are fresh to the company and not jaded to that point of nausea which so many of us have reached now that we have come to the end of the tour. I think, therefore, that you can bring something entirely new to this play, something necessary in its important performance in Stratford a week hence. I am enlisting *you* for the role of Prospero."

I admit that the announcement made me shudder, and in the uneasiness of the moment I found myself on my feet, pacing, looking aimlessly out the window which afforded a fine view of a dismal garden in which naked forms seemed to be struggling with one another in the grass. I hoped that neither of them was the barmaid. S— at length produced another cigar, handed it to me, and lit it from the candle with rather tender concern.

"Well," he said, "what say? Surely this is an enormous honor! Nothing you had expected when you joined, right? You only expected to be part of the chorus so to speak."

"But I don't know," I hesitated. "I mean I'm ambitious enough and interested, but the skill—"

"No skill is required at all!" he boomed. "The skill is all in the lines. I have provided everything. All that you have to do is to speak them, not fight their intention as the principal has been doing."

"I don't even know the role."

"You'll be a fast learner. We won't ask you to do it for another three days yet. Meanwhile, we'll keep this our little secret, even from the detestably untalented Thorpe. But he is in my employ and, consequently, will cooperate when informed. I consider it all settled then. Tell me your thoughts on the role."

"Well ..." I began, returning to the bed and for the first time made the deeper realization that in the long run what had just happened to me could be interpreted as an enormous piece of fool's fortune; it is not every amateur, after all, who is offered the leading role in a new play performed by a respectable touring company. "I will have to get my ideas in order. It seems to me that Prospero is basically not as good as he is supposed to be, if you follow my line of reasoning. He mistreats Caliban for one thing, and he manipulates his daughter's life. And then, when he goes away from the island he does it without caring of what might happen next."

"Precisely!" S— shouted. "That is precisely the point, and I cannot tell you how pleased I am to hear your simple mind disgorge these thoughts. Surely if this is obvious to you it should be obvious to any sane member of the populace. The truth of the matter," he said, and then leaned forward to whisper to me confidentially as if the knowledge should be restricted from the walls themselves, "the truth of the matter as I said is that Prospero, while on the island, functions irrationally. On the other hand, his irrationality is so wrapped up in his imagination that one can never quite be sure that it isn't the one voice but the other. That is what the play is about. It is a simple morality lesson of the lengths to which men will go in order to rationalize purposes that are basically unreal. Why is that so difficult for everyone to understand?"

"When will I be able to find the time to learn the lines?"

"We'll take you out of the supernumeraries; those roles are worthless, and you will never be missed. And then, the performance just before we disband, we'll give you the role. No problem whatsoever. What you have got to understand is the basic relationship between Prospero and Caliban. They—"

"Well," I said, "I'm truly honored, I'm sure. I mean, I'm appreciative. But do you really think—"

"Of course I think! This is my company; I can do whatever I choose with it. I'm putting an inexperienced actor into the role precisely to prove my point: that the play is so lucid and strongly written that any baboon can play it if he simply speaks the lines."

Finding this slightly disconcerting I said, "Well, I do have certain ideas of my own about—"

"Ideas! Forget the ideas! The only time an actor gets into difficulty is when he gets an 'idea.' They simulate thought like little children, and then horrid complications set in. Listen to me," S— said, shaking a heavy forefinger at me. "Just listen to me and you'll be all right. You'll give a sterling performance. You'll be widely admired, and your career will be secure. Well, I'm going to be on my way now; it's been a long evening spent mostly in the contemplation of my dim rhetoric and certain old griefs. I'll have to be back to my quarters." He stood up awkwardly, balancing for the moment against the bedpost, and, breathing heavily, threw his cigar on my floor where he ground it to ash under his foot. "Actually, I'm not feeling very well," S— said. "I do believe I'm getting old—I'm forty-eight this month, you understand, and that's no spring's age. Also I'm finding this tour and company increasingly taxing. Some other arrangement will have someday to be made, but in the meantime there are so many plays to write, so many things to do." These last lines he delivered to himself in a distracted fashion as if he were waiting for some kind of distant audience murmur or response and then, without looking back at me, as if my presence had served its purpose and was therefore necessarily obliterated, he walked out closing the door firmly behind him, leaving me to myself.

It occurred to me then that in some climactic, catastrophic way I might have been used, but there was no use in thinking about that now, not with some other vague dread and apprehension cooking up slowly from my interior. The fact was that I have absolutely no acting experience at all and joined the company on a lark with misrepresented credentials. But that was something to be dealt with in due course, not just now, for coming over me was a kind of storming lust for the barmaid, the lust having no particular motivation, of course, nothing specific that is to say, but nonetheless insistent for all of that. I found myself seized by a kind of brief torment in that room, torment for waste, torment for all the opportunities gone shy, torment for all the connections that had never been made because of unfavorable circumstances. And it was then, at that very moment, that I decided I must possess her, must possess her that evening or perish, must move in fact beyond all conventions and maneuver to a point where I could hold her and gain what had to be gained. There was no way in which I would be denied. It is possible that this siege of demented lust came from the facts of my interview with S— just before, but I tried to humor my mind as much as possible by relegating it to second place; I let desire take hold of me. As far as I was then concerned, I wanted the barmaid for her breasts and thighs, and left the whole matter at that.

I did not even pause in my room to give myself minor physical attentions, deciding instead that dishevelment and the frantic burning aspect of my eyes, their rather hollow cast, might lend enchantment to what would be a kind of insistence anyway. I went downstairs, then, not even bothering to secure the door behind me and found to my surprise and astonished delight that the bar was now almost empty; the barmaid, lounging sulkily in one corner, had absolutely nothing to do except to rest her fair head on the table against the crook of an elbow. A single bald man sat at the bar in a state of numbed intoxication so profound that his moans and whistled intakes of breath were his one connecting link to his mortality.

I went boldly up to the bar and demanded an ale, and when she came before me I put a hand on her soft wrist and looked into her eyes as she placed the drink uneasily on the bar. "You been wanting to talk to me?" I said rather hoarsely. "Here I am. My name is David Perkins."

"You're with that acting company," she said in a rather disconcertingly bleated soprano. "I've noticed you. How are you, Mr. Perkins? Tell me if the ale is well with you."

"None of that," I said. "What is your name?"

"And why be you asking?"

"I want to know your name."

"My name is Jane," she said. "Jane Smith if you must know. Was that Mr. S— himself who departed just a bit ago?"

"Yes it was," I said. "He was up to my room to see me. I'm his lead actor; we were discussing the role I'm going to play."

"That play they're doing in the village? I've heard things about it. Of course I never get a chance to see a play. I have to see this bar all the time, so my work gets in the way."

"Well," I said, "if you really want to see it I'm sure that we can work out a performance for you—at a different time perhaps. As a matter of fact, I'll be happy to read you all the lines of my role right now if you'd like to hear them. Why don't you come up to my room?"

She gave a sidelong glance at the now-sleeping roisterer whose agonized old head rested on the bar atop his folded hands and who was emitting a series of deep snorts into the polished wood. "Oh that's impossible," she said. "I've got to be here until the place closes—to watch over him."

"Nonsense!" I objected. "He's intoxicated, and he's unconscious. There's no need to care for him, and no one else is here. You can close the bar and come right upstairs."

"It wouldn't be honorable," she said and straightened in a way that caused her large breasts to point forward behind her blouse at such an astonishing angle that I could have gasped for the joy of this perception. I wanted to run my hands disastrously over her *poitrine*. "I have to do my job as they see fit, otherwise they won't have me anymore."

"But you *must* come to my rooms," I said and was dismayed to sense the whine creeping into my voice. "You simply must. I won't have it any other way. I'll pay for your time at the bar. I mean, you can close it up, and I'll reimburse the proprietor for your time and his losses. Come up now, and I'll certainly read the whole part to you, complete with gestures."

She gave me a long glance which might or might not have had the hint of a wink in it and said, "I think you've got the entirely wrong idea of me. I'm not that kind of girl at all."

"Of course you're not that kind of girl. I've got no idea of you whatsoever. I thought we might come to know each other—"

"Not at all," she interrupted shaking her head. "I'm neither trollop nor slattern. The trouble with you traveling companies is that you're all the same; I've seen you come by by the hundreds, and you don't understand that everything you do has been done and done before. I'm so bored by the sameness! In any event, I won't be treated like a child."

"I'm not treating you like a child," I protested, and then despair and uncertainty came over me and I said, "I'm not treating you any way at all ... all right, have it that way then. Just give me a drink, then I'll go up to my room and go to sleep."

"Yes, yes," the roisterer mumbled, coming out of his stupor with surprising ease and turning his old flat face in my direction; it wobbled unsteadily on his neck. "Give the young lad a drink and then another one. Send him off to an easy bed, for 'tis a difficult night, a long night, that lies ahead."

"Quiet!" Jane said and made a violent gesture in his direction which might or might not have been obscene, and the roisterer gave an enormous sigh and folded up again over the bar; his hands trembled. "Filthy bugger," she said to me. "The only time you get any life out of him—and he's been sitting here for six hours—is when he has a chance to insult you. Listen," she said, putting a hand atop the back of mine and rubbing it unevenly to and fro, "I didn't say I wouldn't come to your rooms, now did I? There's no reason to be sulky about it. I know how sensitive actors are."

"Women too!" the roisterer shouted with a brusque wave of his arm of such strength that he commenced to fall off his stool. Slowly and dramatically he collapsed in an uneven heap near the footrails of the bar and with an expiring sigh crouched deeply into himself. Any sense of crisis I might have had, however, was resolved by the ragged resumption of his breathing which happened presently. Then he moaned, stirred, and finally adjusted into a more comfortable position and slouched there unmoving.

"But you can't get the wrong idea about me," she continued. "I mean, one thing's one thing and the other is the other. Anyway, I can't close up this minute; I've got to clean him up off the floor. Why don't you go upstairs, and I'll join you presently? In half an hour or a little less, not that I don to want to go now," she amended—and this time there was a definite wink that cleaved through her features and perched with definition on the corner of her right eyebrow.

"Yes," I said. "Yes, yes." And, finishing my drink with one swallow, I sprang from the bar and raced upstairs, two at a time and went into my room. I must have been half naked before I had fully closed the door, the remainder of my clothes followed to land in a discarded fashion on the floor. I leaped into the bed with an enormous jump, my legs all springs. The touch of the cold sheets as I drew them up around me was shocking to my naked prick, already distended to huge proportions. But no less shocking than that was the exquisite cold fire of the sheets as they moved across my asshole, a center of sensation I had never previously noticed. I lay down there then to await her entrance, praying that I had not been too direct.

After a while, however, and because there was need to keep my mind off what I hoped would follow, I noticed that S— had left a copy of the play in the chair near the bed, either on purpose for my study or because he had been in haste to make an exit. I picked it up, noting that it was written out in ink in an uneven shaking hand, carried over some hundred pages; the paper was of a very fine stock, one which held the ink well, giving further evidence of how the inscriber's hand had trembled. I began to read the play without much interest, merely as a means of passing some time but after a short while I found myself somewhat absorbed in it. Despite my presence at all the rehearsals and the rather glib analysis given to me by S—, the fact was that I was only barely conscious of the mechanics of the plot, to say nothing of the movement of the play, so it was almost entirely fresh to me. I found it moderately diverting, but, as is the case with most of S—'s work, too stilted, rhetorical, and windy to really be communicative. Like all of his work that I had seen performed in London there was nothing that much wrong with it that some clean editing and reduction of the flourishes wouldn't have done a great deal for. Certainly I could see what Thorpe had been complaining about: it was almost impossible to tell from the written word whether the play was a comedy or a tragedy, and S— in his unsureness, in his eagerness to touch both bases, had left the thing almost entirely disjointed. This was my criticism for what it is worth. Actually I find plays in general something of a dreadful bore; they have a purpose, I am sure, and they certainly create opportunities for actors, but drama itself, having so little to do with anything other than the simulation of real life could, perhaps, be dispensed with entirely.

At any rate, past my initial concern, I found myself rapidly bored and tossed it aside. It was fortunate that I did so at that moment for scarcely had I put the play under the bed, intending some further study and memorization in the morning, when, without ceremony, the door opened and Jane came in. She was still wearing her costume but it was in a subtle state of disrepair: more of her left breast was showing than was necessary, perhaps because the rosy flush which had entered her body was not conducive to garments. I did not waste any more time in speculation. "I'm glad you came. Please lock the door, will you?"

She gave me a squinting sidelong glance but unprotestingly nailed the bolt home, and as she did so I tore the covers from my frame and with a great bound stood before her; my nudity to her hopefully was at least as shocking as her sexuality would presently be to me, my enormous clout bobbing and weaving before her. She gave a small shriek and started to retreat, but before she could put her hand to the bolt I seized her bare upper arm—a soft lovely construction which had the smooth yielding constancy of the finest velvet—and said, "Please, come on, you know you want to lie with me; that's the reason you came up. Don't deny me; don't taunt me; please, please, please," and similar moans and mumbles. All the time I was engaged in these endearments my hands were working, working on her upper garments loosening, untucking, disassembling, and one vagrant hand was already probing inside toward that lushness; a firm knee went gliding up to the span of her crotch, and I wrestled her against me, pressing my lips against her neck. "Now, now, now," I said or something similar.

She had abandoned her first efforts to escape me, and as a matter of fact had responded with silence and a stationary posture while I worked on her clothing. But now, as I had removed everything from above her waist to clutch her to me in a seizing embrace, she began to struggle with a genuine righteousness, her fists beating my chest, her little legs kicking, and I had to let her go, had to let her enlarge the distance between us. She stared at me across a span of a few feet, her breasts not quite as large as I might have pictured in fantasies but tilted against enormously distended, peculiarly colored nipples the very sight of which filled me with the groans of an imminent release.

Looking at me directly, she said, "You're trying to brutalize me!"

"No, no, no!" I protested, infuriated at this easy and timeless misapprehension of women who can only turn sex, whenever it suits them, toward their own limited purposes. Helpless, pointless creatures all of them—but what are we to do without them? "I'm not trying to brutalize you, I'm trying to capture you, to make love to you, to express—"

"But I'm not that kind of woman! You're taking me for a whore!"

"Oh, no, my beautiful Jane!" I said, "I am not! I wouldn't be so tender with any trollop or tart. You are special to me." And then, seized by moans, my need and greed, I came forward breaching that distance again and put my arms on her. Then, with small tugs of encouragement and whispers, I began to lead her to the bed. To my great joy I could feel her begin to open up. She moved against me, and this counterbalanced my efforts so that we fell in a clumsy, breathless tangle to the bed, and my frantic hands began to work on her skirt, working against the slippery polish of her thighs.

And then she was nude, lying exposed underneath me, the incredible fullness of her thighs and belly in perfect proportion to those luscious breasts. I stood above her from an enormous height, looking down at her like a possessor, and then with a series of cries I threw myself upon her and began to wrench, tug, and stroke at those enormous surfaces. She began to reciprocate, slowly at first, then with greater intensity.

"I don't usually do this kind of thing," she said. "You can never trust actors anyway." Then, "What do you take me for, anyway?" Then, "I'm glad to see that at least you were a gentleman at the beginning." When, "My breasts, give my breasts a good squeezing." Then, "Oh, you've got the most enormous prick, the most enormous prick I've ever seen!" and similar words, all of them blending together.

I was locked in a small, grim web of silence by my need and insistence. I moved over her, feeling the rising and beating of the good come within me, much as if it were a frantic moth scrappling for exit. I was beyond words, beyond speech, beyond rationalization, bending my head in a series of aimless movements to suck and lap at those enormous nipples—bigger by far, it seemed, than the normal span of my forehead—and then working to the underbreast, working to the belly, around the navel, up the line of the stomach and so on.

"Magnificent!" she screamed. "Oh, God, I haven't had it this good in so long, don't stop now!"

Not even needing this splendid encouragement I took her hand and curled her fist around my cock, felt her nails and the tips of her fingers digging deep into the growing length of it which indeed, from her peculiar angle, must have seemed enormous, and then she was moving me into the small nest of her. I could feel it against me, and with a few tender prods of the organ I had entered the wetness, turned the core of her into a gush. I felt myself being drawn up there, slowly, slowly, exquisitely. That first melding in the cunt of a new woman is surely at least as extraordinary an experience as reading the first line of a new play or, the first discovering of a remarkable intention in prosody. All of them satisfactions, all of them rewards—but none so slick, warm, and comforting as this.

"Oh that's good," she said to me enthusiastically, her voice a sudden high chatter as if she were being coaxed into some kind of social conversation at tea. "That feels so good! Get it in there deeper and deeper."

All encouraged I worked my way into the depths of her, my organ supremely confident of its ability to reach her womb—as all external evidence has already indicated, I do have an abnormally large cock. But as I felt myself making that slow inductive passage, all of it exquisite, all of its nerve ends and fibers open to aid me, it felt truly endless. I felt myself being drawn further and further along, and there was simply no end to it, finally I had reached my full length with a bump, and still uncharted seas lay ahead of me! Panting midway between desire and surprise—this being the first woman I had never penetrated completely—I reached my hands forward and began to rub her breasts wildly, pumping the flesh and squeezing it through my fingers. In this position all deceit was gone, her breasts were more than ample, her tiny rib cage in sharp contrast to the full forward thrust of her breasts. Her flesh was as rich and devious as any I had ever touched.

"Oh, get in there! Get in there!" she cried, and I must have made a wince because she added, "Oh, well, there's nothing to be done about it. Everybody's had that trouble."

So saying she began without pause or transition to buck and whinny against me, and I could feel her hips writhing and slamming against me. My cock began the old series of plunges, moving back and forth that familiar distance, and I found myself already on the verge of coming. But I held back, held back through long cunning and experience, trying instead to fragment my thought and diffuse it through my body to save that hard, frenzied concentration. But I was not successful because she began to cry harsh words.

"Finish!" she was screaming. "Get it off, damn it, I can't stand it anymore!"

Thus encouraged I let the full flow of my semen discharge itself. Waves and rivulets poured out of me in a lengthy gush, and the strangeness was that I felt the jettisoning of the sperm before the orgasm itself, a rare experience for usually it is either simultaneous or (less often) before the emission. But this time I was already pouring, snorting, and steaming into her before I felt the throes themselves take me. They were coming on so late that I felt for a moment there might be some intricate deficiency of equipment which had cheated me from the accustomed end, but it was only some trick of her thighs, some dark secret her cunt worked upon the conjoinment, for then I felt the coming seize me, seize me with an intensity that seemed to take me by the scruff of the neck in an enormous hand and dangle me helplessly. I was screaming too, my body coming down hard to slap against hers, all of it pouring, pouring, one hard pellet of nipple absorbed in my mouth, battering against my teeth. And then, for the moment, it was finished, finished indeed, and a most extraordinary fuck it had been. No question about it.

"Don't take it out!" she shouted. "I'm still coming! Can't you see that you blasted idiot?" So I left it in while she continued in some privation of the soul to throb against me, her eyes closed, her breasts swinging, her torso dancing beneath me, her hands biting down hard into my back, not so much scratching as seizing me.... After a time she too was finished, having chased her orgasm as far as she could and, like most women, having in the last moment not quite touched it (which is what makes them further accessible). She panted and collapsed deeper into the bed, gasping and moaning, biting her lips. "Oh, good Lord," she said, "you can really do it. I've never had such a thing like that in me before. It must be all of nine inches."

"Ten I think," I said, "or maybe eleven, but I haven't measured it in years, and it doesn't make any difference anyway; it's long enough."

"Not long enough to get in me all the way. I've never found a cock that could. Oh, it's not your fault, don't look that way, men always think that it's somehow personal. No, I've just got a very long canal, this doctor told me that once. It was good anyway. Oh, it was good."

But the question of how good it was or was not already seemed irrelevant to me, for I felt the idiot desire rising again, a desire that flickered between her lips, her breasts, and the open cunt between her spread legs. I was filled with the consuming rage once more, a rage not only of possession but of discovery because it had been so terribly long since I had had a woman in my bed—it was since I had left London weeks ago. It was also a kind of frustration because, in the last analysis, I had not satisfied her. And so I was reaching, reaching again to touch her. Giggling indolently she was pressing back against the bedspread, one arm behind her head, the other dangling toward the floor when— and oh, how characteristic this is!—that arm which swung so loosely over the side of the bed suddenly touched something concrete and then emerged with the playscript which S— had left for me.

"What is this?" she said, raising it and bringing her other hand up to balance it. "Is this a play? It's full of writing. It looks like a play to me."

"Yes," I said, "it's the one that we're doing next."

"Oh. That's nice. Is your part in it too?"

"All of the parts are in it. But please put it away. Please don't look at it now. I beg of you."

"But it looks interesting," she squealed, "all this writing and all those words. It must be very exciting to be an actor. Would you read some of it to me now? I'd love to hear it."

"You can read it yourself," I said, rather sullenly under the circumstances established.

"There's nothing much to it. It isn't very much of a play after all."

"I want you to read it to me."

"I won't. I've been reading it all day. Read it yourself, if you must. But can't you put it away?"

Her lip trembled slightly. "I would if I could," she said, "but I can't read. I never learned how. Is there so much shame in that? Why don't you read me a part of it?"

I had no words. They are always exaggerating. But there is no question but that the majority of the adult population in the rural areas is indeed illiterate; this is a fact which is difficult to grasp if one comes from enlightened London where almost all adult professionals can read with fluency. I looked at her: the filmy softness of her on the sheets; the soft articulation of her breasts against her chest which possessed a feeling and communicability which no written word ever could; the delicate pout of her mouth which would never parse syllables; and I felt something within myself break. Sighing I plucked the book from her grasp and opened the pages at random. "Well," I began, "this says that it's the beginning of the fourth act. Prospero is speaking."

"Who is Prospero?"

"He's the main role. That's my role. That's what I play, I'm the lead actor in this company."

"That must be very exciting," she said and drew a finger down my chest from nipple to navel, filling me with an unholy shift of consciousness, forcing me to inhale and exhale slowly, deliberately, while I regained control of myself. "Oh, I'm sorry," she said. "I forget the kind of effect that can have on a man. I won't do it again."

"You can do it again right now. I don't care. I want you to."

"Not now. I'd rather hear you read. Show me how you act in the play. Read me your part."

"What part?" I asked distractedly.

"You said you had the main role. Prosperous."

"Prospero."

"Prospero. That's what I meant. Come on. Anyway, you could at, least talk to me. Everything isn't sex, you know."

"Sometimes it can be," I said, but that would have opened up an unprofitable, not to say hopeless, line of discussion so I began to read one of the long speeches having to do with revels ending and dreams and sleep and the end of all things. It was hard to make it sound right because as usual S— had bloated the thing out of all recognition with difficult words and phrases. But on the other hand, I could see how it might be effective in a certain way if given a right vocal interpretation. It is difficult, however, to give any kind of vocal interpretation while lying flat on your back naked, holding a book and reading, while a woman is grasping your cock and drawing the balls up against the base of the prick, tugging on them, running between them with gentle fingertips. Then, moaning slightly, she reaches down to place her other hand across the first so that the entire organ is fully cupped, and the small gestures of erection begin, assisted by her in all ways: her soft groans and pants, the whisper of her breasts drawn lightly across the face, the touch of her nipple gliding past an eyelid and then drooping down toward the mouth, the rise of the bursting cleavage as it billows and sags against the cheeks and ultimately— "Well look," I mumbled against her flesh, "this is lovely, but I can't really read when you do that. It's too distracting."

"Oh, nonsense," she said. "Don't stop reading. It's really beautiful. I don't know what he's saying, but it makes me feel so sad."

"Come to me," I said, putting down the script and reaching that freed hand around her back, grasping, tugging her in, feeling her sigh and cave in to me. "Come on, come on." I began to feel her moving lightly against me, the soft imprint of her skin bringing fire to me, the cleaving touch of her fingers grazing me from head to toe. I felt myself sinking, sinking, into the darker softnesses of her flesh.

"Oh, it's just so sad," she said, stopping her motions for an instant, and raising herself on her elbow to regard me seriously. "There's something about it that gives you the chills. You read it so beautifully."

"Thank you."

"What is the great globe itself? Does that mean he's talking about the whole world?"

"I think so, but I'm not sure. There's a Globe theater where some of the plays have been given. That's where we're supposed to go to perform. Maybe he's just talking about the theater."

"Then there would be a double meaning, wouldn't there?" she said.

"He's talking about the world, and he's talking about the theater. That's nice. I like the way he does that."

"I never thought of that," I said, "I suppose so. I really have to study the role and get into it."

"I like to hear poetry," she said. "You never hear poetry where I come from. Nobody even thinks of it. So people get the idea that just because you never hear it that you can never appreciate it. That's not so. I like the way that sounds."

"All right," I said, "all right," and to abandon the discussion rolled over on her, covering her mouth with mine, reaching with my hands to seize and stroke the soft folds of flesh which curved under her waist. Then she turned her back gently toward me, lay on her stomach, the full smoothness of her body exposed in its anonymity to me. It was true; it was just as they had said: turned on their stomachs all of them looked miraculously similar. But this, of course, was not to denigrate the beauty of that complexion lying like a thick mask on the bed, or the gentle, half-parted folds of her buttocks which she then pulled slowly apart exposing to me an inner redness.

"That way," she said. "Do it that way now. Come on."

"That way?"

"You know. Don't make me tell you. I like that more than anything. Put it all the way in there. My dreams are ending. My revels are ending. Come on! Come on!"

There was no way to mistake the throaty insistence of her voice, nor to be unaware of the gentle, tossing motions of her buttocks as they raised invitingly toward me. Nevertheless, I had heard or read somewhere once that the practice was extremely injurious to the vitality, to say nothing of the latent energies of the male physique, and thus I found myself slightly reluctant, too hurt to tell her, however, that I reacted in this way, too needful of her yet to tell her what I thought. And so I said nothing, only shifted my body slightly over hers and then, lancing down with all my strength, I made the connection, feeling myself slide into her with a liquid rapidity which matched the speed with which I had made the entrance into the original hole. As I did so, I could feel her contract against me, could feel her seize my prick in a clutch of inspiration. At the same time she began to groan, small absent furies of obscenity passed from her, and I found this taking me on to new heights, although it did, all things considered, take me an abnormally long time to come.

"Fuck, fuck, fuck!" she screamed. "All the way up there, all the way!"

I bounced and jostled through her inviting buttocks, a connection so deep that I thought I could feel her bowels, and then my hands snaked around, got all the way under her and grasped the lavishness of that gift in front. Bobbling and jerking them, I could feel the heat of her nipples, a heat that crested and rose up through my fingers and up my arms, could feel her rising, sense the surging, knew her own passion. Then with an, "Unh, unh, unh!" which might have been the sounds of a wounded animal—but not a dying animal, it would live to plunge once again through the forests—I poured into her. My orgasm came before my emission this time, so that only after the agony had torn through me did I feel the anticlimactic, almost pitiable release of sperm as it shot into her, deep into some hidden coil.

She moaned one last time and gave an expiring sigh underneath me as I collapsed, my cheek next to her cheek.... Her breath began to come evenly, pouring from her lips with such regularity that I realized she was asleep, leaving me quite to my own devices. I lay there in the dark for a time thinking of nothing in particular, my prick still wrapped deeply within her, curling upon itself like a sleeping flower as it made its slow, instinctive retraction. Abandoning myself against her in the stupor of oncoming sleep I passed into a long, comfortable alley of unconsciousness where I must have dwelt for quite a long time indeed, for when I woke up it was day, and she had left me. The sheets were pulled up to my shoulders, the manuscript of *The Tempest* was nestling against my cheek, the pages opened with tender concern to the passage that I had been reading.

I had no particular or compelling interest in the stage, but there was the question of that purse-snatching in London along with parental admonitions and the strong threat of incarceration. It was finally agreed that if I removed myself from the presence of those I had made uncomfortable, charges would not be pressed, at least for the time being. So I had to go in search of an alternate career.

Oh, purse-snatching, pig-stealing, procuring, the banality of all the urban evils! But there is so little left for us; the country is obviously harsh and fragmented, and there are only so many things that a young, relatively uneducated young man can do, particularly if he has very little inventive skill and is so ill suited to many of his acts that midway in flight with the stolen purse he will pause to look into a shop to see what, in more peaceful times, he might be able to buy with the money he has appropriated.

I said that S—'s troupe was in London at that time. I was somehow able to inveigle myself into becoming a supernumerary. This leads me to explain that solemn pact I made with Thorpe—to say nothing of the strained situation into which I was subsequently placed.

"Well listen here," Thorpe, the director, said to me in the empty theater after I had intercepted him in flight after the conclusion of the rehearsal, a strangely frail, quivering man of middle years and frail disposition, features pasted indiscriminately over a flat, unmolded pan of a face, "I just have no time, no time for conversation. I have too many things to do. How did you ever get yourself in here in the first place?"

"The doors were open," I said. "I enjoyed the rehearsal very much. It's an interesting play. I've long been a great admirer of S—; I think he's a splendid playwright and—"

Thorpe interrupted: "Enough of that! I don't know how you got in here then or what you presume, but I'm sorry, I have no time to talk. The whole play is disintegrating because nothing's working out right; we have to meet and go over it line by line."

"Let me join the company," I said, feeling it wise to come to the point immediately rather than allow misdirection. "I've done a lot of acting here in London. I'll come along for no compensation at all, merely the honor of joining the company and being part of it."

"Impossible. We have a full contingent. Besides, I have no idea of your talents at all. If you want to join you'd have to go through S—. He makes all the decisions; I only implement them."

"But wait!" I said frantically, seizing him by the elbow before he could dash away, "I'm sure it would be perfectly all right with S—. You always need an extra or two—and I'm willing to do menial tasks as well: setting up the stage, cleaning down the floors, and so on and so forth. I have no objections to almost any kind of labor. Besides it's important for me to leave London in some respectable way. I can't go into details of course but—"

"Aha!" Thorpe exclaimed, and a patient, unaccommodating shrewdness passed across his face. He seemed to be surveying me for the first time, as he removed a large, colored handkerchief from his pocket and began to blot nervously at certain aspects of his countenance to no particular improvement of their appearance. "Now I understand the situation. I have seen it so many times, you understand me that it all retracts to a hideous sameness, a single posture of response which is meaningless, meaningless!" He gestured wildly. "We *cannot*, my friend, be a refuge for felons. The stage is a disreputable pursuit, there is no question about it, and even though S—'s plays have a rightfully held reputation for being blood-spattered, there still must be limits as to how authentic are our professional performances."

"Well listen," I said. "Surely you would run into the problem of many of the men objecting to playing the female roles."

"Not as much as we once did," Thorpe said. "And now you must really pardon me as I must be off. Form follows function after all, and if it is necessary for men to play women's roles, well, then, you will tend toward an increasing population of men who will accept this and be willing to do it."

"I'll play women's roles," I blurted. "It doesn't mean a thing to me at all. I'll even play young girls."

"No!" Thorpe shouted. "This is no longer amusing, and I must be on my way. I have no idea of how you infiltrated yourself, but—"

"I'll do whatever you will!" I burst out without reflection. "I'll do anything you want me to do! Surely there must be *some* use I can be to you. I'm young, intelligent, good looking, and submissive. I tell you, I'll do *anything* for you; you can do *anything* with me."

Thorpe stopped once again, and that strange contemplative expression took over his expression. He carefully folded the handkerchief in quarters and put it in his pocket. "Ah," he said and silently pondered.

"I'm serious," I added, uncomfortable because of his silence.

"Of course you're serious, you young miscreant. But what do you think you could possibly do that would be of any interest to me at all?"

"That's up to you," I said and looked him in the eye. I was taking a chance, of course, but not as much of a chance as all that. One pretty well knows, of course, living in an urban center such as London what the theater is and who tends to make up a large part of that device. Besides my reasons for wanting to get out of London were most unusually urgent, being based upon such possibilities as incarceration and the deprivation of my manhood at the most crucial period possible. Under the circumstances, I rationalized that there could not be much dispute over the proposition since even absurd sex at the breeding age is better than no sex at all. "I'm willing to suit your pleasure."

We gazed at each other blankly for a long time, then. The two of us were suspended in such an absolute and irredeemable moment in time and space that it was possible for the moment to feel context stripped from the circumstance, to feel that we were two neuters confronting one another in a void, so tight was the concentration, so absent the focus. But after a while it was Thorpe—being perhaps more experienced or being, possibly, less courageous; it all depends upon the way you look at these things—who grunted and turning away said, "Well, you know, there's no question of bribery involved here. My chief responsibility is to the company. If you have talent I'm sure we can use you; if you don't, we can't." But then he asked, "Do you have talent? What is your acting background?"

"I acted for Marlowe in a local production," I said. "I played Tamburlaine," which was the wrong thing to say indeed since the plays of Marlowe were S—'s competition. "I believe that my performance was considered most promising."

"But what about S—? Have you ever done any of *his* plays?"

"No, unfortunately. We have trouble getting hold of the scripts; most of the versions which we see in the local company are expurgated versions which we feel do not do simple justice to the original text, so in the absence of a legitimate quarto—"

"Ah, of course, of course, of course," he said. "This is something we do hope to remedy sooner or later." A hand reached out and touched me tenderly, a small beam of concern running through his index finger to my shoulder, and I felt the slight trembling in his arm as he gazed at me intently. "What's your name anyway, lad?" he said after a few moments of silence.

"David Perkins."

"David," he said ruminatively, "David Penkins. I believe I might have known someone of that name a long time ago. No, he had a different surname, David, a splendid lad; we knew one another in a provincial company many years in the past. We had the opportunity to learn the ways of the theater together. Yes, I do remember him well now. I haven't seen him in such a long time."

"May I please join?" I asked, pressing what I hoped was an advantage of sorts. "I could easily camp with the company tonight; it would be simplicity itself as I have very few roots here which—"

"Not so quickly," Thorpe said, and putting a confidential arm around my shoulders led me to a back row of seats, easing me in gently and then following to sit knee to knee against me, his eyes deep and warm in his face. The squeeze of his hands on my shoulders lent a somewhat cheering, brightening aspect to what otherwise would have been a very sober confrontation. "First, we should have an interview of some sort to justify your competence, to learn your background. What play of S— do you most admire?" he began.

"Oh, all of them," I said. "I find them *all* admirable. But *The Merchant of Venice* is my favorite I suppose. I find it very sharply satirical. Of course, I've only come across it in one of those expurgated versions which, I'm sure, doesn't convey the essence."

"Good enough. Would you rather play male roles or female roles in the productions? You understand that our lack, our really criminal lack, is for a number of men willing to perform the female parts. It's this silly law you see, but it places an entirely wrong interpretation on things, so too many men feel that if they act the feminine roles they'll be taken for faggarts. You don't mind being taken for a faggart, do you son?"

"Not in the least," I confirmed with a broad grin.

"I mean, the label, the appellation, the interpretation wouldn't concern you at all, even if you had to work constantly underneath that burden?"

"No," I said, "it wouldn't bother me at all."

He looked surprised and mumbled something under his breath; it was impossible to distinguish the words but they sounded something like, "I'll be damned." A heavy few moments passed before he spoke up: "Well, then, let's see. You say you'd be ready to travel this evening? You see, we're leaving at once. We have an engagement in a week and a very tight travel schedule."

"I can go at once," I said enthusiastically.

"All right, my boy," he said standing and extending a rather solemn hand, "in that case, I'll take a chance on you. This is all contingent upon S—'s approval, of course; it's really his company, I am merely in his employ, but, since he leaves the question of management of the cast pretty well to me, I would assume that there won't be any objection. I'll look forward to seeing you here ready to go at exactly six o'clock this evening."

"I'm very grateful," I said. "I want you to understand that it means a great deal to me. If there's anything I can do to repay your kindness—"

"Oooh!" Thorpe emitted a high, piercing sound strangely disconcerting under the circumstances, even though, of course, it could have been predicted. "I guess that there might be something sooner or later, some way for you to show your gratitude—but not for the moment." And straightening his shoulders he strode out through the doors then, his frame arched against a burst of sunlight which as it glared at him did indeed make him squint. I could sense a slight shudder passing across his frame as he weaved out of sight.

That is how I got the job with the S— company.

There were, of course, problems and complications that arose from our first meeting but nothing worth mentioning at this time; if I am going to be reasonably complete and historically accurate here then everything must take its shape in due course.

This all goes to show that the making of a career on the stage is a relative kind of thing, relative to the situation and the people involved that is. But life is not always—unfortunately—all that damned relative, and there are no easy answers even in this simplest of all possible existences.

There was this bitch in Piccadilly. She liked to be whipped, repeatedly, lustily, usually with a leather contrivance—and if she was in chains well, then, so much the better. I must have undergone that torment with her for a full year before the surprising set of events which precipitated my upheaval and emergence into the craft of acting; I say *torment* because there is no question but that many of my impulses, not to say responses were deeply shaped and permanently affected by that relationship and that even now, to this day, there is an irretrievable sense of loss at the milder forms of the comedy to which I have evolved. Her name was Elizabeth, and I believe that she was a trollop originally descended from good family, although one cannot be sure of this or any of the circumstances. Our relationship was not one based upon much dialectic or the exchange of personal histories. It was Elizabeth who actually got me into this fix in a pretty way ... it would be a most tortured line of reasoning, of course, that would ascribe all of it entirely to her. Perhaps if it had not been for her I would not have ventured into pig-stealing and assorted crimes, but, then, I might only have ventured into another rationalization. It is hard to say.

She stood before me bared to the waist, her high breasts heaving, her face flushing as she said, "Lash me again. Harder you fool! Damn you, harder!"

I stood before her, half naked myself, the steel bracelets which she always made me wear—somewhat of a particular embarrassment because they gave a rather martial air to the endeavor, one which I could easily have forsaken—and said, "I'm resting, now. Can't you let me take my breath for a minute?"

She rattled the chains she had me fasten across the bed keeping her locked to the mattress as she kicked her feet with frustration. "Now!" she insisted. "What's wrong with you? Don't you know how to torture a girl?"

So I lifted the whip again and wincing, brought it down across her body with some simulation of energy, brought it down once or twice hearing the modifying crack against her stomach, and she began to sob and mumble incoherently, asking me to get away from her belly, to whip her around her breasts and higher. Her words blended and merged into a bubbling shriek of sorts, and I felt the revulsion beginning to twitch in me again, a revulsion compounded out of no small amount of horror because it occurred to me after all this time that I had learned to enjoy the ritual, to extract from its pain and terror no small amount of reward to myself. (There is nothing we humans can do, it seems, that we cannot make to pleasure us after a time.) I raised the whip again and brought it down hesitantly on her breasts, always enjoying the way she jumped at the first contact, and yet at the same time feeling a small retreat, a small quiver moving up and down me because of the whole thing.

She began to shriek in a louder and higher voice urging me on faster and faster. The way the ritual went was that I was supposed to chain her up and whip her for ten to fifteen minutes or until she had her first orgasm, whichever came first. Then, after that was done, I could obtain my part of the bargain in more conventional fucking, although she often needed another whipping after my own climax so that she could be ready for a second onslaught. An even trade, a fine barter, the kind of thing out of which all good relationships are born because we had learned to accommodate each other with all the particular necessities.

But it was getting difficult, more and more difficult indeed, and the peculiarly subterranean nature of the relationship which only involved these activities in her apartment three times a week and connection of no sort outside had already become dismaying.

"I think it has something to do with my father," she had said the first night I had picked her up in the street and been taken home by her. Then she had told me what I had to do to give her pleasure: "I think that I really want a man to beat me the way my father used to do it. I'm not happy unless I'm being hurt, but I really don't think that I want to talk about things like that now, do you? It isn't nice. It's usually just a matter of doing what you want to do and not being too concerned with the other." And made naked already by my own need, my own lust, my own rage to touch and knead her fine high breasts unconcealed by the dress she wore, I had agreed and had, after a fashion, shown some genuine proficiency with the whip and other ornaments she had lined up in her closet.

And so it had gone on this way, gone on this way for a long, long time now, a constancy born out of routine. But suddenly, lifting the whip to heave it down upon her once again, I found myself overcome by a remorse as sudden as it was unappetizing but above all a fine, tight air of demoralization spread through me not unmixed with woe, and I tossed the whip to one side, removed the clanking bracelets with a gesture and then, completely disrobing myself, I crouched and leaped upon her, got down upon her body spreading my legs so that my prick hung straight out over her gasping mouth and then, pushing her wrists down on the bed to avoid accident, I began to make a series of wild thrusting motions, attempting to induce myself all the way into her, attempting to plunge my wang all the way to its base root into her mouth that so had shown itself willing only to throw verbal obscenities at me.

I suppose that my idea was to force her through and out the other end of her perversity—ah youth! ah naïveté!—and by so doing to bring her up to a level of accommodation at which we might be sensibly able to talk over this difficulty, but it was hard, hard. She fought me with a lioness's cunning and with an energy that was quite horrible, not to say dangerous, and I had to concentrate all my energies upon not being wounded, upon keeping her under the mask of chains. It was her own sickness that had defeated her: it was she who insisted upon putting on the chains so that she would be tied down with a maximization of brutality, a minimum of escape; she trusted no one else to affix her as securely as she could herself. Now, when she was trying so desperately to work out from under the chains, she could not. Her mouth was closed, set in a tight thin line, and it was almost impossible to make any kind of entrance unless I exerted enormous pressure with my fingers on her throat.

I was finally able to force myself down in there, and after one horrified instant, when it occurred to me—how obvious!—that she might bite me in retaliation, I was able to force some meaningful kind of pumping action. Her mouth was suddenly quiescent; her teeth were not working with me or against me either; there was merely the suspicion of those oral nails digging into me. But I took my hands away from her wrists, taking something of a chance in the doing and circled them down to her breasts, seized them, began to squeeze and depress the nipples, feeling them slide glossy under my palm. The enormous, groaning force of my orgasm was already taking me as I felt the pressure of her mouth against my prick, and I began to scream then, words and moans mumbled together in some kind of an alcoholic stuporous cry, "Do it this way," I was saying. "If you want degradation you bitch, then take your degradation like this!" And at the last instant, just as I was on the verge of coming, I yanked myself out of her with a popping sound—an enormous effort of will—and put myself below, it was difficult to make entrance because of the way her legs were held relatively clamped by the chains but I was so moist and she so unmoving that I was able to slide at least halfway through there. Then at last I had my orgasm, feeble enough it was because of the deficiency of contact but satisfying anyway because it was the first orgasm I had not flayed myself into with whips. So I took it as far as it went, feeling the streams turn into spurts and then convulsive jerks, and I flopped upon her fishlike and was done, done, feeling my exhausted, expiring sigh rack and shape my being.

I clambered off her and looked at her. I don't know what I expected to see in her face—maybe an openness, maybe a kind of exposure, maybe even a wink of new knowledge—but whatever I had expected in my naïveté I was not going to receive. She stared back at me cold, unblinking, her cheeks high in the face, her eyes quite cold and small, contracting even in their glance. "Well, well, well," she said. "Did that make any difference to you? Was that any better?"

"Yes," I said, "it was much better. Was it better for you?"

"All the same," she said. "All of you are the same. I haven't found a one of you who doesn't wind up that way, cowards all. You talk of your manliness and your violence and your swearing and your fights, but when it comes to taking a good whip to a helpless woman you haven't got the strength. You just can't follow through! All you want to do is to act like children, suck and suck on the tits and have yourself sucked off like little boys. I thought you were different! I thought you weren't like the rest, that there was some possibility with you because at least you kept on. But no, even you can't. Get out of here; you disgust me."

"Wait," I said, "you can't really expect to have something like this continuing without any change for months. There's got to be some kind of variety in it. Doesn't there? Don't you feel that—"

"You disgust me," she cut in. "And furthermore you were never any good anyway; I only kept you on because I was too lazy to look for someone else. You whip lousy, and you come too fast, and your scum comes out in a feeble spurt. There's no vigor in you. Think of all the men around just dying for the chance to whip a beautiful woman like me. England must be full of them! Why don't I have any luck, anyway? Why is everything so hideous? Why doesn't anything work out just once the way it should? Why does everyone seem to get what they want except me? Where's the fairness in it? Where's the point?"

To my dismay she began to cry then, moving her face back and forth, her hands clutching and struggling with the chains, and I came forward and quickly released her, hoping that this explosion of effort would convince her, if nothing else, of my compassion, but all that she did then was to whimper and curl herself into a small ball, her face deep in the pillow. She made waving motions with her arms. "Get out!" she screamed. "Get out now! I don't want to see you anymore. You haven't any guts, and besides that, you're not even a gentleman. What's wrong with flagellation? Where's the sin in it? Our literature is full of it! It's harmless. It's as much for men as for women. Why does everybody put the wrong interpretation on it?"

And then she began to spout obscenities considerably less rationalized, but owing to the depth to which she had inserted her head in the pillow I was not able to hear such that would distinguish or particularize them. It occurred to me then that our relationship, such as it was, was probably over. Donning my clothes I tried to make amends, tried to find some way to console her realizing all the time that she had probably indeed unearthed some deficiency which, for all I knew, might approach the worth of a universal insight; there was no way of being absolutely sure but it was something which had to be considered.

"Listen here," I said, stuffing a foot into a sock with dispatch, "there's no need to be that way. You said yourself that I'm no different from all the other men. There really is no point in this kind of thing you know; I mean flagellation may have been esteemed from the conquerors and the Normans, but we're in the age of enlightenment now. This is the age of revolution and the new technology, and besides you don't really think that this kind of thing could go on forever, do you. I mean, I'll do a little flogging like any other chap but you reach a point where you've got to go beyond it if you know what I mean. I can't go on being your father for the rest of my life—or whoever I'm supposed to be!"

This last comment sent her into such an ecstasy of cursing that I realized there would be little enough purpose in continuing with the silly bitch; what she had said she had said, what was done was done, and now was the time to leave. Fully dressed I stood at the door and said, "I'm going to leave you now. You could at least say goodbye to me, you know." I thought for an instant that she would do so and that in one full exchange of glances we could move beyond the dramatics to something simple like, maybe a good carnal fuck. But the moment of indecision passed, and she only buried her face deeper in the pillow, arching her back to give me a truly extraordinary view of her arse—for whatever good that was—and then pulled the covers over her.

"Out," I heard her mumble. "Just get out!" And so I did so then, going down the stairs two at a time into the street and a sodden dusk where it occurred to me that in some vital way she had made me feel that the issue of my virility was on the line and that I had to establish it. She had hurt me in some complex way that I could not even assess, all of this increasing my pain and embarrassment.

But where does one make amends, after all? The boudoir is most complex, and it is not easy to repair its damages outside of its confines, this being something, of course, that I learned much later and under different circumstances. At the time I was merely restless, restless, and, had I been set upon by a passing highwayman at that instant, I would doubtless have turned the tables on him in an explosion of fury or died in the attempt. But there were hardly any highwaymen in that district at that time—highwaymen having learned to stay away from the trollops' quarters from antiquity since they are in a competing business. There was little left to do but to go home.

Three days later my brief, aborted career of crime began. Whether there are connections to that performance and my last encounter with Elizabeth of course are not for me to say. If I catch the notable S— in a soft and reflective moment at some time I might ask him, since he is known to have so much knowledge of human behavior he will doubtless be able to explain away the situation in a trice.

There is no little complexity that has brought me to this pass. I can see that now. Nothing is simple, everything is complex; nothing is concrete, everything is wavering, a strange, drowning mire of purpose and possibility which, blending together toward its own meaning, cancels out virtually all varieties of explanation. After a certain point in all relationships, the only thing left is forgiveness, and I can see that now.

It is probably hopeless, but I wish that the barmaid would come into these rooms right now; I am in need of some comfort.

First rehearsals in the new role today, a difficult day, a strange day, a muddled day, but now, at its end, I see the way clear I think, see some possibility past compromise. It seems as if something might work out after all, altogether my deficiency of experience will not longer remain uninvestigated.

S— presented me to the assembled company before the rehearsals this morning. We were all seated in the first three rows of the musty trap of a building, virtually knee to knee in its confines, waiting for Thorpe to come out and give us what he chose to call his directorial "notes" before we sped into the daily punishment, but S— instead appeared from the wings on stage, a most unseemly hour for him, and stated that he had important news for the company which necessitated this gathering and his own presence. "We have a new Prospero," is how he began.

At this declaration every member of the company began to shift uneasily in their seats, clasping their hands and mumbling absently. There is something shocking, after all, about the sudden and peremptory change of a principal member; it implies that not only is the whole cast liable to sudden change but the entire network of the play itself. Since the play becomes the only reality for the players during the time of its run—I realize that I am talking like S— now—the very rubric of their lives seemed to tremble rather precariously in the balance. "This is not to disgrace Williams," S— said softly, "but we have had some difficulties with this play, as you're all well aware, and we felt that a change would not only be in the best interest of the play but in his own interest as well. I would like to introduce to all of you Mr. David Perkins, a relatively new member of our company who some of you may well know already but who has been performing in a background capacity. He will be taking this role, and with his promise I feel that we will see some very encouraging changes for the better."

As he said this, S— made a few motions at me, and I gathered that I was being asked to stand. I did so rather uneasily, looking at the faces as I did so; they were blank, as blank as death as they confronted me, and yet beneath those professionally trained countenances, that had been taught to reveal only as much emotion as was necessary at a given time, I could sense a sigh of something; perhaps it was contempt, perhaps it was trepidation. I found my legs uneasily shaking under me in a series of gestures that could have moved rapidly toward a loss of control, so I sat down hastily, bruising a hip against the edge of the seat, then folding my hands, and looking down at the floor. It occurred to me then for the first time that I probably had had very little business in joining the company in the first place; it opened up possibilities, that was for sure, but the level and order of experience that it opened up was very possibly one not worth dealing with. It was not, however, a propitious time for metaphysical speculation.

"I do this at my own urging," S— said, "not at that of Mr. Perkins who has merely valiantly agreed to serve in the stead. In the question of succession there would be many of you with more claim to the role by seniority or even by a question of talent, but it is important to get a fresh aspect on the performance. I fear that we are becoming jaded and spiritless and over-familiar. When we go into Stratford in barely a matter of days now we must come in with a play so fresh, so vital, so very much alive in its own terms that we will impress all the audiences and justify this as a new achievement. Therefore, I have felt it best to go outside of context. Isn't that true, Thorpe?"

Thorpe himself suddenly appeared almost spontaneously; it was as if he had been crouching in the wings for a period of time awaiting that cue or possibly and worse yet he had been nowhere at all and simply had been summoned up by S— as an expression of necessity. At any rate, the sidelong glance that Thorpe gave the company which took me in only incidentally and then settled balefully at some corner of the auditorium was indeed something to witness.

"Of course," he said, "my thoughts precisely. Whatever the playwright wants is, of course, satisfactory; I don't think there's any question of that. Of course we're going to get into the question of a newer and more intensive kind of rehearsal, and also we may have to reblock the play. So, as a result of this substitution, all of you will have to work much harder from here on in; we will have to totally rethink and revisualize the play. This is not pleasant, of course, and it may not even be fair, but after all, playwright's prerogative," Thorpe said and went into a deep squat at S—'s side, his hands clasped solemnly in front of him, his eyes down at the floor. He did this all very gracefully in spite of a bad center of gravity.

"Well then," S— said briskly clapping his hands together. "I think that we all understand the situation, to say nothing of our obligations. Mr. Perkins, I would like you to address the company please. I think that they and we would like to hear from you at this time."

I half stood and said, "I really have very little to say. I don't quite know what you want me—"

"Don't be coy," S— said rather sharply, "and don't be evasive, Mr. Perkins; I think that anything you say will be of substantial interest. This is serious business. Stand. Stay standing, that is. We wait to hear from you, then if we may."

"Well, then," I said in a somewhat higher voice not unmixed with quavering; it was dismaying to suspect from the evidence of that voice as to the precise degree of my nervousness. But then with one of those sudden reversals of vision for which the afflicted are so well known, the company suddenly seemed to be retreating; they were a vast distance from me, moving into some dim, faraway area of space; those tiny forms nestling against one another at the outer limits of my vision seemed suddenly to be deprived of consequence, of any means of retaliation in the event retaliation were needed.

"Well, then, I only want to say that I'm very honored by Mr. S—'s faith in me, and I'll certainly do the best I can to be worthy of it. It's a good play, an admirable play, and I think that it can be done well. I have certain ideas about how to do it, but the important thing is that I need everybody's cooperation because I'm relatively inexperienced. I haven't been acting very long, of course, is all I'm trying to say; it's only been a short while. I'm from the London stage, y'know, where we did a little different kind of thing—not quite as good, though, as what we're doing here—simple things in fact, so I might have a few things to learn. But acting is acting the whole world over; as Mr. S— would like to say, 'The play's the thing,' and the only thing and all the others fall into place. What I hope to do is to bring a certain kind of spirit into this and a personal kind of meaning—but of course meaning is all in the eye of the beholder. It all depends. It's a very interesting role, of course. I must say that I've found it very interesting because Prospero seems to be any kind of a man; he could be one thing, and he could be the other, but the most important thing to do is to act him so that he's both. He's *got* to be both, and that takes work, but I'm sure that we'll all want to do it. The thing about it is that you aren't quite sure what is going to happen until it happens. On the other hand, even in real life no one ever knows what's going to happen until it happens; this is the kind of thing you've got to learn. But I'd only like to say—"

"I think that's fine," S— said firmly from the stage. "I think that's quite sufficient, Mr. Perkins, and we all thank you very much for your thoughts and speech."

"May I sit down now?"

"By all means. I think we should all sit now and ponder this play a little bit. Mr. Thorpe will now address you, and then I would like to have a full rehearsal, just a walk-through of course, but a complete reading so that we can see where and how we stand. Good, then."

I sat in somewhat of a haze, perhaps stupor is the better word, while Thorpe came over and began a long, raving monologue about the play which I could not truly understand; I don't think that anyone else was apprehending it either. It occurred to me, sitting in that blind, caring suspension of my personality, which must be the only way that most of us can feel grief or fear or excitement, that I did not really know many members of the company at all. In fact, except for certain of the extras, I knew none of them at all, had had no association with them, had no idea of their functioning or ambitions, had not even a trace of personal contact. In part this had been due to the hierarchy of the company which relegated supernumeraries to the company of other supernumeraries and so on, but in a certain, very real sense, it had to do also with the fact that I denied relationships because certain explosive facts about my history were under less risk of revelation if I were isolated. But I could see now that this, possibly, was something of a mistake and that in any event the game was now thoroughly up, having been up, perhaps, since I had decided to fuck the barmaid. Or perhaps it was even before that. It is hard to say....

Thorpe went on for some time, and then the stage was cleared, and the company went up with bare props for a full run-through. I had to work off the script, of course, unlike the other principals who had already memorized most of their roles and this gave a rather stifling, somehow baroque aspect to my acting, gestures and vocal ranges being continually intercepted by the need to shuffle or catch papers. More than this of the rehearsal I truly cannot reveal. It all recedes from me in a high, fine haze; it is possible that at some buried level of the mind I remember everything, apprehend the totality, but my condition of excitement was such and the conditions were so oppressive at the time to be sure that all of this has been mercifully blocked at that simple level of recollection for me to mention in these scratchings.

The role of Prospero was, inevitably, far more difficult than I had taken it to be; it is distinctly ill-written, ill-conceived, and quite dull in many of its meanderings. The villainies he perpetrates upon the sailors are most indefensible, but on the other hand, the weaknesses of S—'s dramaturgy have been noted before and cannot be repeated. What can

I say? If I could be more complete, more inclusive I certainly would, but I know nothing, I apprehend nothing, I want nothing. It is certainly an experience that makes one question all roots of his ambition, decide that he has probably been functioning in a kind of reluctant insanity rather than through any higher motive, and it gives me the dim feeling that my outcome is at least as muddled as my history. However ...

When the rehearsal was over I stepped down from the stage in a heavy sweat to find myself being roughly embraced by S—; Thorpe stood once again to the side with a rather sullen expression and let the little scene play itself out.

"Remarkable!" S— said, "Of course, there are rough edges all around, and you have some difficulty in reading the poetry, but I think that for the first time we're getting the sense of the role. Wouldn't you think so, Thorpe?"

"He can't *move*. He can't move on stage worth a damn. I can't even block him, he won't listen."

"Well, you'll find this problem with youthful actors almost all the time; blocking is mechanical, and it's a director's job; it has nothing to do with questions of interpretation. As for your interpretation, I applaud you! Of course, we will have to consider this only a start," S— said. "We have, after all, barely established your presence in the role. Tomorrow will be far more difficult, and we give our first performance here day after next, giving you less than two days to learn effectively the role. But this will work out. The basic assumption has been richly proven today; you *have* talent."

"I—" Thorpe was trying to get a word in.

"Be here at seven tomorrow morning, and we'll do some private run-through," S— said. "And for the love of God, try to know most of your lines by then." Without further prompting he seized Thorpe by an elbow and drew him over to one side of the stage in a fierce grip, then led him out one wing. Thorpe's form was somehow rigid, in an arc of protest but for all the effectiveness that this posture showed, his whole body might as well have been gripped in S—'s palm.

I found myself virtually alone in the auditorium. It had been my thought—ah, juvenescence!—that some of the company might stay behind to congratulate me or that at least some of the supernumeraries might have a few words of commendation for the one of their rank who had come upon happier times, but the odd thing was that there was no one left at all except for a few of the stage personnel who were now busily cursing to one another at the back of the stage while attempting to set up some ominous blocks of wood; the company had dispersed so rapidly as to make their very corporeality suspect. But I was not entirely alone I found for as I went to one edge of the stage to clamber down the steps, Williams strode from a wing and came up rapidly behind me, put a fierce arm on my shoulder and turned me fully around.

I was shocked, frankly, to perceive the countenance of this ex-lead actor. He was obviously drunk, highly flushed, and his mouth in forming the syllables seemed to be a few steps before his coercing brain. "Well," he said, "I hope you're pleased with yourself now. I hope you feel triumphant."

"No, not exactly," I said, trying to assume a courtesy, trying to imagine how I would have felt if positions were reversed. (Probably I would not have minded it at all, but this is something I have time to perceive only now.) "I don't think much of the way I did; I'm very unsure of myself. But it was their decision to do it, and I don't know why."

"Aha!" he said, "so you don't know why. You have no idea why they put you in that role. You're just an innocent on the wicked stage, is that right? Well of course; of course."

I began to feel his grip tightening unpleasantly around the edges of my clothing, and with a wrench managed to free myself, then moved away from the more direct encounter and said, "Look, it's nothing personal; you *must* know that. I don't even have ambition that way. It's only something that came up."

"I'll tell you why they're doing this," he said, making an unsuccessful reeling lunge at me and then, sinking to his knees, found himself forced to grasp onto the curtains for support. "The reason they're doing this is because they're out to disgrace me, out to ruin my reputation. They are, in fact, out to get me! You bloody, filthy little bugger, you will not be the means to deprive me of my desire. I'll see you in hell for this!"

"I think you should take it with some professionalism after all," I said. "It *is* S—'s company isn't it, and it's his decision. There's no need to blame this on me; I'm only an object."

"You rationalizing little bastard!" he shrieked and managed to get off his knees to rise like a pendant moon above me, his huge face suddenly distorted by some trick of light flickering across the stage. "You apologetic little fuck! I'll get you for this if it's the last thing I ever do! I know a lot of people in this town, I have influence, I have friends. I'll *destroy* the performance for you. They won't get away with this," he said and staggering to maintain his balance fell full-length on the floor, got to his feet this time with such extreme difficulty, that finally I assisted him and found myself then in an awkward, contrived embrace. (From some distant pew it might have occurred to an ignorant observer who could not hear the dialogue that we were lovers.) "Pointless," Williams muttered, his voice subsiding from accusation to a kind of complex sulk, "pointless, pointless! This company, those fools, these idiotic plays, the merciless tour, the whole thing nothing but the vanity and stupidity of *one* man, that fat little filthy bastard who owns all of us. But you put up with it; you put up with it because an actor's life is supposed to *mean* something, supposed to have a *little* substance. But then you realize that you're forty years old and wasted, *wasted* and that all you've been doing is reciting bombast all your life, and it's going to go on and on. It's going to go on forever, I tell you! The filthy little turd is surely immortal. This has been going on now for twenty years, and it's never changed, *none* of it, and he only gets worse and worse. I won't stand for it!" he said with an enormous, belching hiccup. "I tell you, there'll be some reckoning. I'll fix you too, Perkins! This kind of thing *cannot* be perpetrated. Nothing like this can possibly go on this way this long because if it does there's no sense in life at all. I tell you Perkins, I'll fix you for all of this. I'll lend you the clout to do a proper clouting with." And he disengaged himself from me then and in a reeling stagger moved away, got behind the wings and went off to whatever destination he was seeking, the sound of his sobs and belches mingling with the clatter of his feet.

It was a poor way for a lead actor to make a final exit but, on the other hand, possessed of intimations of mortality as fully as any man, I could put myself in his position and it was most unpleasant, most humiliating. But then there was the question of threats. There is no question but that I will definitely have to tell S— about those threats because the disruption of a performance could be most unsettling to say nothing of actually dangerous, and I have no desire to get involved.

I would, in fact, have gone immediately in search of S— to tell him of all of this had I not been intercepted by the next event which, of course, would be inevitable. Jane, the barmaid herself, suddenly appeared in the auditorium, rising from some hidden seat and waving her arm frantically. I could see from the distance its frantic bareness and above it the small shiny moon of her face. She was moving rapidly out of the row, coming toward me, and although her every aspect was vital, although the sight of her well-remembered breasts filled me with as much gratitude as ever, I must admit that it was hard to stifle an absurd, freakish impulse to run away as she came toward me.

"David!" she shouted. "David! I saw it all. I've been here from the beginning watching you. You were wonderful! What was that awful man doing to you anyway? I wanted to go up and stop that, but I didn't want to interfere. You look so pale, love! You were fine, fine."

I put an arm around her, feeling her languid surfaces sink against me, the faint apprehension of her heat already sinking through my fingers, up to the arm and then to the nerve core, and it dawned on me that all of my fears had been certainly unjustified; there was no question of her availability, not to say my security at the present time. At last, at last I had a rum fuck with no complications whatsoever and without possibility of errors, misapprehension, loss ... or whips.

But why this gloom? Why this apprehension and dread? Why this slow, painful feeling working up from the gut to make me feel at some deep level that I had gone too far, done too much, committed myself too hard and that the end could now only be an extension of every woe concealed in the beginning? Why? Why? And why as her lips tilted up to mine to give me a congratulatory kiss, why was there a slight recoiling shudder in me before I placed mine down on hers and, her body borne as lightly as fragile glass, lifted her into me and began, to run an absent, needful hand over her breasts?

We must have explored, that night, every conceivable variety of human sexual connection. There was the question of learning the role of course, S—'s charge for me to be familiarized with it the next morning. There was the question of having to go into public performance in less than two days, and I, the center of the play, was totally unprepared. There was the question of Williams's threat which was hardly to be denied—in his twenty years of trouping through provinces as a professional actor the man surely made *many* connections. There was the question of Thorpe's dissatisfaction. There would have been enough, more than enough, to have ordinarily occupied me, to have kept me proper lively.

But what the fuck! And what the difference! Breasts are laid out before you, the nipples hard with desire, those spiracles of lust pointing toward you, the skin warm and flushed with its own secrets, the mouth alive and slippery, the thighs parted to reveal the crown, the moistness, that ultimate engine of desire within? Here's to irresponsibility! Here's to fucking! Here's to generation, the act of which is responsible for us all! Us all!

We fucked and fucked in my room past all hours; she had been able to arrange for a replacement at the bar downstairs so there was no question of duties, and she explained to me—oh, how she explained to me!—that she felt so proud of what I was doing that she wanted in every way to give me a night I would never forget. All willing was I to derive benefit from her comforts and it was endless, *endless*. At one time I came full into her mouth, feeling myself spill all the way into that immortal channel while at the same time, due to the pleasures of the particular position we had taken I was able to suck and lap at her pussy and bring her to a quivering culmination of her own. She told me that this position—of which I had never heard before and which I had never previously exercised—was very popular on the continent where it seemed to have originated in Paris and then spread out to all the provinces of France and then to the bordering countries as tourists carried the word forth. *Soixante-neuf* was her term although it seems a poor description for it; sheer numerology cannot evaluate the intricacies or delights of that position nor the way her box opened to me as I slid my tongue in and out rhythmically, feeling her deep explosions within.

But I am getting ahead of myself tra-la, getting far ahead of the sense of the matter, and it is import to retrace and begin at the beginning; this, after all, is my memoirs—and as my memoirs they must contain the fullest, frankest and freest documentation of the facts; no glossing over, no euphemisms. I believe that only through the knowledge and practice of sex can we arrive at any apprehension of our own reality; the rest is all wasteful repetition, sheer posturing; in the heart of the bed we find ourselves reduced to what we are, to how we can function. This is a theory I have developed; it is clear that in the England we know and love so dearly, it is almost impossible to express oneself, to move past the damnation of the walls of self other than through the expression of one's sexuality. There is a clear hierarchy in this land, a hierarchy created by generations of oppression, brutality and inequality which have progressively numbed us, left us without a sense of identity, left us without the ability to function in any individuating ways. In those circumstances there is so little left other than the pursuit of sex that it is not entirely dismaying. I certainly do not consider the pursuit of acting as any kind of just compensation for this sense of isolation, nor can any submersion in the new technology be the answer. No indeed! For a man of modest gifts, background, and opportunities such as myself there is little left but the act of fucking ... but the act of fucking, of course, when performed with skill and abandon can be almost enough; this is something that must be clearly understood.

It can be almost enough, almost enough. Flesh is a wanderer, but when it finds and is absorbed in its own connections it tends to rise to a kind of knowledge; now I can see that there is a similarity between intermingling and the acts of life. But sex goes far beyond the aimless thrashings and posturings of the stage, to say nothing of those of petty crimes; within the small arena of the bed it is possible to enact almost the entire range, limits and possibilities of human behavior, the act of sex being the only one that is done for its own sake and for no other end.

I speculate, I run on. Nevertheless, I feel some need of justification; if these writings survive, if they are ever exhumed with other relics from the ruins of the abandoned state at some time in the future it is unquestionably going to be read by any number of people who will say, "Why so much sex? Why all this fucking? What is the necessity? The social details are very interesting and the portrait of that forgotten playwright S— can be considered to be of some value, but why all this talk of the boudoir, of breast, belly, and lust, of hip, thigh, joint, and cleavage which is, inevitably so boring when set against the rich descriptions and the interesting portrayal of the Elizabethan stage?" never understanding, these people, that sex can never be less interesting than the mind and history of those participants in it and that there be nothing stultifying about the written evocation of the act if done with taste and skill.

On the other hand—and this is a most interesting thought indeed—there is the small but real possibility that I have seen the future all wrong, that at some time in the far, far future should this writing ever reach mass distribution it will be making its way into an audience which rather than being bored by sexual reminiscence or description will be titillated by it, an audience which finds its apprehension of the written act of sex somehow satisfying as either a substitute for their commission of the act or (this is even more interesting yet) something in favor to it.

But it is not likely that this will happen—it would be possible to visualize a society in which sex is not casual but sentimentalized, in which connection is not inevitable but contrived—but if it does, then I would suppose that the questions posed by these far-removed scions of the present day will be of a different order. "Why," they will ask, "Why is it necessary to interrupt all this pleasant sexual picaresque and description with these long, boring interpolations on the state of the theater? Why undercut the fine prurience of thigh and tit with remarks about some long-vanished play by some long-dead playwright? Why pack the narrative with extrinsic details of rehearsal and the physical stage when it is more important and necessary to read only about fucking?"

To this audience, assuming that such an audience might exist—one would hope not; one would not want to contemplate the interior landscape of a society which makes the simple matter of books about fucking the all-important issue—I can only say: Attend, be patient, learn what you will of the times I write of, and be content with the descriptions of the fucking because they are all, all true. There is no single sexual act described herein that is in the least invented: there is no groan that was not groaned, no splash of scum that did not literally emit itself from the tearing prepuce of a living, vital prick. The composition, then, will make up in veracity for what it loses in consistency of vision; a price which has to be paid for any serious, inclusive social document. Indeed. Indeed.

But I digress; I am on the edge of rambling. Let me describe what Jane and I did that night, a night during which, incidentally, I learned absolutely none of my lines. But I think that Prospero would have approved. Somehow I think he would have understood and forgiven my abandon.

I said I will tell now of what Jane and I did during that evening. No reluctance overcomes me. None at all.

We started off with a bit of simple buggery, the question of lubricating her was left for later adventures, my prick sliding up the glazed interior of her ass like a whippet, her little ass revolving and pouting back at me, the only juices being those which my own gland was excreting during that period of excitement. I eased myself all the way into her feeling her grunt and groan, feeling the soft, rising pressure, and sliding my hands around to the front of her, I seized those marvelous breasts and began to manipulate them frantically, bouncing them, juggling them, feeling the little nipples grow to the size of cherries in my hand, feeling the skin jounce and tremble deep in my palms. It excited me into an almost frantic explosion; the combination of soft tits above and hard little girlish ass below caused me to heave my load with the most unseemly haste, and I came into her, deep into the walls of her buttocks groaning and muttering listening with a kind of distant respect to her own screams. Oh God, was she shrieking! Imagine that, a humble barmaid. And although it must have been over, in truth, quite quickly, the blooming, rising, and convergence were so high in their excitement as to make it seem to go on for a very, very long time indeed.

And indeed, while fucking her I found that some small corridor of gloom opened up within me as the act moved past conjoinment toward upheaval; I glimpsed some part of myself that I had never seen before as I lay above her in the hump and throes of my need. Beginning to spill I could see the fear that was within me from all the events of the day and what they portended for the morrow. Easing my scum into her socket I could recognize for the first time that Williams's threats, S—'s sanctimony, Thorpe's hatred had shaken me terribly because I was indeed and for the first time swimming in water which were beyond me. This had not been so during the robberies; it had not been the case when I had traduced Thorpe into offering me place in the company; it had not even happened during my dismal subsequent encounter with Thorpe— about which I recollect little at this time but which I will doubtless in my monomania be setting down later—but it was definitely the case now. And all the time my candle fluttered and wickered out its flame, the feeling of hot, molten wax dripping down the sides—because her little ass, I am sure, could not command the whole of my ejaculation—and finally I gave a dying heave and tumbled off her, lay to the other side of the bed gasping thinly, looking at her body, seeing the swell and rise of her breasts against the flat panes of her stomach, the marks of my fingernails deeply impressed within the globes, streaking down from the nipples and then in an upward arc toward the neck. A pretty set of spirals, a pretty design; I could not in consciousness have wreaked better testament on her body of my desire.

"How was that?" she asked. "Was that good? How is it for a man? I know how it is for me but is it the same for you?"

"It couldn't possibly be. I'm inserting, you're containing. But it's very nice."

"You hear so much about buggery," she said. "All those louts down at the bar talk about when they get drunk is buggery. Bugger this and bugger that; this bugger and that bugger and for all they talk about it you would think that no one in England never does anything else but bugger or think about it—and it can get a girl right curious. Of course, I've done it a few times before. It's not all that it's supposed to be."

"They don't mean it quite in that way," I said. "I mean, they're not precisely talking about it the way I did it just now."

"No I don't understand. What do you mean?"

"It's hard to explain."

"Try," she said, and rolled over to put a full breast in my cupped palm, the nipple winking out its wanton message toward me, the fine, small pores of her breast-flesh brushing against my chest. "I want to understand. I can't be a barmaid forever, you know. I have ambitions."

"What kind of ambitions?"

"Why talk about them? I want you to tell me about buggery. Maybe I've misunderstood the whole thing."

"No, you talk to me," I said. "I feel like I barely know you, for one thing. We've been fucking and fucking—but that isn't the same somehow."

"You sound like some of the guys in that play. What's wrong with fucking? Why does there have to be any more? Isn't it enough? It can be the whole thing; I've learned that."

"Well for one thing you can't do it all the time. Comes a time you've got to do something else."

"That's what a man would say. A woman can do it all the time though. There's no limit to the number of times I can come."

"This isn't getting us anywhere," I said, rolling slightly and getting the other hand on her firm ass, holding ass and breast now in an intense supporting grip that at that time seemed to be bringing me as close to a sense of fulfillment as I might ever be bound to get. "When they talk about buggery they're mostly using it as a way of insulting people or causing them pain. When you bugger someone you harm his chances. They don't mean the actual act itself most of the time. I don't know how they came to use it in that reference, though. Now, why don't you tell me about yourself?"

"So that's what it's all about. There's very little to tell about me. I came from London originally, and I ended up here because the man I was traveling with went off on his own. I had no money, so I was lucky to get this job. But eventually I hope to get back to London and open a shop or something like that. There's plenty of time; I'm not in any hurry because I'm only twenty-three."

"What did you do in London?"

"Nothing in particular."

"Well, you must have done something."

"I didn't do a blooming thing!" she said in a high, piercing voice, yanking herself out of my grasp and spinning to the other side of the bed. "I told you, I don't want to get into any of this! Why can't men be reasonable? Why can't you leave it a simple level. They say that women are the ones who get tied up in explanations and emotions, but it's *not* true! There isn't a woman who can't take things as they come and make of them what she will. What's the difference? Will you stop asking questions?"

"All right," I said, suddenly somber, fearful even because that sudden removal of flesh had stricken me more than I had thought possible; it was only in the ease and warmness of the connection, I realized, that I had been able to have the temerity to ask and to survive the agonies of the day. "I'm sorry," I said. "Come back here. I didn't mean—"

"Oh, it's all right, love," she said, coming back and putting her breast with a small *plop!* back into my outstretched hand; doing something intricate with her thighs so that her cunt, steaming slightly, lay open against my dangling prong. "I didn't mean to get harsh or anything like that. I admired you so much today, the way you were reading those lines and all that. I don't mean to fight, but you've got to learn, sometimes, to keep quiet. A man has got to learn that sooner or later or there will be problems."

"All right," I said. And, "All right," again. Then I moved over her, poised over her, my club at ready again, the break between the bodies having brought me once again to the realization of my need, the depths of my anticipation. And so, I commenced to fuck her, began to work on her in the conventional way, thigh to thigh, belly to belly, my keening, moaning weight slightly supported by the props of shoulders and elbows and the insertion was made delicately this time; a mere twitch of her pouting, spread lips, and I was in there. What I wanted to do this time was to move beyond the banalities of orgasm, thrust into some high, fine place where all mysteries would be ended, search for something so apocalyptic that it would finally be the cancellation of desire. But she was heavy, heavy, almost indolent below me, pumping her hips idly in a broken rhythm, and I could feel with the first seedy rush of scum into the tank that it wouldn't work, it would all retract to the familiar cold sameness.

There are no easy answers. If there were only some way—this must have occurred to me—that I could work on this bitch, work past immediate purposes into some kind of finality, well, then, by the same token I would then have moved beyond equivocation and fear in other directions, fucking being then the simplest and the best thing that was going on. But it was difficult, difficult, and a broken cry compounded by frustration and need must have poured out of me then as I felt the first launches and spillings of my second orgasm of the evening. It was wrenching, clawing, tearing like an animal inside but more complicated still. No easy answers at all, and that is the way that I must have finished into her the second time.

As soon as it was over, I withdrew my prick and sent it into the colder sobering air of the room, and, turning to the other side, facing my ass toward her, I lay there for a while, listening to the still whimpers of her breath behind me wondering how I could lead her to understand the totality of what an orgasm should be and, if I could breach that understanding, break her into a kind of mutuality. But then it didn't seem worth it. It simply didn't seem worth it....

But it had always been this way: women simply don't understand, they don't function the same way. Whatever lies between their thighs and up through the middle areas of their bodies, whatever it is, is something entirely different from what we contain, runs on different fuels, responds to different messages. We are so unalike that for all the connection we can sometimes obtain with them they could be creatures from the moon itself. They are not constructed as we are; the majority lie, cheat. Our evasion of existence is believing that they are all good and then trying to force them to function in that direction. All the trouble comes from that basic misapprehension or, as S— might say, "Let there be no more marriages," no more marriages out of ignorance in any case, marriages wedded of the failure of understanding.

The first girl I ever fucked seriously was named Marcia. She dwelt in a clapboard house not far from my own and became known to me in the easiest and most inevitable ways. Although we only got around to fucking at fourteen or fifteen, we must have known and dealt with one another all our lives and yet, the first time I entered her, lying on the floor of her bedroom, huddled against the possibility of her family's entrance, the strangeness overcame me, the sense of isolation, and the fantastic mingling with the squirming efforts of my prick to dangle in her. I had known this girl in bad ways and good for over a decade but now, as she opened before me, gasping slightly at the impalement on the floor, it occurred to me that I did not know her at all. Her cunt clamping over me viselike was strange, strange, strange; tight virgin cunt, narrow and dry at the beginning opened up into the wet, flat fullness of a flower as I plowed my way in, her hands coming around to seek my back.

"Who would have imagined?" she said and, "Not so fast, not so fast," and similar statements. I tried to give her what comfort I could with absent kisses at the corners of the ears and small, warning mumblings, but she was already out of control this stranger underneath me, wrenching me into my first genuine orgasm, and all that I could do was to let her carry me. Her face, *her face*, it changed as she went into the spiraling motions of her coming; it was not that plain, simple, homely face I had known all my life but instead was flooded with a shrewish cunning, a shrewish knowledge, the face of a small petulant animal trapped in an unspeakable act somewhere, the eyes narrow, the mouth parted, the nose itself flaring. And I didn't recognize her! Even her breasts in the extremity had changed to a kind of rosy, tinctured, bobbling fulfillment, and I realized that had I encountered this girl so suddenly in that position I would not have known her at all so complete the change, so rapid the parting.

But I fucked and pumped and sucked and licked, working out my own sense of cooperation against her distant frame, and then at long last it was over, and I lay engaged within her, her thighs freezing around my cock, her inner lips still squeezing out the last moisture. I had to struggle to break the connection, pain flaring all the way out through the prick and into the body, with a kind of remorse too because my coming had seemed out of all sensible relation to the riches she had exposed to me. Finally I dangled free, and she looked up at me, her eyes fluttered, and then she began to cry. She had changed again: not the woman I had been fucking, not that demanding engine but, instead, the simple girl who I had bedded, the virgin chastised, the innocent ill-used. As the tears came sprinkling down her face, as the words began to come: "Oh, why? Why did you have to do this to me? Why did it have to happen? What have you done to me?" it came to me that there was no way, simply no way that you could deal with them on their own level. To have sex was to open up into a kind of madness and complexity in which the rules were made only on their own terms and had absolutely no relation to whatever was going on outside—which made things very pleasant, of course, which improved the prospects of the act, which gave a lot to look forward to. But I comforted her, such as I could, and after a while her face turned rosy again and went into its already familiar change, and I mounted her again, entered her again, fucked her again, turning the simple face into a mask of desire, turning the virgin's body into the heavy, lush pulp of carnality, turning the virgin cunt into an alley so long, so dark, so mindless and irredeemable that it did indeed signal the beginnings of all desire.

I turned to face my barmaid again, turned to take her face between my palms, and holding her that way I said, "I want to reach you, I want to really reach you *now*." She moaned and scurried against me, raising a sore breast for me to suck, her other hand supporting the bulging twin and I gathered them and drew them deeply into my face and sucked and sucked. Then, moving back to that first and most vital core, the reflex action of the neonate, nothing else, but my prick was growing, growing, entangling itself already in the hard, steely hairs of her bush, and I could feel her legs shift and spread.

"Now," she said, all ready for the taking. "Now!"

"It's too soon. Don't rush it," I said.

"You've got me hot, don't you understand that?"

"I've already done it twice; I can't be expected to be ready again. I'm not a bull you know."

But she insisted, "You're already hard."

"There's another way to go." I heaved away from her, moving into an intricate dance and shift of positions, a flurry of bedclothes, a glitter of sweat at the end of which actions my face was poised between her thighs, my lips buried in her pussy while my big prick dangled and bobbled weightlessly in the area of her mouth. I put my lips into that place with a will, found the spot I wanted and began to work my tongue in narrowly, insistently, feeling the shiny walls part.

"Listen," she said from some far distance, "I really don't like it all that much, so if you don't mind, I don't want to take you into my mouth now. It's so big ..."

"Yes," I mumbled, deep in the discovered mysteries of her cunt. "Yes, you do it now, and make no mistake about it," giving a twitch of my hips to force the organ against her cheek. She gave a heave, and I could feel one of her hands reaching to grasp it, clutch it. There was a slow, gently squeezing, and then I felt myself move into the warmth and wetness of her mouth, reciprocal need driving my tongue further up her little cunt, revolving it, twirling it, and I felt my saliva mingle with her own moisture. There was no doubt about it; the position, once gotten used to was everything she had promised.

"But no," she said releasing me, "I don't want it now. We can't do this kind of thing forever, you know." How she got the words out was something of a mystery since my prick was deeply engulfed within her. But get them out she did, and in response I only thrashed my hips harder, deeper, forcing myself into such conjunction that it would be impossible for her to speak. Then I felt the beginnings of her slow, distant orgasm, a high twitching flutter in her cunt, and I worked to bring out that warmth, worked to bring out the birth cry of her coming. Finally there was a high squeal far above me, and I thought I felt her fluid pour out into my mouth. I drank it, drank deeply as I could of all those substances, and this added franticity to her own motions above. She began to work on me with such sudden enthusiasm that it was almost as if she was eating my prick. Its condiments came out richly into her, a spreading pool, a spreading warmth as I flooded gratefully into her for the third—or was it the fourth or fifth or tenth?—time that night. After this time we were unable to move for quite a while. When we finally did it was very, very slowly, with a kind of reluctance as we shifted positions again to face one another across a small span of bedsheet.

"You know," she said, "I have the feeling that you're just using me. We should talk some. We should get to know each other. I mean, there's more to everything than just sex."

"That's what I suggested before," I said. "Tell me about yourself. That's what I'd like to hear."

"But I don't want to," she said, reaching out and patting me absently on the forearm, a witch's caress. "There really isn't anything to tell. You must have a lot to say to me though. Why don't you tell me about the theater? You're an actor so you should know about it. What's it like?"

"I'm not all that familiar with it. You'd be surprised how little I really know."

"But you know a lot more than I do. What is it like? How do you feel when you're speaking lines for somebody else and when you're talking to people as if you were talking yourself. Isn't it hard?"

"I think you're talking about false spontaneity."

"False what?"

"Oh, never mind," I said. "I don't know very much about the theater. I don't think that it has much of a future, y'know. S—'s plays are all right for what they are but they're cheap, bloody stuff, and he's never made any pretensions that they were other than that. They're just to amuse people and keep them diverted and away from mounting attacks on the monarchy or something like that, but they don't do much more than entertain. Actually I think the whole thing will go out of business sooner or later probably when we get into the next crusades."

"But what is it like to be an actor? You haven't told me any of that at all."

"Oh, it's all right. I mean, there's nothing much to it, it's just a job like being a barmaid or writing the plays or anything of the order where you do something out of necessity rather than spirit. It's as if the whole thing isn't really connected to you at all; you're reading lines and making motions and going through postures and so on, but for all that you're doing you might as well be off somewhere having a drink or cutting some wood. There's nothing very exciting about it because there's so little time that you're actually present, actually feeling what you're doing. And this play is pretty bad anyway, it's impossible to speak it believably, it wasn't written to make sense but only, I think, to be a kind of farce. Half the time I don't understand what's going on inside it, not that it makes much difference."

"But you seem to have such understanding when you're reading those lines. You seem to know what it means."

"Well, that's just professionalism," I said and already bored with the discussion, not to say the dryness of the exposition, moved toward her, not so much for the fucking as for the cuddling. It was strange but as much as I knew of her body I wanted it again; there is always a mystery shrouded beneath the skin, it seems, and it goes beyond all possibility of capture. This may be the secret of the power of sexuality.

"No," she said, "not now. Talk to me. You simply have to talk to me because I want to feel that I'm with you. Tell me more."

"There's nothing to tell."

"Aren't you supposed to learn your lines for the play tomorrow? I heard that man tell you that you should."

"That's right," I said, and reached under the bed to pull out the script. "It's all right here, but I just don't care. I'll learn them in due time."

"But isn't that wrong? Won't they, and you, be in trouble if you don't know your lines by tomorrow? I don't think that that's right."

You travel all through the continent, through untold seas and onslaughts of terror, maturation and knowledge to find that, at the last, it all travels back to the same carping banality, the same maternal querulousness. "In due course," I said, "I will."

"I won't have sex with you again until you do some studying," she said.

"Until you learn some of your lines. That should make you care."

"Listen," I said, taking the wretched manuscript and opening it at random, sitting up cross-legged in the bed then for better compass and fastening upon a speech marked in a childish scrawl: PROSP. "Let me read you something. You tell me if this makes any sense: 'Then as my gift and thine own acquisition/worthily purchased take my daughter: but/if thou dost break her virgin-knot before/all sanctimonious ceremonies may/with full and holy rite be min'ster'd/no sweet aspersion shall the heavens let fall.'"

"No sweet what?"

"No sweet aspersion. That means deliverance or blessing."

"From the heavens?"

"Wait," I said, "I haven't finished: '... shall the heavens let fall/to make this contact grow: but barren hate/sour-eyed disdain and discord shall bestrew/the union of your bed with weeds so loathly/that you shall hate it both; therefore take heed/as hymen's lamps shall light you.'"

"What does that mean?" she said, sitting up beside me and drawing her finger over the lettering as if she could obtain it in that way. "I don't think I understand it. He writes funny, you're right."

"Prospero is talking to the man who has fallen in love with his daughter. Prospero and his daughter and a sprite and a dwarf have been living on this island for a long time until there's a shipwreck and some sailors and nobles come to it and one of the men, this Ferdinand, falls in love with Miranda. That's the daughter. But Prospero cares for her so much that he doesn't want to see her misled or hurt, and so he's warning Ferdinand in this speech that if he wants to make love to her or possess her in any way he has to marry her. That's where all the business of curses comes in. She's a virgin."

"She is?"

"He says she's a virgin. The 'virgin-knot' remember? And he's talking about the hymen too. So what the whole speech boils down to is that he's saying that Ferdinand better marry her or he, Prospero, will put his curse on any relations he has with her."

"Well why couldn't he simply say that?"

"That's the way S— writes," I said. "Everybody complains about it. He can't ever come to the point; he gets all tied up in this prose-poetry, most of which you can't even understand. I think he's outdated, personally."

"And what's so important about being married to fuck? Why does he care? Most people who fuck aren't married—at least to each other."

"Well, that's another thing," I said. "From what I gather, S— is always in trouble with the Crown because they think he's writing dangerous plays that are really about them. You remember the scandals they had about ten years ago with those King plays, don't you?"

"No I don't. I was only twelve then. Besides, I don't really know what's going on; I try to avoid it."

"Well they had a lot of trouble," I said. "I don't know too many of the particulars, but S— wrote quite a few plays that were about Henry IV and V and about Richard III and so on, all people who had lived three or four centuries ago and who hadn't been that well liked anyway we understand. But some people got the idea that S— wasn't really writing about them at all but was really just using them as a means to write about *this* Crown, and he got himself into a lot of trouble in London. I understand that he was banned for a while until he promised to stick to Danish history and Scottish problems and so on; the Crown doesn't give a damn about any of that as long as he doesn't stick so close to home."

"But you still haven't explained all that business about virginity. I don't get it."

"I'm getting there," I said. "You see, S— got in such trouble with the Crown for a while then that he knew they'd be having their eye on him for a long, long time and he'd better do nothing in any new plays to attract their attention. So he built up the whole question of honor and morality and virginity and so on just because he felt that was the best way to pacify them and then he kept away from any real sex on the stage because he didn't want to incite any troubles. So that's the reason for this long speech here."

"You mean that that whole thing is supposed to be said just because S— is afraid of getting into trouble?"

"That's about the truth of it," I said. "Too, you've got to reckon with these damned laws; we're not permitted to have actresses, you know, it's supposed to be immoral, so all the female roles have to be played by men. But I'd like to know what's so moral about a bunch of faggarts taking over the female roles? S— has tried to break that too once or twice, I understand, but he hasn't gotten very far. So if you had any sex or sex relationships on the stage they would have to go on between men and men—and that wouldn't be too pleasing for most of the audience, so S— tries to keep everything chaste."

She put a finger in her mouth and began to suck it intently, her eyes turning inward in the apparent throes of some recollection. "But didn't S— write a dirty play once?" she said. "I mean, I don't know anything about the theater but I seem to recall that there was something about a girl and a boy, Julie and Ronald I think or Julie and Romeo, something like that. It was supposed to be full of fucking."

"You're talking about *Romeo and Juliet,*" I said, pleased that I was able to show this mild erudition, grateful that she would not know that I had only picked up most of this myself third-hand during my period in the company and had been at least as ignorant of S— as she only a few scant months before, "*Romeo and Juliet* it is true had sex—although it didn't show on the stage—and it was romantic but you have to remember that it was one of the very early plays. S— says it was one of the very first plays he ever wrote, and it was almost one of the first produced. But even there the whole point of the play is that they're both killed off in the end along with almost everyone else. And the reason they're killed off is because they had sex without being married; that's the whole point of it, they couldn't get married because they were too young and came from families that hated each other. Even though they had only a little bit of sex they had to pay for it with their lives. So there S— was just showing the perils of having sex out of wedlock. No, all the plays are very moral. I think you have to understand that. Almost everyone in any of these plays who has any fun at all ends up dying. The only ones that survive are those who weren't doing much in the first place. Of course in some of the plays nobody dies, but then the ones that had fun end up by getting shut out of everything."

"I don't think he's very interesting," she said. "I mean now that you explain it, it all sounds a little bit on the dull side. Why use all those words and speeches just to keep people from having sex?"

"Oh, it's not all quite that simple," I said. "He's got other things in mind, I think, or at least he used to when he was trying to overthrow the Crown in his way. But the important thing you've got to remember is that popular stuff like this is for the masses, it's meant to keep them happy; there's no concern about value. S— is a hack, he says he's a hack; he's just trying to run a company and make a few pounds off his plays, and I don't think that in ten or twenty years anybody will worry too much about this stuff. There aren't even any good scripts around, you know, most of this stuff has never been published, and that which has been is all out of shape. S— isn't interested in that; I think he'd be the first man to say that he'd hate to see his plays around in a hundred years. He's a practical man, you know. He's a manager."

"It's all so depressing."

"No it isn't," I said, "it isn't depressing at all; S— is making a living, and a lot of unemployed actors are getting a chance to see the continent, and I've gotten my first entrance into a career, and I think that a lot of people are diverted by the plays; they don't know they're junk or really care; the main thing is that they find themselves titillated by them. Imagine all those Danish princes and old kings suffering so! It gives you hope in your own dull life; if people as important as this are suffering then maybe you're better off being what you are. Actually I think it's rather exciting; it's just that I can't stand his damned plays. I wish they were more interesting."

"Well, what do you want to do?"

"I don't know," I said, "I want to fuck you again if I could. I think that would be pretty good. After that we'll see."

"No, in the long run. I mean I don't know what I want to do either, but at least I have an excuse. You must have some idea."

"I really don't," I said. "Actually I do, but it's not even worth talking about; someday I think I'd like to write plays myself, just for the hell of it. I don't think there's anything wrong with writing plays, that is if you have something to say and you can say it decently. I think that I could give S— a run for his money. Of course I haven't got his connections or his reputation but neither did he when he got started. It isn't very important."

"Here," she said, running her hand up and down my stiffening cock. "What do you think of that?"

"I think that's all right. I think that's very nice. What could be wrong with it?"

"Well," she said with a slight, expert, manipulating squeeze, "S— would say that because we're not married it can't be any good, that's what he would say."

"Nonsense! S— likes a good squeeze on the cock as much as any of us do, he just has to think of the Crown and protecting himself. You talk to him, he's sensible—sometimes."

"I don't want to talk to him."

"I don't want to talk to him either, but I'm afraid I don't have much choice in the matter. What time is it anyway?"

"I don't know. I haven't the faintest idea. Aren't you supposed to know what time it is?"

"I suppose so," I said and went to look for my timepiece with a groan; it had been tossed deep under the bed during one or another of our throes, and I noted with dismay that it was something after four o'clock. "It's late," I said, "it's very late, and I'm due at rehearsal in less than four hours."

"So I'd better go downstairs then, shouldn't I? It's been very interesting, though. I really learned a lot tonight. Now I can see that everybody who knows how to use big words isn't necessarily so smart."

"Not so soon," I said as my lovely arched her soft back, moved up from the pillows, began to make aimless but enticing gestures in the vague direction of her clothing. "Not yet. Wait a few minutes." I reached for her then, and in a state of unbridled lust, started to take her again.

There were small resistances to conquer, small twitches, small upheavals and dodges but with all her soft vulnerability exposed to me, her breasts pouting limpidly over my forearm, her cunt wiggling against my thighs in its frenetic efforts to escape, it was not difficult to turn to stimulation the purpose of suppression. And with a few hearty tugs on the labia, a few patient sucks of the areolae I was able to convert her impulse to flight toward its opposite, was able to cause vast changes and upheavals within her that by some subtle kind of chemistry altered the very complexion of her body until, rosy-hued and soft, her breasts rising toward my mouth, she sank down upon my covers with as yielding, as comforting a sigh as man had ever extracted from woman before. Then I began to work on her, moving hastily to mount, to incise, and in the midst of all her moans and the swooping throes of her hips I took her.

I took her with a few quick thrusts, moving in only to dampen myself slightly the first time and then, that accomplished, came in with a storming heave, split the ripe core of her open. Then, straddling her at an enormous height went in once, twice, quickly and came with surprising vigor for one who had been so drained, my semen an endless rush, all of her flesh billowing and groaning around me, and at the very end, the very declension of orgasm I bestowed upon her right breast the softest, the gentlest of all suckling kisses, an infant's touch upon that brow of her breast.

This must have been enough to set her off because she screamed "*Oh, no!*" in a rapid, garbled way and then began to heave back at me, and it was all I could do not to be unseated, but I kept my posture instead and brought her through to a happier conclusion, the puddles of our spent desire mingling between our limp thighs on the bedspread.

At last she said, "I have to go now," and found no resistance on my part. At last she moved away from me and began to don her clothes slowly, her eyes fixated on some aperture of the window. At last she put a parting kiss on my forehead and went to the door. Spent, I had tumbled in upon myself like a rider on a tired horse and was well launched toward the cove of sleep, but at the door she stopped suddenly and turned to me, said loudly, "But aren't you the least bit worried about how you're going to do in the play, anyway, Prospero?"

"Of course I am," I mumbled. "I'm scared unconscious, but there's really little enough that I can do. And besides if I leave the company I've lost the main means I have of evading the authorities. So there you are. But I assume I'll manage."

"Well I think it's very brave of you," she said and went out, closed the door, left me floating my way toward sleep. I was practically all the way there, sunk into some deep, gray place where only wavelets and elves and beasts of nature tenanted my consciousness, but something occurred to me almost as I had slipped all the way down into that tumultuous pocket; it brought me bolt upright, crosslegged and musing, humming and twitching on the bedspread and made, in its peculiar way, for a very lively night indeed because after this I found myself almost completely unable to sleep.

She had called me Prospero.

An actor's life, methinks, is not for me. But, then again, what is the alternative?

Rehearsal this morning and all through the day, a series of experiences so testing, so obligating, so full in their complexity as to leave me in a position where I barely retain the strength to put down these notes. Nevertheless, once begun, twice finished as the saying goes, and it would be most unfair to abandon the duty at this time; the historical record is, after all so valuable, and this firsthand account of a lead actor in one of S—'s plays will possibly be of high value at some later date, perhaps in the 1800s say, although it is impossible to truly visualize something as remote as this.

I awoke this morning my mind scrubbed, blank and stupid as a child's, was for a few moments barely able to establish such simple details as name, date, place, let alone the question of present obligations. But then it all came to me in a flash and with an accompanying throe of panic; glancing at my watch I saw that it was seven thirty, even later than I had feared, and thus I had less than half an hour to wash myself, dress, eliminate at some length—an excessive bout of sex always gives me unwonted cramps—and learn the complete text of my role to be quizzed by S— shortly thereafter.

What needs to be said of that next half hour? What needs to be said of the woe, the torment, the pain, the remorse, the misery, the racking pains, the coughs and shooting headaches, the sense of guilt that inflamed me much as my poor bowels were under overload? What matters all of it? I dressed, I managed as best I could, I seized the script itself, and I went hurriedly to the theater. Jane was nowhere within my sight as I staggered over there but, then, there was really no reason why she should have been, and if she had it only would have increased the difficulty of the morning because I could not think of a thing, not a single thing to say to her.

I got into the theater, as I say. The theater was entirely empty except for the black form of S—, shrouded by a massive cape as he strode back and forth on the empty stage, his footsteps echoing and clattering in the stillness, his face moving uneasily from side to side, his voice emitting harsh syllables which, in the frail acoustics of the theater could be heard only intermittently. It seemed, however, that he was giving voice to one of his own soliloquies, perhaps from this play, although it could not be entirely determined, having only to do with dreams, death, decay and remorse as most of S—'s admired soliloquies do. I hastened to the front of the theater and motioned to him to let him know that I had arrived, then, stricken by a doubt lest I had intruded upon some kind of self-discovery, sat down in a front row seat and, crossing my legs, took the script out of a pocket and began to read it hoping that I might be able to osmose a particle or two of meaning before the rehearsals began.

But there was no such luck, S— stopped his pacing and, leaping quite nimbly from the stage for a man of his years came over to me. "Ah," he said, "I see that you are early—early for the regular company that is to say. But you are not early for your own obligation; as I recall you were supposed to be here over one hour ago. I've been waiting for you, then, for some time."

"I'm sorry, sir," I said. "I overslept."

"Overslept, hah?" He leaned close to me and inspected me carefully, then collapsed with a sigh in the seat next to mine. "Been doing a bit of jousting, I see," he mumbled.

"Jousting?"

"Euphemisms! Euphemisms! I can see that you've been fucking all night. It's quite obvious; one couldn't miss it."

"Not a bit of it. I went to bed most early and—"

"Stop, stop!" he said, waving a hand before my face. "My powers are dwindling, my very speech is dying within me, but the observation remains keen, unfettered, as sharp as ever. I can tell when a man has been fucking and when he hasn't. You look like a rutted pig. They all do."

"But—"

"But nothing! Don't dissemble with me young man. You've been rolling around the old beast-with-two-backs all night and you haven't learned your role. You have no more idea of how to speak your lines than of how a woman's body is constructed inside. You only hope in the one case as in the other that you can somehow get together with it and make it work."

"Well all right," I said, "but I've been studying the role too. It's a difficult one; it doesn't seem to take. I can only understand a role and work my way into it if I apprehend it first; once I do I can memorize the lines in less than an hour but until I truly understand it it takes me hours to memorize even a word; that's just the kind of actor I am. Of course it's nothing personal. I think the play is fascinating, but I just can't seem somehow to comprehend what's going on and until—"

It was a fair effort under the circumstances; actually it was an admirable response to an impossible situation; even at the moment of my babbles I could congratulate myself upon the ingenuity of the effort. Of course what I truly expected was to be discharged at the instant, not without oaths and curses, S—'s policies doubtless being conducted with as much dispatch as his insights. But instead and to my surprise he only emitted a long sigh, an old man's sigh, and settled back in his seat, grasping the arms of the chair and staring up, his eyes half closed at the ceiling.

"Well enough," he said. "You're quite right, you know; I expected no more than this. Perhaps the ungrateful Williams is merely a victim of the same difficulty. You're right, the play is atrocious, incomprehensible, awkward, a mixture of blends. I don't even know what's going on in it myself. I set out to write a comedy you understand, a little something to give them after *Cymbeline*, which would show them that I hadn't lost the old ability to play at identities and conjure up sprightly scenes, but before I even got out of the first act, the accursed thing had gotten entirely out of control. It turned out to not be a comedy at all; it isn't even a tragedy. The fact of the matter is that I don't myself know what it is except that it's out of control, full of spooks and goblins and nightmares."

"Oh, it isn't that bad, sir," I said. "There are some nice lines in it. And besides it's certainly something that can be acted once you find your way into it; the problem is only that I don't quite understand it."

"Oh, quit being kind, you young felon," S— grunted, "no there, don't twitch, don't start, don't look discomfited. I know all about your interesting career in London—what fascinating crimes! not without humor or true purchase—and the means by which the infamous Thorpe allowed himself to be inveigled into permitting you to join the company without any true credentials. But you must understand that none of this makes any difference to me; I don't care; I am a man of resource. I have seen and comprehended most levels of experience, and at this time I've decided that about the only thing left is patience. No, don't worry, don't worry. I see you think that I'm going to come to terms with this, but the fact is that you amuse and bemuse me. I respect what you are and what you've done, and it happens to be the primary reason I've given you the role: a non-actor might as well play a role that no actor could comprehend, no? But this is all beside the point. I was trying to tell you not to be kind."

"What do you know of what I was doing in London?" I said, my voice possibly quivering a fraction, my entire demeanor certainly physically shaken. I had, after all, been through quite a range of experience in the last twelve hours; intensity was one of my predilections but even intensity can reach a point of diminution sooner or later. "How do you know of this anyway?"

"What I know, I know," S— said with a slight smile. "I'm not without my own sources and connections after all these years you understand, but you must throw from your mind all this anxiety. It is needless, *needless*. I don't care who you are or what you were doing, David Perkins. Don't you see that I've enough trouble with this blasted play of mine? It's pointless. I meant to make Prospero a benign blasted old figure of helpless astonishment before the young lovers, much like Polonius, say—and I even gave him a similar name—but he turned out to be a lout with a conscience of his own. I meant the young lovers to be a sentimental, genuine creation much like Romeo and Juliet and what happens to me? I'm not even past the second act before they're monsters. *Monsters* the two of them, selfish and clutching at one another, existing only in terms of the torment and contempt they can wreak upon the others and Caliban. *Caliban!* He was supposed to be like the porter in *Macbeth*. Here I am, barely forty-eight you see and already I'm rewriting my own plays. But I couldn't do anything with Caliban. He doesn't even have anything to do with the damned play. Oh, Thorpe! Thorpe tried to tell me the truth. He's queer, you know; Thorpe's a raving faggart but too cowardly to have much fun of expression at it. But he's a nice fellow for all of that and a really competent director. The interesting thing about him is that he has no sense of rivalry with the playwright; almost all of them do, you know, they're so damned frustrated and hating, but Thorpe has all his aggressions elsewhere: all he wants is a good cock to suck. Otherwise he's a reasonable man even though he can be tough on people like you.

"Thorpe, anyway, told me to withdraw the play. He said when I gave it to him in London, he said, 'S—, this thing isn't going to work, I can't make heads nor tails out of it. S—, it isn't quite up to the stuff you've been doing. It may be better and it may be worse, but people won't even know what to make of it.' He was trying to do me a favor, Thorpe really was; he was trying to straighten me out and help me before the advent of a public disgrace. But what could I do? I had nothing else in the trunk, and the company was getting sick of the old plays, and besides we can't go out on tour without a new play. That's all there is to it, and I didn't have the patience to write another one. Actually I was afraid that it might turn out worse."

I realized then that S— was drunk. Why this had not occurred to me sooner can only be ascribed to my own state of stupor, to say nothing of fear. But now, sitting, watching him gesticulate and tremble in his seat like a plaintive, ill-manipulated marionette, it was easy to see that he was in an advanced state of intoxication. If this were not enough the fumes which rose gently from his breath to mingle with the odor of the auditorium would have rendered a kind of conviction in themselves. Nevertheless, it was with more relief than dismay that I encountered this phenomenon; it meant that things would be going easier on me certainly as a result. The only question was as to exactly how much he knew of my career in London and, whatever the state of that knowledge, how he intended to deal with it but that was something which was only within the bounds of speculation at that time and might, in any event, be irrelevant. It is quite clear from all subsequent developments that S— himself would incite the curiosity of the authorities no less than I would should he go to those extremes, but I have no expectation that he will.

"Actually," S— said, going on for some time in silence and then swooping back upon that word like a bird in staggering flight returning to a well-known food trough, "actually I think that I may be quitting the stage. I don't mind telling that to you Perkins—this news is too explosive to be lightly divulged—because you are, of course, of the most limited consequence to me. I barely know you personally, and I expect little to devolve from our relationship so I can risk dropping this upon whatever you call your sensibility. I really don't think that I have much more to say; I'm beginning to get frightened, you see, quite frightened.

"I've been playing with demons for twenty-five years now, and they've served me quite nicely; they've honored me and led the pathway to a very pleasing reputation, not to say a couple of pounds. But I'm beginning to feel that he who plays with demons may eventually have to pay them a profit; you cannot, after all, meddle in this kind of thing as if it were a normal business. You can act as if it were a business, and I know many writers who say that they're only a kind of laborer working away as mechanically and as competently as a workman would—but they're entirely wrong because you begin to pay a price after a while, and it simply isn't worth it. It's like they've all come out of their bottles, these bastards of imps, and they're out to get me. They've been paying my piper for twenty-five years, and now they're going to make me pay theirs. Of course, this is all in all a pretty dramatic way of looking at things and may not even be the truth but I'm beginning to feel that way. Maybe I'll go back to Stratford and rest when all this play is over. I mean, maybe I'll stay in Stratford after we do the play there and just collapse.

"Anne and I don't get along, never do get along if you know what I mean, but on the other hand she's never done anything to offend me. The flesh is gone, long gone, distant and deceased that ruddier part of me, so there should be no reason, no reason at all why I should not be able to settle on the level of accommodation. I mean, when you come right down to it, who needs sex anyway? This question I wish, of course, I had asked myself thirty years ago and been the wiser for it. All those rumors about Anne and me are feeble, feeble slander; there isn't a word of truth in it. Besides those sonnets weren't written for *anybody*; they were just written for myself, but I had to make up some initials or it would have looked too narcissistic. Then they pinned that whole thing on me when they got hold of the book years later, but the truth is that it all started in the monarchy in London because they hate me, and they're all out to get me; they figured they'd hang me that way as soon as any other. The wheel has come full circle. I am most unseemly sir, most unseemly full of spirits. It is not those but the time that affects me. Oh, time, wretched fool, death's cheat and nature's folly, trapped in your endless spokes we codify our mortality! For mortality is the child of time that bastard mistress and night the darker scion, and from the two cometh not only mortality but sweet grace, that breeze of flowers which stings our faces into summer. And then—and then—oh, Lord—" S— broke off, and reeling to his feet went staggering out to some alcove behind the stage where, presently, I heard wrenching coughs and heaving sighs.

After a while S— came back, but by that time not only S— but Thorpe and most of the players had arrived. Thorpe found himself too immediately preoccupied with S—'s condition to pay much mind to me. With his arm tenderly around S—, Thorpe led him off somewhere which gave me a long successful period during which, seizing the script and running my hands over it as if to impress the very flesh of its rhetoric into my substance, I found that I was able to familiarize myself at random with a fair selection of the lines.

After a time Thorpe came back himself and taking the stage announced to the company that S— was ill and would therefore be taking the day off. In respect to him there would be a bare, minimal run-through of the play with a dress rehearsal to be done tomorrow and the performance itself tomorrow night. Salvation! But even as I turned amidst the mumbling faggarts to make my exit Thorpe came over to me and seizing me by the collar with an enormous hand said, "Not you yet, Perkins. Not quite yet. S— is ill but he was quite insistent that you do intensive work today, that I drill you on your lines, and block you individually. Besides that, what's your hurry? I said there was going to be a run-through." So I closed my book and yielding to that strange embrace, turned to face my destiny.

But, somehow, I got through it, got through all of it almost as well as I had done it yesterday. All of it becomes a blur composed out of a fatigue of remembered lust, recollected and present pains, and a stinging remorse. I know that somehow I was able to pace my way through the play, sometimes reading from the book, sometimes not, sometimes getting the lines correct, often not but none of it making any difference because Thorpe was not holding up the rehearsal for any reason, possibly having his own urgent reasons to escape. Somewhere toward the very end of the run-through I had the feeling for the first time that I might be getting the play, that it might be making a kind of sense.

It all fell into place quickly enough if you decided that Prospero was completely insane and played it that way. It was the only way which made any sense of it whatsoever because then there was no need to reconcile the sides of the characters, comprehend his relationships, or embrace any understanding of his destiny. Besides, it was perfectly credible that Prospero *was* mad. Whatever he had been doing if anything before he came to the island was quite obscure, it was never referred to other than in an offhand way, and his insistences that he was a "magician" could only be the cries of the lunatic insisting that he can walk upon water. Yes, there was some comprehension of the play if regarded in that way; it was even possible if glimpsed in that way to say that it possessed a kind of terrifying sense. If Prospero was insane, then they were *all* mad: Ferdinand, Miranda, the nobility, Ariel, all of them—except Caliban. If you looked at it in this way, Caliban was the only one who made sense.

He had to. For one thing, he was the only one who knew why he suffered; moreover, he knew how the suffering could be stopped, although it was impossible for him to do it. So Caliban, if he was sane then, was the only man on the island. As for the rest of them ... well, one didn't want to think too much of the rest of them. It was an interpretation of the play which, perhaps, permitted one to act in it but it could hardly be said to have improved one's spirits, outlook, or sense of justification. I felt stricken with a sense of doom.

When we finished the rehearsal, I felt quite limp, but despite this limpness I was exalted in a way because, with all the faults, lapses, and misses it was now clear to me that I might be an actor after all. I had some feeling for the role, some idea of how to move on the stage, and even a knowledge of how to pace out the playing. It was really fascinating. I could see that now; I could see how people could give up their lives and consign themselves to disreputability for decades if they only had a chance to do this because it might be worth it, it was certainly more worth the struggle than most things with which I myself had dealt. And my acting experience was nil! What would all of this have meant to someone who had talent, who had background who—not unlike the author—had spent his life in the theater? It was something to think about.

When it was all over Thorpe put an arm around me—the first time he had ever done this without brutality other than that one strange meeting in his quarters weeks ago—and said, "Well, don't you feel better about this now? Tell me the truth, isn't that a little better now?"

"Isn't what a little better?"

"The whole question. You know what you're doing now, a little bit. You're out there on stage struggling, but you're starting to get something; you're not just floundering out there. And it shows."

"Well thank you very much," I said, trying to push by him, consumed by nothing so much as by a sense of horror at what I had just glimpsed. It occurred to me suddenly that S— was not losing his powers at all, not if what he were saying in this play was as apparent to others as it was becoming to me, and had I had the chance I probably would have told Thorpe that I wanted to see S— about this, but I only said, "I'm very tired. I've done the best I could, but I have to take a rest now."

"But man, it's only noon; you have been at this thing no more than three hours! You just walked through it once! What would it be like if we went through the whole day as we were supposed to? What will it be like tomorrow when you have to work all day and perform in the evening? It's crazy," Thorpe said, "it's crazy. You haven't even had two days to prepare for a role, and now you're supposed to play a lead, I don't see how it can be done. But you've got to show some respect. You've got to stay here and work."

"No!" I said. "No, no, no, no, no!" and pushed past him, "I can't do that," I said. "It's all been too much for me. Tomorrow, I'll manage to make it work tomorrow, but I'm just too tired now, I'll take the script home and study it, but you see I've been listening to S— this morning and then doing his play and I just don't think that I can deal with it any more. I haven't the resources. I haven't the resources!" I screamed at him and fled from the theater, limping slightly, feeling like one of Ariel's broken sprites as I got into the dense, foul air of the village—it was one of those changeable landscapes in which the only constant during certain periods is that of oppression—and made my way back to the hotel.

The bar was filled with workmen of various sorts, Jane in the middle of all of this, gray marks under her eyes, deep hollows in her cheeks, pouring, annealing, mixing, clinking. As she saw me she gave an enormous wave. "You," she said, "I must see you, David. I must talk to you," and disappeared then amidst the turning heads of several workmen as they stared, grinning at me.

I made my way upstairs, suddenly filled with a vast indifference; indifference toward all warnings, indifference toward all devices, indifference toward speculation itself. Going into my room I lay down on the bed for a few moments, knees drawn up, eyes fixated on the ceiling, trying not to think of S—, and yet finding that this was the only image which truly possessed me: the aspect of the man as he had spoken to me this morning; the look of him as Thorpe had helped him stumble from the auditorium. I knew then that the play could be understood fully only as a projection of S— himself; to the extent one knew the play, one might know him, but then that tied into all of my uneasy speculations about the character of Prospero and it was too much, too much. I found a wave of protective fatigue clamping over me, not so damned protective at that anyway because no sleep would come because of the tension. And then, as I was on the verge of sinking into a doze—extended as it might have been fruitful—I heard the door open. Jane, her face flushed, came in and with hands on hips confronted me as I opened one eye to peer blankly at her.

"Well," she said, "that's manners, isn't it? You heard me say I wanted to speak to you and what do you do? You go upstairs. You've made me a veritable laughingstock, do you understand that? All of them down there know what's going on now. You're just lucky that they're a nice bunch and I was able to close up for a little while. Aren't you listening to me?"

"I'm listening," I said. "I'm listening but I'm tired, and there's been so much going on. No offense. I mean, everything's fine. But I've got to take a rest somewhere, I can't keep this up forever."

"Now you listen to me," she said, sitting on the edge of the bed, reaching out with a foot to vigorously slam the door. "I'm going to talk to you—I don't know why, you're not even worth it the way you treated me—but I have to tell you that I've been hearing things all morning and around the bar, and there's a great deal of trouble. There's something about plans to interrupt the performance tomorrow night. That man who used to be playing your role is supposed to be leading this rabble."

"No!" I said in disbelief. "I truly don't understand this. I don't even think I know what you're talking about."

"I *told* you what I'm talking about: the man who was playing your role is going to cause some kind of trouble in the theater tomorrow night. It's all over the village; you can't hear anything but that kind of talk. I wanted to warn you. I don't want to see you get into any kind of trouble."

"You mean Williams?" I said. "Williams wouldn't do anything; he's a member of the company, he's been with the company for years. He's unhappy, certainly, because he lost the role to a newcomer, but I don't think this has anything to do with riots. He'll live with it."

"Then you don't know what's going on," she said grimly, "I know; a barmaid gets to learn everything later or sooner, and I've heard it high and low that he's quit the company. He says he's going to destroy it because of what they did to him. There's a band of rowdies in this place that would take on the Pope if there were a laugh or a beer in it. He's been talking to them and running around with them all yesterday and all last night, and they're making plans! I just thought you ought to be warned."

"Well," I said, "I'm warned. But I'm sure that nothing will happen. The authorities won't let anything interfere with a public performance."

"What authorities?"

"Well, I assume there are police."

"The only police there are is an old man and a young man who is his assistant; they keep order by keeping the drunks out of the roads and the highwaymen down to two or three visits a week. That's the police. Listen, David, I don't have to do this you know. I think it's very nice of me to tell you what's going on. You could show a little appreciation."

I sat up unsteadily, balancing myself on trembling elbows, looking up at her through a glare of fatigue and, yes, it can be conceded, rage. "Well what do you want me to do?" I asked. "You want me to fuck you again, is that it? You haven't had enough of it. Is that the way I should show my gratitude, then?"

She slapped me, moving in an easy, fluid gesture which trapped and closed the distance between us in an instant and left my cheek burning with an intimation of finger marks on it. It is surprising how, for all their softness, they can wreak such damage, but then it should not be surprising at all; they are far more creatures of the flesh than we are. I rubbed my cheek absently, with a feeling of dissolution working through me slowly; I decided that I probably deserved no less than what she had done, although hardly to such stunning effect.

"All right then," I said, "all right, now you've done it. I apologize. But you've got to understand—"

"I understand everything!" she shrieked, "I understand what kind of a lout you are and what you think of me and why you're here in the first place; and I won't have it anymore! I try to do you a favor—"

"But Jane," I said, reaching for her unsuccessfully, "Jane, it's not that I don't appreciate it, I simply don't care. Let them sack the theater. Let them pillage, loot and burn it. The hell with it. The hell with all of them.

I'm just too tired—and maybe the theater doesn't deserve better."

"I hate you," she said and stood up quietly. "You've made a whore out of me, now. That's all you've done. I've never been a whore before. I've been one thing and another thing in my life but I've never been that, and that's what you've made me feel like. So I hope you're very grateful. I hope all of you are very happy thinking so little of yourselves that any girl who goes to bed with you has got to be something of a slut to do it. I should have you thrown out of here. I could do it."

"I'm tired," I said and was surprised to hear the whine in my voice. "I'm just too tired."

"I hope they come down the aisles with sticks," she said. "I hope they come up on the stage and drag you down and beat the pulp out of you. I hope they *do* burn the theater and your precious S— with you. I hope that everything goes to fire because that's all you deserve! I won't do a thing to help them, although I want to. You deserve it!"

And she stood up then, an arch of tension in her back I had never seen before—she would have, I am sure, called it pride, but I could only think of it as something else, something more childlike and gentler, so deeply had I emotionally split open—and left the room, left me to my devices, left my body stinging on the bed. After a time I got up from the bed to lock the door and then I must have gone to sleep, but as to the true meaning of all of this I cannot be sure, it all fades away, it is all dim, no constancy, no meaning, only flight and moving through the center of it on their broomsticks, the crowing witches of fear.

Thorpe hadn't asked for anything dramatic at all; he invited me to his rooms for a drink the night before we left London. He wanted to discuss the theater, he said, but I knew what he was after. It was perfectly all right with me, since it was part of the bargain, and it is only a very small step downward on the human scale from felony to a little honest, manly buggering. So I went there when I should have, gave him my coat and accepted a drink. We sat in the dim, musty entrapment of a traveling actor's hotel room for a time, talking about S— and the company and the plans that we had for the tour, and soon enough— sooner than one would have thought—Thorpe came to the point and made a series of motions indicating that he wanted me to follow him. We went over to the bed, and he sat down on it, sighing heavily, removing his boots. "Comfort," he said, "it's just a question of comfort, nothing else, I just think it's a friendly thing to do, there's nothing attached to it. You're a fine-looking lad, do you know that? You'd look just like my son if I had one."

"I'm twenty-three," I told him but this didn't seem to impress him, and he casually took off his boots and then his leggings and then stretched out on the bed with an expression so complex that there was simply no way of describing it, no way of understanding it and with a slow, beckoning motion, which had such a forest of meaning in it that there was no possibility of ever making one's way through, he bade me to come near him.

I did so, not without trepidation but with determination also, and then his arms came around me and he said, "Please, please, don't go away, just let me hold you for a moment. Don't make a joke of me; don't think of me as a fool. Have respect for me as you would want me to have some for you." And he clutched me and I felt myself being drawn in and in, the very surfaces of me revolved and collapsed under me. Not only could I not get away, but I had no urge to do so, and he rolled against me. Then the two of us were in the bed.

After a little time, I did what he wanted me to do; did it in response to his order working out the rhythms as he asked....

When it was over, in that brevity of interval before all the doors of the ego had slammed closed again I realized that for all the point and purpose it had had—and it had had some, it had had some—I might as well have been doing it with a woman or diddling myself; it was not what you did or who you did it with so much as what it meant to you. That was what Thorpe had, perhaps, been trying to show me, and he might have been right; he in fact probably *was* right. I never forgot the shape of his room or the texture of the bed or the sound of his sighs, although in time I found myself forgetting almost everything else about what had been going on.

I wondered if S— had been in similar circumstances. I wondered if it would have been the same to S— as to me. I wondered at any number of things because I was only twenty-three and in deep trouble and was willing now to admit that. But I knew that it was no time to reminisce or have self-doubt; one had to go forward, forward. And so I did and never did it with Thorpe again. Nor did he ask me. He came to hate me, which shows that there are no answers of any sort other than the simple ones you can construct—but, the constructions themselves are as likely to be lies as any other thing. Because the lies are so satisfactory, so colorful, and so meaningful, we dot out our lives with them, structure our lives against them, and if in the middle of all these lies the truth itself came out shy and peeking it would seem to be only another banality of all misstatement, and we would never take it for that. I see that now ... I think.

After some time I woke up in darkness, not a sound to the right and left and center of me. In the stillness of that room then, drained of even exhaustion I succumbed to that fine, high, almost desperate sense of isolation I have known at certain periods in my life, a feeling that I was the only person left alive and that everyone else rather than being dead had gone to parts unknown. There was no submission to this because if I did submit it would be the cancellation of action, and too much was happening, too much indeed. I found my timepiece; it was two in the morning which meant that I had slept somewhat over nine hours and had yet five hours until rehearsal. I put on a lamp and got up from the bed to prowl around, possibly in search of food, possibly for something as simple as a smoke. Far below I could hear the clashing of glasses and some laughter so it was clear that the pub was still open and I decided to go down there; if Jane were on duty I could, perhaps, make amends, and if she were not I could drink until dawn; either way it would be better than staying in that room and thinking.

I got dressed and went downstairs to find a small knot of people around the bar; there were a couple from the company who I recognized and the usual pair of workmen, people from the village who did some kind of obscure physical labor and spent the rest of their hours recovering from or preparing for it. Jane herself was there, sitting huddled at the end of the bar, momentarily without work to do, and I found an empty space adjacent to her, nodding at the people from the company as I did so. I asked her for a drink.

"No," she said. "I won't give you a thing."

"Oh, come on, I'm feeling a little better now; I just needed sleep was all. Can't we be friends?"

"I think you *are* friends," one of the workmen cackled, having overheard our conversation, and the six or seven of them surrounding him all burst into helpless tormenting laughter which made me clench my fists in a kind of panic. I could see at the same time that Jane was suppressing a nervous tremble only with a terrible effort of will within her body.

"All right, then," one of the actors said—he was the one who played Ferdinand, a slim, delicate youth whose name I had never noted nor wanted to know—"leave us not be unbuttoned. Give him a drink, Jane, and ascribe it to me." When this failed to shock her out of her stupor he said, more loudly, "Come on, Jane, give the man a drink," and hesitantly she managed this time to negotiate the length of the bar toward the bottles at which point she seemed to come once again in connection with her environment. She put a concoction together with reasonable dispatch and handing it to me, "It's a kind of whiskey," she said, "not that it makes any difference."

"No difference, no difference," the young actor said as I tasted the liquor. "The point is that we have been discussing you here for some hours now, to say nothing of your most interesting and credible performance. Do you think you'll be prepared to go on tonight?"

"Tonight?"

"It's well after midnight," he said, which caused the workmen to cackle again, and a most unpleasant heave and rumble set pace in my stomach, causing my eyes to glisten as I took down the rest of the drink in one gulp, "not that it's easy, of course, to maintain one's sense of time. How did you work it out anyway to take the role from Williams? There's going to be hell, you know. He's got all kinds of friends in this town."

"I didn't do a thing!" I said, "It was all S—'s doing. I don't want to know anything more about it."

"Still," the youth said, indolently pouring himself the remainder of a portion of beer from his jug, "what can you do? Traveling actors have no business getting into the difficult provinces anyway. Besides, the play needs a good riot. That's my feeling. What rot! What idiocy!"

"You act in that S— play, too?" one of the workmen said to me. "Is that what it's all about."

"He's playing one of the key roles," the youth said. "Second only to mine as a matter of fact."

"Listen, Jane," I said to the figure slumped once again in something that simulated fatigue, "I want to talk to you."

"Forget it."

"Don't be nasty, Jane," someone said. "He's trying to be nice now, he really is. Can't you tell?"

"You too!" she shouted. "All of you! What do you want to make of me anyway? Get out!" she said to me.

"No," I said, "I've got to talk now." I reached across the bar and through some miracle of gymnastics was able to retain my balance while I pinched her forearm, this bringing further howls from the onlookers, but it was all inevitable and all part of the process; I had to live with it. I was able to jerk her into a kind of attention. "Outside," I said. "Right now."

I was prepared to accept any kind of resistance, any kind of complication, when with a peculiar shrugging of her neck muscles something within her seemed to subside and she only said quietly, "I want to close the place. Be quick now, order up," and something in her voice must have turned them to quiet because no one said anything or ordered anything and so, in a few rapid motions, she cleared up the space behind her and by rearranging the panels of wood closed down the bar. "I'm doing this only so we won't have a scene," she said. One of the workmen giggled, and she slapped him sharply across the face, an experience which brought him to instant and solemn attention, as well it might; I could understand this very well.

"I've got the most important role," I said to the youth unnecessarily as I followed her out the door. "You've got the second male lead."

He said, "That's preposterous! The play is about me. You're the comic relief!"

I would have said something very strong, even perhaps have cursed him, but the door closed behind us too quickly, and we were suddenly in a limitless reach of night, all winds, stars, and grasses, the sound of animals in the fields, slow crows and caws of dismay from concealed night creatures. I only took Jane's hand and began to walk with her rapidly away from there. "I'm sorry," I said. "I'm *really* sorry; I didn't mean them to make sport of us, but what could I do? What *can* I do?"

"Nothing," she said, "that's what you can do, absolutely nothing for me. Do you have any idea of what I've had to go through all because of you and your lousy play and your problems? They all think I'm a trollop; they think that I'm some kind of a slut. I've been fighting propositions all night." And then, strangely contradictorily, her hand brushed down my arm and entwined in mine again, and she said, "I don't know how I get into these situations. I simply don't know. I must like them, I really must, but I don't *feel* as if I do. They're all talking about what trouble there's going to be at the performance. They seem to think it's funny."

"But look," I said, "Williams is part of the company, so he won't do anything against us. Besides that, what's the point? What's the problem? Why would anyone want to have this role anyway, given a choice?" I tightened my hand around hers, feeling her fingers dig into mine, and I felt the first welling, a distant spurt of sexual desire. There was apparently no limit to the necessities for fucking; the night clamping down around us, all the breathing noises of the meadow inside and out. I wanted to join with her there in that darkness. "Look," I said, "I know you've just been trying to be nice about this thing, and I appreciate it but you've got to consider my position."

"Your position," she said, "*your* position? All my life I've been considering the positions of louts and ingrates and adulterers and satyrs; they've all wanted me to understand, see their condition, understand what they wanted, and I've been tolerant; that's me, gentle, tolerant Jane, all the wisdom of the ages even though I can't read. I get myself into these positions over and over again, and they come to nothing. I don't even know what I'm *doing* with you out here!" she said, yanking her hand away from mine and skipping a few steps ahead, "I don't even know what it *means*. What is it supposed to mean?"

I caught up with her in a rapid two-step, seized her hand again, and held it closely against me, the trickle of desire now overtaking me, opening up into a steady, pouring stream of dependency, and I said, "I think that S— wants something like this. I think that the reason S— made all this trouble in the company is that he wants a disaster, maybe he wants to get out of the theater anyway," and it was one of those peculiar moments of utterance in which insight follows upon what has been said rather than preceding it and I said, "My God, that's probably it! There's no other reason that he'd do something like this, he wouldn't do it ordinarily. He took an amateur for the role because he knew that the amateur would screw the whole thing up. He took the professional out of it in the most humiliating way possible because he knew that it could bankrupt the whole situation. He's crazy," I said, "he's crazy!" I saw it all in a flash at that instant, the totality of it: S—'s dread, S—'s fear, S—'s revulsion all tied up in his drunken outburst of that morning. I said, "Well if it's true that he's only trying to blow up the whole thing, then the fact is that he's just using me. I've never had free will from the start!" I dropped her hand, looking up at the muddled sky, the sound of something that might have been a cow erupting out of the far background and said, "That would suit his sense of irony. My God, there's never been any free will here from the start. The whole thing has been manipulated! That's why I probably got into the company in the first place; he probably put Thorpe up to it, I'll wager it, and he was planning to put me in this role almost from the start. Now he's done it in such a way that I can't get out. He hates it," I said. "He hates it!"

"What are you talking about anyway?" she said. "Who's an amateur? Who hates what?" which, at the very least, indicated that my outburst had deflected her from her own petulance.

I said, "S—, he's out of his mind; he's out of his mind and he's going to destroy all of us in the process!"

She made another mumble of incomprehension. It was at that point that I put my arms on her shoulders, feeling the hard, rosy, yielding texture of her body underneath me. I found myself leaning on her slightly, and so we sank to the earth that way, a forced conjoinment of bodies from the stumbling. I came down tightly, wrapped hard around her and put my lips against her neck, my lips into her eyes, feeling the frantic rising of her breasts as she breathed hard and tried to struggle. But then I was fully around her, my hips already thrashing and bucking in necessity.

"What are you doing?" she said harshly, "What are you trying to do to me?"

"I'm going to fuck you," I said, rather hoarsely considering all the circumstances to say nothing of the night air. "I'm going to fuck the hell out of you right on the fields underneath the stars. The reason that I'm going to do it is that I want to do it," all the time my fingers fumbling, fumbling, splitting open her costume and wrenching it down uneasily over one shoulder, one breast peering out at me; the sharp eye of the nipple seeming to wink, the pressure of her hands against my shoulders more inciting than otherwise. "I'm going to fuck you, what's the sense in waiting or playing a game. I want to do it now, and that's all there is to it."

"You're crazy!" she said. "Let me up!" She tried to struggle against me, but her motions were feeble. Already she was sinking against the earth rather than rising from it in her agonies; it was easy to keep her pinned there with one hand while I began, meanwhile, to shed myself of my garments with the free hand, the pants came first, easily and then the underpants and then the shirt came careening off and into the darkness. Then the shoes came, and at last I was naked, no problem to it whatsoever, and I could feel her palm beginning to work against my bare chest. "No," she said, "no, no, no! I have to go back to work; I only came out here to talk things over with you because you made me, I didn't come out for *sex*."

For some reason this made me giggle, and I put the whole plane of my nudity against her and getting the other hand around to her breast began to stroke and squeeze that eye until its winking turned right lascivious underneath me, a kind of purpose in the movements of her nipple. Her clothes were somehow being shrugged off by witchery underneath me, certainly not by my own hands alone, and to the best of all sane evidences not hers either. But they were being discarded to the right and left underneath me, and then she lay nude, all except for her shoes which I nudged off with my heels. I felt the cool, slick softness of her body, as glossy as fine furniture underneath me. Then the welling, the rising, fully began.

"I don't think we should be doing this," she said and, "I don't think that there's any future in this kind of thing." But I was already deeply engrossed in the necessities of fucking, trying to cut a swath into the midst of her, urging my tool into a frantic blending that would be the metaphor for all connection, all mingling.

There is something very satisfying about fucking out of shelter in the middle of the night, a sense of completeness and understanding; certainly our ancestors must have done our fucking this way, far before the creation of interpositions between ourselves and our needs. The needs themselves were the same then, and so I found myself retracing in the fucking the very ontology of existence. I was an insect, then a birdlike creature, a slow blind fish swimming in the depths, a land creature come hideous and struggling to the shore, and then a reptile protected by armor. I was a rooting mammal of some sort, and then an ape, at last ascending to the hairless condition of mankind itself. In my prick were all the seeds of history; in my clutching, gasps, and holding was all of the stumbling thousands of generations, most of them beneath understanding, who had gone into this moment.

She might have felt the same way because her protests and small shrieks moderated into moans, then gasps, then a high, birdlike howl as she felt the first entrance of my shaft. For all the franticity of our further actions, then, we could have been not man and woman at all but any two creatures of opposite sex dangling and sucking and fluttering under all the phases of the moon, blown free from all which separated us from the sheerness of our need, disavowed of all consequence. I felt the sheer meatiness of the connection chasing through my loins: slap of thigh, hint of liquid pouring in the belly, sliding of sweat on the skin, the thud of total connection. I was flapping and flowing on top of her, growing, growing, and she was saying something back to me, retracting, diminishing. The tightness increased, there was a burning, a kind of mounting pain which broke free and open into something else entirely, a new apprehension of existence. The sensation was profound, profound, almost religious in its intensity. The convulsions increased, the tremors worked, and at the end there was such an explosion of feeling, such a mixture of grief, woe, and lust uncompounded that my orgasm seemed to come from the center of the earth. I wept with the jolt of it feeling myself pour through generations and into her loins, the generations seeking all of her. Then we folded up against one another in the blissful meadow, out bodies drenched with the outpouring of energies.

After a long time we stood and dressed, and after a longer time I took her back to the house. During all of this we said nothing to each other, and when we reached the inside of the house we went our own way. There was nothing to say. To say anything would have been to plunge what had happened to banality; anything to mar what had happened would be banal. At least that was the way I thought. Of how she was thinking I had no idea at all, but then I never did. I don't know what they think, I do not know what they want, I cannot even lie about the eventual texture of their dreams which must be seen in shades unknown to all men.

"Flog me!" Elizabeth would scream in the extremity of pain during some of our nights together. "Beat me, beat me! Hurt me! And I would put the lash, with lavish sounds, into the small corridor between her breasts, into her belly, against her thighs while she moaned the moans of climax, and I wondered then as I wondered now how anything that could obviously hate itself so much as to find ecstasy only through torment could possibly carry on all the normal acts of mankind during the day, based upon the tissue of the ordinary, the mechanics of sanity. If we do these kinds of things during the night how can we possibly be called sane during the day? Or does the one permit the other? I have no way of knowing. I do not think that S— would know either, although I would be the first to admit that if anyone could he might; his King Lear, certainly, achieved a kind of wisdom through madness that he might never have achieved the other way; and Gloucester, old Gloucester, had to be blinded before he could see. But then, of course, all he saw was Edgar tormenting him, his own son, his extension. What does it come to anyway? This is not a question which I hold myself prepared to answer.

Thorpe screamed too but for different reasons. Thorpe is more comprehensible than Elizabeth or even Jane, although I do not think that society would hold itself to be in general agreement with this.

The writing of these memoirs has been distanced by all kinds of interpolations of event and understanding. This is fortunate because the night of the performance I would have been in no condition to rationally expand upon the happenings of that evening. A great deal of time, then, has passed; I am not sure whether it is one week or three, we might even be holding to a matter of months, it does not matter. Everything I write about now is already in the past, and I am writing this in far different circumstances from those entertained in the previous parts of the journal. Enough to be said of that; I prefer my future to be obscure. I wish to leave no evidences as to my present capacity, so I will give no dates and details. I will merely concentrate in some length upon what happened, and then this will hopefully end this journal. Perhaps I will throw all of this in the fire and be free. I looked forward only to more interesting felonies, nothing else.

I am writing this at great distance, tra-la; everything is behind me. S— is behind, me, Thorpe is behind me, similarly Williams, Jane, Ferdinand, the members of the company, the actor's life, the Globe, the rhetoric, the cunning, the loss. All of them are gone, gone, gone, quite vanished. Only *I* survive, whole unto myself to narrate these events as they truly occurred, tra-la. S—, you deserved no less, although you might have been taken for better.

The events of the day, the events of the day: I woke up early that succeeding morning in a peculiarly brisk state of mind, a state of mind that can only be present at the moment of salvage from a long, numb sleep, a kind of cancellation of all history and consequence in which the day itself seems to be peculiarly possessed of its own tenor and without any viable connection to proceeding events. But I had not slept that long, to be sure, and I embarked upon a day as seated with consequence and extensions as any I had ever known, yet my mood was oddly out of joint with those circumstances, being composed of a kind of stunned and pert willingness to take upon myself with grace whatever happened, not to say with a certain degree of charm. I am not sure as to exactly how this can be explained; perhaps it had to do with the fucking I had undergone the night before. But fucking itself is not very profound, only what is heaped upon it—usually in terms of most irrelevant inferences—so perhaps the mood has to be ascribed to a simple kind of mysticism and left at that.

I am a bit unsteady. Rereading this previous paragraph I can see that, I am not, perhaps, as reconciled to the events (or as distant from them) as I would truly like to be. There is a hint of disjointedness about the style which indicates that I am only with great effort pushing off to the circumference that kind of dread which I thought at this space of time I had mastered. I am aware, of course, that there are no answers whatsoever, not credible ones anyway. It had only been my hope, starting this off, that I had achieved some kind of basic perception or realization. But this, I suspect, is not the case.

The unwonted briskness persisted even as I dressed, left the house, and went to the theater. It is a short walk from the one to the other even under unpropitious circumstances, but this particular morning I seemed to cover the distance with incredible speed, being aware of bird calls in the background, the sounds of cattle, shouts from the pub where, perhaps, a few of those workmen were having an early breakfast. I came into the theater itself which, incidentally, is a small, hideous building, elongated at the sides for greater seating capacity and with a small stage which sits at absolutely no remove whatsoever from the first row of seats, and found the company fully assembled in the front rows. Thorpe was talking firmly to them; a shrouded glance from his almost hidden eyes indicated recognition of me although certainly no reconciliation. I sat quickly in the rear, folding my hands and was surprised then at the way they all turned to look at me. Suddenly, as if that sense of elation with which I had awakened had been an illusion after all, it all came back to me once again: the primary realization that I had no business whatsoever being here; I was not qualified; I was a fool done up in mockery's costume for S—'s purposes.

"I will repeat for the benefit of your dramatic entrance what I was saying to the rest of them, Perkins," Thorpe said rather nastily. "S— is not with us now; he has gone back to London with a sudden indisposition, some trouble in his family perhaps. In any event, he will not be with us again until we meet up with him at Stratford. He has left this company in my hands, and I have assumed the full responsibility. I don't think that there is anything to be concerned about, but S— does get nervous sometimes before premieres, and this is something to which he's entitled; it's his company after all. Now, to continue, Perkins, we are going to rehearse this play all day; I've got it fairly well blocked out and will concentrate on some line work and adjustments. We are going to stop rehearsing at six o'clock and have dinner, we will then reassemble at seven thirty for a short meeting and the performance itself will be at eight. We have, in short, less than ten hours to put all of this together, and I intend to do so; I have not seen such a disgraceful case of under-rehearsing since *Two Gentlemen of Verona* was done virtually from script itself, but that was a much simpler play. I am the director of this company and I intend to take my responsibilities most seriously. Everybody up on the stage now; places for the first scene. I want to talk to you for a moment, Perkins, so just stay there."

They straggled up on the stage then while I simulated as best I could a posture of indifferent attention until Thorpe came lumbering over to me. Seen close up his face was wearier than I had ever seen it before; it seemed to convey its aspect only through a series of deeply etched lines, a network which stretched from one cheek to the next and down through the neck, a grayness over his skin, a heavy, sagging bloodless look in the eyes complementing all of it. It occurred to me that Thorpe was probably far older than I had ever taken him to be; he was an old, old man; he must have been as old as forty, not as senescent as S— then, but still a heavy burden to carry, not that it created any different aspects to our relationship, of course. What is done is done; there is no returning.

"Listen, Perkins," Thorpe said, "it's not going to work. You haven't even learned your lines yet, have you?"

I shrugged. "No," I said. "I just can't seem to interpret them."

"Forget that garbage: You've been fucking that barmaid all night, that's why you haven't been doing your reading. Don't shake your head; it doesn't matter. It would have been a fiasco anyway. S— is crazy. He was crazy to do this in the first place."

"No," I said, "he spoke to me yesterday and I just thought that he was drunk."

"I know he spoke to you yesterday. That's neither here nor there, and it doesn't matter anymore. I would have put Williams back into this except that he's unavailable. And I'd scrap the whole production if we weren't committed for rentals. Under those circumstances though we have to go ahead. It's a disaster, that's all."

"It's not my fault."

"No of course not; it's not your fault, it's not my fault, it's not S—'s fault. No one is to be blamed; it just goes on and on without any sense of causality. Elizabethan England, you know," Thorpe said, covering a belch with a sudden gesture of his right hand. "That's the way it is these days: you just have to live with the situation; they haven't had any mature sense of causality since the Normans and Saxons. Barbarians overrunning, that's all. At any rate, Perkins, what I've decided to do is to give you the script. You can walk through the role reading the thing, and we'll explain to the audience that you're filling in because of the lead actor's indisposition—but the show must go on. We'll try to build you up as a sacrifice, as a brave and gallant attempt to save a production. You might even get some applause."

"That's not fair to the others."

"That's the first and last thought you'll ever have of the others," Thorpe said, "because listen to me, Perkins, the second thing I want to tell you is that after this performance tonight, you're getting out. I'm giving you traveling money, and we'll settle up the few pounds for your being with us to date. You're taking the next coach to London. You are fired. You're leaving the company.

At this I managed to rise, this was quite difficult because I could only subsequently support myself by flexing my shins against the seat giving a certain unsteadiness to my demeanor as well as voice when I said, "But you listen to me. Now that's not fair. I had nothing to do with this. I didn't even ask for the role!"

"Nonsense, Perkins, this company has been in trouble since the day you came into it. S— was upset; he's been needing a long rest—but he hadn't been anywhere near crazy until you came along. We had a perfectly decent lead actor, not particularly talented, but he did his work and knew his lines. Then you came in and, I tell you, the whole company's falling apart. S— is going to stay in London and says he never wants to write again, my lead actor is somewhere out in the provinces plotting murder, and you yourself haven't even made an attempt to become an actor. You don't deserve even to be here this morning; I should have thrown you out days ago, but now it's too late. No one else would have the gall to get up on that stage with a quarto and read the lines, but you're going to do it, Perkins. I'll *make* you do it. And don't give me those looks either, those looks don't affect me, and they have nothing to do with me. Whatever happened between the two of us happened once many weeks ago. I don't even remember it, besides, you didn't even know what the hell you were doing. You understand me, Perkins," Thorpe said, and thumped me rapidly in the chest two or three times, causing me to sink back against the seat for support. I felt the rage beginning then, the fine, dead rage which in a twinkling restored the severed connections of the awakening, and I knew who I was and what I was and what I was probably doing there. "You'll understand me because I am in charge now—and I'll be in charge for a long time. If I see your face around here after midnight tonight for so much as a glimpse or a moment I'll have you set upon and devoured! I can do that you know."

"You son of a bitch," I said and it was a pleasure to watch his face turn from gray to a kind of distant white. (It is not only in folklore but in truth that the relationship between actors and directors is only a thin overlay for murder.) "You son of a bitch, you're the one who wrecked this company in the first place, not me, not S—. I heard the poor man yesterday, and I think that it's all *your* doing. He doesn't even know who the hell he is anymore or what he wants to do. What he tried to do was to fire Williams because he had to do something to prove that it was his company, that he still had some kind of control, but even that didn't work, you've had this thing by the throat now for years and, you've squeezed the life out of it and him. Now you're going to blame *me* for it? Why you lousy faggart, you have no more idea of S— and how to direct his plays than you do of how to handle a cock."

My voice might have arched toward something of a rant over the last lines but Thorpe gave no indication that this might have been the case, his face only becoming colder, windier, more distant, setting upon itself like a demolished sun as I spoke. When I was finished he said, "I take it you have nothing more to say right now."

"Not right now."

"Good. Then you'll go up on that stage and get a book and finish this goddamned rehearsal, and then tonight you'll act in the goddamned play, and then you're going to get the hell out of here, just like I told you. And as far as that goddamned whore of yours is concerned, you consider yourself lucky if you don't come up with a good case of the clap."

"Go to hell," I said but it was a poor exit line, he had beaten me fairly in that regard for he turned and walked away from me briskly, back arched, facing the stage, really leaving me with no position to undertake other than the one I did which was to seize the script from its place underneath my arm and follow him slowly up on stage. The ship scene of course had no reference to me so I joined the rest of the standbys backstage, noting that none of them would look toward me or say anything at all. I crouched against one of the stage supports and watched while Thorpe started the play.

And then memory once again binds, there is little to recollect, the play was started, it was played through, it ended. Thorpe stopped it constantly for adjustments or reiterations and thus doubled its playing time but since he had absolutely no comments to make to me I was able to work the thing out in a fine, dead, suspended haze of purpose, all six hours of it. It went on for at least that long, a deadly, extended, crucial period of time, but for all the significance or point it had to me it might have been six minutes. I walked through the role mechanically, holding the script before me, not even trying for inflection let alone gesture, and the play, interestingly enough, seemed to be going on around me; it was being conducted by a group of actors who were using me as an audience but one of my functions as the audience was to read dialogue myself. If I merely followed the script and said the lines the principals could go on with whatever they were doing.

This time, unlike the other day, there was very little meaning at all; Prospero might have been insane but his insanity was only conditional, an extension of the deeper madnesses which might have given birth to the role. In any case, I had lost all patience at that time with S—'s rhetoric. If Thorpe did not address me in those terms there was little enough reason why S—should use it in the mouths of his characters. The whole thing was unreal, unreal! There was even the possibility, I could see that now, that I too was unreal, that everything was as insubstantial as S—'s plays usually said that it was, in which case, of course, there would be no question of consequence whatsoever. I wandered through the role, then, filling a certain cavity of space on the stage, filling certain areas of silence with words, and as far as I could tell or care this was as close as I was going to get, after all, to being an actor. It didn't seem to matter too much.

This seems as apt a place as any to give a summary of the plot of *The Tempest*; I have been writing about it at some length, of course, with no dearth of critical opinions to the contrary yet I can see that in neglecting a summary of the actual mechanics of the play I may have made this journal needlessly confusing to say nothing of slighting a work which in its various confusions, alarums, and mysteries probably stands with anything of Marlowe's for sheer obscurity.

The Tempest has to do with an old seer of some kind named Prospero who, with his daughter, is living on an "enchanted isle" with a sprite named Ariel and a man-beast named Caliban; precisely what Prospero did before he came to this island or why he had to leave his place of prior occupation to go into isolation is entirely obscure. At the time the play opens they have been on this island for some time. Ariel helps Prospero perform feats of magic while Caliban, who appears to have occupied the isle since before Prospero's coming, is not very happy about the whole process, feeling, perhaps, that Prospero has taken his rightful locale from him.

To this island come a group of shipwrecked sailors and passengers. A young noble falls in love with Miranda while meanwhile the members of the crew plot to overthrow Prospero and take over the island. (Why they want to do this is never made quite clear.) In so doing they are aided by Caliban who finally finds a way in which he can make amends with Prospero for what has been done to him. But, of course, the plot is hopeless; Prospero possesses magic and there is no way whatsoever in which he can be overthrown; he casts all of the plotters into spells except for Ferdinand the young noble. He renders Caliban helpless, and finally he changes all their natures from bad to good with the help of Ariel who enjoys the process enormously, being somewhat of a malicious as well as benign spirit whose powers can be used in any direction.

Ultimately, the engagement of Ferdinand and Miranda is consummated, meanwhile the crew of the ship, now benign, place themselves in Prospero's service, but what he decides to do is to leave the island and, with all concerned, take the fastest route back to London where he says he will "drown his book" and abandon magic forever. Why he wants to do this—why he wants to give up his powers, that is to say—is never made quite clear, but he frees Ariel who, it seems, has always been in his command and embarks, leaving the place to Caliban who, having been given the power of speech and conscience now, presumably, will uplift it slightly.

This for all intent and purposes is the plot of the play, although it pays little regard to the many amusing scenes of the plotters falling into stupors or having hallucinations, or for the boiling resentment of Caliban (and even Ariel) who, after all, resent being servants in command of a lunatic magician.

It is a very strange play, of course—I have said that already—and a most frustrating one because for all the fact that he is supposed to be the hero there are very peculiar aspects to Prospero's behavior: he torments Caliban, imprisons Ariel, makes insane declarations to Ferdinand, performs cruel jokes upon the crew, all in the service it would seem of a certain sense of proportion, a certain sense of humor which are, perhaps, not entirely normal; then too there is something very peculiar about his decision to go back to England and give up his witchcraft. Would any man who is such a force for good want to do this? And if he got his magic not from his own nature but from a "book" why would he want to "drown" it and where did the book come from in the first place?

Well, I feel hardly capable of answering these questions nor will I deal with them again; the role, even for an actor of some talent and background, would be wholly unactable, and there is a most unpleasant overcast to the play as if it were being performed in a dungeon rather than in the clear, open spaces of an "enchanted isle."

We staggered through rehearsal painfully, Thorpe making constant adjustment of the actors around me—treating me as if I were no more than an indolent piece of furniture around which the play would flow— and it must have gone on for several hours, four or five anyway, the indifferent, dappled shades of afternoon were already creeping into the theater and casting the stage into a kind of off-yellow pallor when, somewhere in the throes of the next-to-last scene, I heard vague shouts and clamor from the back of the auditorium, figured that it was only some private wayfarer's disputation among individuals who had found themselves mistakenly in search of a pub, but the shouts increased in violence and tempo and were superseded by what sounded like a series of thumps, clangs and bangs which made our speech almost impossible to distinguish, even on stage and so we had to stop. Looking toward the rear of the auditorium in the off-light it was hard to see for a moment precisely what was going on.

Then, suddenly, S— himself emerged, moving with great speed from back toward the stage, his entire lumpish body in a posture of lunging attention. He might have sprung upon the stage had not Thorpe at the last moment come from his seat and blocked him, forcing S— to stumble back a couple of paces and then attempt another assault. But this one was no more successful; he stopped in midaisle and began to shout at us, this time quite distinctly, the motions of his hands frantic conveyances. As he did so we could see the source of the other sounds because he was alternately kicking and smashing his fist down upon the row of seats next to him with a strange clashing sound that made the wood shudder and seem to disintegrate. "You bastards," he was screaming, "you're ruining my play, don't you understand that? Ha, ha! Thorpe thought that he could exile me to London but he doesn't know the cunning of this mind, the shrewdness of this intellect. It was nothing to evade the coachman and spring back here through the fields bent upon this awful confrontation. Thorpe thought he could take all of this away from the old man and made him a-rotting go but heigh-ho, it won't work! It *won't* work because I'm back now. You're ruining my play you bunch of faggarts. You've all been ruining my plays for thirty years now! One way and the other way you've managed to destroy almost everything I've tried to do, but my secret is that in spite of all of you, I've managed to get a little bit of my work done, a little bit of my work seen. I tell you, I'm shrewder than all of you because I know what I've been dealing with, that puts me ahead of the rest of you. You're atrocious but you won't get away with this."

"Look S—," Thorpe said, standing and trying to push S— off to one side, "enough of this. I won't work under these conditions. Now it was agreed that you would leave the play in my hands."

"Get those hands away from me!" S— shrieked and gave Thorpe a violent push which toppled the latter past his original row of seats and almost head-over-heels to the next where he lay there panting, his eyes suddenly round and astonished, looking numbly at all of us on the stage. For the first time, in that instant, I saw Thorpe bare; it was the face of a child, pleading helplessly for a kind word or remission. I might have been able to have expanded the insight further, but S— was not stopping, he was screaming, "I'm taking this thing over again, Thorpe. I'm going to run the company now, this is my play, not yours and it's going to be done my way; I will no longer be in the hands of idiots!"

He was leaping then up to the stage, the smell of his breath terrifying me as he lunged in my direction, but at the last moment he turned and seized Ferdinand instead, began to shake the boy in his fists, mumbling and cursing, some of the words indistinguishable now but the sense of the message was clear. He was telling the boy that he was playing Ferdinand as a lover when the fact was and he had selected the boy for the role because Ferdinand was a faggart, having no more interest in Miranda than Miranda did in Caliban; he was only using the guise of romantic involvement in order to entrap her but in so doing he entrapped himself more deeply because Prospero's sole purpose in permitting the adventure on the island was to get some kind of a match for his daughter who he was otherwise afraid of fucking. Ferdinand was being thrown in deeper and deeper to a situation so ugly and complex that he could barely comprehend it. But no matter, no matter, and then S— broke away from the boy and began to dart over the stage screaming, cursing indiscriminately, foul words, terrible words and it was at that moment that I broke from frieze, the only member of the company to do so and lunging stage left seized him just as S— was about to throw himself on one of the sailors. I pinned him by the shoulders.

"Stop it!" I said. "You've got to stop this now. You may even be right and the play may be all wrong the way it's being done, but you wrote it, you were the one who made it this way, and maybe this was the only way that we could act it. Actors are simple creatures, you know; they can only act in terms of feelings, not abstractions, and you've got a responsibility too. You can't carry on like this! You've got a reputation to protect, and besides, the play doesn't matter. Can't you understand that nothing that we're doing now matters at all? It's all going to pass away, just like you say in your own plays. In a few years no one will be able to know the difference; we're all going to turn into dust except the plays, and if the plays have any sense then they'll stay, and if they don't then they won't. But you can't act like a child! You've got responsibilities to yourself, you know."

And as I said this, holding him in a grip composed of desperation and admonition, I felt him begin to relax, felt him cave in on several levels as if the very layers of his body were collapsing in sequence one upon the other and then he was lying in my arms quite limp, his face contrite, his eyes closing and he said, "Yes, yes, but it is my work. I've got to live with it you see, you don't."

I felt myself on the verge of some climactic insight, some insight so vast that I would, in an instant, be able to render to him the full sense of what had been going on, tell him at last exactly what it was for and what it meant and where we were going. It was so close to me that even as I opened my mouth to begin speaking I found myself with a kind of stunned self-reproach because I hadn't seen all of this far earlier; if I had it would have been so simple, would have saved so much trouble, would have rescued the totality of the situation. I tried then to talk to him, to deliver upon him the message that would rescue the whole situation and listened with curiosity indeed to what I would be saying because the words seemed not to proceed from myself but from some distant orator who was at last making the situation clear. But before I could say anything at all there were a series of shouts from one corner of the stage and then a group of rowdies, Thorpe behind and directing them, sprang upon us and seized S— and, with many protests, squeals and shrieks dragged him off into one wing and, despite his thrashing, seemed to be in the act of pummeling him into some kind of submission when they faded from view.

Thorpe, breathing rapidly, said without giving us a chance to think about this, "All right, that will be the end of this now; now you know the truth. He's had a complete case of nervous exhaustion, and that was why it was decided best to send him back to London for recuperation, but now the ugly facts of his condition are spread out before you. There is nothing, after all, to be done about something like this except to place it in its right perspective. Of course it will be my responsibility to run this company through the performances; there should be no question of that at all. We will have a one-hour break for lunch. I want *none* of you under any circumstances to do any drinking. We will reassemble here for some final comments after we complete the run-through of these two last scenes. That's all," he said and clapped his hands rapidly. "Dismissed!"

"Wait a minute," someone said from stage rear, one of the sailors half hidden beside some aspect of the foliage. "This is S—'s company, isn't it? I don't really think that it's fair to treat him in this fashion."

"What else could be done?" Thorpe said, and shrugged. "At this point, producer playwright or nothing he was purely disruptive. You can see his condition. It is a great tragedy for sure but, then, he has been working too hard."

"What are they doing to him back there?"

"They're not 'back there'," Thorpe said, "they have already removed him from the theater and will take him directly by coach under supervision to London." He sighed and said, "You see, I envisioned something like this might have happened. It is most regrettable. But one must take measures."

"I don't like it," said the sailor and came forward a couple of paces, hands on hips to confront Thorpe. "I've been with this company for five years; it hasn't been a picnic but it's been a way of life, and I never seen anything like this happen before. S— was always sensible about things. Now, all of a sudden, this happens in two days. I never liked you, Thorpe. I thought ever since you came to this company that we'd have problems. I don't know if we want any more part of this, just speaking for myself, of course."

"Now listen here," Thorpe said as a mumble built up in back of the sailor, "I think this is ridiculous. His condition is obvious. All of you can see it. I've been acting only in his best interests."

"Have you Thorpe? I don't like the way you work in someone's best interests; nothing personal, of course, but if this was the way that you acted in my interests I'd be looking for some protection. S— seems to have been right screwed if you don't mind my saying so, and I feel right suspicious myself. I don't think anybody wants any more part of this thing. I vote that we just leave right now, all of us, and go to London and look for S—."

"That's insane!" Thorpe said.

"No it isn't!" the faggart playing Miranda piped, moving up in his flowing white robes to confront Thorpe and making quite an astonishing picture indeed as he gesticulated. "I think there's a lot of sense in this. What a thing to make us witness! What goings-on! I don't think that we should go any further with this until we know what's happening."

"I'll relieve both of you," Thorpe said, "and pack you out of here on the first coach as well. I tell you, I won't put up with this kind of thing. What more do I have to say; what do you have to see? S— is unwell, he's needed a rest for a long time and hence these unfortunate incidents."

"Unfortunate for you, Thorpe," the sailor shouted and there was another approving mumble behind him. Then, it seemed as if the whole company, acting in some unconscious concert, moved toward him, only one hesitant step at first but in conjunction it made a most unseemly shuffling noise on the floor and probably lent them all a kind of courage because they advanced—some of them—a few more steps. Thorpe's complexion changed slowly from a difficult white to one of purest cinder and the trembling began in his upper body, an uneven beat that spread slowly down. I could see the foundations of a very profound scene indeed, one that would, no doubt, lend no little to my increasing education, but one that might at the same token, become entirely uncontrollable.

"Listen, all of you!" I said, moving to Thorpe's side and speaking as loudly as I could to overcome the hissing and jostling noises which came from before me. "I'm a new member of this company and haven't got much say but I say that there's nothing going to come out of all of this but a lot of trouble. S— may have been in an unfortunate position, what you say might even be true but there's still a question of doing the play tonight, and if we don't do it, if we just break this whole thing up, then the company's going to fall to pieces. We won't have *anything* anymore. Besides that, there's no point in dealing with Thorpe, he has no answers, and he's not going to give us any. Besides that, he might even be telling us the truth. S— after all hasn't been well the last couple of days. Let's stop this; let's act like actors. Actors are professionals! Let's do the play tonight and fill out the engagement, and then tomorrow we can see where we stand. We've all been rehearsed, we know what we're supposed to be doing. We don't even have to listen to Thorpe! I tell you, gentlemen, be reasonable; we don't know what we're among now, and when you don't know that you'd best to walk very carefully, walk quietly."

It was a close thing; I could sense in the short silence following my speech that there was an actual and almost mechanical question of balances involved; the sharp, uneven intake of their breath around me could have led to either capitulation or a shriek and the trembling of Thorpe's hand against my shoulder as he reached out to graze it was sound enough indication that he understood how close it was. After a moment, somehow, the trembling was contained, and I could see that it was going to be all right, that there was not, at least for the present, going to be any kind of violence. "Well, then," I said, seizing whatever advantage there might have been, "Let's all take a break now; let's take as much time as we need, and then we'll come back here and do the best we can. We don't even need Thorpe anymore," and I strode rapidly off the stage, wondering if they would follow me because if they didn't it had all been accomplished in perfect futility. But after a moment, somewhat surprisingly, they did follow with a series of moaning and shuffling sounds which seemed perfectly normal to me, the usual noises that actor's made as they came off after a long siege of rehearsal. I went through the doors, out into the air, over to the other side of the building and went in a stage entrance finding as I leaned up through the aperture to the stage that, just as I had expected, Thorpe was now in the theater, perfectly alone, the phalanx of retreating backs capturing his rather indolent attention as he leaned himself against the stage wall. When the auditorium was clear I came out behind him and said, rather abruptly, "Listen, Thorpe."

He trembled and seemed to rise into the air at least a few inches, then, coming back on his feet to wheel and face me, his face passed from astonishment to a kind of gratitude and he said, "Perkins! Perkins, I don't have to tell you how grateful I am. You saved—"

"Forget that," I said. "I'm leaving the company tonight, after this performance. I'll save your neck by reading it once, but then I'm leaving. I didn't do it for you, I did it for S—."

"Well of course you did it for S—, we all did it for him. It's a great tragedy what's been happening here but they all misunderstood."

"Don't give me that nonsense, Thorpe. I know what you're doing to S— , and I think the company has a pretty good idea themselves. Why are you doing it anyway? Wasn't being director enough for you? Did you have to move on to this kind of thing?"

"But I tell you, the man is under terrible pressure; it's only a question of a small collapse, a fast recovery, and then he'll be back with us. I've only been trying to hold things together."

"Shit, Thorpe," I said. "I've been there myself now and then; you know that I came into this company under the most doubtful of circumstances, and my origins are at least as murky as yours. All in all, there should be a total reconciliation of understanding if not of attitude here. Come off it, Thorpe. Why are you doing it? Why?"

"I tell you—"

I slapped him once, sharply, an excellent extension and reiteration of Jane's slap of the night before, one which had all of her nicety of expression in addition to a certain crude, masculine power. He seemed to break under it, his face curving open into a series of distorted planes, his eyes black and staring.

He collapsed then into a seat and ran a hand across his forehead, moaning. "No," he said, "no, no, no, no, no. You had it all wrong, all of you. It wasn't that way at all. I don't have anything against him personally, never did. I just can't stand it anymore, can't stand his tragedies, can't stand his rages, can't stand his arrogance. How much of this is a director supposed to put up with! Who can direct that stuff? I tell you, it's undirectable! And then it was all of the things he was doing to me. Oh, Perkins, you have absolutely no idea of what the man was doing to me, the corruption, the horror of it all; no one could understand that. I couldn't take it anymore, I don't think that *anyone* could stand it anymore. He was getting worse and worse and the plays were getting worse and worse, and he was denying me all due credit, just taking the whole thing to himself. Who do you think *made* those plays? Who do you think put them together, made them have any sense at all? He was always cheating on salaries and getting the worst possible people from the provinces to act just because he could have them cheap. It's at a point, I tell you, where I can't stand it anymore! There's just got to be an end, eventually to anything, and this was it—but I didn't do anything that horrible; I didn't want to really hurt, just to get rid of him so that for once I could do something in peace, but the drugs didn't take, and none of it took, and it's all such a mess! I can't stand it anymore, Perkins, why did I ever get involved with him anyway?" Thorpe said and in a distinctly unmasculine way, put his head down between his hands and wept, loud, uneven choking noises somewhere between sobs and coughs.

I let him do that for a while looking at him with a complexity of attitude which mingled revulsion and other emotions in almost equal parts. After a time I said, "Get out, Thorpe, just get out. The play is in our hands now, not yours. I want you out of this town when we open tonight. You can take a coach or walk or crawl for help, but you will not be in this town when the play goes on tonight because I won't stand for it anymore either, I won't stand for you. Get out."

"You don't understand," Thorpe croaked. "You don't understand, I *can't* leave, and it wouldn't make any difference anyway if I did, there's going to be something happening tonight in any event and—"

"I know all about it," I said, "I knew you started it. Forget it. We'll handle it. Whatever happens, happens. There will be no more dealing with anything on your part. You are out of this company."

"You're a presumptuous little bastard, Perkins. One would hardly know it in bed, of course. In bed all of that presumption turns to water very quickly, doesn't it, Perkins?"

I raised a hand to slap him again, then put it down—upon consideration there is a fine line to be drawn between remonstration and bullying—and said, "That's all, Thorpe. I'm leaving. We will carry this on ourselves as we must and you are not to be here when we return. Goodbye, Thorpe. Goodbye, Thorpe."

And left him sitting there mumbling, astonished, walked through the doors and into the air not knowing exactly what I had left behind: whether I had left lover or foe, assailant or victim, possibility or history, knowing only that I was irrevocably as I had never been before, cut off from all sense of purpose. As I turned toward the pub looking for nothing more elaborate than a short rest and a time of passing it occurred to me that never, if I lived to be a hundred, would I exist again in that solidity of conviction with which I had addressed Thorpe because I already felt myself tumbling, tumbling and tumbling from that high precipice of insight to some low point of outlook where consternation and surety—those two wrestler's in the body's cavern—fought with one another to no outcome whatsoever. I was tired, tired, tired. I thought that I could hear the sound of Thorpe's choking sobs before me but that, of course, was an illusion. All of it was an illusion, and it came to nothing, nothing, nothing, nothing, nothing, nothing.

Raising the lash to whip her in that long ago time, I had an insight and the insight was simple, it mingled with the sweat and heat and noise of the room, the smell of her as she opened her body to me crying for the lash, the tearing sounds from her mouth as she begged for pain. The insight was very simple and utterly final, and it was this: we wanted it; we were a nation built upon pain; we had come from pillage and destruction, ascendants to a throne and a country that was really not ours, all of us sprung from the loins of thieves and barbarians who had sacked the country and taken it from the gentle folk who created it, and now, generations later, we could pay for our evil only in terms of loss, the sting of guilt, the stroke of pain. We needed this pain terribly because it was the only way in which we could truly assure ourselves that we were still alive, the only way in which we could pay the penalty which we felt should have been exacted a long time ago. All of us, standing to be buggered or waiting open for the sting were only acting out that first and crudest need. Planted deep in the seed of her body Elizabeth had a need for that pain as I had the need to give it, and the two of us conjoined with our cries in a small room that could have been the duplicate of that room in which so long ago the Normans performed the rituals that gave them their country; those barbarians had taken out their lust and property in a small room. And so, then, condemned at the remove of vast generations and to the same end, we were enacting in rooms all over the nation the same pillage and terror except that this time, instead of taking we were giving, giving up with our souls and flesh all that we had painfully acquired. It was too much, too much to sensibly bear.

I brought the lash down hard across her time and again and then in an animal's heat leapt like a monkey to spread across the sheet of her body like a bear and fucked her once, twice, and over again, the steam and semen of my rise mingling with her cries. Nowhere in merry old England that day was there such a conjoinment of revelation to say nothing of reparation, of that I can be sure. And I loved it too; that is the stricken admission.

Could this be what S— had been trying to tell us in *The Tempest?* That all we could understand was pain, that we could only come close to feeling in pain, trickery, and the slow torture of the broken beasts; that this simulation of vengeance was all that we could have; and that the end must be the drowning of all our lies in the sea of expiration? Or is there something else to it; something more to this damnable play that sinks beneath the level of apprehension and, like a woman, is always beyond reach, always vanishing in the muddle of the next purposes, the final destiny?

Who knows? Who knows?

I came back to the pub and found it empty and went upstairs to my room to find Jane naked on the bed, her legs spread, her arms open, her lovely breasts bobbling. "Fuck me!" she screamed. "Fuck me for England!"

And for England I leapt upon her, tearing off my clothes and growling as I did so. For England I grunted my need into the strange hardness of her ear. For England I grew my tool to enormous size and felt it peeking at the slyness of her cunt. For England itself I leaped upon and fucked and fucked her, burrowing deep between her breasts, rising in spurts to the ascension of her thighs, raising and lowering myself, Caliban upon the hump of the earth struggling for manhood and subsiding to the moan of the beast as I came and came into her, bit her nipples, squeezed her shoulders, screamed my song into her ear, plunging and plunging. There was no end to it, no end whatsoever; I fucked her all afternoon, no time for refreshment and renewal; no time for anything but the pouring and pouring into her until night slammed over all the aspects of the land it had overtaken and it was time to go to the theater and hold a book and be Prospero.

Or was it all a construction, a loss, a dream? And did I only lie on my bed entrapped with the pity and anticipation of all of this? And if this was so, where could the line be drawn? What did the difference matter?

What did it all come to? What did it mean? Did S— know it all, or was he madman shouting out his own confusion and terror? Did he see what had to be seen plainly and finally, or was it all a mime, a dumb-show for the peasantry? Was I felon escaped from apprehension or genius reaching to the soul of his torment?

Who knows? Who knows?

I went to the theater that night.

There was a crowd already gathered in the seats, a sodden, mumbling crowd of townspeople of indeterminate ages and history, filling the seats and spilling over into the aisle. Shouts from the rear of the theater, strange apprehension, strange anticipation which must have touched all of the company clear into the place where they were standing, huddled against the wings. Thorpe was not there of course, and without even thinking about it, I took his place, stepped in front of all of them and motioned them onto the stage, then, behind the drawn curtain I said, "We have to do this for our own sakes, because it deserves to be done; there's no other reason, and tomorrow it will have all gone away—but for tonight it has a purpose consistent unto itself. So I beg you, for your own sakes, to give this performance."

And as they listened to me, their expressions sad and yielding, their countenances folded into the solemnity of loss, I realized that so bad was this company—so stricken its leaders!—that I had already become the motivating force in it simply by the act of assuming it. It was distressing, frightening, but there was no time to think of all of it because someone from the management came back and said that we had best begin the play.

There was vast restlessness in the theater which could be best served by getting on with the performance, rumors of difficulty, vague intimations of disaster moving through, so we took our positions as best we could and the stage manager made his way in front of the curtain for an announcement we could not hear well—it seemed to have something to do with "pride" and "performance" and "manners, ladies and gents" from what we could pick up. Then the curtains were drawn aside and somewhere in the wings I huddled with my quarto, feeling the sweat pour from my palms to stain it as the ship scene began.

And the play began, the play went on: that was the amazing thing about this play, it went on under all conditions. I had a thought just as I strode out on stage for the beginning of the second scene. The thought was that the play had to have some value after all because even under these circumstances we were all playing its roles. Yes, one could see that now, for S— was Prospero, and Thorpe was Caliban, and Jane—who else but Jane?—would have been Ariel but the question was, then, that if all this were so and the parallels were so consistent well, then, who was I? What did it all come to?

And I read on, feeling myself vanishing into a high, dim haze, the actor's trance in which the only consequences are those of formation within the limitations of the role. I found that as things proceeded I knew what was going on so well that I could put the book away. For the lines had more than been driven into me by reiteration. In fact, I *was* the lines, those lines being the only way in which I could understand or truly express the sense of what had been going on during these past few days. S— had written with cunning and understanding because seen this way there was nothing foolish about the rhetoric at all, it was the only way of saying these things, no paraphrase possible.

And so I roared and bellowed and twisted through my lines, kicking the oaf playing Caliban, flirting with the faggart who was Ariel, clutching the boy who was Miranda and seeing all of their faces from this angle, the tension, the distortion, I could feel that I, as much as Prospero, possessed them all, that, in fact, I was them truth to tell, and they were me. I held onto them that tightly, with that enormity of grasp. And the audience too, was seen only as an indistinguishable gray blur of attention—and the audience must have known this because there were moans and shouts, coughs and screams of approval, curses and encouragements called in at the right time, and the fullness of the play, its absolute spirit began to overtake the stage. I felt myself sinking into this, sinking more deeply than I had into anything in my life. It seemed that I reached some kind of private culmination—and then I smelled the smoke. I smelled it coming in in various waves from all sides of us. And felt then, almost absently, the heat of the fire.

The fire was coming in from some direction toward the back of the theater; it was coming in such an intensity that it was possible to feel the heat far before apprehending the blaze itself. We could not, from the stage, see it for several seconds, before that, however, we could hear the panicked screams of the audience, the sounds of thumping of chairs, the scurrying of legs and then, still holding on to some vestige of the performance calm, as I opened my mouth to utter a line, I heard the voices begin.

"Get out!" they were screaming out and, *"It's all coming down around us!"* and, *"Help!"* and similar cries. As I turned from the audience momentarily to confront the faces of the actors on stage I could see in them a terror that could only have been the mirror of my own, their faces poised, shining in their anticipation of that final disaster. Ferdinand shrieked, abandoning all fidelity to his role which at that moment

called for a kind of submission. "Let's get the fuck out of here!" he yelled, and at that point the screams, the horror, and the running began.

We bolted for the wings, all of us, indiscriminately running without regard to role or precedence, not even a pretense then at performance and the fire then became truly visible for the first time, snaking down one of the aisles, whistling through with enormous force so explosive as to utterly consume as gratuitous those bodies which were hopelessly standing in its path; one moment there were people jostling and standing in line, trying to get out and the next there was nothing at all, only an incandescence of light and a smell of soot, a wicker of ash. I heard the other shouts, someone was saying, "Serves you right! That's what it all comes to!" and, "This'll show them!" mixing and mingling with curses and obscenities so enormous as to deny any kind of paraphrase.

I was surrounded by bodies; there were bodies on all sides of me, huddling, groping, scratching, clinging. I reached out for some kind of hold that would drag me through to backstage and maybe into the air and caught only the insubstantiality of flesh that slipped away. And then the rest of my impressions all spiraled into a high numbness of terror. I was moving, moving, driving through an enormous space of ground, fighting desperately to find some kind of clarity. Then everything blended and muddled together; I know that I was running, that I was achieving some kind of support between feet and skull which was holding me together, but as to the specificity of the condition I had no grip whatsoever. The voices were rising, rising, the heat was increasing and then at last I burst free into a large, airless space where there was only coolness, and I passed into a grateful unconsciousness, a passage of time and space so enormous that for all that was happening outside I might as well have been locked swinging into a womb where no one could touch me. Behind me, of course, the really crucial events of *The Tempest* disaster of 1612 were only just occurring, the bodies, the deaths, the flame. But of these I can give no credible account whatsoever because I was not aware of them; all that I was aware of was that in due time I woke up in different circumstances altogether, absolutely drained and devoid of thought; what happened was an absence of sound, an absence of sensation which contained as much horror as the other.

But then I was alive and had the rest of my career to fulfill which was something, of course, and gave me something to look forward to. I have not, even at this date, discovered whether or not Williams perished in those flames or, for that matter, whether or not he even started them but it does not matter; the conflagration has an absence of history as profound and numbing as its negation of consequence, and somewhere in that small space between we exist and perish, rise and fall, looking for our own little bit of ground, a piece of ground on which we can sculpt out those things we do, we wish to do, and that we have never done...

I have now finished this journal. Looking back upon it it strikes me as being satisfactory, somewhat absent of detail of course and somewhat surrealistic as well, perhaps, in its final passages, but all in all as apt a summation of those tortured days, that hideous anticlimax, as we are apt to get, considering the fact that like most actors I am devoid of outstanding creative skills.

Nevertheless, my companion is not satisfied. Passing the manuscript back to me a few moments ago after having read it in its entirety she said, "I don't think that there's enough here. You haven't really made it clear as to who set the fire, what happened to S— after all this happened. What happened to Thorpe and Ferdinand and the rest of them? You said that this would show why S— left the theater in 1612, but I don't really think it does, it just seems to explain why *you* left the theater, if you know what I mean."

I know what she means. It is possible, in fact, that she has a point. But I feel an inability to explain this out along outlines foreign to its original purposes which were, perhaps, more fully purgative than otherwise. However, my lady to your satisfaction and for some measure of my care for you, let me try to finish all this out as rapidly as possible, as irrelevant as it is.

I believe that the fire was set by Williams although there will be no way of ever knowing this, he died in the flames as did ten members of the company and several hundred of the audience. Among those who perished were Thorpe who was found, to my astonishment, in the rear annex having apparently been unable to resist attending, when all was over, the performance of the play. A director to the last he paid the supreme penalty for his curiosity.

I left the theater because I found all these events insupportable. S— on the other hand—and I can see this more and more as we move further and further away from those terrible days—probably left the theater precisely because he did *not* find these events insupportable, that, to the contrary and very much on the other hand, he found them entirely comprehensible. I do not think that seen in this perspective his play—which happily survived, albeit in a tattered manuscript—leaves any doubt whatsoever as to this quality of sensibility.

One wonders where S— is. There are tales that he is in London, that he still stalks the streets at night, that he can be seen in certain pubs that, in fact, when some local company performing his plays is in rehearsal—for they have, to my surprise, acquired a mild reputation—

or puts on a particularly vigorous performance, a strange, gnarled man will emerge from a corner of the deserted balcony to doff his hat and call strange opprobriums down upon them. There are tales that in the back streets of London where all the complex rabble of the world unite toward another day, a dwarfish man with piercing eyes can be seen circulating through the crowds at sundown singing archaic songs. But this, I believe, is all rumor born of guilt and incomprehension, for S— himself, were he alive today, would indeed be living as a recluse. I know him; I feel that I know him that well. I feel that I know almost everything there is to know about him; one way or the other I have touched that vessel of him through those strange days of many years ago.

This witness, this girl for whom I have written all this says to me, looking over this epilogue, "But you still haven't given any sense of what he is, what he wanted, where he is going." If that is all that she can, after all, say to me, I believe that this time I will merely sit back a little deeper in my chair and taking another drink of stout will say, "Well, we'll never know, don't you understand that? None of us will ever completely understand what he was like; there was never such a man, do you see? Never such a man, and there never will be one, like him again, not that his voyage will really touch any of us or in the long run make any difference, but he has been there, wandering through all the seas himself, and he will paddle them forever, a vanguard without a fleet, a dolphin without a school, a God without a following. And we can't touch the real him, none of us, because we don't even know where he begins or ends. And it is our great loss, our loss because he taught us everything—if we could only learn to find it."

THE END

Into Air, Thin Air
By Barry N. Malzberg

Two specters float through, over, inside, outside this misbegotten novel: William Redfield whose *Letters from an Actor*—published in 1967, the novel preceded the film by about a quarter of a century—records his experience as an observant Guildenstern in the famous and notorious Gielgud-directed, Richard Burton *Hamlet* of 1964 and the Harvey Weinstein-produced *Shakespeare in Love* which won an Oscar in 1999 for its portrayal of—well, Shakespeare in love with the very young Gwyneth Paltrow who sneaks her way into the first performance of *Romeo and Juliet* and creates a stir within and without the odyssey of its author, masquerading as Ralph Fiennes. The plot of the novel, framed as the memoir of a young actor entranced by one of the eponymous maidens reads in sections like a parody of the memoir-as-diary of Redfield; of course the novel preceded the film by a quarter of a century and it would be staggering far beyond credibility to accuse the screenwriter of plunder. The kind of novel requested for Lancer's brief Oracle Books in 1969 had little to do with the aspiration and tragicomedy of Redfield's memoir; the events of the novel might have been Shakespearean but not the Shakespeare of *Romeo*. It is *Timon of Athens* who haunts this product of a few weeks' industry, the Timon of the second half who watching his treasures depart goes quite mad.

Madness was the default of most of my Olympia protagonists; the narrator of *Screen*, my movie-going lead of *Screen* was throttled by sexual obsession, not perhaps as lucrative as its economic variety (my advance was $1500) but as profoundly centered and so were the central figures of the other eight books I produced for Girodias from 1968-1970. What partially separated this Lancer production from the Olympia works was the centrality of Shakespeare, modestly known in its pages as *S. S* rather than my narrator was the true protagonist but after a mistaken three or four pages opening drafts in which *S* was the narrator, I was overtaken by humility; even though the Bard was in public domain I simply could not summon the gall to attempt his voice. Arrogance of even the young writer in early, throttling possession of his gifts simply would not go to that limit. So *S* was a character and my hapless (as usual) narrator was the observer, the acolyte, the figure of assessment.

Redfield depicts Burton at both the height and depth of his fame, overtaken by stage fright, fatigue, self-doubt, self-loathing as he and his new bride Elizabeth led world journalism on a self-destructive, extravagant chase. The posthumous Burton diaries, far more self-aware than the young actor's memoir and surprisingly, blazingly well written, reveal a scope of character, action, inaction and disaster perhaps unparalleled in Shakespearean performance history. Redfield settles for the self-doubt, the self-hatred, the astonished disgust of one truly famous who is asked by himself thirty times an hour "What am I doing here?" It is a question which fountains of whiskey were employed to answer but they were as illusory in the main as the advice of Polonius and the brilliant Burton, sporting perhaps the most brilliant mind ever to be broken by talent, came to an abortive and partially tragic end. (No man with whom Elizabeth was in love could find a wholly tragic end.)

All of this both relevant to and somewhat distant to the novel at issue, the fifteen hundred dollars of blood money which left me at the end as saddened as Prospero when he broke his spear. It is *S's* final play, the play in which he followed Prospero into silence and, living out those mysterious years, left public life. Perhaps the play represents the struggle between Caliban and Ariel, opposed spirits, broken spirits, both of whom can achieve apotheosis only through utter separation; Ariel departs, freed, to other and distant adventures, Caliban is granted the island itself by Prospero but faces an uncertain future. He had been given language but the only good he ever got on't was he learned to curse. Prospero's future is uncertain; he has divested self of self. Redfield had a successful career, mostly in television, but died of leukemia very young.

And more... Girodias by the time *A Way With All Maidens* was published had been more or less destroyed by vengeful publishers, brutal circumstance, Maurice Girodias himself. Oracle's imitative attempt at the Girodias route lasted through only ten novels or so, about a year and Lancer, the creator of that misbegotten line filed for bankruptcy in the Summer of 1973, sending its two owners on to very profitable careers (Walter Zacharius was financed for Zebra Books to the astonishment of his rather shady backers, Irwin Stein got out of publishing altogether) and its authors to varied fates. I was pretty well done with the pornographic market by 1973, the market was pretty well done with itself. As Girodias had predicted in conversation in 1970, written pornography had no future; it would be supplanted by visuals easily acquired and by slightly graphic romance novels which would be sold to the women's market. (As almost always his brilliant predictivity was of no use to his own career.) *A Way With All Maidens*, then, a kind of dying fall.

"You don't know something's good 'til it's gone"/Joni Mitchell/*Big*

Yellow Taxi. Actually in this case I did. I could never have written let alone sold this novel anywhere outside of its actual market; it was too graduate-English-student for porn; too porn for anywhere else. So I had to go out and make a living with works like *Scop*, like *Galaxies*, like *The Falling Astronaut*. Prospero granted me language and all the good I got on it was I learned to curse.

—5 August 2021: New Jersey

A SATYR'S ROMANCE

by Barry N. Malzberg

This novel is for Stephanie Jill:
the good parts

January 2

A new year. Tra-la for the new year! Ring a bellow or two. Slam a knocker for the new decade while we are at it! Of course it is all the same: one year, ten years, the important thing is growth, flourishment, the extension of old habits, old methods into new terrain, an expanded sense of function. Superbly fulfilled as always—my groin literally sings of fulfillment—I look forward to the 1970s with no trepidation, knowing as always that my own destiny will move in solemn pace with this expanding decade: everything is in ascendance. Of course, there is always the possibility that so much fucking will make my prick fall off or become coated with a cheesy substance—I am thinking here of various horrifying medical texts I picked up recently at the library, masquerading as a graduate botanist looking for some "allied readings"—or cause the prostate to leak embarrassingly. This would be difficult to come to terms with if true; nevertheless, co-existent with all alternatives I shall certainly co-exist with this one—thank you, sir—it being a strange life after all. Highly in flux, almost impenetrable: we might all be snuffed out tomorrow or, for that matter, find that the steady inhalation of smog fumes in this city will render us wholesale without sexual powers or given only the ability to procreate monsters. Politicians! One must, nevertheless, take chances. The angle of the dangle is all that truly matters; to it, all thought, all action, all consideration must be subservient. This and little else is worth stating as truism; to engage in a bit of that small pedanticism to which I find myself gravely inclined during terminal dates in history.

History! The sweep of it overtakes us; we are all swimmers in the flotsam! A new year, a new decade, a new life style … and therefore a fresh diary. I have decided to continue my journal-keeping straight through the 1970s; the 1960 notes have been placed in a large, brown manila envelope and sent on their way to a publisher, surely they will sell and demand a sequel. I believe passionately in journals anyway; there is so little patience, so little knowledge, so little history seemingly available in these difficult times that one must do all that one can to hold off the welling flood of nihilism which would, in a rush, destroy all institutions, all accretion of culture, all sense of common respect for the past. By piling up these notes carefully, one by one, against the onrushing tide of the century, I will perform my little gesture (or so I like to think) for a sense of perpetuation. Someday some historian will look back upon all of this from his shelter, breathing evenly through a gas mask and realize what a truly strange time it was. On the other hand, perhaps it is only vanity that drives me to these exercises: vanity and too much free time. I have been out of work too long, for instance, and my sexual accomplishments even to the contrary, there are long dull patches—color them blue and green subjectively—during which the rooms of this apartment seem somehow oppressive, the air strangely dense, the sound of the streets particularly clinical and the mind—then moving within toward its own channels—finds itself confronting in its corridors a small shrieking beast—color it brown with red spots— which in its peculiar jawings and ravings seems to signal, however faintly, the onrush of perversity. One would want to bugger the beast or at least to engage it in a long, slow squirming dialogue; something like this, of course, cannot possibly be, it having grim inferences for the mental health. It is better, far better, to try to systematize neurasthenia than to accede to it; and it is in this mild and gentle spirit with which I begin my new volume, a careful document on which I can float slowly this raft of purpose, navigating all of those difficult channels to a roseate conclusion. I expound a bit.

Yes, a bit I do expound: I can see already the slow rise of rhetoric, the dangerous, circling wander of pun and metaphor. And I mean this to be a conservative work, a documentary tool, nothing more, a coldly organized prologue to an auspicious decade. I must tone things down. I must be reasonable and precise. I must not allow impulse to desert virtue. I must keep an even course. I must pass strange beggars on the street without complaint. I must be wary of clap. I must massage my genitals at least twice daily so that they do not shrivel and desert me. I must nod briskly to old ladies. I must cut down my drinking and smoking. And so on. And on.

I was talking about New Year's Eve.

Well, of course I was talking about New Year's Eve; it was only some twenty-four hours ago or a little more and as was the case so many times before, I found myself once again in Times Square, that crossroads of the world, surrounded to the right and left, bottom and center, up and down by perhaps some 200,000 companions: some of them drunk, some of them sober, some of them old, most of them young, a few attractive, not a few of them repulsive, all of us bound together in the cold by the common apprehension—not to say human warmth of clustering and in the clutter of lights, the scream of the sirens, the slow whining drone of the overhead lights, television equipment, clubs of cop and whinny of horse we stood to let the New Year in, a golden ball at a far range our guide, the clutch of our bottles the symbol, and the ball began to fall slowly, slowly, then with increasing speed, moving down toward that apocalyptic moment of connection which more than anything else both warns and reassures us of our mortality and, at that precise moment, some son of a bitch set off a firecracker behind me. I was most deafened and confused, and found myself instantly sweating warmly within my grey tweed overcoat, my tight hat, my silken scarf that I had cast on so idly only hours before around the various chiseled delicacies of throat and feature. "You bastard," I said without turning and found, as if in response, a lovely young blonde girl tossed to my arms, stretching, as a matter of fact, almost perpendicular to my body, her eyes closed, her features expanding evenly, a slow flush moving up and down almost idly on her cheeks. She had fainted, it would seem.

"I'm sorry," a voice to my rear was saying, "it just kind of got away from me, the little son of a bitch," and I bent my neck in order to see this dangerous idiot, unable to confront him full-face of course because of the lovely burden now slowly collapsing her full weight against me. "I didn't mean to excite anyone; I didn't want to hurt—"And then there was the sound of impact, something like a fist meeting features and I heard no more. A hearty madman disengaged himself from some hubbub behind me, came past me briskly, flexing his knuckles and regarding his hand with some satisfaction. "You've got to watch these college kids," he said absently and adding some more generalized curses, thus pranced from my life forever, taking with him, no doubt, any possibility of explanation for my good fortune, this sudden explosion of luck which had been so abruptly visited upon me, almost as if the heavens and the populace itself had collaborated in a sudden joint decision to recognize my gifts and potential to their fullest worth and had thus passed on to me, if rather crudely, a contribution to my general well-being in light of my well-performed past services to the cause of mankind.

For it *was* good fortune; there is no question about that whatsoever, the kind of fortune I have had very rarely in my life and then always brought about by a kind of accident—as if I had intercepted luck duly assigned to someone else. The girl ground herself absently against me, stirred, rubbed her eyes with small, well-formed hands ungloved for all the cold and then looked up at me with a certain poignance and wistfulness which would have been moving if they had not been so quickly wiped out by confusion and the kind of slow, roiling shock which is always so disturbing to see in them; they only have aplomb when they have it but when it is lost the loss is complete. As if I could ever do them any harm. As if it were not only love's first load that I carry for them, forever, forever! As if I did not depend upon them, all of them, for my very sustenance and sense of purpose.

"Oh," she said in a low, modulated voice. "Oh, my God, I think I've fainted. What happened? What was that terrible noise?"

"It was a firecracker, 1 think," I said. "Don't move. Just stay there. I'm a graduate botanist with some very extensive medical background and a good knowledge of fainting. I've seen some terrible cases whereof people fainting. I've seen some terrible cases where if people tried something like that, dreadful things happen. Pardon my syntax, I seem to be a bit excited. Usually I parse."

"Purse?"

"Parse. Just relax now and let me hold onto you. I think you'll be fine." My efforts, even at this early stage of our relationship, were already dedicated toward a sense of retention then: one thing that I have never done—granting the fact that good luck finds me by accident and always with a kind of sullen overcast, as if having found itself cheated of recipient it will make itself as difficult as possible—is to forsake opportunities.

"Where are my girl friends?"

"Your what?"

"I came here with my girl friends. They were just here a minute ago when that sound went off. Where did they go, anyway?"

"I don't know," I said and to my pleasure was able to say this with a certain honesty, a certain sense of rising conviction which added pleasure to my insistence; in a stroke she had already denied what was, for me, the only element which could have instantly aborted our eventual connection: that is, the presence of an escort. I had already pictured him, a dull blond man chewing gum wearily, the light of intelligence slowly sinking like a ship behind his stunned and fluttering eyes, one hand outstretched to pull her from my grasp and out of her faint, but if she had none … if indeed, this startlingly attractive girl had come to Times Square alone on New Year's Eve or better yet, in the company of girl friends similarly bored and lonely, then there could be nothing to lay between me and the eventual accomplishment other than my own bumblings and haste which I knew I would be able to control. This was, after all, the start of a new decade. "I honestly don't know where your girl friends are," I had said meanwhile. "It's a big crowd, you see, and people move around quite a bit in it."

"But they were just here a moment ago," she said and seemed upon the verge of commencing a serious series of efforts to locate them; at that precise moment, however—oh accident of collaborative biology!—she swooned again and fell into my arms with a heaviness even more fervent than the first time, collapsing against me indeed in such an extremity of weight that if the soporific could be classified as the enthusiastic she certainly would have fucked me on the spot. At that moment, most instinctively, I clasped my arms around her and drew the full heaviness of her within, feeling for the first time the faint perception of the outlines of her body, smooth and soft; heavy and of a peculiar lushness it was as if I was feeling them here at that moment, apart from clothing, apart from scene, even separated from any question of context. Oh, the joys of frottage! Would that we would commit frottage upon the most unspeakable of our ambitions and be done with it! Context, context, the enemy of the natural being!

It is difficult to communicate any true sense of my responses at that time. Oh, my excitement, my trepidation, my glee, my unease! Oh, if it were only possible to use this pen to make—instead of words—certain figures, perhaps I would sketch in a series of representations: circles, stick pictures of spheres invaded by pointed objects, all of this doing far better than the poor medium of rhetoric ever could to arrive at some conviction of what sped through me so recently. But one must use the word; it is, of course, the only means available to me at the present time. I make no apologies for what I did then. I made hasty efforts to leave the vicinity while not losing possession of the girl, all the time holding onto a certain muffled dignity and sense of aplomb which, I have been assured, is almost always superb and the secret of whatever moderate—and I do not underrate them—successes I have had. Unfortunately, under the conditions of the density of the crowd, the weight of the package, the pressures of the moment, it amounted almost immediately toward a kind of excruciating waddle which was my primary means of navigation out of there, a waddle not unwitnessed, of course, by the beaming eyes of thousands of spectators, almost all of them as drunk as I but not a one of them nearly so involved. I found the sweat to which I have already referred increasing and becoming somehow rhythmic, a slow, gleaming sense of pallor moving up and down my cheeks ... but all the time I was moving, moving, my humble object and I speeding toward the subway, my destination my home, my considerations even at this hour strictly of the most concrete kind. How she stirred in my arms! How her little eyes blinked! How I feared she would desert me! Oh, all of this, it is almost too difficult to communicate; the anguish of the moment, the uncertainty of the outcome, the scream of horns, wicker of flight, drum of traffic, patter of wind. Nevertheless, I did it. Yes, I did it. I led her all the way down the steps of the subway station and, having tokens already in hand—these were of the old type, the presumed strike not having yet been called or settled—was able to escort her through by the subterfuge of nodding at the clerk in such a way as to indicate that she was drunk and I, her drab, faithful escort, was merely taking her on her way home. At the second flight of stairs, approaching the trains themselves, there was something approaching a minor crisis when her eyes opened with a lolling roll and it seemed that she would, for one instant, attempt to resist my gentle probe and push but then, with a moan, she collapsed against me again and juggling her in my arms like heavy, swelling fruit, I was able to negotiate this second flight as well and come onto the nearly deserted platform where, shortly, a train appeared and onto which train we proceeded. I mean, we got. The transit strike, incidentally, was avoided by last-minute negotiations.

It was then, in the empty train itself, roaring and rattling comfortably uptown that the true circumstances of my feat began to assault me for the first time; what I had done unquestionably—what I was still doing as a matter of fact—was nothing less than the act of abduction of a stranger, abduction being a crime punishable in this state by not less than five nor more than twenty years. Yet criminality could not have been further from my thoughts; my only interests were succor, release, assistance, possibly communication. On this declaration I now repose. My intentions, although not strictly honorable, had been formed only in the instancy of a moment which had occurred coincidentally and had it not occurred it is certainly against the grain of my nature to abduct strange girls from familiar surroundings. Gentlemen, my whole record speaks this! My entire sexual biography! Every element of psychology, cell of heredity within me shrieks a wistful song of gentility; a horror of the ungracious, forcible act. Surely I do not need to further justify myself, even when the hilarious consequences of my evening's work now lie spread before me, a virtual blanket over the decade, and compel me to walk carefully amidst this rubble lest, by a false step, I bring upon myself a certain attitude which would be the very obverse of what I now seek ... calm, tranquility, that is.

No: no abduction, no rape, no forcible entry, no assault, nothing at all, merely the simple peasant's desire to take advantage of a piece of good luck lest, by the ignoring of it, luck should desert me for all time. Had I seen the girl's friends, had the girl not swooned for a second time, had she not swooned the *first* time, had a ruddy-cheeked escort in ascot, muffler and top hat intervened to take her off my hands ... Had any or all of these things happened, I certainly would not have worked myself into this position. Nevertheless, what could I have done? How could it have been otherwise? How could things to any different pass arrive? I understand, of course, that these are questions often raised in more dreadful historic circumstances.

The train moved with gathering speed past 50th street, past 59th, heading like a bird or an arrow for 72nd, my very stop, two blocks from which these simple rooms are presently located. As it did so, some feat of engineering or possibly only the lapse of time, caused the girl to awaken for the third time that day and, as she did so, as she turned towards me for the first time with a kind of full knowledge in her eyes, with the first flush of implication guiding her mouth toward her cheeks in a high, pursed concentration which might, for all I know, have been preliminary to a rant, I faced myself on the instant with one of the few truly crucial decisions of my strange and lamentable career—that is, to say, the necessity to keep the girl with me while at the same time doing nothing so forceful as to lead to flight. "What's going on?" she said. "I don't know where I am. Is this the subway?"

"Yes; yes; we're on the subway. I thought it would be best to get you out of that crowd. You see—"

"Well," she said, "well, what right did you have doing something like that?" And sat up with a jerk so abrupt it took all of my energies, indeed, all of my concentration, to keep the pose from falling fully askew to disastrous outcome. "You could have been severely injured," I said. "Even hurt, for that matter. That's an enormous crowd in Times Square; every lunatic in the city comes out looking for trouble and if you do get separated—"

"Where's the firecracker?"

"I don't know," I said and risked a small caressing gesture on the nape of her exposed and adorable neck; a fine white surface it was indeed, gleaming with far more purpose than her muddled features could yet assume. "It went off somewhere behind us."

"And now you're taking me home on the subway."

"That's right."

"To *your* home."

"It seemed the nearest and the safest place to go. After all, I don't know where you live. You had a dangerous medical shock and—"

"Will you try to fuck me?" she asked and blinked and the cars wept to a halt and we were at 72nd street, the groaning and gasping of air infusing the empty space around us as the doors sighed back and the motorman, giving us a pointless glare, shuffled from a crouch in the corner to create certain banging noises in a hidden sector of the car.

"No," I said. "Now, come on; that has nothing to do with it at all. Actually, I have this very strange condition, I wouldn't call it a disease but it limits my function; well, it's all too embarrassing, some other time I'll tell you," and pulled her unresistingly to her feet. "You've got to understand that I'm only thinking of you," I added, and guided her from the car, her weight somehow cooperating with, rather than working against me, and that is how we became disgorged upon the scant platform at 72nd street on the IRT West Side subway. The uptown side. The train hissed away, the motorman having deserted his cubicle to fix us with a mighty wink as he pushed and pulled handles, having somewhat the aspect of a man tugging hugely on lavatory chains as the train moved slowly away. "A seduction is not for me," I said sadly. "I just wanted to make sure that you wouldn't get hurt in that crowd; it's really a fantastic—"

"Why weren't you with someone there?" she said with engaging clarity. "How come you were alone? Are you one of those nuts that people are always talking about? The New York ones that go to strange places and feel up girl's asses?"

"Asses?"

"And the other parts too. The breasts and the thighs. I read all about it in this series report in the *New York Post*. It warned—"

"I should say not," I said. "I happen to have had a lovely date prepared but my girl friend—she's practically my fiancée as a matter of fact—my girl friend, I said, came down with a miserable cold and couldn't make it. She invited me over but I didn't want to be contagious; that's when a cold is—in the first days, you know. So all I had to look forward to was spending an evening on my novel and on New Year's Eve I hardly think that's an appropriate gesture; the whole decade is changing, you know, and besides the novel has hit something of a snag. I'm a writer, you see? It's a western, this novel, I'm something of a pulp writer in my spare time, I supplement my income from botany that way and until my real novel sells I want to write only junk for the fast buck." I must say that I have something of a tendency to rant under pressure, an affliction that I share with most American politicians although hardly to such advantages and long-term benefit. "But that's neither here nor there; the thing is that I thought I'd go down and see the New Year in at Times Square because you can get your best insights in crowds and get first-hand material and that's why I happened to be there. And then there was that accident with the firecracker and you fainted in my arms and we couldn't find any of your girl friends, so the safest thing to do was to get you out of there, out of that crush, because they get pretty wild down there after midnight on New Year, there's a lot of looting and so on. And then we came up here and here we are."

"Ah," she said with a slow, gathering poise, and began to fumble in the large grey pockets of her overcoat; what she took out, to my surprise, was a mirror and she opened it in front of her, inspected herself carefully and then, with one of those absent, pondering, lip-curling nods which women seem to give themselves when they are under investigation, shrugged and flipped the case away. "And now you want me to go to your apartment," she said. "Just like that."

"Just like what?"

"I don't know why not. Are you going to come on strong though the minute you close the door?"

"We already went through that," I said. "I explained all of it to you. Now look," I said with that affected jauntiness which is one of my very best faces, a combination of irony and whimsy which, in the proper circumstances, is as close as I can come to a true gradation of mood, swinging through to a high, clear space now because I began to see an end to it. "Do I look like a rapist?" And took her by the arm without further ado, half-led, half-prompted her from the subway platform, up the flight of stairs and into the cold, stinging air of the New Year itself, all of it coming down with humidity and blankness, wrapping us into the chill in a sudden intimacy as she gasped and folded herself against me, moving into my coat. "Oh, it's cold," she said. "It's terribly terribly cold." And I said, "Yes, it is but it's only a little walk to my apartment now," and took her west, along 72nd Street, toward the river; and the whole unresistant weight of her, stunned by the cold, stunned by my briskness, began to fold around me with such a certain submissiveness, such a great suggestion of softness that I could feel an emotion close to love rising within me, love for her vulnerability if nothing else, all of it heightened by sex, the smell of her, the perception of the planes of her cheek tilted toward the moon. "Oh, it's cold, Goddamn it," she muttered, "it's so terribly cold." And I mumbled something abstractly comforting and so we came into my apartment building, all seventeen floors of it, shaking off the weather as we came into the lobby, her hand still dangling in mine; and I led her down the stairs toward the basement as for the first time, however subtly, she balked. "Where do you live?" she said. "In here?"

"Of course."

"In the basement?"

"Right ... this way. Right near the boiler: you can hear it shuddering like a big heart in the night. Except when it freezes up."

"I never heard of anyone living in the basement of one of these buildings before."

"The superintendent used to live here," I said. "He lived here until October but then he demanded the penthouse because he said he and his wife needed more room. It was either that or he quits so they gave the tenant up there a summary eviction and moved him. That meant the basement was open and that's how I got it. I just moved right on down from the second floor to save sixty dollars a month rent. It isn't too bad and the boiler keeps things so hot down there that there's no roach problem. You'd be surprised at the degree of—"

"God," she said, "it's loud!" And so indeed it was because it is necessary to pass the boiler in order to reach my two-room apartment at the rear of the cellar—this is where I lay out the floor plan, so to speak of this little memorial—and the sound of heating water, rushing steam, leaping figure, compressed oil was almost unbearable as we scurried by, the flames from the apparatus moving out with such speed and force–it has a defective gauge—that a stray wisp of clothing or girl would have been in danger if it had happened into an intricate but predictable kind of luck. She moaned, putting her hands over her ears and ran ahead of me; I followed her at a slight remove, observing with some delight the convulsions of her ass, the sedentary twitch of her buttocks as they receded from me; even clad in thick winter's grey this was apparently a girl for the ages, or at least for the evening; certain subtleties of construction which had evaded me to now seemed to emblazon themselves like moving ticker tapes across my brain as I followed her, keys extended, one hand moving caressingly to touch the notch as I pursued her to my door, blocked her deftly against the panels and then eased her in with a swift, careless clout of belly, following her to slam, bolt and double-chain the door. One cannot be too safe in these New York apartment houses, particularly on the West Side and in such close proximity to the boiler room. One of these days a disgruntled ex-tenant is going to come down here, I am sure, with several shimmering packets of nitroglycerin and succeed in sending not only the residents of the building but that aged boiler itself to a destiny so deserved and so lurking as to make any of this overdue.

"It's quieter in here," she said unnecessarily as I stamped feet, flicked lights, mumbled greetings, gave the parakeet cage a brisk returning nudge, went into the kitchen to make sure that all of my notes, jottings and cryptograms were still in order. You never can tell. "You wouldn't think from the outside that there would be any peace in here but—"

"They put up double-proofed walls," I said, moving gracefully behind her and taking off her coat with a whisk, all of this rendered facile by the fact that she had somehow opened the buttons already. "The superintendent insisted on it and you know the truth about those New York superintendents."

"No, I don't," she said with a sudden, rather charming poignance which all at once moved me, not in the way I had already been struck by her (which, when you come right down to it had been rather banal and conventional—excellent impulses, strongly crystallized of course, but still very much of the ordinary, nothing to differentiate this from a hundred other such instances) but toward a kind of need to envelop without holding, so to speak. "I've only been in New York about three weeks, you see, and living at a hotel. So I couldn't tell you."

"Really? Just three weeks?"

"That's all. I mean, I'm not ashamed of it or anything like that; it's just the way that things worked out."

"I've been in New York for thirty-five years," I said. "I don't think I know much more than you do."

Oh, then you're thirty-five years old?"

"Well, close enough to it. Actually, I came here when I was a couple of years. Before then, my parents lived on the continent in a rather disastrous way. But that really isn't very important and besides they haven't been around for quite a while now."

"Oh," she said vaguely. "I'm sorry I'm sure."

"I don't mean death. They live in Brooklyn now as a matter of fact— in a very old hotel. I mean that there simply isn't much contact among us, that's all. We never got along too terribly well."

"I'm sorry about that, too."

"But forget it," I said and put on, with a feeling of quick weariness, the faithful mantle of cheerfulness, briskness, purpose; that vital, cherished compound which must always precede even the most modest of my successes. "That has nothing to do with the holiday. The spirit of the season! The necessity of the loss! The flight of time and the adventure of mortality! A drink! What can I get you to drink? I have the usual—"

"Oh, I don't really drink. I mean, not seriously or anything like that. I mean, I can only stay a few minutes, really; it was awfully nice of you to pick me up the way you did and save me from the noise or something but my girl friends will be really worried about me if they don't hear and I will have to go back to the hotel and—"

"What's your name?"

"Huh?"

"I said, what's your name? My name is Harry Walters and I'm kind of a civil servant aside from the botany and the novel writing. I just do that for the money. Shouldn't we know who we are, already?"

"Oh," she said. "I'm Rona. Rona—uh—Smith. I'm not really anything just now, but I'm an actress. I worked in stock and upstate and—"

"I'm delighted to meet you, Rona," I said and extended a hand, grazed her palm, winked at her; then, on vagrant memory, impulse—color it red—drew her against me with an even pressure and put my lips against the cool plane of her forehead, dropping them down then to make conjunction with her nose and moving past her mouth by surprise, took the point of her chin in my teeth, nipped it once and then moved her away. "Hello."

"Listen," she said. "My girl friends. My girl friends will be—"

"Rona Smith," I said, "let us begin our relationship at this time of the new year, the new decade, in that spirit of honesty, frankness and meaningful communication which made this country great before it capered onto the wrong path not so many years ago when it neglected to leave its troops in Europe at the end of World War II and exterminate Stalin and the rising brute horde of stinking communists. You have no girl friends.

"There are *no* girl friends."

"What?"

"There are no girl friends," I said. "None at all, Rona," and took the graceful, spare slackness of her upper arms in my hands, began to knead them slowly, a delightful gesture which has in the past given me almost as much pleasure as I obtained from her then. I have neglected to mention—how could I have neglected to mention?—that she was wearing a black sleeveless dress, high at the collar, simple strand of pearls, the dead whiteness of her skin contrasting most meaningfully, albeit bleakly, with the silk and, as is often the case in such dresses, witchery of construction, making the breasts seem higher, firmer and fuller than they often turn out to be, even a suspicion of nipple winking at me under the cloth. The dress was very short, falling somewhere above the knee. An extraordinary looking girl, sir. I must remember to include such details earlier on in the future; this diary is, after all, intended as a document of inclusiveness.

It must be disciplined!

It must be concrete!

It must be objectified!

It must speak to the point!

It is not subjective; oh, no, gentlemen, there is no such thing as psychopathology. Clear lucidity, reason: the light of understanding, the clear, swinging dawn of the decade. Better fucks, clearer minds, calm genitals, sweet breasts, antiseptic cunts! Reasonable, gentlemen, reasonable! Pain! Pleasure! Sweetness! Amelioration!

I see where I had best pause and have a drink or two before I continue this. Things are starting out somewhat less coherently than I had hoped. I will have a seven and seven on the rocks and prepare then to describe how I fucked her. She was a splendid fuck and

Somewhat later

Considerably better and back to this now. It is possible that my rather agitated state of a few hours past was merely a consequence of events which have recently occurred rather than tracing back to any deeply sequestered and long-held fault of personality. I am not of inferior stock but on the contrary have a certain psychic sturdiness which allows me to resist almost all those temptations toward breakdown which would be the dissolution of a lesser man. At any rate.

Seven and sevens are, of course, a drink for juveniles but nothing, taken to excess, can be said to be against maturity and I have had a good many—say, seven or eight. There is something about the nature of the seven and seven, a sensual stickiness—color it limpid—perhaps it is only the nostalgia to which I am referring, the strange *nostalgia* of the associations which this exciting mixture brings back to me. One thinks of fraternity rushes, cautious expeditions to a bar while still in one's middle teens, the taste of stolen sweets in the back seat of a car with a girl too young, a car too old, an evening too late, a drink too mild ... I wander.

I was going to speak of the fucking of her.

Well, ho! And right to it; there is no point in attempting discretion—this is, after all, a private document circulated privately for modest personal reasons—nor in attempting that kind of careful structure and ordering found in the "socially redeeming" novel, that kind of book in which both protagonists can come to the matching of genitals only if they have "reasons," an "identity," a "history," a set of explicit rationalizations for this otherwise amazing conduct. Enough of these! Enough of this poison and pollution! Enough of these frail, wandering books, some long, some short, all of which would further propound the illusion that fucking is any more meaningful, prolonged or sacramental than a random meal or the retchings of the fervid drunk over an incautious counter. I do believe that these "serious" and "socially important" works have done us more damage than any other given item in the popular culture; how many pretty girls, otherwise perfectly suited to their possibilities and function, have been led to loss and total misdirection of purpose simply by junk like this, junk turned out by mindless writers and ignorant publishers in search not only of "the fast buck" but of "reviews" in which these girls, perfectly valid material from the start, found themselves coached to neuroses, obstruction and disentanglement by a point of view propitiated in which the simple act of glands was raised to the holy altar of Relationship—to enormous loss for all the parties involved. No, enough of this, enough of this indeed: this work, being private, need be by no means "socially redeeming" or "carefully structured" but can, in fact, concentrate on things more important and useful: that is to say, it can tell the truth. I am very high on the truth, gentlemen. I wish that there were a little bit more of it in our world or at least a little less of its obstruction. I do not mean to get into politics here.

So, I fucked her.

Our clothes came off with a tumble and a wink; one moment I was solemnly coaching her to an admission and the next, with almost no sense of transition whatsoever, all the clothing had fallen apart and we were on the bed, naked, pumping heavily, mouth to mouth, joint to joint, trying to join one another in that oldest and most necessary of all acts while, due to some strange power failure, the lights in my apartment flickered and tumbled and the refrigerator went on with a mechanical click! which encouraged the immediate and further insertion of my prick into her delicious and quivering cunt. Ah, yes. Ah, yes!

"This is incredible," she said, and "I don't even know you," and "I can't understand what we're doing," and all the time I was assisting her with the removal of clothing (all right, all right, it didn't quite fold away; I helped her with it; there is no great shame in this; besides she wanted me to) and as I did this I talked to her, soothingly and at great length, all the time flipping a breast, squeezing a thigh, encouraging her with my eyes to respond to my feelings of ardor with all the shallow requisite of which she was capable. "Oh, Rona," I said to her, "let's stop this, let's stop this simple dissemblance; it means nothing, there's no future in it; it isn't fair to either of us. Here we are, just the two of us, alone in my apartment on a New Year's Eve and a very comfortable and eloquent apartment it is indeed, almost as comfortable and eloquent as its speaker although a damned sight more temperate, and there is no point, simply no point, in letting social circumstances or lies get between the two of us and the magic we can make with our limbs on this very bed. We have within us, you see, this gift: the gift is the ability to create ecstasy for, being human, we carry within ourselves both the best and worst of all potentials and can realize either, are driven so often to the worst because that seems the only ability which we are allowed to bring into play but there is another part, a world of wonder, terror, beauty and excitement in which, cleaving nipple to nipple, heart to joint, navel to pubic we can rise far beyond the simple and pointless obligations of the social circumstance and by the joining obliterate them. Oh, you have wonderful breasts, really wonderful, I've never seen anything like them; they seem to come up rather than out, you must have done exercises to make them that way or perhaps I am only imagining that and cannot believe their reality; you must have a darling cunt too, oh, let me take a look at it, there, just let's get these down now, oh, look at it, look at it," and at this point or shortly thereafter interrupted my speech by burying myself to a point somewhat slightly beyond the lips in her cunt which was indeed of a certain majesty although not nearly as small as I would have wanted to think or as she might have permitted me to convince her. Because of my efforts at this time to jam both tongue and teeth all the way up her hole, my speech was cut off and my hearing as well seemed to suffer because I could hear her only dimly and as if from a great distance murmuring things like "Oh, don't," and "This is impossible," and again, "I don't even know who you are," and in some attempt to bring matters to a kind of fruition I desisted from my vigorous eating of her just long enough to pick her up, sprawl her over my shoulder and carry her to the cot where I put her down heavily and then divested myself of my own clothes in a flash, rushing down to meet her as she rose, either to meet me or in search of her own garments. In any event, our contact, shocking and with a slightly corporeal bump was so harsh as to forestall any efforts she might have made to leave the couch and, without much further thought, I took my tool in my hands—which had grown to enormous proportions—not my hands, of course, the tool; my hands are delicate and white, neatly-shaped and even at the fingernails, *and in no way whatsoever* are the hands of a compulsive masturbator and showed it to her with a flourish—the tool I mean, catching certain absent dazzles and twinkles of light in its uncircumcised folds which glittered in a way I hoped she would find as enticing as I always did myself and then bobbled it a few inches above her open and busily speaking mouth, indicating with a series of flourishes what I suppose might be called in one of those novels of social redemption my "perverse" desires. "Oh, no," she said with a moan and thrashed against me. "I don't do anything like that, not on the first date anyway," and I brandished a finger at the calendar on the wall, indicating with my motion that this was no ordinary first date but was as a matter of fact the inaugural encounter of a decade, to be inevitably marked by such dramas and convulsions as we could but dimly apperceive and said, "Yes, yes, you want to, you know you do and besides that, it's a very rare girl, a very rare girl, mind you, who I will permit to do this until I know her very well," and with no further comment, slid it down her mouth caught in mid *O!* and shoved it down the slick warmth of her throat to its full and majestic penetration of some five and three-quarter inches in the erect state, and when she gathered around me instinctively began to pump mildly, encouraging not so much the flow of semen as the rise of some procreative substance special to the esophagus and other digestive organs, a much milder concoction to be sure—one specially prepared for the act of generation done out of its normal orifice. I am a man to fit to all occasions.

I have, as a matter of fact, have had for a long time, the fantasy that I have not one breed of seminal fluid as is the case with "normal" males but indeed five or six, a different brand for each occasion: there is the usual acrid blend of course for the usual, spontaneous occasions, there is a sweeter, lightly-scented kind, bereft of actual sperm, for the act of fellatio, there is a hard, winy substance, smelling faintly of oak and old cellars for buggery, and then, for various notions like ears, armpits or breasts there is a thin, roseate substance with the consistency of skimmed milk, only lightly perfumed, which is meant to reside with the female flesh and indeed brighten it and render it more wholesome and desirable in the morning's light. I realize, of course, that this is nothing other than "wild imaginings" and that actually, no more gifted than other men, I can slip into them only the same old banal substance, firm at the beginning and loose at the end; but if the mind is allowed to control the actions of the involuntary nervous systems as we all know that someday it will do—modern physical sciences are performing wonders—then surely my idea must be an inevitability. In any event, no wine, no champagne, no firm, glowing foreign beer could have had the brightness and irresistibility of that substance which I allowed myself to think was bubbling merrily in my veins as I slid my cock gently up and down her throat, bumping her a little bit with my knees as I did so, to encourage her toward reciprocal action.

Reciprocity, gentlemen, reciprocity! The giving back unto the giver as it is given with its own interest! It is this which is needed more desperately than any other quality in this sad, ruined old world today and so I encouraged her to replace my offering with one of her own, put my hands gently around her wrists, drew them up, her hands that is, to the pendant charm of my wavering balls and then she cupped them for me, cupped them with a gentle gesture which belied any lack of experience which she might later protest and—as she was doing this— encircling them, squeezing them, bringing them up with a gentle swinging gesture until they seemed to conjoin their congestion with the very implosion of prick which was central to my being, she was saying, "But I don't even know you, I don't even know you at all, I never do this with people that I can't say I know." And I said to her with considerable pedanticism, at least in relationship to the rather exciting juxtaposition of hands-and-cock. "But why worry about that, my dear sweet, I mean,

Rona, where did you ever read or hear that it was necessary for people to know each other in order to enjoy fucking?" And she said in a dim flat wee voice so small that it might have been miles and miles away from me and perhaps indeed it was, "But the movies, that's what they say in the movies." And at this gentle admission tenderness filled my heart, semen my prick, love and remorse my chest, convulsions my scrotum and I ejaculated into the swoon of her hands an unusual agglomeration of semen, tears, joy, remorse, the frail white slave containing these gifts dripping thinly to her wrists and then to the smooth, flat sheen of her belly where it lay to congeal against her seat. Oh, my shame, gentlemen, my embarrassment, my almost sophomoric disrapture as she looked upon me then with a glance both condescending and pitying and—removing her hands to run them down the strange pool on her belly—said, "Oh, for God's sake," in the most moving tone imaginable; it was as Elizabeth Taylor or perhaps Sophia Loren might have said it to a strange masher in a bar making obscene gestures in the presence of husband and cameramen alike. "Oh, dear God, I never knew of anything like this! Say it couldn't happen!" And I said, "Oh, my dear, there is so, so much more in this world and time as well than could be imagined in all the stars and bars of your philosophy!" and fell upon her, there to join her lips against mine and sealed in that ancient compact comprised of woe, mystery and excitation I began to work on her in the conventional way, urging with happy slap and gather my prick to a new erection while my hands danced in and out of the disappointed cup of her cunt. Oh, strange, strange! But soon enough I fucked her and a randy burst it was.

I waver, I wander, I fail to chronologize. But this is logical enough; I have always felt during fucking as at no other time as to the co-existence of being at several levels of time: time present, future and past seem to mingle as with the single cleaver of the prick I work out the various pulsations of *internal* time, there is no sense of development as such, no sense of structure: the whole peculiarly western sense of plot is obliterated and I am able to fuck at all levels in many ways, am able to join the tentative caresses of the foreplay with the rousing bounds of the Act itself, the gentle turgid sucks of nipple in the preparation with the heavy gasping drooling sighs around that nipple of the post-coitus; thus it is possible for me, during the act of sex I am trying to say, *to physically leap out of time*, meaning that working through me is not one experience but several and I am able thus to fuck most pleasingly, in many ways, and with that utter fusion of purpose which is so foreign to the ways and limited cunning of most Americans, limited creatures that they are and always will be. But before I can carry the message to them (I am a missionary creature after all, humble out of all relation to my potentials, my gifts, my glory, my accomplishments, my irresistible ability to seduce girls of any gender or age to my purposes) I must carry it to you, through the medium of these notes.

Aha.

Yes.

And thus—

And thus I wrapped the coil of my prick around her breast, literally catching it in that strange pulpous state midway between turgidity and flatulence which can be the most exciting of all because you can feel the semen literally *forming* in the coils of the testes, wherever that is and bent it into a half-bow, framing the nipple, winding it around her in a half-state of suspension while she, regarded me with moderate whimsy and interest; then I wiped that whimsy off the bitch's face, wiped it right off, yes indeed, by dodging my fingers into her cunt and entering her with enormous speed and force, spreading out lips, inner lips, membranous sheath, and going to the very heart of her organs, above the clitoris, above the tunnel, right into the womb itself (or what I took to be the womb; one must understand the constant necessity to confuse fantasy and image in the act of sex. What is it otherwise?) and there I tweaked and pulled on that long distended stem, imagining that I was its occupant or perhaps only a practitioner attempting to dislodge the occupant or better yet I was *both*, giving birth to myself so to speak, pulling myself out of the vortex of burial and my prick uncoiled, moved to its fullest hardness, extended toward her pretty and pouting mouth and as if to lend the obstetrician courage she began to suck on his tool, knead it with her lips, apply to it her tongue, hint of teeth, suspicion of molar, echo of bite and the obstetrician was quite pinned in her, quite helpless and at her mercy but, at the same time, with his tweaks and jerks controlling her motions just as she controlled his and then the obstetrician began to pant, began in his customary manner to announce the onset of the Nativity itself in his incomparable way as only he could.

"Oh, it's coming!" he moaned, referring to the Child, of course. "It's coming, it's coming right now, it's going to come out all the way, I can't stand it anymore," referring of course to the enormous pressures of his obstetrical practice. "Your breasts, your breasts, oh, God, your breasts!" referring to the patient's need to prepare her breasts for the act of nursing the Child, to be sure, and dropped then his scalpel from the patient's anterior orifice, taking it on its strange, wending journey to the Delivery Table itself where he removed his pincers and forceps quickly and inserted the scalpel then to ease the patient's way toward a fast birth. "Oh, it's coming, it's coming!" the obstetrician, referring to the child again, screamed and then began with his scalpel to work in his most effective surgical manner, bringing about the act of delivery with all the speed and skill at his command, using his scalpel to open up the passage and at the same time murmuring those wicked roguish encouragements which have made the obstetrician famous in all of the continents, which have made him at least the occasional toast of several cities within and without the continental states. "Your breasts, your breasts!" alluding again to the lactational function and then, to test the breasts so to speak for their resilience and ability to perform the wonderful act of suckling which is so pivotal to the health of the neonate in the important early months of his development, seized them in his two investigatory hands and began to press and knead, plead and suck, turning the nipples ever darker through his efforts until the very veins seemed to congest around the aureolar area and the very appearance of maternity was given them; then inserted his scalpel to its deepest penetration and with a deep hush and medical swoop the obstetrician brought forth from within himself the equipment and materials to perform his ancient and necessary act while the patient writhed and kicked under him, the consummative pains of labor wracking her of course and then the obstetrician, uttering a dim, final diagnosis, "Oh, it's finished, it's finished," poured into her with all the emphasis at his command the sum of his skills and—in a series of quicks and shudders which might have been less medically detached than, strictly speaking was necessary under the circumstances—the surgeon with a final moan laid down his knife, laid down his tools, took off his mask and lay beside the patient steaming coldly in the after-ardor of love. I mean the delivery. They are the same thing.

"Oh, Good Lord," murmured the obstetrician. "Oh, Good Lord, I've never known anything like it."

"I don't understand you," the patient said, "I mean, I never met anyone quite like you. I've never known anything like this before," and for a moment the obstetrician does not know whether it is love or bemusement or cunning or whimsy which leads her to this statement, nor does he care; he is circling darkly, settling dimly, moving forward slowly, falling inexorably into a hollow pit of purpose congested with slumber and dreams in which he places himself for just a little while as the patient sighs and settles against him, the panels of her flesh hard as boards, soft as cloth as he runs his hands over them, feeling that if for all the world her body was the only thing in it, it would be time and enough, and drawing slow familiar comfort from her skin and odors it could be said that the obstetrician sleeps or, at least, his mental state is at a lower level of activity, awareness, dedication and song than it is customarily, breathing slowly, breathing evenly, moistening to sleep as it were as the boiler in some far-off place hums for him. And for her. The conjugal boiler.

Somewhat later

In his sleep the obstetrician or perhaps now it is the patient, has a dream: it is hard for him to tell exactly who he is, shedding and switching roles progressively as is his wont. In his dream he is lying in another room next to a girl, a girl not entirely different from the one next to whom he is sleeping except that her face is somewhat younger, her eyes brighter, her breasts a shade smaller ...but the dreamer is not thinking of breasts now; his mood can be said to be one compounded now of fatigue and shame intermingled as he dreams he sits with covers wound around him, in a semi-fetal posture, smoking and looking out the window. The girl is talking to him and as is so dismayingly often the case in dreams her voice seems to alternate in levels of communicability: first harsh, first soft, cutting in and out of his consciousness like a scalpel so that the act of gradual attunement to her words is made only slowly and then with a series of efforts that the dreamer does not truly want to make, so immersed is he in the simple biological act of smoking, the consideration of glass, the attunement to various noises in the landscape so to speak which function as an excellent objective-correlative to his own sense of exhaustion which has come over him somewhat in the aftermath of fucking. He does not mean to be ungrateful but fucking puts him at a disadvantage at least temporarily; it drains him and leaves him somewhat out of rhetorical form. "Look, Harry," the girl is saying to him. "Harry, I tell you it won't work. I wanted to tell you that before but I didn't have the heart. But I have to now, Harry. It can't go on. I won't be seeing you anymore."

"Uh," says the dreamer. He is perhaps replying to her, more likely he is trying to frame his lips into a perfect *O* around the ridge of the cigarette which ever so gently he is inserting in and out of his mouth, perhaps trying to ascertain the true qualities of the tobacco.

"No, I mean it, Harry, we've got to talk now. Because I just can't go away and leave you, that wouldn't be fair; I have to tell you why I'm doing something, I know that. But you've got to give me a chance. Now look—"

"Why talk?" the dreamer says. "I mean, who told you that you had to give explanations? Do what you want to do, that's all."

"But I'm leaving you, Harry. Didn't you hear me say that? I mean—"

The words *leaving you* seem to elongate themselves like snakes in the dreamer's consciousness, torpid as it is and somewhat smoke-obsessed to say nothing of drained by sex. *Lee-vee-ing yoo-hoo, lee-vee-ing yoo-hoo*, he finds himself murmuring and the words have the not entirely unpleasing aspect of the conclusion to the chorus of a popular song; the dreamer has always been interested in popular music although lacking both compositional and performing ability. Nevertheless, as great as his desire is to vacate the subject of discussion as such, as it were close up the doors of the rhetorical apartment in which he now seems to be rattling, turn the lease over to the landlord—a small, squat man with a beard and orator's mustache—he is willing, for the sake of simple dignity if nothing else, to try to continue. Leave it never be said that the dreamer is discourteous; he is, as a matter of fact, so well-known for his good manners as to have received the International Courtesy Award of a minor private foundation in the year 196- in a presentation held on the steps of the Foundation's offices which were, of course, located in a rather cluttered building somewhat north of the dreamer's regular haunts.

"Go on," he says. "If you feel better that is. I mean, I don't care."

But the girl is, in fact, already speaking. "It isn't just the lies, Harry," she is saying, "because everybody lies a little bit and I only know that you do it because you want those things to be true so desperately that you actually frame them that way in your own mind; it's like a gift that you're giving me because you don't think that you're worthy of me as what you are. I've worked the whole thing out and I understand this now, past the defensive hostility. You don't really mean anything by it because each lie is a confession of love. So it's not that."

The dreamer, still meditating on his cigarette—it seems to have lost a little bit of its fine cool taste; perhaps he needs a switch of brand but there is in this room no hearty co-fatalist to pass on one of his own Relaxing Brand and thus he has to make do with what he has, lights another. The dreamer has had the feeling for some months now—color it grey—that each cigarette may be his last, not so much because he is on the verge of quitting smoking—he knows he never will, it is too easy a distraction—as that the inhalation of fumes may result in his "sudden death through heart exhaustion." The dreamer has been watching a series of public service commercials on the television networks which fascinate him morbidly: the idea that almost as much money is being spent to persuade him to stop smoking as was spent to get him started and keep him going, fills him once again with that gloomy knowledge of the duality of human motive which America—oh, America!—has heightened and deepened past national chasm into a mood as bright and glorious as any of the great principles on which this magnificent

Republic was co-founded. "You really should get out of analysis," he sees fit to say. "It just fucks you up worse than you were before. A little knowledge. Fools rush in. Bolt all the doors."

"Oh, stop that, Harry. You know perfectly well that that's only defensive hostility. It was the best day of my life, I finally understood, that I had to face up to my problems and stop avoiding them and come to terms with myself. Before that I was in a fog, just in a fog. Watch your ashes, they're dropping all over the sheet, you'll burn us alive. It isn't the lies, Harry. It's just that you won't ever seem to face yourself in any way whatsoever. You won't make admissions. You won't come face to face with yourself. You lack a sense of identity."

"Says who?" the dreamer murmurs in a civilized accent and, reaching for an ashtray, cautiously dumps in the remainder of his cigarette. "I have a compelling sense of identity and anyway, who has the right to assign values? What I'm doing is fine."

"No, it isn't, Harry," the girl says to the dreamer and seems on the verge of hurling an irritated pillow at him, thinks better of it, checks herself, settles back on the sheets with a languorous gesture believed by the scurrying motion of her fingers as she reaches against her will for a cigarette from the dreamer's pack, then thinks better of it and sits up abruptly. "Oh, this is getting us nowhere, Harry," she says. "Absolutely nowhere; you won't face what you are and I can't make you face it and besides I'm just beginning to find out who *I am*. I can't let you hold me back. I've got to think of myself now. The doctor said I should think of myself and try to be good to myself and that's why it can't be any more. Harry, I'm not coming back."

The dreamer sits up himself, folds his hands around his knees, looks at the girl. She is really a very pretty girl although her breasts are both too small and a bit sagging but otherwise her body has riches which he takes at this moment to be unfelt and he permits himself a flicker of gloom, one knife-trace of woe coming at him as if from a far distance and then sliding by, past bone into the visceral organs. It occurs to him that the girl is serious and this fills him with the greatest pain of all because he has always believed that the major problem with women is that they cannot resist fumbling attempts to see themselves as serious creatures, creatures with rational motives, definable histories, occupiable roles and so on. Perhaps it is the media which are the sole culprits for this but the dreamer does not really think so; all through recorded history they have had this feeling, it is only that the modern media have tried to convert it—along with just about everything else—into coin. "You really ought to stop this psychiatry mess," he finds himself saying. "It's a terrible thing, it's just leading you into the wrong paths and besides that I know the major reason you went into it is to try and get at me. Going behind my back to spill my secrets."

"Oh, Harry, you're so damned defensive. We've discussed this though and we think we know why it is. The reason that you're defensive is that—"

"Stop it!" the dreamer cries with somewhat more emotion than he had perhaps intended; the girl looks at him with shock and then subsides, against the bed-sheet, not at the same time making any efforts to find her clothing; the dreamer wonders abstractedly whether it was the vehemence or the simple truth of his reaction which has so disconcerted her. "Stop it, it's a pack of goddamned nonsense!" he goes on, fumbling for his cigarettes again—oh, the dreamer is a very heavy smoker although he does not believe at this time that standard conceptions of mortality are relevant to him, rather he is to be considered somewhat extrinsic to them at least until he dies. "You know perfectly well that it's an evasion, psychiatry, the real evasion, you see some guy who only got there because of his own projective fantasies and fumbling inept curiosity but now shielded by degrees, shielded by his role, and you fall into a situation where you can be told that nothing you did is your responsibility. It's the absolute removal of culpability, that's all it is; for the bloodstain of guilt, responsibility, causation, the cause-and-effect structure of human action which has controlled all deeds for thousands of years is substituted a dim set of sentimentalities in which the flesh and circumstances are heirs to what has been imposed on them. I tell you," the dreamer shouts, half-rising from the bed in the excitement of his insight. "I tell you, that wasn't the solution! Why didn't you listen to me! Why didn't you get involved in the occult or scientology or mysticism! There are your answers! They can tell you what you want to hear at one-tenth the price and beside that they can give you an education too. Oh, terrible, terrible," the dreamer mutters and subsides. He seems to be thinking, not an uncommon trait. A bit of sunshine bounces through the window, cleaves the hair of his companion, seems to turn it into a slab of golden in a momentary illusion; then the light metaphorically winks out and so does the dreamer, settling back on the cushions, sighing, brushing some cigarette ashes from his frame. "Of course I could be wrong," he says. "Suit yourself."

"I mean each to his own and so on," he adds.

"That is to say that if it gives you pleasure you can do it, what the hell," he pursues.

But the girl is not listening to him or if she is, she is not responding; rather, she is crying now or perhaps this is only some phenomenon of set and actually she is laughing; in any event, head cradled in arms, shoulders shaking, she seems to have departed into some maze of her own and the dreamer, caught by certain waves of sympathy which under other circumstances he might find suspect, puts a hand on her shoulder and draws her to him. She comes, sliding, easily, her eyes glistening with an emotion which might be fright or desire and she says, "Oh, Harry, it could have worked out but you're just so hostile, so hostile, Harry, you know what I mean? I mean I wish that things were so simple that they could be resolved that way," and it occurs to the dreamer then, for the very first time—and the dreamer is thirty years old at this moment, it is to be understood that he is not a Young Dreamer, at least not as young as he might have once taken himself to be although he is not, as he has been assured by certain random bartenders, taxi-drivers, employers and so on, exactly senescent—that the girl literally cannot help herself, that she is not saying what she is saying, doing what she is doing out of any misdirected efforts to be nasty, that there is nothing personal in this series of gestures but instead, in her attitudes, in her immersion, in her very life-style this girl is only being what she can—and that psychiatric jargon, such as it is, is as close as she can come to the rhetoric of love: the sound of love is so unfamiliar to this girl, so unfamiliar to all of the people and all of the ways she has known that she can only approach it through "emotional attachments" and "close relationships" and "deep needs" and "defensive hostility" and "compensatory withdrawal" and the dreamer feels a rush of sympathy for her so profound that he feels himself moved to the core of his being. It is not her fault after all that it has turned out this way but can only be blamed on Society or perhaps on himself, the agglomerate of people like himself who also have only enacted their own necessities and he huddles over her then in an anguish of longing, his impish prick uncoiling in contrapuntal response to this profound metaphysical insight and he feels his prick restored as it were to its fullest potential, charging and snorting, moving and growing underneath him, the lash of his prick somehow comforting to him as he rides it home, guiding it up her thighs and into her hole and he buries his head in her breasts then and murmurs strange words, words which the dreamer could not believe himself to be uttering were not the circumstances so corporeal, his prick so necessitous, the girl so fleshly. "Oh, God," he is saying. "Oh, God, I don't want to be this way, can't you understand that; I'd give anything if it could be different but it simply can't, I can't help myself, I can't, I can't," and perhaps he is sobbing although this is impossible—the dreamer is not known for his sobbing—and he gathers her to him loosely like a heap of clothing and putting himself into its deeps begins to screw her. It seems to be the only appropriate response.

The dreamer on his bed shifts. He dozes, he dreams, he twitches, he convulses. Perhaps it is only a random itch that is bothering him, nothing so profound as recollection, perhaps it is only some malfunction of limbs in juxtaposition to Rona's which have introduced his restlessness but he feels now as if he were sliding up from the cave of sleep, moving up that lightening pipe rapidly, all space and wind around him, all event waiting outside and he mutters "No, no, not yet, not yet," and tries to retreat where he was; tries to bring himself back to the sense of the girl that he was screwing and Rona beside him murmurs something which sounds like "Goofl", two flies batter the window pane, a strain of music from the boiler aborts his consciousness, he moans and flexes his limbs, somehow returns to sleep again but the context has changed, the very dream itself has shifted and now he is not fucking the girl, no, something else is happening, he is standing with his hands on his hips and she is eating away at his cock, crowding it, bobbling it. In this strange illumination he cannot tell whether the girl eating him is the same one who was undergoing psychotherapy; perhaps it is, perhaps it is not but in any event it is no great technique of insight for him to understand that both are the same, all of the girls are the same and in any event she is doing a superb job of sucking his tool, really ramming it all the way up her mouth, biting and teasing and licking and sucking, drawing him into her with strange plopping sounds which seem to be more echoes of his own pulsations than sucking and he bends his hands down, touches her shoulder, feels glide and sheen of skin and murmurs "More, more," or perhaps he too is only saying "Oofl"—a strange phrase which seems to cover all necessary contingencies, and "Oofl" again and "Oofl, oofl," and he dodges his hands down to her breasts, squeezes them, holds on with prayer and for life as she draws his semen deep into her cheeks and begins to raddle it around, huffing. Yes, this is a different girl. The breasts, among other things, are considerably larger and the nipples of somewhat less delicacy than those of the other: coarse and roughened they seem to rise in his palms as he skirts them in the throes of orgasm, muttering to himself. The girl drinks all of it down and then with grace and precision stands and walks to the basin in the room, giving him a proprietary tug on weakened prick as she leaves him, and spits everything out, then runs water, sighs, dashes it over her body, checks the cleft of her buttock, touches her breasts, winks in the mirror, comes back to him. "Did you like it?" she asks the dreamer.

"Yes," he says. "Oh, yes, yes," and touches her weakly, feeling the very essence of him having been torn out by the act of fellatio and she huddles for an instant, then breaks and heads toward the bed which is a very pleasing modern double job in the corner of the room, all sheet and glare, lying there all primed for screwing, the ornament and centerpiece of her apartment and what a shame! it has not been used yet, easy distractions having diverted them from those purposes. The girl straddles on the bed, holds her breasts, smiles for the dreamer and he smiles back more out of courtesy than feeling because what facial expression he seems to have retained is more suited for moans than for jollity. Nevertheless, the dreamer will do the best he can. He is always courteous, always willing to please, always willing to go along with a situation to the best of his ability. This as a matter of fact may be why he is a Dreamer rather than a practitioner. He is not yet ready however for such difficult thoughts. He falls against the girl, feeling her flesh rise like steaming cake against him, fastens mouth to mouth, begins to work on her with his hands while meanwhile she toys with his so-recently imploded prick, urging it into certain reactions and actions of its own so that once again he finds himself rising. Oh, fortunate dreamer! Oh, strange biology! Oh, marvelous circumstance that presents this omnipresent renewal! The dreamer would certainly shriek his gratitude to nature if he were capable of words.

But he is not capable of words, no words for him, only touch and sobbing, slow animaline movements in the darkness and he darts his hand to her cunt, feels it heave and open underneath him, inserts a hand and fist then into the most voluminous cunt he has ever felt in his life or so he tells himself: he is not inexperienced with cunts, this dreamer, has petted and sucked and banged a few in his life but of all of them the one at issue is certainly the most exceptional; to reach into it is to be absorbed by a most dark cave full of specters and longing, opening and retreating against his hand and incautiously he closes his fist and pokes it up further, still the cunt accommodates him, his *whole hand* so to speak and the dreamer thrills although whether it is with the size of the cunt or only with the accommodation he does not know, now he is sighing and lurching, easing his arm up there; he engages, the dreamer does, in the fantasy that he will be able to sink himself up to his shoulder, the very shoulder and then create an ornament of her that he can dangle from upraised fist; well, the dreamer's somewhat excited mental state is to be forgiven, he has not had much screwing for a long time now and has built up in his mind a reservoir of dreams, longing, morbid insanity which fucking is meant to purge, all of it hammering at the gates of the cerebrum and he stretches, moans, implodes, offers, lunges and puts his lips against hers, concentrating on that welding contact—and at that moment something disconcerting happens, the girl slides from him and tosses her head free, leans back with a gasp, squeezes her thighs, looks up at him and says, "The money."

"The money?" the dreamer says. He is quite lost, quite stunned. This is after all quite a jolt, a certain declension and he is not sure for a moment who he is or where he has gone; he feels as if he might be insane. "What money? I don't know what you're talking about," and tries once again to enter in that absorbed state but the girl says, somewhat more loudly, "The money, you promised me the money, the fifty bucks, remember?" and then it all comes back to the dreamer although too rapidly to have any achieved sense of discovery and he says, "*Oh, the money,*" relief and disconcertment mingling in his tone. "You mean, the *money!*"

"The money," the whore says and the dreamer staggers away from her, several extrinsic flourishes in his movements and wanders over to his pants which appear to be somewhere in the middle of the floor, leans over gasping, extracts his wallet and begins to fumble idly with bills, drops the wallet, bends to pick it up, loses his balance and, arms flapping, falls to the center of the room which accommodates him with a lurch and only with some difficulty does he regain his feet. His cock seems to hurt, the balls of his feet make inaccurate contact with the floor, his breath is irregular, he has pains in his eyes. He brings the wallet over to the girl, hands it to her. "You take it," he says. "You take it, I can't seem to get it."

"That's all right," the girl says, fumbling expertly. "That's okay, I understand. Now, you watch me so that you can see that I don't take any more than fifty dollars. That's what I said it would be and that's what it's going to be. There's a lot of girls, you know, who take advantage of their customers, they get them in a certain condition where they can do almost anything they like to them and then they do terrible things but you don't have to worry about that with me. I'm honest. Besides that, I want you to check me careful," she says, extracting two twenties and a ten from the wallet or perhaps it is five tens or perhaps it is two hundreds, the dreamer can hardly count, let alone reckon, and slides this money under the pillow while, with the other hand, she puts the wallet back in the dreamer's grasp. "I wouldn't want you to think I'm any kind of a cheat," the whore says. "I'm honorable. A lot of men think that there's some shame in being a whore but there's none at all; we're honest and we do our work and we don't ask no questions."

"Me neither," the dreamer says, tossing the wallet heedless back to the wall. "Me neither, I don't ask nothing," and plunges on top of her again but somewhere during this the edge has been taken off his excitement and he finds himself distracted, scuttling away from her at great speed, off-angle like a frightened animal, his consciousness swimming uneasily in his being, the very spaces of the room seeming to open up in a strange way which seems harsh and unaccommodating and he finds himself wondering what he is doing with a whore and what he expected to gain and what he had wanted to lose and why precisely after all of his adventures to the contrary the dreamer, at this late stage of his development, would take up with a prostitute: it would make the most solemn judgments on his abilities, history and inner life if the dreamer did not already know himself, *know himself* perfectly capable of having sex with almost any girl of his choosing if he is disciplined and puts his mind to it. He seizes one of the rough breasts, rubs his hand over the large pores, inserts it in his mouth like a cigarette and sucks meditatively while he considers this. Surely there are good and ample reasons for him being in the room with a prostitute now but for the very life of him—or perhaps for the very death of him, depending upon the way you looked at it—the dreamer cannot understand why. "What am I doing here?" he mumbles, his mouth salivating around the tit but this of course cannot be understood by anyone so he removes it from his mouth and tries again. "What am I doing here?" and the whore answers as if this were an inevitable question and one which she had handled with ease many times before, perhaps from the dreamer himself. "Why, honey, you know the answer to that? I was just drinking and minding my business in that nice little bar and you asked if you could keep me company and I couldn't think of anything that I would like more, you being so attractive and all. You remember that, don't you?" and the dreamer returns to suck the breast; it is easier to suck than to talk because the fact is that, for the life of him, he cannot remember any of this but can only accept it on faith; for the moment it is as if history, sense, motivation have all been obliterated in favor of this small cubicle which he occupies and in which he will pace out or perhaps suck out, his last years. "You were very sweet to me, honey, and you're being even sweeter now," the whore says and puts her arms around his neck to draw the dreamer in even deeper, thrusts out her breasts, blows in his ear, does something with the involuntary muscles to make the nipple seemingly dilate and the dreamer is touched by what she has done for him; it is not, after all, as if this was something which any woman would routinely do but is rather a special offering given him in honor of his personality and having nothing to do with the situation. And so he returns to fucking her, feeling his prick growing and growing, feeling her cunt open up into an alleyway so enormous that it could be the corridor of all revelation and at last he removes his wrist and inserts his prick, feeling it balloon further but instead of swimming around pointlessly he finds to his gratitude and surprise that his prick exactly fills her hole—a snug fit, a tight fit; either he has gotten much bigger or she smaller and he begins to fuck her with enthusiasm then, back into the ancient, trustful motions, his body colliding with spirit on the familiar course and in due time he feels his semen rising, rising, it is cresting for him and he puts it into her as deeply as possible, hearing her groan of reciprocity underneath, hearing her dim sounds as if from a great distance and, when he is fucking and fucking her he is also talking— this is a habit he has gotten into recently and it is almost more disconcerting to him than to any of his partners—and what he is saying is, "I'm 27 years old, I don't know what the hell I'm doing here, I can't understand what I'm doing here, won't anybody tell me what I am doing here?" and the dreamer would go on and on, would go into a rhetorical burst of such dimension and length that it might, just possibly, explain everything—but the logical, rational thread of his monotone is interrupted by the seizure of orgasm which carries him completely out of control and so, to his disgrace, the dreamer finds that instead of lecturing the whore mildly on purposes and meaning he is instead screaming with extraordinary vigor and with a range of tonal quality so florid as to be embarrassing, "I need it! I need it! I can't stand to be without it! Tits! Tits!" and all rhetoric interrupted then grabs the shelf of her bosom and shoves it into his mouth, sucking and sucking, thinking perilous and magical thoughts indeed as she leads him into the far reaches of his excursion, the feeling of North around him, snow drifting aimlessly to the right, the left and the center, the sound of animals baying somewhere in the woods, a song of loss and majesty, pacing out the measures of their pain while he the hunter, storm-stricken toward silence, heaves and heaves, his mouth crying strange incantations which might be, for all he knows, mystical in their origin, religious in their background, prophetic in their purpose.

Later

I woke to Rona staring at me. All cheers for women's stares! There is no give in them whatsoever but only an empty and total kind of penetration which might look into the very center; on the other hand, they might only share with cows the qualities of penetration and somnolence which have made these humble animals so famous. "Are you still sleeping?" she said. "I mean, it looked like you were sleeping."

"No," I said. "I'm not. I wasn't, either. I was just resting."

"I mean, I didn't want to wake you up if I didn't have to. I hoped you might be up."

"I'm up," I said. "You can see it. There's not a chance I'm not up."

"I want to go home," she said. She was still naked but her eyes were clothed, so to speak, her body retracted into those very attitudes it might subsume if bundled in layers of cloth. "I mean, right now. Is that boiler going to explode?"

"It never has."

"It sounded terrible about an hour ago. Like it was going to shoot right through these rooms."

"That's just an aural illusion. I mean, a fact of hearing. It's perfectly safe. The other superintendent, after the accident, had an entirely different kind of boiler installed for the new one."

"Accident?"

"Don't worry about it, Rona," I said and put my arms on her to draw her down again, seek the soft, winding somnolence of fucking, oh, I was hot, no question about it, all genes restored in the flush of the new decade and pointing toward the act of generation. "Just come here, come here and let me hold you again." But she fought me off then with a skillful, wrenching gesture and pulled herself to her knees, glaring at me almost birdlike, darting her glances around the room, then, sighing, got up from the bed and went to the window, looked out for a while while I had an excellent opportunity to inspect the curvature of her ass. She had a remarkable pair of buttocks, tight and inwardly curved; I could taste their sweetness as my tongue would move in to penetrate, separate, sniff and discover. "No more," she said, returning to the bed. "I want to go home now. It's not snowing or anything out there."

"Who said it was snowing?"

"It would be just like you to say that the weather was bad so I had to stay. But there's nothing wrong with the weather. You know, it gets very warm in here. If it's like this during the winter, I wonder how you can stand it when it gets warmer."

"They shut off the boiler on March 1st. How would you know how I would try to keep you here? You don't know me at all."

"Ah!" she said with a faint gasp of triumph. "That's just what I was saying. Listen, Harry, the thing is that I'm not so good at one-night stands. I mean, I've done it before, once or twice in my life, but there's no future in them, you understand? Now it was New Year's last night and we were both a little drunk and maybe excited or lonely but now it's the morning and everything looks about the same as it did yesterday, you know what I mean? I mean, there isn't any future in it."

"There's a future in everything," I said, still thinking of her ass. "You can devise a future out of anything you want; form it out of whole cloth, history can become the future—to say nothing of the present." I leaned forward, my mouth in a precarious, lunging pout and tried to grab large handfuls of her to sink amongst them. But too quick and clever for me she darted away and began to ransack through her clothes. "I don't know what got into me," she said. "I just don't know."

"Rona," I said, with the evening's sharpness on me, a forced attempt to make myself rational under stress which has never yet, thank the Good Lord and all the machinations of desire, has never yet failed me, "Rona, there were no girl friends. Right?"

"I thought we settled that last night," she said, taking her brassiere, inspecting it, shaking it a bit as if concerned that a random dog coming in unbidden during the night might have been testing it for flavor. "I don't want to talk about it anymore."

"But there weren't, Rona," I said in my best cajoling mood, at the same time trying to convince her of the seriousness, that is to say the asexuality of my new purposes by standing myself and taking a pair of trousers from the closet which I put on most discreetly, not taking my eyes from her. "Isn't that right?"

"All right," she said. "All right, there weren't any girl friends and if you want to know what I was doing down there I got stood up on a date and I was lonely and thought I'd at least be able to see something interesting in New York when I went on down. I haven't seen anything in New York that's interesting since I got here. It's all a lie. There's nothing going on when you're on the outside. It's just a big dirty place with a lot of congestion. I was supposed to go out but he got sick at the last moment and—"

"Stop!" I said, wagging my finger. "Enough! We've penetrated thus far to the truth with the girl friends, don't you see, Rona, there's no need to go beyond it. *Stet.* Let it stay. Let it remain that way; there are no explanations necessary. But don't you understand what it means that you went down there alone?"

"It means nothing."

"But it means everything!" I said with perhaps a bit too much enthusiasm and bounded on the bed where, with some excitement, jumping up and down alternately, I bellowed out the following phrases, "It means everything! It means that you're vulnerable and solitary and that you came to this city to have it shape your life rather than the reverse, you've come to it open of experience, drained of the power to manipulate, you want life to make *you.* And here you are! Now, why screw the whole thing up—"

Fully dressed now, she backed into a corner of the room with a wary expression, her hand toying with the inside of her panties, the other hand holding out the sweater which she was trying to get over her head without taking her eyes off me. It occurred to me for the first time then that her emotions were fearful and that she was reacting to me not out of my primacy, my uniqueness, my talents and my enormous capacities; no, it was none of this, she was responding to me out of simple fright and as if I were some sort of dangerous lunatic which, of course, could not be further from the truth. Nevertheless, all power lay within her to disgrace or disconcert me now, I was willing to concede, not for the first time, that women were not able to follow the various perambulations of my intellect well enough to keep me entirely out of trouble. "All right," I said, sitting down on the bed and working with a free hand to dress myself as well as with the other I made a series of comforting gestures. "All right, I can understand where things may seem a little strange to you. Would you like me to tell you a little about myself? Would you feel better if you knew me?"

"I don't know," she said. "It was only a brief thing. I mean, there's no future in it. It was all right but I really think I'd better go out, you don't even have to take me home."

"Look," I said. "I'll tell you something about myself. No obligation, no commitments, nothing, just to try to help you get to know me so that we can start off feeling that there's a relationship. No obligation, okay?" concentrating at that moment with that wonderful mimetic ability of mine on speaking the jargon she would want to hear, the jargon of the "integrated," of the "rational," of the "coordinated" man who would come to her out of a universe of meaning and motivation and sculpture out purpose from it: it was very important, vitally important I might say, that this girl not leave, rarely had I found myself so obsessed with one of them so soon after meeting—perhaps it was due to the dramatic and fortuitous way in which our accord was made—and in the bargain the possibility of her leaving filled me with the echo of an old, blocked rage; it was simply impossible, incredible rather, that she would do this to me. No, she could not leave, she had no independence of action but was linked to me not only through circumstance but through stronger and superior personality and I would hold on to her, hold on to her by force if necessary but long before the exercise of force I would have exhausted the other pathways; I would have tried "relationships" and "pleas" and "promises" and "gifts" and so on, wanting nothing other than to hold her in this apartment, hold her to my will and so I said, "You want to know about me, don't you?" And she said, "Oh, I suppose so, I think so, but it's not very important," and I wanted to but did not say, "If it's not important then why must I go through this perversion of dramatic narrative in order to hold you?" But did not say it to her of course: circumspect always, circumspect now, to this moment. I padded to the door, opened and closed it on the wicker of the boiler to make sure that all things in the cellar were as normal, no signs of infestation or of random tenants coming down as they sometimes did to tap the boiler and plead for sustenance, no, no problem with that today because it was a New Year's morning, the dead of a New Year's morning and nothing ever goes on before noon of this horrid date except a little chaste sleeping, a little extrinsic fucking and now and then the splitting moan of someone trapped too deeply in the consequences of liquor. I never drink myself, other than in a mild way and to be somewhat sociable. It is too dangerous. One can lose one's control that way.

And came back to her, after chaining the door unostentatiously, came back and smiled and went to the stove, engaged in a series of actions which must have looked even more efficient than I had hoped, for she sat down quietly as I made her coffee, a steaming cup full of dregs and then one for myself and I sat down opposite her and passed her one cup, held the other and said, "I mean, it's an impossible city, just a terrible place in which to try to live and feel and when two people who could make it together meet it would be a tragic thing, just a tragic thing for them to let misunderstanding drive them apart, wouldn't you say?" Just the kind of bullshit which envelops them because it plays into their deepest fantasies and imagings and those f & i are the belief that they are meaningful creatures involved in a situation of dramatic import and personal weight, and once you understand this and begin to function with them in that way there can be no losses because *they are not rational*. They are not rational. "Well, I suppose I should tell you what kind of work I do to begin with," I said, this exercise of cleverness coming from my realization—the realization of an intelligent, detached man— that in this culture at the present time one can only be defined by the work that one does and when someone casually asks you "What do you do?" he does not mean to ask you how many times you have been laid or by what quality of ass, more's the pity. We shall change this; we shall change many things.

And so—oh, picture this gentlemen, if you will, I realize that this is not any easy request to make, my rhetoric running as it does all to threads and snatches, pastels of language weaving in and out, so to speak of the scenery, great gobs of language sitting somewhere midway between apprehension and communion but my gifts are limited; I never made pretensions to being particularly good at this sort of thing in the "socially redeeming" sense now accepted picture then if you can this scene on a cold New Year's morning in Manhattan; in a room in a basement near the bottom of a boiler, a young man and a young woman are talking, that is to say that the man is not so terribly young nor the woman doing a great deal of talking but the fundamental outlines are there, are there: the man is intense, his intensity refracting from all the curves of his being which are, lamentably, a bit more rounded than they really ought to be. And imagine that as the young man talks, over an extended period of time and in perfect contrapuntal frame, his clothes come *off*, that is to say that the more words he lays upon the girl the less clothing he seems to be wearing until, at the penultimate moment with words adance and aglitter in the warm, warm room the young man sits in glistening nudity and as the venal verb or perhaps it is a noun comes out, his arms jerk up in the puppet's snatch and he reaches toward the girl, mouth gleaming, eyes gleaming and virtually gathers her unto him, she in somewhat of a state of undress herself and hungrily, mouth frozen to the glitter of his glasses, lowers his limbs upon her and begins to pump her enthusiastically and, oh, gentlemen, miracle *diaboli*. She begins *to pump back* so that the two of them are pumping together, heaving up and down and through your telescopes equipped with auditory devices you may hear their sounds and sighs. "Oh, fuck me," and "Oh, God, you're beautiful," and "I don't care, I don't care, just give me a great big fuck", etc., etc. But that would be surging ahead in time perhaps too much for this simple chronicle, this plodding pedantic document which must try to make order out of disorder much as it can be presumed that the boiler by shedding heat as well as light on the roaches in this basement can be said to disperse them to a better reward. *Oh mirabile dictu!* Oh, storming flesh! Oh, sweet, sweet fuckery!

But in time, in time, let us not run ahead of ourselves. I told her then—that is to say, the independent, detached young man or as we shall proceed to call him, the *idiom* proceeded to tell her then—the following astonishing and never-to-be-before revealed elements of biography: the idiom was not a humble civil servant in whose mere guise he walked out the unimportant part of his days but was a serious dedicated young *artiste* out of decadent continental stock who was seeking in one fell swoop, as it were, to redeem the family title prestige and bloodline through his created efforts. The idiom's parents had been cast out of a minor European country's aristocracy and border's during a secondary purge many years before and, renouncing estate, jewels, contracts and various connections to the corridors of power themselves had come in disrepair to America—America!—where they had set up their humble tenancy in a two-bedroom apartment above a candy store owned and operated by the husband of the pair who paced out his days torn between loathing for the military of his country and affection for the neighborhood youngsters who would come into the store to steal candies, misappropriate cigarettes and set profitable fires late at night—the insurance for which was his major means of sustenance during all these difficult years. In due course to these parents—who we shall call for the sake of this narrative Joseph and Mary although these are not their real names but only Americanizations of complex European appellations which to the untutored ears of young actresses would sound like Olifschitzyn and Eznkopfaum—came a child who they named Idiom because he would spring them loose from their wilderness of isolation and by immersing himself in the wonderful mainstream of America—America!—bring them joy and amelioration and Idiom had shared the humble life of his parents with an eager inner fire, his destiny whispered to him gravely during hushed evenings at fireside, his future made apparent to him in stark declamations in police precincts during which the family was occasionally obliged to seek shelter during some of the more spectacular conflagrations. "You will possess this country, you will show them what Joseph and Mary are capable of doing," Idiom was assured and in due course, having completed the public schools, high schools and selected optional religious instruction during the afternoons Idiom was able to take a full scholarship in one of the most prestigious of the Eastern colleges, a scholarship won through pluck and luck combining in a certain fortuitous encounter with the Dean of Women of this great institution some months before his prospective enrollment. At this institution Idiom continued and extended his study and apprehension of American moves, moving on from simple wonder to the more mature realization that this country—his adopted country!—was completely insane and that the only way one could function in it was to somehow make his own insanity dovetail with the larger madness. Idiom decided to do this by becoming a Creative Artist and Television Personality but in the interim, before he achieved these goals, so to speak, decided to work in the civil service since Joseph and Mary had assured him that most of the artists whom they admired came out of the civil services of countries very much like the one from which they had been exiled. "It will encourage your alienation," Joseph counseled his son, "and will give you a clear metaphoric basis for your intellectual pursuits, a visible metaphor so to speak through which you can encounter the enemy bare and stripped or ornament." And Mary added, "Besides that, it pays a decent wage and is always very secure and is the right place to be in when hard times come as so many people have learned. If the aristocracy had only been aware that hard times existed and were surely coming to our humble country they would have all been civil servants and the *civil servants* would have been the aristocrats, then being exiled to this sewer of a nation where they would have gotten, you had better believe, everything they deserved for being the misfits that they were." Idiom took all of this to heart and became a civil servant, operating as a minor functionary in the Bureau of Cleanliness and Public Standards where, for the further propitiation of the Republic and his own salary, he was assigned to review prospective pornography cases; he was to visit various bookstores which specialized in this kind of item and after diligently reading huge random samplings of the work decide whether or not a given book was actionable and if so refer it on to the Investigations and Morality Division for further study. Unfortunately, Idiom learned early on that the Bureau of Cleanliness and Public Standards was maintained only for the nourishment and ease of a small cabal of Southern politicians who had made it a necessary codicil to the Negro Human Rights Act of 196- which had admitted Negroes to the standard of servitude in return for submissiveness; the Southerners had given into this grudgingly but in the last analysis with a certain low good will, demanding only that the Bureau of Cleanliness be established and so, some eight years after its inception the Bureau lived on; one could say that it flourished and was staffed by several hundred investigators, all holding the same position as Idiom as well as forty-five hundred Senior Supervisors and eight thousand, six hundred and forty-three Case Unit Commanders who passed on the recommendations of the Senior Supervisors and forwarded them on to the nine thousand, eighty-nine Case Heads who were responsible for the final decisions being referred to the eighteen-man Board.

In the first instance, some mere eight months after his employment at the Bureau, Idiom found professional cause to read a book called *GOLDEN THIGHS GRIP HOT DICK* and even though he had been cautioned by older workers and supervisors as to the limited nature of his job and its possibilities and had supplemented those cautions with an aristocratic wariness of his own, even in spite of this, Idiom could not repress a virtual charge of longing and excitement from steaming slowly through his frame as he read this book, doodling on a pad unconsciously, the pencil making marks which later turned out to be *actionable, actionable* in the middle of a hangman's noose. The book, which dealt with the attempt of a chimpanzee to find normal warmth and companionship among humans, was written in a high, lyric style which was a virtual celebration of animaline sex and the chimpanzee himself, an engaging creature named Roll Over, had one of the foulest mouths which Idiom had ever encountered in one of these books; in the scene which gave him the longest pause and the greatest deal of excitement, the following events and dialogue occurred:

"Fuck it," Rollo said and put his enormous fucking ape's cock deep into the twat's twat, squeezing and sucking her tits cruelly at the same time. "I said fuck it, I don't care, so they'll send me to jail," and with that he began to give the poor victim's cunt an enormous workout with his huge dong, now swollen to the hitherto unprecedented height of TWELVE INCHES while underneath Sally groaned and writhed. "Oh, you are killing me," Sally said, "you are killing me," but the ape was remorseless, sliding it up inch by inch into her painfully constricted but always beautiful cunt. Deep up his ass, behind him, he could feel the penetrating raws of faithful Tige now moving swiftly toward his climax and the barks and snuffles of his eager friend rushed him madly toward his own achievement. "Oh, fuck, fuck," he screamed and put his teeth down on the nipples, biting them cruelly and succeeding in rending one of them completely severed from the now white and formless breast underneath him. He chewed the nipple lavishly. "Arf, arf!" barked Tige quickening and Rollo felt the enormous jets of his companion's semen filling him; at the same time, Angela purred from underneath the girl and unsheathed her claws, bit them cruelly into Sally's back to draw the bright, beautiful jewels of blood from there which the excited cat licked and slurped eagerly. "Mew!" went Angela. "Mew! mew! mew!" and Rollo could see the dark spot of womanhood between her legs that signaled she was ready for an orgasm. "My nipple, oh, my nipples, you're killing me!" Sally exclaimed and Rollo bit down on the other, bringing it stirring to life inside his thin ape's mouth and then came, Tige's barking all around him, Angela's mewing while above them on the silver cord dangled Jack who, flipping his tail angrily back and forth, growling with exposed lust, forced Sally to take his bull's cock in her mouth and drink down all of his semen. "OH, NO, STOP IT GUT I LOVE IT!" Sally mumbled and flesh and fur alike they dove together on the floor, quivering and jerking as they came simultaneously in the most furious and finest orgasm that any of these poor creatures had yet received.

Idiom took this book, his thumb down on the passage at issue to his Senior Supervisor and said "Look at this now." His eagerness and somewhat abrupt manner might be explained by the fact that he had had to wait the requisite four days for an appointment with the Supervisor, all of this time being required to stop all his other duties and read and reread the one book at issue over and again, at half-salary, so that he would be prepared to defend himself during the interview. The Senior Supervisor, a kindly old man in shirtsleeves and with golden spectacles neatly firming out his features put down his newspaper, tossed a half-eaten doughnut into the wastebasket and without a word took the book and read the passage carefully, his lips moving, muttering to himself. Idiom, despite his intelligence, background, attitudes and training, almost beside himself with excitement, sat with his fists clamped in his pockets and looked with taut tension at the wall, wondering if the Case Head would be able to appreciate the clarity of the arguments he would make, the sheer beastliness of a passage which would surely corrupt and devastate any fragments of the population unfortunate enough to come into contact with it.

"Sorry," the Supervisor said when he had finished, and tossed the book into the wastebasket with a flourish, the standard procedure for any book which had been "passed." "It's socially redeeming."

"Socially redeeming?" said Idiom. "How can the book possibly be socially redeeming?"

"How not?" the Supervisor said, taking off his glasses and cleaning them vigorously, blinking his eyes rapidly to ward off a case of what he had once conceded to Idiom in a private moment were probably "incipient cataracts." "Don't see any problem there at all."

"But a chimpanzee, a dog, a cat and a bull are fucking this girl, all at the same time."

"Don't mean nothing. Got a lot of birds in these books too. Seen one with a frog. Even a couple guppies. You got to understand the nature of the medium, it's just a one-for-one swap with reality but it's got to go further and further out to give 'em the illusion that they're reading something new. Tragic but that's show biz so to speak. It's an entertainment culture; even the guys who don't get laid got some rights."

"But listen," Idiom stammered and in a rush twenty-three years of careful breeding, continental background, paternal coaching, maternal assurances deserted him and he began to fidget like an old uncastled Lord. "Listen, this really goes too far, I mean it. I mean, I know the ropes; I wouldn't bring you anything usual. She says she loves it."

"So?"

"It's a scene of degradation but the girl says she loves it. She's dragged down to the bestial level but flourishes. That's corrupting. It has no socially redeeming—"

"Oh, shit," the Supervisor said with a sigh and retrieved the book from the wastebasket, leafed through it until he found the passage and then, with his finger on a certain line, handed it over to Idiom and said,

"Looka here." After a moment Idiom gave it back to him with a wondering expression and a shrug. "It's just the last line," he said. "It's as bad as any of them."

"Poor creatures?"

"What's that?" Idiom said, at a genuine loss. "I don't understand."

"The last line '… furious and finest orgasm that any of these poor creatures had ever received.' Keyword is *poor*."

"Huh?"

"I don't know about you, kid," the Supervisor said, leaning back in the chair and sighing. "I'd bring you up for charges if there weren't such a waiting list. Listen, I'll say it once and then no more: the keyword is *poor*. They are referred to as 'poor' creatures. In other words, the author is not glamorizing them. He is showing them for what they are: poor, twisted grotesques. By using the keyword 'poor' he is tipping off the reader to the fact that he is by no means recommending their behavior to anyone but is instead only holding it up as an example. He disapproves and the book can thus be considered to be cautionary, a fable or case history so to speak which is intended to show the reader the perils of uncontrolled sexual behavior."

"There are animals in the book."

"Doesn't make no fucking difference at all if there are falcons in the book. Purpose is purpose. Listen, son," the Supervisor said rather kindly and took the book again from Idiom's moistening palms, tossed it in the wastebasket and then leaned back to confront him with a benevolent expression. "Son, there's nothing to this department if you just go along in it for the ride. The thing to do is to read the rules and know the system and just get along. You dig? You follow what I mean? There's nothing to it at all," he said and, standing, ushered Idiom out of his offices with what Idiom in retrospect took to be unseemly haste but then too it was 11:10 which meant that the lunch break for Senior Supervisors was fast approaching and Idiom did not want himself to cut in on that all-important three-hour period when the Supervisors huddled with one another in a local cafe and decided which Investigator would be brought up on charges and which would be permitted to stay for a while, until, at least, the very next conference.

Needless to say, this damaging but educating experience made Idiom far more cautious and it was, as a matter of fact, some two and a half years later that he came again across a book which he truly believed to be worthy of referral. His spirits had admittedly been raised by the fact that earlier in the year there had been rumors in this particular locale of the Bureau about a book which had actually been sustained on charges in the Bay Ridge section and the Investigator promoted to

District King; this had filled the workers with a virtual explosion of morality and they had involved themselves far beyond their normal efforts for quite a while, trying to duplicate this astonishing success but even Idiom had given up hope and things had slipped back to their familiar level when with a trembling of hands and eyes—it was these sensors that reacted before the mind did; at a certain point in the job, usually after about a year, the Investigator no longer knew what he was reading until his secondary sex organs took over for him—Idiom came to the realization that he was once again holding a book which might become a Case. Because of his sobering early experience he quieted his excitement and allowed the book to rest before him for several hours while he read the offending passage, took careful notes, and finally decided, toward the close of the workday, that this was worth risking; he was never likely to have such a good chance again and in the bargain nothing sold or published in Bay Ridge could possibly duplicate this. The book was called *THE BABY FUCK BOOK* and consisted of obscene drawings of infants copulating, their sex organs drawn to hideous adult proportions and usually colored blue and with veins, frozen obscene expressions on their faces, pure panic in their eyes. It was by reason of the panic that Idiom might have been tempted to let the book go but the text, he was convinced, after reading it several times, was sufficient to put the work Over the Line. In any event, he knew he would never have a better chance. The text was written in parody First Reader style and the passage which drew Idiom's particular attention was this one:

See Dick.
See Dick and Jane.
See Dick and Jane Fuck.
See Dick and Jane Fuck with baby Sally.
Baby Sally is fucking Dick.
Dick is fucking Baby Sally.
"Faster, faster," screams Baby Sally.
"Slower, slower," says Dick.
Dick is a good fuck.
He is named Dick because he has a big dick.
His dick is colored orange. Jane's cunt is colored blue.
Dick touches Jane's cunt.
Dick fucks Baby Sally's cunt.
"Oh fuck, fuck," says Baby Sally.
"Oh, fuck me too," says Jane.
"Yes, yes," says Dick.

Dick puts his prick into Jane's cunt.
He puts his finger into Baby Sally's cunt.
"Faster! faster!" shrieks Baby Sally.
"Slower, slower," says Dick.
"Faster, faster!" screams Jane.
"Slow, slow," says Baby Sally.
"See them fucking" says Daddy. Daddy is in the room.
Daddy is fucking mommy.
Mommy is fucking daddy.
Mommy and daddy are fucking each other. So are Dick and Jane.
So is Baby Sally.
They are all fucking.
Fuck and fuck.
"I love it," says Baby Sally.
"I love it," says Dick.
"I love it," says Jane.
"I love it," says Daddy.
Mommy loves it too.
All of them love it.
They are very happy.
They are happy fucking.
Everybody fucks.
Fucking is good.
Fuck and fuck.

After he had considered this passage for several hours or days—it hardly mattered; Investigators, in these more recent days of the Bureau had been cut down to a quota of one book to be covered every fortnight in order to do the job thoroughly and at the highest level of competence—Idiom got up with an expression of determination and went into the office of the Senior Supervisor, the same Senior Supervisor, by coincidence, that he had seen the first time around, although in a different locale since Idiom and his entire division of the Bureau had been transferred out to Coney Island in the beginning of March as part of an overall Departmental Expansion which would eventually put an office of the Bureau on every major intersection as well as in every public school. Because of a recent alteration of Bureau policy, Idiom was allowed to see Senior Supervisor immediately, five hundred and fifty Senior Supervisors having been promoted from the Investigatorial ranks in July in order to contribute to the expansion of the Bureau. Idiom, not having any long-term plans had not taken the test for Supervisor although he was sure that he could have passed it or, for that matter, the far more testing examination for Case Head.

"Sit right down," the Supervisor said amiably. His personality had taken a surprising turn for the better in recent weeks, due to the fact that he was to receive his pension and permanent retirement from a grateful public in December; until then he had been reduced to the supervision of only two Investigators which gave him a good deal of free time to refine his thoughts for that massive Essay on Pornography which he intended to write for the *Men's Home Entertainment Magazine* as soon as he was free of the department and thus able to speak his mind. The fact that three hundred and fifty ex-employees of the Bureau submitted such essays to the *Men's Home Entertainment Magazine* every day of the week did not disconcert him and, as a matter of fact, would not have disconcerted him if he knew about it. He figured deep down that he was a better writer than anybody he had been reading during his years in the Bureau; in any event he was as good as most of them, better than quite a few and inferior only to the very top ones who were the most Socially Redeeming of all. "What can I do for you?"

Without any words, Idiom handed over the *DICK AND JANE FUCK BOOK*, his thumb, just as it had been years ago, on the offending passage. It should be pointed out that by this time the Supervisor and Idiom had become very close friends, even doing a certain amount of drinking and chasing together although, in the case of the Senior Supervisor it hardly mattered anymore since he was so feeble. "Is that what's bothering you?" he asked.

Idiom nodded again and handed the book to the Supervisor, settled back and lit a cigarette with concentrating fingers, all the time looking at the walls of the Supervisor's office which had been plastered with cutout pictures of tits: there were tits of all sizes, descriptions, hues and dimensions on these walls, all of them apparently clipped from the pages of the *Men's Home Entertainment Magazine* and Idiom had never ceased being fascinated with the Supervisor's taste and diligence although, of course, he would never had gone in for that kind of thing himself. Still, if that was the kind of thing you were going to go in for, you would definitely want to do it in this way: the Supervisor had no prejudice for or against tits of any size, he like them big and small, heavy and sausage-like and for good measure he had put in a couple of pictures of his wife when she was much younger apparently, breast-feeding what Idiom supposed was the Supervisor's child although the back of the head, in certain suspicious shots, might have been that of the Supervisor himself. It was very difficult to tell and it hardly mattered; Idiom found himself resisting with difficulty the impulse to get up, walk around the office to handle and fondle the tits. They looked so extraordinarily realistic on the wall that it was hard to keep a true sense of perspective and in the bargain the Supervisor looked up occasionally from his reading to make inviting winks and glances, making it clear that it was perfectly fine with him if Idiom were to avail himself of the opportunities in the situation. But holding on to his professionalism, to say nothing of his increasing sense of anger at the kind of mind which would write and/or publish the *DICK AND JANE FUCK BOOK*, Idiom stayed in his seat, clenching his wiry fists and doing everything within his power to avoid getting an erection which the Supervisor would surely suspect, take as credit to his portfolio, and use as a means of putting a black mark into Idiom's record. Even though they were friends, the levels of approval in the Bureau were murderous and for the length of time that he decided to hold onto the job, Idiom decided that he did not want to take any chances.

In good time the Supervisor put down the book, sighed, removed his glasses, scratched his crotch and then, with a strange flourish, put his feet on the desk, parted the feet and stared at Idiom through the aperture. "Well, then," he said, "what seems to be the problem with this one?"

By this time Idiom was wise in the ways of the Department which demanded an eloquent and precise defense of a given objection to a book, regardless of how obvious defection might seem to the "common reader." "Degradation," he said crisply. "Children involved in gross physical activity, children degraded, the image of the Child ravished, the idea of parental consent along with equivalent degradation invoked to give a portrait of the complete dissolution of the society, of the moral code, of all the values of the culture, of any sense of respect, of social control and so on. A celebration of bestiality, without any redeeming value whatsoever. Neither pity nor terror illuminating."

"They do say they enjoy it. And there are no perversities involved."

"But it's pederasty."

The Supervisor looked quizzical and said, "How can there be pederasty if only children are doing the fucking? There are no adults involved."

"Mom and Dad are fucking."

"But they're fucking each other! They have nothing to do with the children."

Idiom shrugged and said, "They express approbation. It isn't implied, it's explicit. They say that it's good. Baby Sally urges going 'faster' and so on. I don't think it would stand up."

"Why not?"

"I just damned well told you why!" Idiom said with some irritation and then settled back in his seat, aware of the fact that he had let bad manners and frailty interfere with simple sense and yet somehow obscurely shamed and angered. "I mean," he said, "if this damned thing isn't dirty, then nothing is and we have no function."

"Who said we did?" asked the Supervisor.

"But we must."

"Not necessarily. Anyway, this is perfectly protected by the first amendment to the constitution of the United States. It falls fully within the purview of free speech. It is a simple transference fantasy in which the desires and vague lusts of the reader take on the form of children and the childish sexual manipulation functions as both expression and amelioration of those desires. Perhaps I mean the trivialization. In any event, there's nothing we can do with it."

"It's disgusting," Idiom said. The fact was that at this moment, despite his training, background, high intelligence and overall sense of competence which had been nurtured in the virtual fires, so to speak, for all this time, he felt himself overcome by a new sensation: one of despair and a feeling of disillusionment so enormous that it might have come close to that of Joseph and Mary when, landing in the strange ports of a mad country they beheld before them the gleaming visage and bobbling features of a customs investigator who assured them that there was absolutely nothing of value which they had and therefore there was no need to do any checking. "I tell you the book is foul."

"Well, so it is," said the Supervisor with a calm, almost beneficent smile and leaning back lit a cigarette—everybody in the Bureau smoked at least two and a half packs a day; this was where Idiom had picked up the foul exercise in the first place, having come there with high resolve not to pollute his body or his internal humours. "So it is, but there's absolutely nothing we can do. Now, if there was a religious overtone to all of this: I mean if they had nuns and priests mixed in, that would be something else. That would be an implicit religious condoning of the affair and would definitely put the book in another category. You can always look for something like that. If you find something like that, I know I'd be very interested."

"I had one with priests and nuns a few months ago," Idiom said glumly. "But I couldn't put it into you. They were all married."

"Well, that's the way it is," the Supervisor said cheerfully and with an almost winning smile stood from the desk and draped an indolent, cigarette-holding arm around Idiom's neck. "Listen," he said, "don't worry about it. It doesn't mean a thing. You're young, you're enthusiastic and furthermore, you're convinced just as I am that an end ought to be put to all of this stuff. It really should you know, it makes sex even more horrible than it necessarily has to be. But you learn to temper your youthful idealism with maturity, that's all, and then, strangely enough, you become more effective rather than less so. You become level-headed, not eager, and can make detached judgments. We'll get what we want, we really will. But it takes time."

"I think," said Idiom, "I think that it will take more time than I'm willing to invest."

"But don't say that!" the Supervisor said with a tone of horror and looked nervously through the open door of his office to make sure that no one had overheard him entertaining a visitor-employee who had indicated that he was not interested in the Bureau's long-term objectives. "You've got a wonderful career here and a very bright future. Together we will make America free again in the Bureau, release her from the agonizing scatology of her polluted history and into a new age of confidence, morality, and sex behind locked and barred doors once again occurring between clothed and furtive people. We'll have all of that, that's what we're really working for. But it takes time. You've got to be patient." When he spoke of his ideals, the Supervisor's eyes gleamed and he stood up very straight but when he had finished and with another glance at the door had assured himself that no one was, after all, listening, he sighed and dropped back to his seat again. "Ah, fuck it," he said. "Look, take this piece of shit out of here and write a report and pass it through, will you? I don't have time for this crap anymore; I'm not getting any younger and my heart is bothering me." He tossed the book over to Idiom, made a waving gesture of his hand which was surely unmistakable and then, eyes nodding, head bobbling, dropped himself comfortably across the desk from which position he shortly began to engage in a series of heaving snores. Idiom left the room quietly, holding the book loosely in his hand, feeling the flap of pages almost doglike between his thumb and forefinger, on the verge for the first time in his not inconsiderable intellectual experience, of an insight so large and vast that it would take him beyond simple dialogue and into the possibility of larger actions.

It was this and many other factors which caused Idiom to leave the Bureau within the fortnight to apply himself to other tasks, primarily that of free-lance writing. He came to the decision that since the authors of all the books he had been studying apparently made good money— there were a lot of repeat authors in the work he had covered—he would try to make some of that easy cash too but, having no intention of writing filth and yet knowing that the markets were primarily oriented toward pulp-and-paperback he would become a fulltime writer of Western fiction, until such a time as he would have established such an income from these paperbacks as to go on to something larger and more serious. He never doubted that he had a novelist's gifts and found from the start that it was much easier than he had thought it would be; there was really nothing to it, you just put down what was on your mind and kept the clichés of the category firmly in mind and that was the end of it. He had chosen Westerns because he knew that science fiction was a fantasy literature written for the most part by certifiable lunatics who had a reputation for being actually dangerous in public gatherings— and mysteries, being obsessed with murder in a strange way which always made death *clean* depressed him; there was something about reading a mystery, to Idiom, that sent him into a state of almost wild depression because the books not only had nothing to do with reality as he understood it but, indeed, seemed to be inimical to reality in a way which was peculiarly grotesque and sickening. At least, in the case of sex books, there was some one-for-one relationship far in the background; people *were* fucking or at least trying to and those that weren't were quite interested in it anyway, whereas no one—absolutely no one—was walking around in America without any sex drive whatsoever, thinking of executing or solving a perfect murder without blood. Since the occult, astrology and historicals had always left him cold, Westerns by a process of elimination were the only category of fast-selling literature which Idiom could write and, after a while, as he got into them, he began to find all of it most interesting, intriguing even, there was something both prurient and healthy about a Western because no one could possibly have ever lived this way, yet the imagined American past was far more baroque and provocative than any reality and the manipulation of it fascinating. Idiom found both success and disaster in the writing and marketing of his Western novels but at this point I feel that I am getting somewhat ahead of matters and should return to an earlier and more crucial instance in Idiom's career, that is to say, his very first sexual experience. Just as the very nature of conception-and-birth is supposed to stamp the individual personality indelibly for life, exactly in such a way is the first sex experience, in America, supposed to be both the paradigm and the prophecy of everything which will come later and Idiom's first sex occurred in a particularly interesting and provocative manner; he was deflowered— using *deflowered* of course only in the poetic or poetical sense—he was deflowered, I say, in a drive-in movie located in a valley between two motels, three used-car lots and fourteen hamburger stands, while in the virtual act of trying to consume a quick-cut cheeseburger and focus his attention on a romantic film dealing with two important but now forgotten stars. Let us talk of the manner in which Idiom lost his virginity.

I said, let us talk of the manner in which Idiom lost his virginity.

His virginity! His virginity!

Well, perhaps in a few moments. This is all very tiring. Not tiresome, but tiring. I was not aware how difficult it would be to sustain this. It is time for another seven and seven. Rum and coke? Reminiscence? Whatever. Tra-la! Heigh-ho! Fickety-fuck! I am not unbalanced Not unbalanced.

Later

"But I'm not sure I want to hear any more of this," Rona said to me, chastely exploring the inner surfaces of her cunt with a concentrated expression on her face, faint twist of tongue, flutter of eye, wink of brow as she looked up at the ceiling in an abstracted manner. "I think you hurt me a little bit in there."

"It's just sore," I said, "just sore, nothing to it," making no reference therein to the dimensions and outlines of my turgid prick which, in its fullest state of luminescence is indeed quite a fat organ, modest in length but gigantic in circumference, it has been the heart of many a heated discussion at other times. "Anyway, you wanted to know all about me, so I'm telling you."

"I really should get going," she said but there was no conviction in her statement, no commitment in her tone, no energy in her movements and I knew that she would stay, there was no way whatsoever in which she would leave this room until I had said to her everything that was necessary, had done to her all that was convicted, had consummated, so to speak, all of the dire necessities of relationship and had then wandered beyond this to a new free area where we could begin for the first time to approach one another. I should explain that during the interim between chapters I have had several rather thick and sweet seven and sevens, a bit high on the seven, a bit low on the seven, some rum and coke as well, binding all things at the edges and throwing me into a high, almost frenetic state of drunkenness which, if I were not concentrating so hard on these notes, would probably blow me out of this room and onto the literal streets where I might do something disastrous like pissing on the pavement or equal disgrace. Oh, I explode with energy: like this America itself I am full of unused expenditures, accounts unbalanced, small thrusts of eagerness which, if they do not find objective-correlative on the outside will begin to thunder at my insides like small animals rattling in a cage; fortunately, I have these notes which keep me sane. I had never realized what an excellent writer

I am. I am not drunk, merely slightly giddy. I can handle huge quantities of liquor. It is January 2nd. I can do everything I want to do. While not quite King of the Universe I am at the very least a Crown Prince, a bastard one at that. There is nothing to fear. Watch out for small disturbances in the corridors. Listen carefully for sirens. Attend to the sounds adjacent, they might consist of people on the prowl. Cautious, cautious. Control, control. Watchful, watchful.

"Yes, let me continue," I said to her and without further ado began to speak at some length about Idiom's first sexual coupling which, as I say, occurred in a drive-in movie encompassed by several hamburger stands, etc., and during the lower half of a double feature consisting of a mystery retrospective involving the gifts of one of our country's Own Major Actors, now long dead, alas, although the center of a small cult which puts his photos on posters in strange places and leaves notes for each other on the street like GET HIM NOW or HUMPERDINCK DOTH LIVETH. The girl—there is always a girl; this is the miracle of heterosexual sex and who would say a word against it?—was named Gloria and was, in fact, an Older Woman, no longer a student at the high school which Idiom attended but a graduate with a vocational diploma which allowed her employment as a waitress in this very drive-in theatre's Hot Shoppe from which employment she now had a day off. "I love the place, I can't think of anything nicer than not having to do work but just to sit in and take a movie for once," she had explained to Idiom when that youth had tremblingly requested a "date"; and to his surprise he found that in Gloria's mind or what passed for it, "date" was synonymous with "fucking" for, not five minutes after he had pulled his father Joseph's ancient Dodge into a deserted area very near the screen, Gloria had removed brassiere, sweater and jewelry, had disarranged her skirt and—quite naked except for certain appurtenances near her thighs—had perched herself on Idiom's lap where she proceeded to stick a wicked tongue into that worthy's ear and said, "Oh, come on, let's do it. It's the greatest thing in the world and anyway, there's nothing else to do in this place." So saying she presented him a breast with a queenly gesture while Idiom, all agape, proceeded to meditatively suck while he considered his fortunes: they were good and bad, good in that "fucking" as the obvious objective of every "date" could not be denied as a benefit in imminence but bad in that Idiom had never "fucked" before and thus had a certain trepidatory overcast to his feelings as he began to work on the other breast with only moderate enthusiasm. His experience with breasts, thanks to the mass media, was excellent, and he knew exactly what to do with them but he was not so good on cunts and tended to wonder, if brought quickly to the threshold, if he would know exactly how to "stick it in."

Forgive Idiom, if you will; these slight crudities of thought and expression are not to be ascribed to him because of weakness of personality, banality of mind, flaws of intelligence, etc. No, it must be understood that Idiom, no less than any other young man of his time had been so exposed to and anesthetized by what were popularly called the "mass media" that he was able to think and function only in terms of definitions and experiences described by them and ascribed by him to various experiences which he might otherwise have had to struggle to identify for himself. At the time of which we are speaking, these "mass media" had taken over a good deal of the waking consciousness of most "Americans" who were consciously forced to meditate between the impressions of reality given by the devices and their own assumptions, the near-impossibility of coordinating the two, of course, was one of the reasons why the country was completely insane. Thus murmuring to Gloria in the car, Idiom could find nothing to say other than "This is really too much for me," or "Your breasts are fabulous," or "I don't quite know what to say," while she in turn muttered "Kiss me, my sweet" and "Touch me with your lips all over" and "My body is on fire" whereas, left to their own devices, they would have been more likely to have said things like "I don't know what the fuck is going on," or "Do breasts really hang that low when they're out of a brassiere?" or "Where are you supposed to put your hands when you suck a breast?" declamations far less romantic and thus potentially more effective than those which they actually did speak but, on the other hand probably superior, at least in quality of feeling to what they actually and with some moderate astonishment, found themselves saying. They are not to be condemned, however, less and less can there be assumed to be any culpability in America by virtue of these "mass media" and who cannot say but what their screams, cries, murmuring and sensations were superior, because more coached and less mysterious to them, than any of the screams uttered by the famous Bacchanals in Rome who probably, after constant trips to the vomitorium preceding their other exercises, were probably rendered impotent anyway?

In any event Idiom found himself progressing rapidly from breast-sucking to more detailed fondling and exploration of the "erogenous zone" of the breasts, the term "erogenous zone" being used because it was Gloria herself who reminded him in that exact term that her breasts were extremely sensitive and all during this the sounds of a developing mystery epic were filling the car through virtue of the loudspeaker, "Come on, you rat, come and get it," and "I can't imagine who would have done this to him?" and "Mary, you're tough, but deep down you're just a little girl" and "I'll fix them," and so on and so forth, all delivered in an actor's intensity which unfortunately the speaker reduced to stentorian monotone thereby managing to cancel out what feeble efforts the actors had undoubtedly made to induce a sense of realism. From time to time there was gunfire, scuffling, patter of feet, shrieks in corridors but Idiom and Gloria perceived them only as numb counterpoint; now Gloria's hands had dipped down to Idiom's thick and growing rod, grabbing purchase on it in a series of uneven squeezes which showed enthusiasm no less than inexperience and Idiom, wrenched into a peculiar position in the corner of the seat, pinned almost under the steering wheel found himself almost incapable of movement, his panic being in no ways alleviated by Gloria's own insistence which rather picked up in tempo to the sounds of gunfire and consisted of a series of huffing and sighs, pants and snorts which would have moved him more if he was not vaguely aware of the fact that she was doing it less in response to his presence and his own movements than to certain distant events on the screen. "Oh, this is terrific, terrific," Gloria moaned, baring his prick for all the world to see and running her hands over it while she performed a series of butterfly motions with her thighs, enabling her to somehow sit in his lap and yet maintain this conjunction. "You're a tower of love, do you know that, baby? Oh, I want to take it, take it, take it," and on the screen an actor said with horrid clarity. "You can dish it out but you can't take it, son," and Gloria said "I can, I *can*," although whether she was addressing the actor or her own conscience Idiom was never quite sure, perhaps she was talking to both of them simultaneously. "I can, I can," she said and began to wedge him inch by inch into her clamorous hole which was very tight and hot, surprisingly so under the circumstances since she had informed him during the breast-sucking interlude that she was a "fountain of love waiting for his tower to come in." Tower or fountain, the two of them found themselves in a peculiar tangle and Idiom was able to make his entrance only with a difficult series of winces, tics and gestures which might have been disconcerting had not Gloria's attention been focused tightly on the screen where, Idiom could dimly see, two detectives were struggling with a large demented man who they referred to as "the maniac." "The maniac's coming, the maniac's going to get us," the detectives counseled one another and the senior of the pair, the Cult Idol, pulled out an ancient gun from a concealed pocket and shot the maniac neatly between the ears. Meanwhile Idiom's own maniac was squirming its way, inch by painful inch up the vaginal walls and he could feel himself dimly scrappling and heaving within like a trapped animal; then a breast dropped into his mouth, expanded, seemed to inflate and he

sucked it intensely while on top of him Gloria began to engage in an
uneven squeaking series of pumps which carried him along toward
orgasm: they were carrying her somewhere too although exactly where
he was not sure because rather than moaning in what Idiom would have
hoped to be "painful ecstasy" or whispering "words of love" into his ear,
she was singing, was singing a ballad which happened to be popular that
year and which Idiom to this day has never forgotten, so bound up is it
for him in the imagery of sex, its necessity, its vigor:

> *"Oh, to know the God of love*
> *As the Venus de Milo*
> *Or the Devil of Hate*
> *That's my Milo.*
>
> *He's strong and good and wonderful*
> *His arms do hold me tight*
> *But the river and flood of sighs he sings*
> *Haunt me during the night.*
>
> *Oh, to know the God of Love*
> *As the beautiful Venus de Milo*
> *Or to know the Devil of Hate*
> *The Devil of Hate is named Milo."*

All of this sung with a certain vigor and attenuation of crucial syllables
which made Milo come out as *Mi-hy-holoo* and beautiful as *bee-yoo-yoo-
ti-tee-tu-tom-fool* and love as *lo-ho-hoho-ho-hohoho-uh-uh-uv!* which
Idiom might have ascribed to faulty diction or hearing if he had not
heard the words of this "popular song" so many times already himself
and was not, as a fact, as he fucked her, singing the lyrics along with
Gloria—although whether he envisioned himself as the God of Love or
the Devil of Hate is something which will have to be left to the
historians. God of Love, Devil of Hate, Milo or Idiom, he slapped her
buttocks and coaxed his turgid prick along and was rewarded finally by
a thin flaring pain which began at the base of his scrotum, went
through the anterior vesicles underneath the prick (Idiom had a weak
or faulty sense of biology but cannot be blamed for this; like most
American men he believed until very recently that orgasm was the
result of semen being pushed along various nerve-centers rather than
understanding, thanks to the wonders of modern research science,
that it is the *tremors of orgasm* which induce the movement of the
semen and for these miracles the scientists are still out of the jury box;

perhaps an orgasm results from coming and it can be left at that although, in America, it probably and unmercifully won't be) and then flaring into the seemingly-expanded tool itself which seemed to flare and fly up into a wedge and he groaned, "Oh, God! Oh, God," and squeezed her breasts with renewed energy, urging out of himself an orgasm which in retrospect stood midway between inferior jerks he had had and a couple of sublime masturbatory experiences with a stuffed green dog (He had never told Joseph and Mary about either pole of course but the green dog would be tied up with his subconscious for a long time to come) which had been given his mother once as a prize at a "bazaar" and, as he worked on her energetically his partner moaned "Love, love, love, oh, you're a tower of power, a million of billions" and on the loudspeaker three actors began to rant at one another in a high jargon which seemed to be a combination of the Chinese and Teutonic accents and which had to do with a set of "missing precious jewels." At the conclusion of his thrusts Gloria had an "orgasm" of her own or perhaps it was only a simulation; in any event, she gave a deathly series of whimpers and jerks and fell heavily into his arms weeping, her eyelids fluttering, her face strangely inclined toward his so that he could get a good close look at the effects of the faint on her delicate features which seemed to be suffused with a brilliant yellow color amidst the flushes. Then she fell all the way across him, causing a certain whimper of agony to float through his prick and, kissing him on the neck, told Idiom that he had been "terrific, much better than any of the others," which confession filled Idiom, he was pleased to find, not with jealousy but with the kind of smug satisfaction which comes from having joined a large circle of men in an Initiation Ceremony. He figured that if this was all there was to it: the getting and enacting of it that was, he could certainly stand sex; in any event it expanded his necessarily limited horizons rather nicely and gave him an entirely new set of principles and goals to pursue. He never, after this initial experience, found it necessary to ask Joseph and Mary what particular advantages this continent held for him—he had shared their simulated nostalgia for the country of exile—and became, as a matter of fact, a rather insular and reserved person, quite different from the enthusiastic and somewhat repellent youth he had been. He took to taking long excursions on his own through the city, occasionally going into certain "book stores" and "motion picture theatres" and also took to giving long, lingering glances at women in innocent circumstances—supermarkets, wheeling perambulators in the park and so on—in a way which brought these ladies much embarrassment because they thought that Idiom was in some way being sexually offensive. They could not understand that he was merely regarding with wonder these strange, ordered creatures who concealed, one layer beneath their soft complacent skin a network of meaning so profound that Idiom wondered if he would ever work it out. Of course he was only eighteen years old.

This being then the sum of Idiom's first sexual experience: he is not sure nor am I whatever became of Gloria although he heard rumors some years ago that she had gone "West" to try to make it in the "movies" but had instead found an "office job" and a "husband" which he vaguely hoped would make her content. He bore her no ill will. He came to understand in due time that most men brought to the memory of the women who had initiated them into sex an almost unparalleled and embarrassed kind of loathing but he never shared these feelings; he figured that Gloria would have done it with anyone as likely as with him and the sheer lack of personal intent then, in her coupling, indicated that she bore him no malice of any sort and would not be responsible in any way for being blamed for certain unfortunate sexual experiences which Idiom later had. Or thought he had had.

It was some twelve years later that Idiom began his first Western novel. It was entitled *RANGE RIDERS WITH JINGLING SPURS* and at the present time is some 30,000 words long. Since the minimum requirements in the paperback Western field are for a novel of 45,000 words minimum, Idiom has 15,000 words to go, but he figures that he will be able to wrap this up, no strain, by next winter.

Idiom feels a little bit uneasy now. Idiom feels a little bit rocky. Idiom feels a little bit strange. Idiom is going to go to the bathroom and make wee-wee. See Idiom make wee-wee! See him go to the bathroom! See him stagger and lurch! See the plaster fall from the walls! Listen to the boiler huff! Idiom is making wee-wee! A pure jet of semen comes from his faithful attendant, old peter, who has served him so well on so many missions. The water is turgid. Idiom is turgid. Idiom is making wee-wee. Idiom is tired.

Idiom is drunk.

Idiom gonna quit for a moment and try to get his senses in order.

Idiom confused. Hurt, lost, dismayed, unsure. What the fuck!

Later again

Much better now. Many hours have elapsed, of course. During this period I have done many things, have passed out for a couple of hours, have relieved myself several times, went out an hour ago and picked up a whore in the street and fucked her in her furnished room as a matter of fact. Just back from that one and to these notes again. Must remember to stop drinking, at least until I am finished. And this was supposed to be a diary, a calmed, reasoning assessment of a year in stilted, varnished prose! What an explosion of event, however! Well, perhaps this, when completed, will be the Final Installment, I believe that I am through with diaries. Better to stick to Westerns. Better to save the rhetoric for two cents a word. What would I have made from this so far if I had written a Western instead? Five hundred and forty dollars?

The whore is interesting.

Sinking over her, pouring into the rich folds of her flesh I believe that I had an insight, one of the few genuine and important insights I have had today: Sex is *all. Everything else is compensation.* She had enormous breasts which seemed to throb and pick up the beat of her circulation as I screwed her, sticking my prick deeper and deeper into her huge pillowing mound and at the end she barked, one small sound of glee and snorted in my face, then thrashed back and went into one of the longest and most involved orgasms I have ever seen in a woman, far past my own relatively banal coming she was still thrashing and screaming. Her breasts were enormous: huge, white thick cylinders—delightful, and she must have known with what glee and desire I ravished them because after we had finished the first time she said with a look of wise, tolerant cunning, "Do you want to try something different? I can give you a better fuck between the two of those than you can get in my hole! Try it and see?" And without waiting for my response, which would have been enthusiastic assent in any case, slid herself deftly underneath me, seized my prick and stuck it between herself, grabbed her breasts in delicate hands, squeezed them against my rod and then began to pump back and forth with a hissing, swishing excitement which in no time whatsoever generated my own response. I felt literally smothered in tits, the world was breasts, there was nothing else inside or outside and with what enthusiasm I screwed her like that, what whoops of astonishment I gave, what tentative and tickling nips she gave the glans as we pumped, using the up of every stroke to deliver a small delicious bite to whip me further along. *Quelle* whore! *Quelle* experience! *Quelle* vie!

(I have not explained nor do I find it necessary to explain how I picked her up. Why should I give away good information? Just rest assured, gentlemen, that there is at least one excellent whore in New York City willing to work in the residential district of the Upper West Side on cold holiday afternoons and that she gives back in better than due coin anything that she receives. Eat your hearts out. Find it yourself. It took me long enough to manufacture my own luck, I ask no less of you.)

"Oh," she moaned, "I love it between my tits, that's the best place for it, I can't think of anything I like better," marking herself thus as irretrievably breast-oriented, what we do to women in this culture as well, and then went into a shaking, shuddering orgasm which made her completely lose visible contact for a moment although not, I am happy to say, oral contact with my eager prick—which she continued to bite with increasing intensity; the combination of sucks, licks, pressure of breasts, increase of flesh, turgidity of nipple, whiteness of sheen, uncoiling of cock was entirely too much and with a scream I came myself, pouring yards and yards of semen into the valley, looking with astonishment at my manufacture, surely more copious than could be dreamed considering it was the second such within a few moments and she relinquished hold of neither breasts nor prick but continued to work me enthusiastically, only switching off at the end to massage the last agonized spurts out of my organ with her two careful hands, the breasts falling unbidden to her sides. Enormous breasts they were.

And then I was finished and got up from her with a sense of relaxation and relief I have rarely known, a sheer sensation of *thankfulness* inflating my limbs and paid her her coin with a kiss (she did not even, tender spirit, ask for it beforehand) as well as with several bills, put on my clothes, blew her several impassioned kisses at the door and left her, a delightful experience, surely a *ficelle* but for all of that not to be disregarded when the final accountings are made. Who is not to say that when we look back at all of it from the roil of the deathbed many (or not so many, it all depends) years later, it will not be the insignificances which matter and the larger events—or what we have taken to be the larger events—which will be revealed as slender intrusions, nothing else. A good whore, a good fuck, a brisk walk, a crisp day, a happy decade, a refreshened possibility. There is little more to ask. Yet I still tremble with sheer *uncomfortableness* as I get back to this and I am not quite sure why this is so. Surely it cannot be the effects of the liquor which wore off slowly during sleep and rather rapidly during the fuck. Perhaps it is the strangeness of these quarters, the odd intrusion in these rooms, the whining hum of the boiler which seems to have taken on rather more of an insistent note.

Ah, well. At any rate. Back to this with renewed energy and the resolve to be disciplined. "Come here," I said to Rona, at the conclusion of the narration of the drive-in. "Come here." And reached out my arms and, to my surprise, she tumbled in unresistingly, a stray wisp of hair tickling my face, her cunning palm coming up to wipe it back, tickling my cheek; then she was kissing me with a strange remoteness which yet kindled me and underneath her insufficient clothing I could feel again the already familiar rising of her breast. "What are we doing?" she asked.

"Come on. Kiss me."

"I don't even know what's going on," she said. "You're so strange. You're such a strange person. I never met anyone quite like you before. I don't believe half of what you're telling me, you know."

"But it's all true."

"I think you made up the whole thing just to impress me but I can't figure out why. I mean, who could be impressed by stuff like that? That Bureau sounds insane and that girl you were with, I know girls like her, just like her back where I come from and they're all impossible. I mean they're crazy. And a Western novel! Who reads Western novels these days anyway? I thought it was a dead form."

"But that's the whole point of it!" I said with some excitement. "It's so archaic! It's such an anachronism! The whole thing is an exciting groove! What could be deader than the mystical image of America, the myths and clutter on which we have grown up?" And slipped my hand underneath her sweater, crawled it up her belly and seizing her breast with some enthusiasm began to work on it. An extraordinary breast, an extraordinary girl and I could feel the faint lushness of her body opening up underneath me, a sensation of *openness*, of yielding, and knew then as I know now that I could have her again and any time I wanted. I mean, I could have this woman any time I wanted. There is always a certain point in a relationship, if it works out, when one undergoes this realization and it is to everyone's credit that it can almost make it, the relationship I mean, worth it. To increase the pleasure, to subsume my desire, I held back, aware that for all the city cared she could be dwelling with me forever and no one would ever know. Certainly not her girl friends. There were no girl friends.

"That's the groove!" I said again, lowering my voice and slipping into my "hippie" shade of rhetoric, another one of my exciting masks and simulations which comes from my ability, probably already noticed in these transcriptions, to mimic the style and substance of any writer or speaker living or more happily dead. "That's the scheme of the whole bag; now you consider the Western novel, it deals with a mythical America, right? The range, the past, something that never truly happened. Livestock, branding, rustlers, covered wagons, pioneer women, busted-up old marshals and so on. That's the network. And then you've got to consider the scheme, the ploy."

"I don't understand."

"But baby, it's easy: it's always one man against the mob, standing up for conventional morality. The town is under threat because a group of vigilantes have broken the code of the Old West, whatever the fuck that is, and the marshal, you dig, the marshal can't rustle up anybody on his side to fight the good fight. All he can get is maybe a couple cripples and a girl who as we know don't really count in the Western structure. Then he takes on the vigilante group and reinforces the moral code. It's a groove! And he always wins, the vigilantes are brought to heel and the crowd—the witnesses in the town, you dig?—always come back to the understanding of their cowardice and the supremacy of conventional morality. You follow what I'm saying here?"

"Not at all."

"Why, it's the last form of literature standing up for America! That's all it is. You take the sex novel, it's saying that the puritan ethic is half dead and the science-fiction novel is saying that the quality of life here, when you get right down to it, is so intolerable that you've got to break ground any way you can or die and the mystery is saying that there's murder, nothing but murder, blood and death and terror lurking at the fringes of existence and the Gothic novel is saying that there is always something, *always something* dark and terrible and hidden away and besides the heroines never fuck and the nurse novel says that life is surrounded by disease but the disease is so intolerable that it can't even be mentioned so all the patients in nurse novels just have broken arms or something. And the commercial novel is just a hyped-up sex bag, you dig, and as far as the literary novel, the hell with it. There hasn't been a literary novel to stand up for America for years and years, probably since *THE LEGEND OF SLEEPY HOLLOW* and that was more like a novella, 20,000 words and what could he have gotten paid for it? Two hundred bucks. So I say you've got to stay with the Western and gather for America. You dig?"

"No."

"But it's simple really," I said and with a flourish gathered her into my arms and recommitted myself to the fucking of her; I had not fucked her for some six or seven hours which necessarily had caused my loins to once again cramp and constrict with desire, raging lust it was or at least a pleasant simulacrum that lent urgency to my trembling hands, pulsations to my caresses; her sweater dropped away or maybe I mean was simply pulled up her neck by my clumsy hands, her lower garments fell apart, I bent my head and began to suck and suck at her nipples, finding within those bright cores such substance as I had never known before. My own frail clothing of course departed and then, huddled knee to knee on the bed, we addressed one another in the sexual position, lip to lip, thigh to thigh and I kissed her in the space between the breasts and then brought my head down, down her belly, all the way across her pubic hair—thin and wiry, stabbing me with the hearts of a thousand needles—and then I proceeded to eat her lavishly, with a great deal of enthusiasm and profusion of gesture, making occasional grunting comments which sounded like *good good* but were really saying *delicious* while she dug tense fingers into my neck and gathered me in, inflating her breasts, ballooning her thighs and my tongue, then lips, teeth and veritable jaws disappeared within that splendid tunnel as I ate and ate at her. Oh, gentlemen, did I eat!

Oh, gentlemen, did I eat! I just said and eat I did, coiling within and without, tasting the gelatinous substance of her walls, feeling the membranes constrict, the faint, salty taste of her come roiling in and out of my mouth and she began to rock in reciprocity, her fingers clawing deeply into my head, pain and pressure from scalp to toes, moans and screams, sighs and caresses, warning and admonitions and then she went off into climax, forcing my head to be the helpless trapped rider between her thighs and so it was; I rode it out with my usual aplomb, sucking and blowing, staying with it as far as I could and then when she had subsided on the bed— The hell with the novel of social redemption.

When she had subsided on the bed I kissed her in reverse, up the thighs, across the belly, between the breasts, harshly in the neck and then threw my tongue into her mouth with enormous and speeding force as I entered her, a clangorous, clamoring entry, my prick hungry for her, burning for her, extending and extending to enormous length, searching and prowling and I went into the motions of sex, lunging and biting and she said to me, "Oh, I can't stand it, what are you doing to me? Why are you doing this?" and being without answer I only fucked her harder and she said, "I don't understand this, I don't understand you, I don't know what is going on here," and I fucked her harder, building up the rhythm with strength and persistence, ass flapping, thighs beating, neck stretching, mouth moaning and I felt the orgasm coming upon me as if from a great distance, then increasing in speed and size, it was as if I could see it, a ball of filaments glowing with fire and it sped into my consciousness, growing and growing with a power no less than that of at least a minor star and I screamed, whether for interplanetary travel or for simple climax I do not know but screamed again and poured into her vast foul jets of oozing substance which I saw murkily in mind trailing away into her, fish darting, sperm sifting, eggs searching and the hell with all of that, who cares about consequences? Fucking, Fucking. Oh, fucking. It is really induplicable, there is nothing quite like it, at least within the moderate circumstances which I have described for myself, related for Idiom and ascribed to Rona about whom more will presently be heard.

When we came apart she rolled from me, her eyes large and confused in her head, then turned back and with a curious blinking gesture said, "I don't care. I don't want to play games anymore. I loved it, I loved what you did; nobody ever gave me a fuck as good as this," and I laughed but whether for joy or remorse I could not be sure and she said, "The trouble is that nobody wants to fuck anymore. Do you know that?"

"Yes," I said.

"They're all hung on different grooves," she said, doubtless influenced by my jargon of some minutes before and more power to her, more power to it, more power to any rhetoric which can be so simultaneously banal and yet such an excellent simulation of thought; politics, not to say international relations, would be better if certain leaders called the Present War "a fucking groove" and let it go at that. "They're all hung on different things, some just want to impress you with how good they are and how easy it would be for them to fuck you if they only wanted to but they don't think that they're in the mood right now so the hell with it and some of them are just hung on insecurity and don't really know whether they can fuck you or not so they don't; the real thing is not that they're insecure about fucking you but whether they're able to fuck anyone, period, and then there are the ones who just want to have "relationships"; I'm not even mentioning the goddamned faggarts of course, and when you finally find a man who knows how to fuck and doesn't mind doing it and would just as son fuck you as talk to you, he wants it to be significant and wants to know if you came good and wants to know if you're breast-sensitive or how your cunt muscles are taking his thrusts and by the time the bastard's finished you're so sick of the whole thing that all you can think of is whether or not you're pregnant. It's something when you find a man who just wants to *fuck*. I thank you, Harry," she said and gave me a graceful, glowing tap on the elbow which, I do admit, gave me something of a thrill of pleasure at the reception and I nodded at her, perhaps a bit more solemnly than was necessary under those seemingly lighthearted circumstances and said, "Well, I always did like fucking, you know. It seemed like the natural way to consummate a date. What I'm trying to say is that there's nothing wrong with it; it's what you make of it."

She nodded enthusiastically and said, "You're right. That's just the way I feel and I bet it's the way every girl feels when you get right down to it; fucking is something that you do if the circumstances are good. And that's what everybody says but the thing is these men don't believe it, they get so hung up on morality or relationships or dynamic orgasms or something like that that they never get around to just doing it and then they're always asking you afterwards how it was. Who cares how it was? Does anybody ask you how a drink was after you've got drunk?"

"What men?" I said.

"What's that?"

"These men you're talking about. The ones that get hung up or morality or orgasms. You know a lot of them?"

She shrouded her eyes, blinked, fell back against the covers and said, "What is this anyway, an Inquisition? We were just making conversation."

"I just wanted to know."

"Don't tell me you're hung up too and you want to know who I've been with and what I've been doing and what my sex life is like and all that crap. I just met you twelve hours ago."

"Oh, it's not me," I said. "Not me, I couldn't care less. No. It's Idiom who wants to know."

"Idiom?"

"Yes, he's curious."

"Now look," she said, shaking her head. "Look, buddy, uh, uh, I don't know what's going on here but all of a sudden I don't like it very much. What complications? What are you trying to do? Are you another—"

I could see at once with my splendid, almost precognitive ability for reading personalities, tendencies, reactions and response that I had come to the verge of making a dreadful error, had, in fact, lurched far ahead in psychic time to some space where I might be able to make all kinds of uniquely disastrous statements to her but this time, such as it was, such as it is, was sufficiently in advance that I had done myself little good with my sentimental leap. There is this tendency in me to dissolve time through the force of my own emotions and to try to simultaneously exist—I believe I have mentioned this earlier in relation to sex—to try to exist simultaneously I meant to say at all chronologies of the relationship, the far limits, the near caresses, the tentative shy discovery and the frank exhaustion of the end, a projection upon the partner of my own feelings so profound and so harshly unsettling as to be somewhat disorienting both to the partner and myself. I have had this trouble before and I saw that it was coming hard on me again—oh, no pun intended, gentlemen! a pun was the furthest thing from my mind!— and so what I did then was to endeavor to soothe her, launched upon her apologies, pleas, murky explanations which although wordless were supplemented with grunts, groans and caresses and all through this, in one way or the other I was trying to convey that I meant her no harm, that I carried for her only the burden of love—enormous love, gentlemen! felicitous love! binding, hungering love!—and in due course, whether or not this had any effectiveness I could not tell, but in due course she subsided, her eyes becoming clear again and she said something like "Well, it just seemed very strange but I still gotta get out of here soon, you dig?" and I said, "Yes, yes, I know that but let me go on telling you about myself. I barely got started, I mean there are other important things to understand."

"You don't have to," she said.

"But I want to," I said. "I want to tell you more about myself or at the very least about Idiom, that one-for-one paradigm of reality who may embrace truer explication of the common reality than this humble speaker."

"What's that? Huh? I don't dig you. I mean, sometimes, I just feel—"

"No matter," I said and jauntily lit another couple of cigarettes, handed one over to her, and laid back puffing. (I feel that this is the time to interpolate that I realize that there has been a lot of smoking, huffing, puffing and blowing in these pages but what can I do? The cigarette has been given a bad name in the "socially redeeming" novel as a mere piece of bad stage business employed by inept or bored authors to keep the characters trotting along physically at the same time that enormous dialogic chunks of absolutely worthless exposition are continued, but the fact that the device has been appropriated or misappropriated by hacks cannot be said to cast any aspersions on my own narrative which is, first of all true—there was a great deal of smoking going on—and secondly superbly rendered, neatly paced and operating, as you probably have noticed, on three distinct structural levels: time past, time present and time future. We shall get to time future in due course, have no concern. In the meantime, permit the writer to allow cigarettes to wind their gentle, sulphurous, metastatic way through his pages: he has so few other indulgences, so few vices, so few true releases that these pale metaphors for death should be allowed, as would any young and promising writer, to Find Their Own Direction.)

"Sure you dig me," I said. "You'll even learn to groove on me. Let me continue. Let me tell you a little bit now about Idiom's Western novel."

"It's awful warm in here."

"They turn the boiler up to its fullest intensity during the day," I said. "Or rather, the boiler turns itself up. It's on a self-guiding mechanism which allows it to adjust the temperature so that it becomes warmest on the warmest parts of the day and then cools off when the temperature drops. You can save a lot of trouble that way,"

Idiom's Western novel (I then went on to say) was begun immediately after he left the Bureau to devote his attention to full-time free-lance writing. His original intention had been to write the novel extremely rapidly so that he could pick up enough in advances to live comfortably while he wrote another one but he quickly became dismayingly aware of two facts: firstly that he was not a quick writer and would have to struggle over his production as he never had over sex and secondly that it was almost impossible for a previously unpublished writer to sell a "portion and outline" of a book, no matter how oriented to his category, to a responsible publisher. In these days the custom was for hack writers to write an opening series of "chapters" plus a "brief outline," a total package of some 10,000 words or so and then send it out to a publisher who would hopefully on the basis of the submitted material decide that the hack's idea would become a novel indistinguishable from any other that he had ever published and would hence offer a contract and a check—say for one third of the total price for the book—immediately. Idiom had envisioned himself moving grandly from portion/outline to portion/outline for a couple of months, raising enough money for him to easily finance the writing of several books but he quickly found that publishers were unwilling to take a chance on a newer writer, even in the familiar Western category which less than any other deviated from accomplished marketing norms. Thus, after having spent three weeks of considerable agony and without income painfully putting together the first "forty pages" of a "range novel," Idiom had sent it out to the most likely publisher, one whose works had been long famous in the paperback field for their banality and dreadful garish cover paintings and had then waited out four interminable weeks expecting a check to come almost instantly while, in order to give himself some income in the meanwhile, he reluctantly accepted a part-time free-lance position in the Bureau in which, for one quarter of the salary he had received for office work, he read the books at home and submitted brief reports on them. It was not nearly so interesting as work at the Bureau itself had been because the Bureau was engagingly and always unpredictably insane whereas Idiom was quite familiar with the kind of insanity he could generate left to his own devices and was thus fairly bored with it. However, he was able to sustain himself in poor circumstances until one bleak morning he received back his portion and outline with the following note stapled onto the title page of his manuscript, written in a strange, uneven scrawl and with a certain unevenness of characters leading Idiom to the feeling that the note, if not the staple (which was bright brass and fairly glowed in the dark) had been administered by an idiot:

"Your work while interesting in certain ways does not quite fit the needs of our market at the present time and must be returned to you with regret. We assure you that it has been read with great interest and we will be happy to see submissions from you in the future. Please remember to attach a stamped self-addressed envelope in the event of future submissions inasmuch as if you do not the manuscript will be destroyed unread."

And underneath this someone had typed poorly and on a machine apparently in great need of a new ribbon, "Have you read any of the Westerns we've been publishing recently?" In something approaching a high rage, Idiom sent off an obscene unsigned note to this publishing firm which even to this day he cannot recollect, knowing through his retrospective embarrassment only that it had something to do with genitalia coupling in proscribed positions in the presence of witnesses from one of the world's most important religious organizations, one of whose participants was the owner of one set of the genitals at issue. He then put the Western into a clean envelope and sent it out to the next most likely publisher on his list, one who had become famous for his "quality science-fiction" but who every now and then, just for the hell of it, published a Western with a title like *Singing Spurs* which instead of having a standard Western cover painting seemed to use one of the science-fiction overstock so that the Westerns were issued with pictures of rocket ships or snakes on their covers—very disconcerting, Idiom would have imagined, for any "science-fiction" readers who picked it up expecting their usual jolt of megalomania to find that instead they were tenanting the menacing but entirely puritan landscape of the Old West. This publisher was far more prompt and responded within a couple of days as follows:

> "Thank you very much for submitting your material (title) for our reading and appraisal. This has now been considered closely by our senior editorial staff but I'm afraid that in the final analysis the reluctant final opinion has been that it is not quite right for our list and we are therefore returning it with our best wishes for your success in placing it elsewhere."

This second response yielded Idiom some real encouragement inasmuch as it indicated that somewhere rational people were trying to come to rational decisions on his work but he decided at that time that his chances as a unknown Western writer were probably not so good for portions and outline and therefore, on the famous Reckoning Day which will occupy an important place in Idiom's pivotal Turning Period when the final memoirs are written, Idiom decided that rather than resubmit the portion elsewhere—there were only a couple of possibilities left and neither of them were very likely—he would simply sit at home and finish up the book and then try it once again at the two initial houses. In order to now devote full time to his novel he quit the Bureau for a second time by mailing in two books with a covering note saying *FUCK OFF JACK I'VE HAD IT* and then, although this was extremely difficult for Idiom who, due to his background and relationships had always been somewhat insecure about money, he decided to live on his accumulated savings for the length of time it would take him to finish the book and sell it. A small legacy had been bequeathed to his mother by an exiled uncle of a duke and she in turn had turned over a half of it to Idiom on his 21st birthday with a touching note saying that she hoped this would send him off on the "royal road or the road to royalty" and this one hundred and fifty dollars, along with the five hundred and thirty-eight dollars and sixteen cents which Idiom had managed to save from his years of employment at the Bureau, he decided to use as his "sinking fund" while he threw himself with a frenzy of dedication never previously experienced into *Jingling Spurs and Lariats*, the new title he had selected since it seemed to be closer to the level of his perceptions, to the tone of his purpose than did the old title.

It might be relevant at this time to quote at some length from Idiom's Western novel; it is almost impossible for you to understand exactly what this brilliant writer was attempting and why, unless you are afforded the opportunity to glimpse the work, so to speak, at the first hand. With no further objection, therefore, Chapter II of *Jingling Spurs and Lariats* is quoted at some length to make it clear that Idiom was not a simple "hack" in pursuit of the "dollar" but was indeed, as he said in his "novelist's notes to himself" (which he was saving against his memoirs and critics someday) trying to do nothing less than to reconstitute the American dream in terms which would be highly relevant to today's restless but hungering audience.

(At this point I stood up, went to the secret cabinet and removed my carbon of the manuscript, bringing it back to bedside with something of a flourish and riffling through the pages until I had found the appropriate section. Typed on pink carbon paper with certain blue streaks of age running through it, the manuscript had a rather veinous, that is to say, peculiarly and sexually repulsive aspect, but the words were clear enough and I was able to read them with clarity, pace and vigor, once again showing the unusual range and versatility of my gifts. "Do I really have to hear this?" she said. "Of course," I said, "aren't you interested in knowing all about me?" "But I never liked Westerns," she said "As a matter of fact, I was never much of a reader, I was slow in school and there's something about books that puts me off, like there's so much words, you dig? I mean, I don't have to hear it." And I said, "Of course, you have to hear it," and she said "What if I don't want to?" and I said "But you do, you do," and she gave me a peculiar stunned look, began to wipe her palms over the bedclothes with a strange resigned gesture, much, I suspected, as if she felt herself somehow at bay with an individual who was literally uncontrollable and therefore had the potential for almost limitless alternatives of action, some of them dangerous. How wrong she was, how gentle I am! But of course there was no way to explain this to her without further endangering the situation; certain things after all, motives, slashes of history, touches of cunning, fires of desire are inexplicable in any terms other than themselves, just as, so I am informed good novels can also be. This is why I take pains to include the following excerpt in my notes.)

JINGLING SPURS AND LARIATS
by Harry Watkins
Author's pseudonym: Chet Roscoe
Chapter Two: The Bunkhouse

When Jim got into the bunkhouse, the first thing that he did was to unpack his gear and put it away. The horse neighed and whinnied in the stall behind him and he went over and patted the creature gently, giving it a lump of sugar from his pocket. It was a tough ranch. There was no doubt about it. The Brady boys had it shut down cold. Jim knew that he had walked into a tough situation but with Amanda dead and in his past and with no sense of hope for the future he didn't much care. Let the town get what it deserved. He didn't care. The Brady boys had it by the throat—Joe, Tim and John. They always would. It didn't matter.

He went over to his bunk and opened his marshal's uniform, took out a small piece of hardtack which he began to chew meditatively. Cows in the background gave the scene a peaceful aspect. Suddenly the door opened and Martha, the mistress of the ranch to whom he had just been introduced was standing there. She was naked except for a thin shirt which covered but did not conceal her breasts and a pair of jodhpurs which showed her fine thighs and ankles.

"Hello, big man," she said. "I reckon to have found you in here. You settled in good?"

"Yes," Jim drawled. "It's kind of lots of animals here but nothing not gettin' used to."

"How you feel?"

"Tired," Jim said. He stood up, since he was getting an erection which dangled uneasily in his pants and which embarrassed him. Martha must have seen it. She smiled and drew her arms way up over her head, showing him the distended outlines of her breasts, an impression of hard, fiery nipples, nipples the shape and color of the sun Jim suspected.

"I don't like bein' married to Tim Brady," she said. "I just reckoned I ought of told you that."

"Don't matter to me," Jim said. "Don't care who you married to?"

"He's not interested in a woman," she said in a strange voice. She came over and put a hand on his shoulder. The hand trembled and Jim's shoulder trembled. The bunkhouse seemed to be trembling too and there was the sound of chickens cawing as if from a far off distance. It was the clucking of chickens that brought Jim back to other memories, memories of him and Amanda and the chicken house feeding them, the chickens in the morning and he felt a pang of loss as he thought about this and a growing flush of embarrassment at his desire. He tried to pull away from her but suddenly her grasp was strong on him and instinctively, not knowing what he was doing, Jim drew her into his arms, making sure that his marshal's badge did not prick her. She came against his leather easily and lifted her mouth.

"Oh, Jim," she said. "I'm so hungry."

"I don't know," he said.

"I'm so hungry, I haven't really had anything good down at this ranch in so many years. Tim doesn't care anymore and his brothers hate me and do you want to know something? He's a bad man. A bad man," she said and dropped her hand to the front of her shirt, opened it quickly and then, pulling away from him, took it off, exposing her two breasts to Jim's frantic eyes.

They were large, full, dappled as with sunshine, they had the beauty and energy of young colts galloping in the meadow, they were as proud and upstanding as two baby lambs and she inhaled deeply to show them, then put her hands around and cupped and squeezed them, showing them to Jim like the headlights of a buckboard stagecoach, moving hell-bent through the Great Canyon.

"Jumping whillikers," said Jim.

"Oh, please," she said. "Oh, please don't play with me. I'm so lonely. It's so terrible here at the ranch. Please tell me that you want me. I'm a woman, Jim, I'm young and desirable. Time—"

"Oh," Jim moaned, "Oh," and took off his spurs, then removed his large boots and stood before her only in his informal range costume, then stripped down the front of his jacket, removing the marshal's badge, to stand before her only in long underwear. He could feel the pulsations of his prick galloping like a wild stallion inside his clothes. The sight of her was as pretty to him as a field in May with flowers weaving gently amidst the grass and the sound of birds in the tree.

"You're sure you want this?" he drawled.

"Oh, yes. More than you can ever know."

"I wouldn't want none to take no advantage of a lady. I mean, I'm a spare and lonely man and I try to go my own way. I want to feel that what is right is right and what is wrong and wrong. The code—"

"Oh, Jim," she moaned, tossing herself into his arms, her jodhpurs dropping like little bears' paws on the floor. "Oh, Jim don't talk anymore. Just fuck me. Fuck me good, Jim. Make me your woman. Give me a good fucking."

He guided her over to the bunk carefully, gently, side-stepping his mess-kit which lay in a tangle on the floor and put her down amid the blankets, lying her back so that her skin gleamed in the thin light of the kerosene lamp the way his marshal's badge caught the fire of the sun. "You shore are purty, ma'am," he drawled and then he was upon her, his massive cock inflating to enormous size as he ground his lips down on her and she felt her tongue come between his teeth.

She began to fuck him with her tongue between her teeth moving it in and out, out and in in a wonderful strange rhythm and he felt as if she had made his mouth a cunt which she was entering. "Oooh," he gasped. "Oooh," but then was unable to speak anymore as she continued and expanded the wrenching soul kiss and he seized her breasts, one in each hand and began to squeeze them.

"Oh, yes," she said, breaking the kiss. "Oh, yes, do that! Really hurt them. Tim never touches me there anymore. He think it's dirty. You don't think it's dirty, do you, Jim? It isn't. It's wonderful."

"It shore is," Jim said and squeezed the massive apples painfully, grinding and kneading them, one against the other until she howled like a coyote in a trap and said "Oooh, ooh, more, more!" and then he put his thumbs deep into the nipples, literally indenting them and worked harshly with his nails, bringing her to a frenzy of response as she put her mouth back against his and he felt her underneath spreading open like the doors of a stagecoach to accommodate him. He gasped, not releasing his hold on the breasts and feeling as if his prick was the largest part of his being, even bigger than a Winchester rifle, he allowed it to guide him into her hole. She was wet, dark, moist, as wild as a raging river and he felt her eddies and sea-currents drawing him up and up. "Aah," she moaned, "Oh, that's good, that's the thing I wanted, that's what I needed, give it to me, give it to me!" and he gave it to her, uncoiling like a lariat, cracking his tongue as if he were chewing tobacco and entered her freely, fully, all the way. She grunted and began to work back against him and he felt the cow-town of his orgasms beginning to build as he bayed at her like a bull in heat. "Oh," she said, "Oh, you don't think I'm bad, do you, Jim?" and he said, "Sure enough not, you're just a lonely woman and in all the world there's nothing as soft as a lonely woman unless it's a heifer that done lost its mama," and began to fuck her, easily, sliding in and out, accelerating his motion. "Once had me a heifer," he reminded her, "just a little thing and they took its mama away for slaughter and the little thing went around nipping hands and crying but it didn't mean no harm. It was just lonely, it was hurt," and as he told her the story of the heifer he increased the thumping beat of his pumping, stopping at the end of this sad story to suck and bite at her breasts, spongy and rubbery they had become in the intensity of her need. "Aah, God," she said. "Aah, fuck. Fuck, fuck, fuck," and he felt himself beginning to pour into her the way that Haycox had poured into a Western or Dillon into a town, all the heat and need of him and he was so lonely, he had not had a woman since Amanda, three years ago and he had forgotten how soft they were, how wonderful, how resilient, he had almost forgotten and his meat throbbed out an enormous Brand as he put his mark on her, fucking and pumping and sucking and biting as he held the animal down for the iron and she poured back at him full force and at that moment Joe Brady came in, right through the bunkhouse doors, looked at the two of them with astonishment and then turned around and clumped out angrily.

Jim knew that he was in for more than a heap of trouble and knew from the expression on the rat's face as he had left the room that he bore him no good will and probably would now try to find out all the facts about the new ranch-hand.

But somehow he didn't care. Martha who had not seen Brady come in, shot into her third orgasm in succession with gusto and he slammed his wedge into her chuck wagon, his eyes closed in intensity, thinking how truly wonderful she was and how she had enabled him to discover what he had truly come to the range to find.

It would all be worth it.

He knew his mission now.

He would bring the Brady boys into gear and set the town of Rustle 'n Spurs straight again.

Through the woman he had found himself, Jim Perkins again, the man he was.

And he hoped he never lost it.

When he had finished, Idiom put down the script with a slow, meaningful gesture, and turned to face the girl, his eyes still alight with the power of his own rhetoric, still moved by the force of his own vision, this a familiar trait which he had picked up from his days in the Bureau—call it excessive self-involution—and for a moment found himself so deep into what he had read and written that he was disoriented; then he came back to himself slowly to see the girl sitting, blinking her eyes, doing things with the sheets in a frantic effort to cover her breasts, closing her thighs instinctively at the same time and breathing harshly, unevenly, rapidly. He put the script on the floor and said, "What's the matter? What happened?"

"I don't understand it," the girl said. "I mean I just don't understand it."

"I explained to you—"

"I don't mean about that," she said and tried to stand and if Idiom had not then committed certain forceful actions to keep her in her place it is possible that she might have made an effort to leave his apartment. He hoped not but it was possible. Anything was possible. Anything is possible. In any event, he held her in place.

To hold them in place, ah, to hold them in place, this being the mission of the race! I am getting unbalanced again, it is time for a little drinkie wee-wee or is it the one or the other which I truly need? I feely a little unsteady. Surely it couldn't be the liquor I'm fine but something seems to be wrong why did she look at me in that way, the strangeness in her eyes, the heavy lifting blandness, the cold sheen of her face, the murmur and curve of the lips she looked at me in a certain way not as if she thought I was insane because this was not possible but in a different way it seemed to open up to a new level and murmur of meaning oh God I think my head is going to split where the fuck is that chapter I dropped it right on the floor and forgot about it oh there it is right over there well I'll just pick it up and get it back into the cabinet I mean I'll pick it up after I wee-wee, got to wee-wee, piss is the word, I should have picked it up before, goddamn it the pages are a mess now, I'll have to retype everything or at least the whole chapter and it's awful, why didn't I think I'm not really very well at all and I need to get up well I'll just get up now and

And still later

Considerably better. The strange cyclical nature of my passion, the strange binding throb of my entrapment. Nevertheless, a certain levelheadedness once again has shyly extruded and I have not had anything additional to drink. I think that it is primarily the lack of sleep which accounted for my last breakdown; there has been such a profusion of recent event with no time given to turn off and try to assemble it that at times it seems to overlay me and tend to implode that fine, high, rational perspective which is my major contribution to Western myth and society. In any event, I really think I should try to get some sleep shortly and perhaps after I do a little bit more on this latest section I will. I am very tired. Why didn't I simply try to sleep before?

Well, we know why. I went back to the whore again.

Went back to the whore, tra-la! The same whore, already my very favorite living person on the residential West Side of Manhattan; apparently she chooses to double up her work, so to speak, on holidays, for when I returned on vagrant impulse, more out of curiosity and the faint fatigue of fugue than out of any genuine hope or conviction that she would be there, so was she there indeed, perched comfortably between the half-open doors of the huge apartment building in which she dwells and works, twirling an accomplishment handbag in the cold and—oh!—the smile of greeting she gave me when we met again was such a smile as I have never received before—gleaming, open, hopeful and wise, it confronted me in the gathering darkness with the aspect of a pennant waving merrily and happily over the breeze in a victorious football stadium and I came over to her with something of a bound, an answering grin on my own face and waved a finger at her for sheer joy and seized her hand. The sheer *permanence* of her! It was so reassuring as to be immense; the thing about New York is that it is possible to walk a given city street at the same hour every morning for a year and never—*never,* mind you!—see the same face twice. It is not for nothing that our sociologists have pointed out the anonymity, overpopulation and increasing anonymity of our Inner Cities as one of the primary contributants to social breakdown, loathing, suicide, murder.... As a matter of fact it was all those dreadful qualities that seemed to be circling in my mind during this rather unhappy walk and to see this whore was to at once obliterate them and lift me to a new level of circumstance where, for the first time in quite a while, I sensed that life could have meaning. No existence could be entirely hopeless if it would cough out the same delightful whore to a stranger twice within a mere eight hours; this happy collaboration of circumstance seemed to cause space to close around me warmly and with something of a glow. I walked to her with a grave solemn gaiety to no extent unrelieved by my prodding around in my pocket for a fresh series of bills. Her fees, incidentally, are quite modest, but as a gentlemen and as one who wishes to savor his sweets for himself, I do not believe that it is within my purview to reveal her price or, for that matter, to be more specific on her location than I already have been. There isn't enough of it going around as it is; I intend to save it for myself. I realize that this is selfish, gentlemen, but this is intended only to be a metaphysical document, you understand: I am not really trying to do anyone any good. Not to my own detriment, in any event.

"Hi, again," the whore said with a gracious, gleaming smile, and I took her by the arm, wordless, touched her cheek with my lips and led her into the apartment building silently. Oh the way in which she clove against me, the way in which her body made light contact with mine as we walked to the elevator, the sheer ease and familiarity of it! Gentlemen, I do not exaggerate, it was like coming home after a long trip. And I really had been gone for such a short period of time.

In the room—just one large furnished room as I may have remarked, with that splendid, ponderous bed rooted in the center to give it meaning—she reminded me again of her fees, at the same time showing her trust in me by divesting herself of her garments with great rapidity and ease, at the end of which her fee had been placed on the top of her trusting bureau and she stood before me naked, her breasts falling and rising evenly with a quality that I could not interpret as excitement, and I took off my own clothes rapidly, lying them in a neat huddle on top of hers, then took her by a thin, white wrist and escorted her over to that exquisite mattress and guided her down gently. "I want to bugger you," I said.

"Buggery?"

"You know what I mean. The rectal—"

"Oh," she said with a perfect understanding crossing her faithful features, and her little nipples seemed to congeal with comprehension. "You mean pegging. That's what we call it, pegging. It's all the same thing."

"Pegging?"

"Yes, in Brooklyn—"

"I want to *bugger* you," I said. "Egging, cornholing, whatever you call it. Is that all right with you? I want to do it very badly."

"Oh," she said, and laid back, her breasts falling to her sides evenly, exposing the valley between them to me, the other, smaller valley underneath as she flexed her thighs, "Oh, that's fine. I don't mind it a bit. It's something that I like to do if it's okay with my customers. I mean, with the men."

"That's good," I said. "That's fine. Do you know why I want to do it so much? I only do it occasionally, you know; I've really done far less of it than I've wanted to. I've led a rather disadvantaged life. For me it is the perfect and sublime sex act, uniting in its perversity and its thrust all which we have come to know and fear about sex: the spilling of ourselves into the secret places, the unimaginable scatology of the act itself—a scatology, I might point out, which is absolutely American in all of its details since this country and no other unites this wondrous and simple chain of life with the bathroom—a simple, splendid act which in all of its outlines as well as its performance—"

"Listen," she said, humping her legs up, smiling at me, shaking her head, running her tongue across her teeth. "Couldn't we just, well, sort of *do* it? I mean, do we have to talk about it? ..."

"But I *like* to talk about it," I said. "I mean, what is sex without rhetoric? For me, the one completes the other, I don't mean necessarily that you have to talk when you're screwing but certainly before and definitely after and even in the middle; language is the soul of love, after all, the only thing that separates us from the beasts—"

"Has anything happened since the last time? You didn't talk so much then."

"Oh," I said. "Oh, I've been a little bit excited. I'm putting together a treatise on American socioeconomics you see and I've reached a key part—"

"You do run on, don't you?" she said and then said quickly after that in response to my own facial expression, which, I suspect was rather on the dramatic side, "I mean, that's all right, I didn't mean to hurt your feelings or anything like that, it's just that sometimes screwing is better than talking and anyway, nothing personal, but time is money, I mean, I like you a lot and all that and I wish we could really talk a bit but I'm trying to make a few dollars today if I can and I can't get too involved. I mean, if you would pay me for the time, that would be something different and then I'd be happy to listen to you all afternoon but it wouldn't be right to charge you and I'd feel very guilty—as if I was getting away with something or something like that if you know what I mean—so what I'm trying to say is that if maybe we could just sort of, well you know what I mean, if we could just sort of *do* it, well then it would be a lot better, do you follow?" And saying no more put out her unresistant arms and, tumbling, I grabbed purchases and clambered between her thighs and in an instant was lost, gentlemen, lost!

Lost, lost, lost! Although hardly, I do wish to assure you, by the wind grieved. No, no wind to soothe me, no palm or unfound door either, let alone a father's face, only the hotness and depth of her snatch and I began to caress at her with my cock, feeling an alarming warming sensitivity spread through all the outlines of my tool, began to feel the rush and fires of congealment and once again she offered me her breasts, one by one, to suck—how the breasts of whores are able to put up with the continual fantasies lavished roughly upon them I do not know; surely every obsession of America must sooner or later end up in teeth marks on those poor innocent surfaces—and I did so with enormous enthusiasm, feeling myself beginning to already grovel in the excess of sexual need and then turned her over, vaulted away from her at enormous speed and height, feeling the room seem to contract as my body filled it with air, with space, with speed, with light, turned open the flowers of her ass underneath me, just a hint of redness within, but whether membranes or the rosiness of her love I could not know, turned open her ass as I said and then my enormous cock, lunging like a rabbit with desire and fear, buried itself deeply in that trap, moving inch by inch, forcing itself up those cheeks, spreading and spreading her so that I could sink myself within and then, gentlemen, ah then, well, then I-

I buggered her.

I buggered her: no apologies for this obsession, no explanations either, only the moderate and rational ones will do: there is nothing in this country quite like buggery, it is the perfect objective-correlative to the American lust, the American obsession, because it is not only scatological and faintly perverse but it is *complete protection against generation* and what could be of more interest to any satyr, particularly an unmarried one working on Western pulps which have not yet quite gotten through to meeting the needs of the contemporary market? No, no pregnancy, no conception, no complications whatsoever—only the pure, incredible tightness of her tiny hole clamping itself around me as if she were in agony which, I knew, she distinctly was not and she heaved herself by the elbows up from the mattress so that her breasts swung free, swung free indeed, and I snaked my hands around to cup them, feeling that strange softing fullness press back against my palms and moaned and sighed, groaned and ached as I felt the orgasm beginning to *wedge* itself out of me, not a straight, strange rising as is customarily known in screwing but instead a kind of forcing off-angle, as if the constriction of the body causes the orgasm to come only as an incidental factor and in any event I was involved, involved indeed, huffing and puffing and biting on her back and squeezing and tweaking and nuzzling and screaming and she worked back on me with genuine enthusiasm, more conviction than skill in her movements certainly but willing, willing for all that had been inflicted on her to try, try again and that is the way I came—fluttering, cawing, hissing and squeaking like a bird pinned in mid-flight, my elbows flapping, my thighs descending, my neck straining and through it all I held her breasts, held on to them, desperately manipulating and stroking and extending the nipples until at last I fell on her exhausted and in all the sweetness and quiet of that room then, for all the peace which descended upon us, it might have been the end of all time and we the only people who dwelled in it. Her eyes danced against my palm, she stretched and sighed. She kissed my hand. She drew a finger down my arm and told me how good it had been, what a nice change of pace it had meant.

Buggery is splendid, gentlemen.

And when I left her finally, I left her at peace, that is to say that I like to think it was at peace that I left her, peace in her limbs, peace in her face, peace in the quietude of her limbs, peace in the silence of the room, trailing down the hall in heavy woolen overcoat and scarf with the silence and high precision of the assassin, only the strange pennant of my shoes waving from one indolent hand, shoes removed in the interest of silence. Because she deserved it. Because there was no less that I owed her. Because I wanted to.

And came back much refreshed, aha, aha! Back to this journal with a will although, alas, I do not believe that I will be seeing this pleasant whore again; I simply cannot afford her. No, I will have to spend my next break more conservatively, passing back to seven and sevens or perhaps to catching up on the daily newspapers which as I note in a casual sweeping glance across this room, my keen features set in determination, are several weeks backlogged. Conscientiously I buy them, conscientiously I toss them into a corner of the room, conscientiously I aver that I will surely be getting around to them ... and yet, for some time now, I have not. It is not that I dread the news—in fact, I flourish on it, I increase, I feel America singing in my literal soul as I read of these engaging disasters—no, it is the horrid sameness of it all that is beginning to depress me, nothing indeed ever changes. This war, that murder, this threat, that playgirl. A new show opening. An old show closing. Nudity. Burlesque. Assassination. Pornography. Indeed life is a cycle but cannot it get, perhaps, onto a slightly larger wheel?

I digress. There have been, in the last few hours since my last return, strange noises in the cellar outside; noises as if creatures were prowling around, scuttling in the area, checking out my room among other things and carrying whispered reports to one another. I know that this is impossible, there is no problem of vermin in this locale and the only tenants who come down to check the boiler are invariably elderly, much advanced toward senility and hardly in what I might refer to as the Communicable State; they are people whose dialogue, if at all, runs to things like "Fuck 'em up, Jonny," or, "Sure thing, Willy boy got a cold one today," or "Chester, you betcha, I watch them feet," and "King is coming to town today" and so on. The particular shame of this dwelling, which I might as well admit and be done with it is that it is occupied by a large and seemingly growing population of people who have outlived their rightful tenancy on earth and are now descending (or ascending, it all depends upon how you look at it) toward incontinence, drooling and slow ranting monologue, they cannot, however, be taken to nursing homes because their rent-controlled apartments rent for something less than one-fifth of what they would bring on the "open market" and younger relatives can only keep the aging tenants in until they die so that they can then take over the lease... whereas if the tenant is exiled to a nursing home he will of course lose his right to the property and the relatives, because of some obscure proviso in the rent code, cannot take over quarters that have not been died in unless they are willing to pay the market rent. All very puzzling and confusing, in any event it is neither the pensioners nor their elderly pets who are prowling around outside but someone or something *else* and although Idiom has always kept—excuse me, I meant to say that *I* have always kept of course—his paranoia within reasonable limits it is exceedingly difficult to maintain one's calm in the face of this strange situation.

In any event, the door here is well-bolted and double-locked, I have at arm's reach a telephone to call the police—not that I want to call the police at this particular time—and I will hold onto myself and finish this. I have decided not to make it a diary of the decade after all. Make it a diary of the first two days of the decade and be done with it. All America known within that microcosm, all span and swoop of life perceived in that tiny space. Besides, I am becoming rather bored with it. I can understand now that I have for too long been wrapped up within myself; have been listening and attending too greatly to the tinny, tiny, slightly piercing and almost dwarfish ring of my own voice which, after a time, has become a paradigm of what I take to be "life" and which may indeed be no such thing. It is time to get out into the world. It is time to put away childish things. It is time to cast aside journals, notes, mutterings, mumblings, vague communications and embark upon the bright spaces of possibility. "Relationships!" "Mutually satisfactory arrangements!" "Therapeutic binds!" "Meaningful encounters!" This is what we must look for as the decade's days increase and swell toward the apocalypse of the eighties. Or of the nineties. It is hard to tell.

But not journals.

In any event.

After *Jingling Spurs and Lariats* had been so engagingly read to her, Rona commenced a series of efforts to leave the premises hastily. "I tell you," she said, "I just don't want to talk anymore. To hear anymore. It's all been very nice and I appreciate it but I've got to go now. I think it's best."

"But why?" I said, having dropped the novel in astonishment (as I believe I have already mentioned) in a set of uneven sheaves on the floor. "Did it frighten you? It's a perfectly reasonable piece of writing, you know."

She shook her head violently and said, "No, it didn't frighten me. Really it didn't. I never get frightened, I wish I could. I just feel that it's time to go now. I mean that—"

"Not yet," I said.

"What's that?"

"I said not yet. I still have a little more to tell you, Rona. Then you'll know all about me and we'll be ready to do anything. But you can't leave until I've told you."

She stood up straight, dignified for all her nudity (or perhaps because of it) and said, "Are you trying to say that you'll stop me from leaving this room?"

"Of course I'm saying that!" I said. "But that doesn't mean I'll have to; it just means that you'll be nice and reasonable and that way we won't have any problems at all. Of course I can't speak for my actions if you do the unpredictable but really, who could? Besides, there's no such thing as the predictable."

She subsided slowly on the bed, a dull film coming over her eyes and shook her head, then did something with a loose sheet across her forehead, mopping it slowly. "I knew it," she said. "Somehow, I knew I'd always wind up in something like this. They warned me. Everybody warned me. Everybody saw it coming except me; I was too smart and couldn't wait to make it happen. So it happened to me. Do you know?" she said and looked up at me brightly, "I think you're enjoying this. I really think you are. That's the truth of it."

"Not necessarily," I said. "Remember, I'm doing this for you. You were the one who wanted to know all about me, who insisted on qualifiers and background and so on. I would have been perfectly happy to have left it at the immediate level. But you wanted to be 'socially redeeming.' So you're getting your goddamned social redemption!" I shouted at her suddenly and with quite a bit of surprise because I did not think that ever again I would allow myself to "blow my cool" so to speak in a public situation. "And I hope you like it, the hell with it!"

She shook her head again and said, "No, you're wrong. I didn't want to know anything about you. I knew everything I wanted to know almost as soon as you went to bed with me. I knew it all then. But you wanted to tell me, you had this compulsion to tell me everything about yourself and so you made me sit and listen. You'd really stop me from leaving this room, wouldn't you? I mean, you'd use force and all like that. I didn't really faint, you know. I was lonely and frightened and embarrassed by being in a place like Times Square alone on a New Year's Eve and I was a little bit drunk and I thought that everybody was looking at me wondering why I was alone and when the firecracker went off I just kind of fell back on you. I had noticed that you were alone too only it didn't seem to bother you too much and you were kind of interesting looking and I figured if you turned out to be some kind of a nut, why, I'd find out right away and be able to lose you. Well, that will teach me, won't it?"

"There were no girl friends."

"No," she said, "no, there were no girl friends," and in silent and apparent confirmation of this, lifted up the sheet and snuggled down into it, drew it up under her armpits and sighed, rolled around in the bed, stared at the ceiling although not with any great interest. "Of course there weren't any girl friends; I've been in New York all by myself for just three weeks, the only people I've met are silly gross sons-of-bitches who want to feel me up or get me into bed—those are the normal ones; then I'm getting the bastards who just want to go somewhere with me and have a relationship by talking about their pet dogs or something. I haven't met a single man in New York in three weeks who had anything on his mind except some kind of sex but that's all right because the girls don't either, it's just that I haven't met any of the types who would be interested in me. What did you expect? I mean, what *could* you expect?"

"So why did you come to this city?" Idiom said, suddenly quite interested in the girl and her story. "Socially redeeming" or not Idiom found himself curiously piqued, not only by curiosity, but by a simple idiot kind of necessity to "know it all," to understand what he was dealing with not only as a fundamental abstraction but as a "person." It was a totally new experience for Idiom who had for a long time seen people as "abstractions" who had to be "dealt with in a disciplined way" in order to yield any meaningful results and at times he had wondered with a wry detachments whether this was simple common sense or a clear case of schizoid functioning. "I said, why did you come?" Idiom said rather sharply to the girl who had stopped talking and, in a complete kind of languor, seemed to be assessing the size and profusion of the cracks on the ceiling, of which there were indeed many since the owners of Idiom's dwelling were not conscientious landlords and tended to let repairs lapse in the hope that they would kill off at least a couple of the pensioners suddenly in the night, before the relatives could come in.

"Oh," the girl said, "oh, I just wanted to be an actress. Doesn't everyone? I had this bit in college, before I dropped out, in the drama society and so on and then I had a little bit of stock and there was this girl I knew who had hard-knocked it for a while and said it wasn't too bad if you could get a couple of commercials, one good commercial could keep you going for years and in any event you could connect with them easily if you were willing to fuck the right person. Oh, I have nothing against the *fucking*, you see," she said flatly, "I mean, it's not a new thing or anything like that; I've been around and I know fucking. It's just finding the people that you need to fuck and then making them want to fuck you; you see, the problem is that you can't tell the ones who will do you some good from the ones who just want to use you and can't do a damned thing but you have to put out in all ways to get anywhere and then, where the hell does it get you? I wish I could get out of here. I don't feel well. I mean, you're not the kind of nut who would imprison me and keep me on a chain to bring me food and hide me from the outside world, would you? I saw a movie about that kind of stuff once and it got me sick. I'd rather be dead than that."

"You've got me wrong," Idiom said hoarsely. "You've got me entirely wrong. It's nothing like that at all. I just wanted to talk to you, that's all."

"Yeah, well that's what happened in this movie. The guy just wanted to talk to the girl and he wound up talking to her for six months and she *never* got out of there. Those are the ones you really have to watch, the ones who want to just talk. Let me tell you. Let me tell you a thing or two; I could tell you a lot."

"So go on," Idiom said. "Tell me more. I want to know. I can't say I know everything. I'm just a part-time botanist and a Western writer with a little background in the social services. There are whole things I don't understand. I'll listen to anything you have to tell me. Please. I don't mind. You tell me everything you want to say and I'll just listen," and wiped a hand across a forehead which seemed, to Idiom's blunted, muzzled judgment to be virtually agleam with sweat; a feeling of quaking up and down his armpits, strange disconcertment quite foreign to Idiom who, he was sure, had never quite lost control of a situation in the way that he saw himself losing control of this one. Everything for Idiom had always been too easy; he had lived a circumscribed life—this much is true—but within its limits he had defined things pretty well:

he had carried within himself for a long time that peculiar sense of destiny and imminent salvation which are so close to the sense of America and it had never occurred to him, not even for a moment, that a time might come, a situation might evolve, when he would not be bailed out by some extrinsic force of enormous beneficence which had been concentrating on—and in fact guiding—his personal destiny for a good long time. In part Idiom supposed that this was because of the movies; he had seen more than a few in his adolescence, and they gave you a certain way of looking at the world which was not entirely inaccurate but in any event was certainly pervasive, in part it had to do with Joseph and Mary who had always referred to him as their "special son" and their "path of redemption" and so on and had never quite forsaken the illusion that someday Idiom, at the head of a colonnade of white horses and shouting generals, would lead his parents back into their small home country in triumph, right straight to the Ministry of Government offices where he would shoot the present administration dead and put his parents back in their rightful custody. The trouble was—and Idiom had learned this only much later and in a rather dismaying third-hand way—that Joseph and Mary were not royalty or even aristocracy in their country but were in fact, menial stock of the most disaffected and abused type, the kind of people who would till fields in an agricultural economy and in an industrial arrangement would probably run candy stores. It was only the haste and bitterness of their "exile" and the very name of their country itself, odorous and faintly glamorous, reeking of the scent of castles and dogs baying on moors which had allowed them to convey the impression that they were in any way "special" people. In any event, coming into his 34th year, Idiom was just beginning to be able to judge the degree of damage which Joseph and Mary had done to him: they had done it in the best of spirits, of course, and they had given him the feeling that in any given circumstance he would be able to get control, but they had not prepared him well for a world which was totally unreasonable, a country which was completely insane and Idiom found himself now and again trembling on the verge of an insight: an insight that he was beyond redemption, cold, frozen and stricken out of purpose and that in no way whatsoever was he going to be able to "retrieve" any kind of special destiny because he had done. Destiny was only for people you saw walking around in the movies or heard lecturing you on their manifest, but it was not for Idiom himself, the humble persona and recipient of all these convictions. All of this came forcibly back through Idiom as he listened to the girl speak and he found that it was only with a great and increasing effort of control that he said, "Well, that's the way things work out. You have to understand the kind of city this is."

"I don't want to talk anymore," she said, having turned sullen during Idiom's intricate chain of speculation. "Now let me go home."

"Not just yet. I told you, I haven't finished. I want to tell you a few more things. Don't you have anything to tell me yet?"

"No. No I don't. Not a thing. Why is there so much noise outside this place? I thought you told me no one ever came down here."

"I thought so too," Idiom said. "I can't explain it. Maybe it has to do with the weather. Maybe they're huddling near the door for warmth." But he did not go to the door to check this out because Idiom did not want to see what was out there. If anything was out there.

I want to tell you (Idiom then went on to say, making sure that the girl was comfortably ensconced on the bed for the time being, even going over to plump a pillow for her, set it under her feet, give her another for her head and then step back to look at the portrait she made: one of engaging indolence, well, she deserved no less) about Idiom's most crucial and therefore final formative incident which had to do of course with the incident of the Fraternity Orgy and the Great Traveling Whore. In order to understand this it is necessary that you travel back both some years in time and some distance in spirit to envision the nature of the "public college" during the time that Idiom attended it which was, perhaps, in the middle years of the decade before last when sex, except for married students, was a very rare and exceptional thing and where an Orgy with a Traveling Whore coming out of the network of purest fantasy, so to speak, would obviously have the most critical effect upon the life of any participant. As a matter of fact, Idiom knows that of the forty-odd people in attendance at this orgy, no less than thirty were changed by it in some serious and quietly desperate fashion. He was one of them and the way in which he was affected was perhaps in its profundity the greatest shift of all but he had no reason to be sure of that; now and again, Idiom would meet or hear reports of his "fraternity brothers" as they made their way in the "outside world" and by reason of the various disasters, alternations and occupational shifts which seemed to occur to them he had reason to believe that, no less than he, they lived in a state of perpetual astonishment, being in a world where the unalterable could open up at any moment to disclose a crevice filled with a pack of faces in greasepaint, gross clowns stumbling around in that pit, fooling around with the various manipulations of outcome. It was a strange thing for Idiom to think that the episode of the Fraternity Orgy and the Great Traveling Whore may have been for him and his "fraternity brothers" what the army was supposed to be for an earlier and gentler generation—that is, the first great common shared experience.

Idiom attended the "public college" in his district and commuted to it daily by subway; this college which he attended was famous for the fact that during the years of the Depression or earlier it had been attended by a large number of poverty-stricken people who later went on to become financiers, authors, economists or Presidential advisors and were invited back to the college now and then to tell the more recent crop of students exactly how they could do the same thing. Idiom found himself wondering, time and again, how any man who had to go home every evening and face his parents could possibly come to a large destiny from his college years, but none of this seemed to bother the financiers or advisors, none of whom ever referred to anything as banal as a "sex life" during their tours to the college; apparently for their generation sex was an incidental like subway fare which was simply extrinsic to the whole series of larger purposes which drove them and could thus be dismissed. For these reasons as well as many others, Idiom found that most of his experiences at the college drove him into a wild depression, the same kind of depression which he was to encounter years and years later from mystery novels—which similarly seemed to have nothing whatsoever to do with the common realities of the reader. The girls were mostly drab, enclosed sorts: no less than the men they lived with their parents and came trailing into the college at various hours in a state of stunned disarray but floating behind the drab aspect of these girls were a series of rumors that such and such a given man was "getting it from something good" and Idiom, although he found himself hard put to imagine anything good coming within ten miles of this public college, allowed these rumors to flay him into states which for sheer color and emotional excitement went far beyond his normal reactive depression. He and his fellow students knew that there was no action whatsoever; anything that was going on occurred in the huge private university some half a mile to the south and separated from the public college by much more than space; in the private colleges people had money, not to say "privacy," and Idiom was only to find out much later and in rather soporific circumstances that things at the private college—in fact, things at *all* colleges at this time—were essentially no different. But this insight, like most of the truly important insights Idiom had ever had came substantially too late to do him any good ... or to give him, when it finally descended, any feeling of epiphany.

Idiom was fortunate enough, however, to be able to join a fraternity in his sophomore year. This particular "fraternity"—like all such organizations at the college—was not to be associated with the kind of organizations which he read about in books and for the private-university members of such appeared to be a continuous tumult of fucking, drinking, camaraderie and shouting, all of it relieved by occasional dismayed visits from the Dean who, once he saw the error of his ways, would join in for a bit of fucking himself. No, this "fraternity" consisted of three dismal furnished rooms on the fifth floor of an old walk-up dwelling about half a mile from the college; the rooms were furnished with a couple of desks, mattresses on the floor for members to "flake out" and a small assortment of liquor bottles, almost all of them empty, which the members quarreled over for deposits. The major function of this fraternity, due to its mattresses, was to allow various members to "flake out" in its room during pauses between classes and Idiom quickly found that his initiation dues and ceremony had only taken him into some kind of Sleeping Society but twice a year, out of desperation, the fraternity threw a "party" on a Saturday night, a major affair during which girls were supposed to join the fraternity members in an unparalleled explosion of fucking, drinking and conversation which would enable the fraternity, the ensuing Monday morning, to take its own place in the rumors pantheon.

Unfortunately, the overwhelming majority of the members neither knew any girls or were capable of inviting them to a "party," and there had been a number of disasters in this fraternity in the past: at one party several years ago the members had arrived for their "blast" to find only one dismal coed sitting on one of the mattresses, surrounded by a heap of beer cans—and her heavy, trembling fiancé who kept his arm around her throughout the evening and refused to permit her to even go to the bathroom, much less talk to the fraternity brothers who were able to work themselves into a state of drunkenness only through the diligent application of beer which eventually left them sick and reeling and the apartment, if not the coed, rather in a shambles. After this cataclysm and the stories of it which had spread through the campus and made the fraternity a laughing stock—nobody at this college was getting laid but precisely because of this, those who weren't getting laid *publicly* were in even deeper trouble than they would have been at a private school—there had been a high policy meeting which had even included a visit from the vice-president of the fraternity's impoverished "national" (which saw this particular unit of the fraternity as something of a disgrace and refused even to list it in its year-end reports and fraternity newsletter although everyone knew perfectly well that the fraternity's first chapter had been this very one) and which had resulted in a shift of the party's auspices and purposes so that now, instead of inviting coeds, none of whom for the brothers existed or would have come, prostitutes were invited for the Spring party, two or three of them, at a fee decided upon by pre-arrangement and pool, and then made themselves useful throughout the evening getting the brothers drinks and screwing the few who were interested in doing so. The prostitutes who came, of course from the neighborhood of the college which was one of the most impoverished and disadvantaged in the United States, were generally rather ugly, desperate women who looked upon their duties with mingled contempt and hope: the way they lived, they found that the parties put them in contact with what they took to be a great deal of "money" and the fraternity brothers themselves found that the new arrangement was a very satisfactory one because they were now able to let it be known through the college that these parties, rather than being "social" in nature, were purely "stag" affairs where a number of healthy, hearty nicely-functioning heterosexual males could get away from the bodies of their girl friends for one Saturday night and indulge their simplest and most ancient desires. By proxy, so to speak, Idiom found that this reputation rubbed off on him and when he was initiated into this fraternity he found that people regarded him and its pin with at least a moderate awe and told him that he had got into "the best place in this damned hole." It was a valuable lesson for Idiom; the fraternity had failed worst by trying to accomplish what the new arrangement lied about whereas it was a brilliant success simply by denying all reasonable chance of helping the members socially, and Idiom never forgot it although he did become an inactive alumnus shortly—upon his graduation—and never met the yearly dues tithe which the fraternity was seeking in order to build the largest fraternity house in the world at the University of Wichita, a building which, they assured the alumni, would give them international prestige.

At the particular party at issue, the one in his sophomore year, Idiom arrived somewhat earlier than most of the brothers to find that the apartment was occupied by the "President" of the house and the "quorum" chairman, two thin nervous youths who were in the process of passing in and out of the engineering school rapidly, and a rather striking whore in a strapless gown who sat between them on the couch with a can of beer in her hand and regarded Idiom rather sullenly while he took off his coat, put it in a closet and went to get some beer of his own. Idiom was nervous because he knew of the reputation of the parties and what he was supposed to do but found it all a shocking newness; the fact that, by virtue of Gloria, he was not a virgin, did not seem to him to be of any particular help in the present circumstances which were quite tense and strained. He nodded to the whore, trying to make it a civilized, detached gesture and was on the way to the bathroom—where he intended to sit and solemnly drink until more guests arrived—when the President called him over to the couch and nodded at him and said, "Let me tell you what's going on tonight? Marcia, this is one of our new pledges, Idiom Lament." (This is not what he said of course; instead he gave Idiom's real first and last names but in the context of this memoir it will have to serve and 1 will not tell you the whore's real name either except that it definitely was not Marcia. I wish to protect the lady's reputation, you see: there is no telling how far she might have gone by now.) "I'm pleased to meet you, I'm sure," the whore said with a tired shake of her head, extended a pair of crossed fingers and put them limpidly into Idiom's hand, then sighed and settled back on the couch again with a rather confused shake of her head. She was not the ordinary turn-of-the-mill whore, that was damned certain, and even though Idiom had not been at one of these parties previously he suspected that the President and initiation head had made the same judgment. "Listen, Idiom," the President said hoarsely, "I'm glad you came a little early so we could ask you something. Do you have twenty bucks?"

"What's that?"

"Twenty bucks," the initiation head said. They did indeed look remarkably similar, head and President, flanking the whore; only the whore provided an odd, somehow anachronistic centerpiece, her gown not only sensual but imparting an air of *style* which rather uplifted the whole tone of the rooms from their more normally dismal aspect. "I mean, we have to ask everybody who comes here that. Those who don't have it on them, well, maybe we can advance a little money but it has to be twenty dollars a head."

"Why?" said Idiom. "I don't understand," although of course, in his best mode—even at the age of twenty—he was being duplicitous and did indeed get the drift very well. The whore and he exchanged a drifting look of pure apprehension over the heads of the other two and one eye, in stunned languor, seemed to wink, then she patted her breasts back in place with a free hand, took up a can of beer from the floor and began to sip.

"You see," she said. "I'm taking on all of you. That's the arrangement. But it's got to be twenty dollars a man, nothing less."

"She's a showgirl," the head said with a kind of horrid confidentiality, lifting a palm to shield this information from the whore which was peculiar since, of course, she would have to know it already. "She works down on the East Side and she's absolutely tremendous. It's a fair deal, don't you think?"

"It's only because I need the money," the whore said. "I got into a little spot of trouble and I've got to get a few hundred bucks. I mean, that's what they promised me and it's worth it. Of course if it can't be worked out ..."

"It can be worked out," the President said heavily. "Believe me, we'll work it out." He seemed under stress for some odd reason and the whore smiled at him, raised her shoulders in a tentative giggle and then, in a strange gesture, ran a hand along his forehead, bringing gleaming sweat to his engineer's brow, then ducked the finger down into her cleavage where she poked around for an instant. Her breasts were quite large, quite well-maintained by the gown; Idiom wondered vaguely if they would live up to their promise in the nude but decided that whether they would or wouldn't, this knowledge would come too late to change the situation.

"Twenty dollars," Idiom said. "That would be about six hundred bucks if everyone comes."

"I know," the President said, "I know it's a lot of money, of course it is, but the thing is that when you get it down to a price per man it isn't so much at all and it's worth everything. I thought that it would be a good thing to do because the party last year was lousy. Besides, I *know* Marcia and she's really good." The initiation head gave an assenting groan when this was said and seemed to sink down further on the couch, then flapped an indolent arm around the girl and drew her into him. She came rather easily, turning her face toward his neck which led Idiom to the logical conclusion that both the President and head had already probably paid their share; either that or the inducement was that they had promised to use their influence to raise the money in return for free services. It hardly mattered. While it is to be clearly understood that the Idiom of this time was not the superbly detached, intellectualized and mature Idiom of such extraordinary accomplishments today, he was, at the least, a good version of the Artist At A Younger Age and suspected that the situation, fraught with menace or veniality or simple ineptitude was not one which was to be taken entirely without suspicion ... Nevertheless he said, in a high voice that hardly sounded like his own—when some angle of drapery in the bending gave him an excellent view of the whore's left breast, right down to the nipple, and an excellent breast it appeared to be—"All right, I'll go in for it. I have it on me. But I can't put up anyone else's share, that's all that I've got."

"But that's fine," the President said in a voice equally high, and the whore flounced around on the couch, patted a small space open and Idiom wedged himself into a crevice between the President and the whore where he found himself suddenly caught in her embrace; her softness enveloped him and she kissed him with real interest, saying,

"I knew you fraternity boys were just going to be wonderful to me. I just knew it," and dropping her hand into cleavage, gave Idiom a splendid and almost uninterrupted view of her breast for the next five minutes during which time Idiom stared, the President and the head chuckled to one another in uneasy boyish giggles and the whore sat with her head high, an expression of unusual placidity and warmth—which seemed to literally fill the room—flooding her features with what Idiom thought then and now was the greatest look of perception which he had even seen on a person's face.

And the thing was that it all worked out very well: much easier than the President or the head had probably thought it would; with Idiom now converted to the cause of the whore it meant that there was solid phalanx of three of them now to convert the others as they came and one by one they yielded to the girl's smile, the President's persistence and Idiom's own frail wink which indicated that he had seen the girl and she was good. Of the eighteen men who came, all but three went along with the idea: one of them, put under pressure admitted in terror that he was a homosexual and while he had always been *interested* in girls and wanted to *learn something about them*, he did not feel that these were the proper circumstances for what would be his fumbling initiation, one said that he did not have the money and in any event had never paid for it in all his life and never would and wouldn't have to and then had tried to interest a couple of the others in abandoning the party for a "beer blast" in a neighboring tavern where they could watch a baseball game in progress, and the third, another pledge, had made the insane choice to bring his girl friend to the party, a heavy, unhappy girl with a mustache and a frenzied expression when the drift of the party was gradually made apparent to her: this would have been bad enough but what made things even worse in that case was that the girl suddenly began to get very interested in the proposition and started to say things to the pledge like, "Aw, what the hell, Marvin, let's give it a try," and "It's not as if you'd do anything, we'd just watch," and "How many really interesting things ever go on in this place anyway that we should pass one up?" and "She's really pretty, isn't she kind of built, Marvin?" and so on until Marvin finally took his date forcibly out of there, causing her to scuttle with great rapidity out of the door still making offers, propositions, calculations, until the door closed with a slam and the President went to lock it and said, "Well, anybody else who comes tonight is out of luck," and then a large amount of money, in cash, was put in front of the whore who took it with a placid expression, smiled gratefully at them and tucked it into her handbag, which handbag she gave to the initiation head and said, "I get this back at the end of the evening with everything in it. If everything isn't in it I'll leave and come back with a gun and kill you all," causing the head to shake his head in frantic agreement and take the pocketbook with trembling fingers, looking frantically for a place safe enough to hide it. "All right," the whore said to the room at large, standing and with unusual grace and facility, unzipping her gown from the back, dropping it to the floor and letting them see that underneath it she had been wearing nothing at all and that she had not been cheating on her breasts in the slightest. They were, in fact, rather magnificent although Idiom lacked at that time standards against which to compare them and settled dimly for thinking that she looked "something like an actress" or some such nonsense. It is to be understood that at that time Idiom's standards of comparison in the matter of women were almost nil and it is possible thus that he tends to exaggerate today not only the whore's body but her very beauty; possibly she was not very much at all and has only attained a kind of retrospective attraction which might be obliterated if he had a good cold look at her today at the age of 33 with all of his superb accomplishments and background behind him. This does not matter.

There was, then, a very embarrassing moment because for a definable period of time after the girl had removed her dress, patting it neatly into an even heap on the floor, no one knew exactly what to do. They had read about orgies presumably, they had certainly talked about them, but the sheer etiquette, the stage management of the orgy was beyond them at this stage and for quite a while men stood in embarrassed nodding clusters and looked at the whore, checking the look of each other's eyes until the whore said suddenly, "Well, for God's sake, isn't anyone going to play? The bedroom or right here?" and seized the nearest figure which happened, unsurprisingly, to be Idiom's and drew him against her with a groan, tumbling back into the couch, cushions flying in the air, and a crack of laughter in the room. Everyone, it seemed, was delighted that Idiom was going to be the first. "Go to it!" and then someone else said "Do it, man!" and Idiom felt the whore wind and flex against him and she whispered into his ear, "Come on, let's show them how to do it, they're all afraid to be the first" and giggled at him rather harshly and Idiom felt a flutter of sensation in his stomach; it was hard to define, hard to know exactly what his metabolism was up to but it might have been far. Behind him he had the impression that there was a kind of increased attention, a moving in of bodies and when he looked up briefly he saw that almost everyone in the room had come to circle around the couch, looking at the two of them with solemn expressions which seemed to have less lust than sheer *curiosity* on them; they seemed to want to know what it was like to copulate. A hint of puzzlement shone in their engineers' eyes, their apprentice-architects' faces, their pre-medical visages and Idiom fluttered against the girl and said, "Couldn't we do it in the bedroom?" and she said "Of course not, what would we want to do it in the bedroom for, they want us to do it right here, be a sport now, come on," and because Idiom's most obsessed desire, as long as he could remember, was to be a "sport," someone who in his simple acceptance of the insane codes and various convolutions of his country could be understood to be someone who would never, ever try to meddle with its understructure, Idiom felt his resistance ebb and he bent his lips to the whore's ear again, beginning to bite and nip tentatively. He wanted to say to her, "All right, what the hell," but somehow couldn't quite make the words come; he settled for a series of groans and hums which he hoped sounded sensual and then put his hands inside her cleavage, feeling and fondling the empty space between her breasts, then spread them and cupped her breasts fully and began to squeeze. For the first time it occurred to him that the whore was naked and that, granted the rather public mode of the situation, he was perfectly free to do anything he wanted to her, a rare circumstance which he had never previously enjoyed with any woman. "That's good," the girl muttered, "that's good," whether out of reciprocal encouragement or real desire he did not know and he began to work on her breasts in either event with somewhat more interest and intensity and someone said, "Look at that, look at that!" referring, he supposed, to what he was doing with the breasts although it might have only been in reaction to some casual disturbance in the room, some flurry of activity, because there was a rustling of bodies and someone in the background screamed incoherently and then Idiom, still trying to maintain his concentration, heard a series of running sounds much as if someone were being hustled out of the room with great speed and force, there was a violent slam of door, flush of toilet, gurgle of water, things he could not possibly assess because the thing was that he was beginning to become very interested for the first time in what he was doing. Instead of being impotent which had been his chief fear about the whole thing he took himself to be enormously functioned with her and here, given the benefit so to public, in the vanguard, so to speak, of the evening's revolution, only whipped him into a further excitement. "Oh, oh," Idiom gurgled in a high, strained voice, thinking perversely of Gloria and wondering vaguely what she would think of him now; he supposed that she had not been entirely pleased by the way that he had functioned with her and her, given the benefit so to speak, of a second chance, he would have tried to make it up to her but the whore was now working under him with a passionate, monotonous intensity and, rearing up on his elbows to look at her as she began to struggle with his clothing, it occurred to Idiom for the first time that she was quite stoned, quite drunk, that is to say or maybe it was merely drugs, her eyes bleached and wide in her face, staring numbly, her forehead wrinkling in a nervous intensity, her nose whiffing out uneven pants of breath—and her mouth was murmuring things like, "Don't stop, just let me get them off," and "Isn't this the craziest?" and "Look at all those bastards being jealous," and similar statements which to Idiom's rather limited mind at the time spoke to him as evidences of either her insanity or her submission to a state of drugs more profound than any awakeness he had ever known. He figured that any girl to do the things she was doing with him would have to be quite drunk or worse, not understanding until many years later that he had done similar things cold sober or at least, in Idiom, what passed for "sobriety" but there was little enough time for reflection; by a series of careful adjustments and calculations she had managed to get most of his clothing off and then Idiom moved heavily on top of her, hearing the couch creak in either protest or lust, it was hard to tell, and then with concentration and facility he began to fuck her, feeling with astonishment the ease of the conjoinment she made and then allowing himself to follow his prick blindly, moving all the way into her and there with swooning ease and enormous pride Idiom accomplished the act of generation which is to say that he fucked the whore.

Through the room now there were sounds, shouts, cheers, remonstrances, bellows of joy, greed, sadness or loss; men—although Idiom's blinded senses could hardly assimilate this but only left a series of impressions which he was then later able to dissect—were standing around him in a gallery of response which included, as far as he could tell, every conceivable emotion: it ran from lust to revulsion and all the states in between not excluding boredom, curiosity, joy and sanctimony and the faces, seeming luminescent in the thin, streaking light of the room, seeming to hang in uneven rows before his eyes, seemed to have rather the aspect of bulbs in a subway car, winking and blinking off-angle as he allowed his little train to speed him home, rocking and buffeting within her and he bent his lips down to her neck, bit her with intensity, squeezed her breasts, patted her thighs, sucked a nipple and came into her with the vanishing sigh of an imploded balloon, falling, falling, petals curling in upon themselves as he collapsed on her body in a state of exhaustion, only a strange, sifting querulousness at the center of his purposes seeming to extrude on a thin branch from which a face peered out and asked him: *Why? Why anyway?*

What's the point? What's the difference?

"Don't know," Idiom said aloud to the voice. "Don't know, it's just something that has to be done, isn't that right?" and in his youthful ardor not to say his reawakened lust, tried to screw her again but his dick was limpid or at least somehow pulverized and in addition the whore made a series of vigorously non-cooperating gestures which, in his weakened state, were sufficient to dislodge him from her interiors and he bumped off the couch in a state of shamed awkwardness, prick dangling heavily, semen still oozing in thin trickles from some disappointed vesicles unrelieved outside and stumbled away to a corner of the room, feeling himself in an obscurely equivocal state where it was almost impossible for him to frame any kind of reaction; he simply did not know how he felt. It had been one of the most dislocating experiences of his life but in what way he was not quite sure, whether it thrust him to a new level of insight or only to a kind of abysmal stricture where for the rest of his life a fuck would be an event contracted in a corridor tenanted by strangers he did not know, but at that moment the President said from some other corner of the room, perhaps stuffed in an alcove, "Son of a bitch, let's give him a cheer!" and there was a thin crackle of rowdy, rising applause which spread throughout the room until it enveloped Idiom. It was only much later that he understood that the applause was without irony and that more than anything else what was being cheered was his sheer ability to function which, under the circumstances, had been remarkable and which each of the applauders had reasons, in his individual and forthcoming case, to somewhat doubt. The whore, coming in at the dead stopping-point of the applause, caused it to build anew and to even a higher level by saying "Okay, men, who's next? Next!" and the room for Idiom then seemed to dissolve in streaks of light and pulsating darkness as a reassembly of witnesses began and someone else took his place on the Infernal Couch. It seemed to be the President this time, as was only fair, but Idiom was not watching too closely and could not be sure.

("So what?" his audience said to Idiom. "So what? So you got it for the first time at a gang-bang? It doesn't mean anything to me. I mean, you talk about it as if it's the most unusual thing in the world. Most girls get it for the first time within ten yards of their parents when you come right down to it. So what's what? I can't see that it makes anything of anybody."

("You don't understand again," Idiom said with vast tiredness. "You've got to understand that this is a *public* country. Everything takes place now in the open arena, is manipulated in that direction. So you'd have to see that to find sex for the first time in that way—"

("You know what I think?" his audience said and leaned up on an elbow, "and I'm not even scared of you, the hell with you, you're not going to scare me with your cheap tricks. I think that you just have a tendency for self-pity and self-dramatization. You think you're so exceptional. You think that everything that occurs to you is so important just because it happens to you and you have to dress up the whole thing with a strange way of talking and putting things in order, but you want to know something? It doesn't mean a damned thing. There's no difference at all. You've got to learn to live in the world."

("I do live in the world," Idiom responded. "I'm trying to educate you to that small portion of it in which I dwell; remember, all of this done in answer to your own request. You got it started. It would have been perfectly well if you had left it at the initial level. But you wanted to be 'socially redeeming'."

("I think you're insane," his companion said, flouncing back on the bed and looking up at the ceiling with a graceful pout, "do you know that? I think that you're completely insane and also you're beginning to bore me. So why don't you finish the story already?"

("There isn't that much more of it to tell. It's almost all finished."

("So just why don't you go ahead and finish it up and be done with it?"

("I will. I was in the process of doing so when you interrupted me."

("You always say that you're finishing up but you never do. It's just endless. Don't you ever stop? Doesn't there come a time when you can't stand it anymore and you just have to stop talking?"

("You don't understand," Idiom said, "it's so difficult. I live so alone and it's so hard to find anyone to listen and then when they do they're not really listening, they're just waiting their turn. And there are no easy answers. You must not render unto me unjustly. I deserve the complexity from which I came. I tell you, nothing here is easy, there are no easy answers. In fact—"

("Oh, for God's sake—"

("All right, then," Idiom said, regaining his control with a grunt and giving his companion a careful pat on the surrounding sheets, trying to smile at her with a smile which would relieve her unease and bring him to his own superb level of accommodating function and realization. "All right then, don't worry about it. Idiom is almost finished. I mean, I am almost finished."

("Is there any difference?"

("I don't know," he said. "Can't you understand that? I simply don't know.")

The point of this incident (Idiom then continued after only a slight pause during which he got up from the bed, strolled to the window of his apartment so that he could look at the greyness of a grate sopping with snow and filtering ash down to the level of his rooms, walking over to the door then to check the thump of the boiler, finally coming back and resuming his easy, narrative stance) is that all of his life, Idiom had been directed by the heart and soul of America which was to be found in its technology and media to believe that sex was a private act which somehow exalted and ennobled its participants and the act of having sex—any kind of sex, anywhere—somehow made its participant superior to the ruck of humanity but what he had gathered in a flash was that this was not necessarily so and that sex, as an act, could become as routinized and public as eating or going through the corporate tumult of the stock market. That was the point: it could be anything, it was only a neutral quality, sex was, like life or death or madness it could be shaped in any way whatsoever by the occupant, it could be glimpsed in any fashion and there was no way to say that it had any particular qualities whatsoever other than those of sheer presence: and if this were so—Idiom guessed that this was so—it meant that sex could literally be anything, be used for any purposes, take on any guises which the participant wanted. Coming as it did so highly at variance with that fine sentimentality which had so distinguished Idiom's predecessors and ancestors from the run of humanity, coming as it did with a rather shocking force beyond Idiom's ability to subsume and intellectualize it, this insight left him quite numb and drained although not incurious: past the first moments of his astonishment he began to feel his interest returning in small bursts and quivers, much as a sleeping child might slowly pull itself together and make pleas for food, Idiom found that the events in the room began to come back into more and more intense focus, color was added, noise, streaks of light and temperature and he saw that the whore, having passed on from the President, was now taking on one of the pledges in the front entrance while in the rear a senior man was avidly buggering her, squatting dog-like on the floor, his face a mask of astonishment to equal Idiom's own as he huffed and pumped. The whore had managed this spectacular double entrance by getting down on hands and knees, squatting dog-like then and even the sounds of the intercourse were animaline; the boys yelped and whined like puppies in a pound, the one who was buggering squeezed and kneaded the whore's breasts with the kind of desperate clawing gesture of an animal working unsuccessfully on a cage, mewling, yelling, the one in front, meanwhile, had managed to make his entrance by lying fully on his back, legs slightly flexed and extended and was trying industriously to pull the whore down upon him, being resisted by the buggerer who, of course, was holding her up.

The men were, thus, struggling less against the girl than against themselves: to Idiom's rather palsied and inaccurate gaze it looked as if it could be said that the men were not fucking the whore so much as one another—with the whore only a kind of medium and interposition to keep things rooted at a rationalization, at a heterosexual level of some sort. More device than participant she submitted to all of this with a smug, bleak expression, her eyes seeming to roll and half-retract in her face, her mouth twisted into a fine line, her cheeks showing sudden creases and lines of strain and the noise continued, the pumping continued, there were squawls and yells and at one point one of the men must have come because he groaned and crawled away but then he was replaced immediately by someone else and things continued; then the buggerer finished with a whoop and dislodged himself with some modest struggle and was replaced and then—

And then it became apparent to Idiom that things were getting somewhat out of control: whether it was the question of the extrinsic events or only his own breakdown was something that he could never quite resolve, perhaps a little bit of both, because what had started out one way began rapidly to take a different direction altogether, some kind of intensity building up in the actions of the men, some blind submissiveness discovered in the whore and no longer taking an initiatory role, in fact quite silent, she submitted over and over again to lines and lines of staggering men while Idiom—who in a certain sense could have been said to have started matters and thus was responsible for their development; this was an old fallacy in Idiom's thinking which he has, incidentally, never quite corrected, he still insists with lunatic persistence as seeing himself somehow as the *manipulator* of actions and therefore responsible to almost all of them in some degree, this has nothing to do with megalomania but only that sense of self-importance which was built into him at a delicate age—found that it was only by some massive application of discipline that he was able to prevent himself from calling "Halt, halt!" or its parodic equivalent and trying somehow to stave matters from their development, "Stop it!" he wanted to say. "Don't you understand that none of this will improve your social lives in the slightest and will, in fact, reduce your academic achievements while at the same time only giving you enough of a simulation of experience to disregard them; I tell you there must be an end to this!" and similar Calvinist pejoratives; all of them Idiom knew would sound somewhat out of place in the given circumstances and could rapidly make his position untenable. So what he did, still keeping one shallow, fascinated eye on the proceedings, all that he tried to do was to find his clothing and put it on and get out of there but he somehow couldn't concentrate on it, he found against his will that he could not stop looking at what was going on and as the bodies multiplied on top of an around the whore, as simultaneity of entrance seemed to become the cause of the moment Idiom could hardly resist shouting, "You goddamned idiots, in a gang-bang you take her *one at a time*, each man does what he wants to do and then passes on to the next, it's a social contract, a democracy!" because he had read about gang-bangs in various of the "socially redeeming" novels and knew that there was something wrong with this one but he said nothing, he kept his mouth closed, one could say if one were sentimental that he kept his heart closed too because his awareness of what was going on and its disastrous potential for the whore somehow traveled only as far as his brain stem and then stopped there in a kind of imploded blankness, below the neck nothing, no feeling, no action and the bodies swarmed, there was moaning, grunting, and at the low dead-center of this he thought he heard the whore cry, babbling, wordless, a long extended shriek which might have been only a cry of lust but might have again been a plea for help, you couldn't tell about things, you simply couldn't know; what you had to do was to try to disassociate yourself and Idiom got his clothes on and the cry resounded again, higher, more urgent this time and Idiom fastened his belt and someone grunted and there was the sound of a slap and a curse and, the cry again, although somewhat feeble and Idiom tucked in his shirt and put on his tie and there was silence and the movement of bodies, trickle of limbs, shifting of figures white and glowing in the hard bulb and Idiom got his coat and was fully dressed and what he did then, what Idiom did was to leave: he went to the door and he went out. He closed the door. Outside it was very quiet—the soundproofing in these old buildings was always excellent—and the hall seemed to tremor with insects and with precognition of a different sort, it was all very detached, it was a long distance off, it all did not seem to matter so much with the door closed and Idiom went down the stairs, trot-trot, clump-clump, went through the door, swish-bang-and into the street, hiss-roar and stood there for a while and Jesus Christ almighty I thought I had this thing licked but it's all starting again I don't know if I can stand this anymore what the hell am I trying to do what is going on? Oh well, I guess I should get another drink now but what good is a drink going to do me I should go to sleep the whore was screaming oh I'm so tired the girl was screaming, she looked up at me in the lostness of that small space, swimming at time-center and her eyes opened then to the youngest most engaging expression that I had ever seen, the child in her revealed at the moment of extinction, the child that is always there, the vulnerability that we spend our lives promoting or avoiding but never understanding and her mouth was open oh boy it's hot in this room and her eyes were open oh God I wish I could stop this now and she lifted herself up at me and said what she said and I couldn't stop myself she said it she didn't have to say it it is time for a drink it is time to stop the street was quiet, Idiom did not know where to go, he did not care about the whore anymore I don't care about the girl anymore I don't know about any of this and they are vaulting at the door now all of them coming to get me and I think I'd better quit now but I've got to finish this no why I've got to finish it look at that roach scuttling in the corner, where the hell did the son of a bitch come from? There is a kind of quiet knowledge in that scuttle, direction in his leap, conjoinment in his bounce as with insane precision and a geometrical sense of control he vanishes into some clear dark space at the other side of the room and is gone.

And later again. Later!

Well, there will be an end to this. I am sick and tired, sick and tired, I say, of interrupting this lucid, contained, beautifully structured narrative level of these notes with occasional frenetic bursts of what I must refer to as insanity which force me to interrupt my jottings and typings for an indeterminate time when I recoup. Apparently I lack the discipline of the professional novelist who is able to keep his mood consistent, his rhetoric even, this whole stunning explosion of *literacy* leaves me weakened and an irregular condition and has forced me into the embarrassing panegyrics which occasionally conclude sections. Such as the one previous. I have reread it now with cold, sober and detached brain and have seriously meditated its excision but have decided in the last analysis not to. Let it roll on! Let everything be contained! Let the fullest expression cometh forth! But there will be enough to this.

There will be enough; I am tired, tired, back in control of course and quite calm and contained but nevertheless too tired to continue this much further. This will be the last chapter of these notes. Not because it is an ending but because it is as far as I choose to go. I can see that my original intention to write a carefully segmented diary of this decade was completely or at least moderately insane. There is simply no way that these things can be compartmentalized. No way at all. Things are not locked into separate cubicles of chronology, there is what we would refer to in the industrial technology, a kind of machine waste. Pollution! Dispersal! Engine loss! In any event, we will wrap this up and call it an ending. There is more than enough material here to point in various directions. Everything will only be a re-enactment of the basic proposition. Yes indeed. Yes indeed.

Some hours have passed: I have slept. In a clotted deep slumber I felt myself diving into a tunnel of purpose, felt that I was sinking deeper and deeper into some kind of void of comprehension and woke up stiff and surprised on the bed to find that for once sleep had not been a cheat: I had learned something, I had seen a way out of it. Got up then, stretched, made myself a drink, went into the cellar to check out things again—there was no one down in the cellar at all, it was only my frenetic, projective consciousness which yielded that illusion—and then came back, sat meditatively on the bed, finished my drink, felt myself coming into a kind of order. After a while I felt strong enough and I looked at her. Once I had gotten my mind around to that point there was nothing to it. She was easy to look at. Now I can look at anything.

She lay before Idiom stretched in that final frozen sleep, her limbs now quite peaceful, relaxation seeming to flood through her dead thighs, her dead shoulders, her dead breasts and in an extremity of tenderness so enormous that it came as close to love as anything ever sought, Idiom went over to the dead girl and kissed her, once gently on the cheek, on the forehead, holding her wrist which in death had a peculiar kind of grace and said to her, leaning close to put the words into her ear, "I'm sorry, I really am; but you see there was no other way it could be worked out. You know that now, don't you?" The girl did not respond and after a time, Idiom got up, sighing, and went back to his desk and picked up his transcript once again. He looked it over, made a fresh drink, sipped it, considered things and in time went back to his diary again. It seemed to be the only fair gesture. Slowly and then with increasing intensity he began to write while the boiler hummed on with a click, the lights flickered and the glass trembled in its perch on the desk. He continued. He pushed on. American to the last, he attempted to fulfill his destiny even when that destiny had been shown to be false. Scandalous. Ah yes. Ah yes indeed.

"And that's all," Idiom said. "Now you know everything about me. There is nothing more to say."

She stretched on the bed, sat up and said, "I see. Can I go now?"

"Go where?"

"Go home. You said 1 could go home when you finished. You promised me."

"But don't you have anything to say?" Idiom asked. "Isn't there anything to all of this that seems worthy of comment? It is not for nothing that I have told you all of this you know. I thought that something might come of it."

"What might come of it?"

"I didn't know," Idiom said after a pause. "I simply didn't know. But something. There can be no action without a reaction after all, can there? A reciprocal action, an unwinding of causality, a—"

"So you've lived a tough life," the girl said. "So have a lot of other people. There isn't anything special in that. What entitles you to think that you've had it so tough? Look at me—"

"That isn't the point," Idiom said flatly, with enormous determination. For the first time with this girl he felt himself spinning on the verge of a dangerous and vaulting kind of rage because she had missed the point, had totally missed it, it was as if everything he had done had been for nothing because the simple clarity and fixation of purpose which lay at the dead-center of everything which Idiom did (he was an organized man) had not only been ignored but mocked, something with which he could hardly bear to deal. "That isn't the point at all; do you think I told you all of this to show you how tough I've had it? We are not talking about the *difficulty* of Idiom's life which in that sense is only typically American; once you understand that there will inevitably be a delimitation and foreclosure of goals, a cutting off of all sense of purpose at the core, a kind of darkness in the center of everything American which the media will not admit in their rhetoric but can hardly deny in their gesture, once you say that you have said it all. I was talking only about the particular metaphoric value of Idiom's life. The microcosmic significance so to speak."

"What's a metaphor? What's a microcosm? Why do you have to use those big words and speak that way? Can't you speak like a normal human being? No one will hurt you, you know, if you just try to talk simply. No one will laugh at your ideas if you express them so they can be understood. I think you're hiding behind words, that's what I think your problem is."

"Oh, God," Idiom said and groaned, ran a sopping palm over his forehead, muttered to himself, bent over, stood up finally and with a painful old man's shuffle went over to a wall and began to bang it idly with his fist. "Oh, God, you don't understand. You don't understand a thing that's been going on here. It's just been words and you've tried to make them 'socially redeeming'. It was all for nothing."

"Listen," the girl said to Idiom and stood up from the bed with vast determination, put the sheets back with a vigorous sweep and went for her clothes, this time with a kind of determination which almost touched Idiom, so shyly confident she was of finally bringing things to a conclusion. "Listen, that's the end of it. You don't know anything, do you understand that? You can keep me here for a thousand years and screw me and bore me and torture me and starve me but that doesn't mean that you know a thing. You do not know where it is at, my friend, because you've never tried to learn. I came here with five dollars in my pocket. My parents don't know where I am. My fiancé who runs a shoe store does but I told him that if he ever comes to get me I'll destroy his life. I came in to be an actress and I found that they'll eat you up alive here. I've only been here a few weeks and I understand one thing already: *they'll never let you out of it alive*. They'll take it away from you in small and big pieces and destroy everything that's there and make you give away little parts of yourself until you're no longer the same person and by then it's too late to ever try to get even with them because you aren't what you were. And you live in cheap hotel rooms and take phone calls from men in just as much trouble as you who think that a screw will solve their problems and incidentally yours and you write letters all over the place which are never answered and there's always someone feeling you up on the subway."

"I never did it."

"You never did it, then you're the only one in New York who never did. There's always an arm on your back or a hand accidentally touching your breast or a knee coming into your ass and when you turn, looking for a face, you see nothing, just a body, a body with hands moving in the opposite direction and the air stinks and the food stinks and you find out sooner or later that it doesn't make any difference what you do, there's no way you can touch it—"

"The anonymity of our cities," Idiom said reflectively. "The multiple pressures of urban existence, the fainting, humbled and lonely crowd. *Anomie*, alienation, isolation, drift, chaos, hatred, hostility, schizoid detachment, finally the great riots beginning, the slow, burning cataclysms at the center of experience, the shift and dislocation, the moving of the various parts into and against themselves, the fires, the burning, the panic, the dispersal—"

"It has nothing to do with cities."

"You're right," Idiom said, after a moment. "You know, you're absolutely right."

"It only has to do with people and you better get hold of yourself, Harry. That's the last and only piece of advice I can give to you, you'd better straighten out. There are a lot of people who wouldn't put up with this, you know. You better watch it, Harry."

"My name is Idiom," Idiom said.

"What's that?"

"I said, my name is Idiom, not Harry. Why are you calling me Harry?"

She backed off from him then, putting her sweater into place, her eyes rounded and said, "Oh, forget it. It's hopeless. Just hopeless."

"No, it isn't. Nothing's hopeless. But why did you call me Harry?"

"Oh, come on—"

"Why did you call me Harry?"

"Because your name is Harry, you told me your name was Harry, Idiom was just a character in this story that you were making up and furthermore—"

It is at that moment that Idiom lost his control. He had held on to it for a long time, had doubtless gone far beyond what might be called "normal expectable limits," had, as a matter of fact, even managed to surprise himself seized as he was with an ability to communicate far beyond his modest level but at that moment a pure, shattering streak of insanity shot through Idiom, a total thrill of madness and he plunged toward the girl, bellowing thickly, mumbling chaotically, making strange, frenzied gestures with hands and feet, arms and legs and he fell on top of her, literally seizing her and plunging her weight toward the bed, moving his hands up under her sweater to palm her breasts and then he grunted thickly in her ear in a voice so strange and forceful that it hardly seemed his—oh, Idiom, Idiom!—"I'm going to show you now. Do you understand that? I'm going to show you, because the fact of the matter is that I simply can't stand this anymore, can you tell me a single reason why I should be able to stand it?" and she gave a squeal somewhere midway between fright and astonishment and began to fight him then. She fought him with a strange and terrible effectiveness, showing a precise knowledge of what angles to make, what areas to lash at and it took all of Idiom's superb physical gifts not to say his sense of interior control to subdue her which he finally did, rolling over and over on the bed and then with a *thump* and *whack!* to the floor where he pinned her arms solemnly and rose above her, removing garments right and left. The air seemed to flower with clothing which moved swiftly through the spaces of the room and then she was naked and Idiom was naked and he said in a perfect, hollow voice, "I'll show you now, you bitch. I'll show you. I don't have to take this, do you hear me? I can't stand it anymore and there's no reason why I should, give me one simple reason why I should, you bitch, all of you bitches, the whole lot of you," showing a tendency for generalization which was perhaps a bit extreme and unfortunate under even the complex circumstances and then Idiom removed his own clothing, still swearing and mumbling strange phrases to himself which, lapsing into his Private Language as they did, are probably unparaphrasable although they sounded somewhat like *glum ontoffen* and *misercordia dominis* and *fulliar lux* and *sons of bitches*, and so on and then, swooping down on her like an enormous bird trapped in flight he rammed his prick against the safe, steady interior of her thighs, anchoring himself there and then penetrated her with a mighty burst, squeezing on her nipples as he did so until she grunted with emotions inexplicable and then, right on the floor, Idiom gave it to her, fucking with enormous speed and skill and above all accuracy, aiming himself as it were so that his semen would collide with her womb in just the right way to penetrate her body right through to the undiscovered places and he forced her arms around him and dug in deeper and deeper, panting, moaning, gasping, biting, thrusting himself deeply, trying to literally impale her on the scavenger of his prick and—

Oh, Idiom! What is there to say, gentle spirit? What can we tell you? You committed rape, you of the questing spirit and modest aspirations, you who had prided yourself on never taking a girl unwilling. How unfortunate! Tra-la, how grave! For this was not the solution, Idiom and you above all should have known it.

But nevertheless, you did it, ramming your prick in deeply, listening to her rocketing moans, talking to her, biting, nibbling, sucking, tonguing and all the time you drove it up deeper and deeper and your orgasm began, coming as if from some far-off distance, a mountain in disintegration somewhere beyond the horizon, rocks clambering, stones sifting, mud melting, animals running from the forest as if it were not mud but fire which awaited them and you drove it in deeper and deeper and then it came on you, thunder and roiling, mystery and lightning, sifting and driving and it poured out, you poured out everything into her, every little bit, gasping, wedging, moving in deeper and squeezed out the last drops, bitter, bitter, dropping it into her from some distant height, weak now and gasping because rather than having made it into her womb you *piddled off*, piddled off, you silly son of a bitch, won't you ever learn? and dropped away from her falling, falling, distances, heights, falling-action, disaster, collision and lay there and she lay there and then you did it.

Well, you did it good, you stupid son of a bitch, what else is there to say? Surely I cannot grant you any approbation. It is not for me to sit in judgment on Idiom but this does not mean that I have to *approve* it either; I suppose you had your motives and they seemed reasonable to you at the time but that does not mean that I have to share them, not me, I do not condone what you did at all. I would not have done it in your position, let me say that. On the other hand, if I *had* done it I would have done it differently. Somewhat. Oh, you silly, silly son of a bitch and you did it, well you had been waiting in one sense 33 years to do it so that was all right, what can you expect? How much tension can you take, how much of this is really exportable and how much of it winds up roiling within? It's not my problem, that's what I say. A keen, reserved man, I live my life according to its own plan and let the devil take the others. Live and let live, that is my motto. Distinctly.

So you did it nevertheless, you son of a bitch, don't ask me for explanations or for forgiveness, I'm not in any position to do so, no you have to make your own life, your own judgments, court is in session in the deepest spaces of the human heart perpetually and a goddamned grafted court it is too—with the plaintiff always bought off before he can truly reach the dock? But what can you do, things are tough all over and when you were finished you scuttled away hands and knees and went to your desk still naked and began your writing. Well, that's your business. Each to his own. *Ony socki mali pons.* Did I spell that right?

So you started your diary, you bastard, and that's okay and now you're finishing it up which is splendid too but what do you want me to do? Do you expect any answers from me? No sir, I haven't had a thing to do with this anywhere along the line and I refuse to get involved at this point. I've stayed out of it.

My plans are simple, schematized, referable, unalterable: I am a modest man of limited gifts and attainments. You do what you want. In due course I am going to get dressed and have a cup of coffee and take a walk.

Perhaps I will stroll uptown past the desiccated river and to the steps of the private university; perhaps I will go downtown and to Times Square where I can witness, so to speak, the scene of the crime. Perhaps I will merely wander a little bit west and search out your whore. It all depends upon how I take the air.

But those are my plans, I have nothing else to say, I really didn't want to get involved from the first and I'm getting disinvolved pronto.

Now you're crying, you son of a bitch. Well, as far as I can take it, that's your problem. Go ahead, there's an easy childish purgative in that.

Me? I've decided what I'm going to do, after all, I'm going to make it to Times Square. And Times Square will be deserted, only filth and paper blowing amidst the cops and clubs and horses and dazzle but somewhere in the vicinity of Times Square perhaps there will be a girl and she will come into my arms. Graciously, gently, the smell of leaves on her she will tumble against my face and I will hold her and she will look up at me and in the freshness, warmth and essential decency of our communion I will talk to her gently; gently, gently, always gently and after a while we will come back here and in grace and valor commit our love. And commit it again. And there will come a time at the end of passage when it will be possible to look back upon all that we have seen before and know that it is truly over and all answers divined, all goals collected, all mysteries known, we will huddle against one another, plane to plane, skin to softness and in all the partitions of our knowing will absorb with cunning and spirit the scheming night.

January 24, 1970
New York, New York

The World Snake
By Barry N. Malzberg

Clearly in 1970, only two years since I had sent my first proposal to Olympia, Maurice Girodias, the six or seven novels already in the tank and I were already circling the drain:

"...Concentrating at that moment with that wonderful mimetic of mine speaking the jargon she would want to hear, the jargon of the "integrated", of the "rational", of the "coordinated" man who would come to her out of a universe of meaning and motivation and purpose."

"At this institution Idiom continued and expanded his study of American movies, moving on to the more mature realization that this country—his adopted country!—was completely insane."

This novel was clearly conceived as anti-pornography (a phrase in Lehmann Haupt's *NYT* review of *Screen* which my mother told me on the day of its appearance "Enabled me to hold up my head for the first time" but which did not further enable its distribution after the London police raid on the warehouse containing copies of the British edition) and one can sense, or at least the author can, the use of convoluted and occasionally almost incomprehensible language and description to render the very production itself of pornography ludicrous. Here was a demonstration of the world-snake at large; finding different quarters—like the USA Constitution itself—in which to self-annihilate. I cannot, half a century later, look at this novel without shudders of relative and challenged incomprehension: What the hell did I think I was doing? And for what purpose?

Institutions and individuals have been devouring themselves since at least the *Book of Jonah*, in fact we might as well start with *Genesis*, but Girodias and pornography were perhaps a union gathered in and sanctified by hell; it was Maurice's conviction that pornography was the cutting edge for the toppling of a corrupt, repressive society and pornography, as pioneered in *The Decameron* was from the start focused upon the uses of sex to reduce all human desire and ambition to a kind of perverse inventiveness. Henry Miller, the first arrow in the quiver of Jack Kahane, Maurice's father, was expert in denoting sexual union as the most colorless, destructive and ultimately anti-stylistic of all human endeavors; the flood of works which followed in France and ultimately the United States consisted of substantiation. *A Satyr's Romance* was serious stuff, an attempt to use the devices of pornography *against* its intended purpose and as the narrator a/k/a "Idiom" staggers from one maladaptive and spiritlessly violent sexual union to the next the reader is taken by the hand and escorted through the wilderness of the object lesson. "Don't try this at home" was the implicit message and I was as earnest as I could be in clarifying why this would be so.

Olympia under Maurice's shaky and luckless guidance was stumbling in the same direction. The clank of rusted machinery and ill-fitted garbage cans could be extracted in every season and it seems to have been my intention to make the experience as distasteful as possible. Disaster accompanied Maurice—who took her clawlike hand and escorted her through all of its highways and byways—with a kind of elegance, Maurice trotted in her grasp with an eagerness occasionally interrupted by flickers of remorse and self-hatred. He published an imagined sex diary of Ilsa Koch; he published the pseudonymous *Homosexual Handbook* depicting destinations for grubby romps in the forgotten coves of the New York and Angelo d'Angelo included an appendix listing a hundred indifferently famous and three-quarter closeted homosexuals. He published *Moscow Nights* purportedly by a Communist regime insider which graphed the listless sex of the Gulag State. These drawing perfunctory attention, he published *President Kissinger,* an alternate history in which the eponymous protagonist achieved the position he had always desired. Far too much attention.

It was this of course this last work (the author's true name suppressed) which, finally, led to Maurice's deportation; the State Department bestirred itself (under heavy application of its leader's whip) and galloped Maurice and his latest mistress to France which, having no apparent alternative, took him in for the final struggling decade and a half. A string of small disasters (he lost Olympia to bankruptcy; J.P. Donleavy's Gingerbread wife*** got news of a secret auction, appeared and won; her husband led the company to oblivion. Volume II of his memoir, never published in the United States was the subject of an author television interview; Maurice died offstage minutes after its conclusion. Everything for him was too early or too late and at the end Barney Rossett and other USA pirates cleaned the boards.

A Satyr's Romance, an angry but misbegotten novel was of course dead on semi-arrival; it may not be the weakest of my ten for the Olympia Press but it is the most refractory and the angriest. I look upon it with equivocation but with a bow to Stephen Sondheim, *Follies* and the beloved Elaine Stritch,

> "Lord knows, at least I was there, and I'm here
> "Look who's here, I'm still here."

—August 2021: New Jersey

***This reference is surely too obscure. J.P. Donleavy, author of the once famous *Ginger Man*, hated Girodias with a passion deeply engaged and true. Girodias had been the first publisher of what became ultimately a famous novel, never obtained a USA copyright, misdirected most or all of what tiny royalties might have been due and like Nabokov with *Lolita* allowed a festival of publishers throughout the world to further enjoy life. When Girodias, bankrupt, put up the Olympia Press as part of a forced divestiture, he made sure that the mandated auction took place with only the minimum publicity law allowed and found the most obscure rural location possible. Unhappily for the ever unrepentant Maurice, Donleavy, a stalker for decades, got the location and sent his wife who, with Girodias became the only bidder for this particular property and for a very small expenditure, obtained and presented Olympia to her husband, leaving the flabbergasted Maurice with nothing but astonishment and anger.

Barry N. Malzberg Bibliography

FICTION (as either Barry or Barry N. Malzberg)
Oracle of the Thousand Hands (1968)
Screen (1968)
Confessions of Westchester County (1970)
The Spread (1971)
In My Parents' Bedroom (1971)
The Falling Astronauts (1971)
The Masochist (1972, reprinted as Everything Happened
    to Susan, 1975)
Horizontal Woman (1972; reprinted as The Social Worker, 1973)
Beyond Apollo (1972)
Overlay (1972)
Revelations (1972)
Herovit's World (1973)
In the Enclosure (1973)
The Men Inside (1973)
Phase IV (1973; novelization based on a story
    & screenplay by Mayo Simon)
The Day of the Burning (1974)
The Tactics of Conquest (1974)
Underlay (1974)
The Destruction of the Temple (1974)
Guernica Night (1974)
On a Planet Alien (1974)
Out from Ganymede (1974; stories)
The Sodom and Gomorrah Business (1974)
The Best of Barry N. Malzberg (1975; stories)
The Many Worlds of Barry Malzberg (1975; stories)
Galaxies (1975)
The Gamesman (1975)
Down Here in the Dream Quarter (1976; stories)
Scop (1976)
The Last Transaction (1977)
Chorale (1978)
Malzberg at Large (1979; stories)
The Man Who Loved the Midnight Lady (1980; stories)
The Cross of Fire (1982)
The Remaking of Sigmund Freud (1985)
In the Stone House (2000; stories)
Shiva and Other Stories (2001; stories)

The Passage of the Light: The Recursive Science Fiction of Barry N.
   Malzberg (2004; ed. by Tony Lewis & Mike Resnick; stories)
The Very Best of Barry N. Malzberg (2013; stories)

With Bill Pronzini
The Running of the Beasts (1976)
Acts of Mercy (1977)
Prose Bowl (1980)
Night Screams (1981)
Problems Solved (2003; stories)
On Account of Darkness and Other SF Stories (2004; stories)

As Mike Barry
Lone Wolf series:
Night Raider (1973)
Bay Prowler (1973)
Boston Avenger (1973)
Desert Stalker (1974)
Havana Hit (1974)
Chicago Slaughter (1974)
Peruvian Nightmare (1974)
Los Angeles Holocaust (1974)
Miami Marauder (1974)
Harlem Showdown (1975)
Detroit Massacre (1975)
Phoenix Inferno (1975)
The Killing Run (1975)
Philadelphia Blow-Up (1975)

As Francine di Natale
The Circle (1969)

As Claudine Dumas
The Confessions of a Parisian Chambermaid (1969)

As Mel Johnson/M. L. Johnson
Love Doll (1967; with The Sex Pros by Orrie Hitt)
I, Lesbian (1968)
Just Ask (1968; with Playgirl by Lou Craig)
Instant Sex (1968)
Chained (1968; with Master of Women by March Hastings
   & Love Captive by Dallas Mayo)
Kiss and Run (1968)
Nympho Nurse (1969; with Young and Eager by Jim Conroy & Quickie by
   Gene Evans)

The Sadist (1969)
The Box (1969)
Do It To Me (1969)
Born to Give (1969; with Swap Club by Greg Hamilton & Wild in Bed by
   Dirk Malloy)
Campus Doll (1969; with High School Stud by Robert Hadley)
A Way With All Maidens (1969)

As Howard Lee
Kung Fu #1: The Way of the Tiger, the Sign of the Dragon

As Lee W. Mason
Lady of a Thousand Sorrows (1977)

As K. M. O'Donnell
Empty People (1969)
The Final War and Other Fantasies (1969; stories)
Dwellers of the Deep (1970)
Gather at the Hall of the Planets (1971)
In the Pocket and Other S-F Stories (1971; stories)
Universe Day (1971; stories)

As Elliot B. Reston
The Womanizer (1972)

As Gerrold Watkins
Southern Comfort (1969)
A Bed of Money (1970)
A Satyr's Romance (1970)
Giving It Away (1970)
Art of the Fugue (1970)

NON-FICTION/ESSAYS
The Engines of the Night: Science Fiction in the Eighties
   (1982; essays)
Breakfast in the Ruins (2007; essays: expansion of Engines of the Night)
The Business of Science Fiction: Two Insiders Discuss Writing and
   Publishing (2010; with Mike Resnick)
The Bend at the End of the Road (2018; essays)

EDITED ANTHOLOGIES
Final Stage (1974; with Edward L. Ferman)
Arena (1976; with Edward L. Ferman)
Graven Images (1977; with Edward L. Ferman)
Dark Sins, Dark Dreams (1978; with Bill Pronzini)

The End of Summer: SF in the Fifties (1979; with Bill Pronzini)
Shared Tomorrows: Science Fiction in Collaboration (1979; with Bill
  Pronzini)
Neglected Visions (1979; with Martin H. Greenberg & Joseph D. Olander)
Bug-Eyed Monsters (1980; with Bill Pronzini)
The Science Fiction of Mark Clifton (1980; with Martin H. Greenberg)
The Arbor House Treasury of Horror & the Supernatural (1981; with Bill
  Pronzini & Martin H. Greenberg)
The Science Fiction of Kris Neville (1984; with Martin H. Greenberg)
Mystery in the Mainstream (1986; with Bill Pronzini & Martin H.
  Greenberg)
Uncollected Stars (1986; with Piers Anthony, Martin H. Greenberg &
  Charles G. Waugh)
The Best Time Travel Stories of All Time (2003)